Secrets

Satisfy your desire for more.

On Kathryn Anne Dubois' story: "Start building your jungle tree house now gals, Tarzan is due to swoop in and carry you away on a to-die-for fantasy!"

—*Suzanne Coleburn, Reader To Reader Reviews/*
Belles & Beaux of Romance

On Kimberly Dean's story: "An FBI agent is hot on the trail of a smart woman accused of selling top secret military computer codes. And **hot** is what he gets!"

—*Brenda Passow, LORE Reading Group*

On Bonnie Hamre's story: "Captain Yancy creates the ultimate fantasy for Chloe on his yacht *Fantasy*. It's scorching hot…I almost fainted dead away while reading, almost, but not quite since I was too riveted by the action, and my imagination was working overtime."

—*Suzanne Coleburn, Reader To Reader Reviews/*
Belles & Beaux of Romance

On Lisa Marie Rice's story: "If you feel like dying and going to heaven on an unsurpassed sensual orgasm then being sequestered with Nicholas Lee in his unique hideaway is the ultimate highway to heaven. Nicholas is a special hero that will blow you away!"

—*Suzanne Coleburn, Reader To Reader Reviews/*
Belles & Beaux of Romance

Reviews from Secrets Volume 1

"Four very romantic, very sexy novellas in very different styles and settings. ... The settings are quite diverse taking the reader from Regency England to a remote and mysterious fantasy land, to an Arabian nights type setting, and finally to a contemporary urban setting. All stories are explicit, and Hamre and Landon stories sizzle. ... If you like erotic romance you will love *Secrets*."

— **Romantic Readers** review

"Overall, for a fan of erotica, these are unlike anything you've encountered before. For those romance fans who turn down the pages of the "good parts" for later repeat consumption (and you know who you are) these books are a wonderful way to explore the better side of the erotica market. ... *Secrets* is a worthy exploration for the adventurous reader with the promise for better things yet to come."

— **Liz Montgomery**

Reviews from Secrets Volume 2

Winner of the
Fallot Literary Award for Fiction

"*Secrets, Volume 2*, a new anthology published by Red Sage Publishing, is hot! I mean *red hot!* ... The sensuality in each story will make you blush — from head to toe and everywhere else in-between. ... The true success behind *Secrets, Volume 2* is the combination of different tastes — both in subgenres of romance and levels of sensuality. *I highly recommend this book.*"

— **Dawn A. Long, America Online** review

"I think it is a fine anthology and Red Sage should be applauded for providing an outlet for women who want to write sensual romance."

— **Adrienne Benedicks,**
Erotic Readers Association review

Reviews from Secrets Volume 3

Winner of the 1997 Under the Cover Readers Favorite Award

"An unabashed celebration of sex. Highly arousing! Highly recommended!"

—**Virginia Henley,** *New York Times* Best Selling Author

"*Secrets, Volume 3* leaves the reader breathless. Each of these tributes to exotic and erotic fiction offers a world of sensual pleasure and moral rewards. A delicious confection of sensuous treats awaits the reader on each turn of the page. Sexy, funny, thrilling, and luscious, Secrets entertains, enlightens, and fuels the fires of fantasy."

— **Kathee Card**, *Romancing the Web*

Reviews from Secrets Volume 4

"*Secrets, Volume 4*, has something to satisfy every erotic fantasy… simply sexsational!"

—**Virginia Henley,** *New York Times* Best Selling Author

"Provocative…seductive…a must read! ★★★★"

— *Romantic Times*

"These are the kind of stories that romance readers that 'want a little more' have been looking for all their lives without crossing over into the adult genre. Keep these stories coming, Red Sage, the world needs them!"

— **Lani Roberts**, *Affaire de Coeur*

"If you're interested in exploring erotica, or reading farther than the sexual passages of your favorite steamy reads, the *Secret* series is well worth checking out."

— **Writers Club Romance Group**
on AOL Reviewer Board

Reviews from Secrets Volume 5

"*Secrets, Volume 5*, is a collage of lucious sensuality. Any woman who reads *Secrets* is in for an awakening!"

—**Virginia Henley,** *New York Times* Best Selling Author

"Hot, hot, hot! Not for the faint-hearted!"

— *Romantic Times*

"As you make your way through the stories, you will find yourself becoming hotter and hotter. *Secrets* just keeps getting better and better."

— *Affaire de Coeur*

Reviews from Secrets Volume 6

"*Secrets, Volume 6* satisfies every female fantasy: the Bodyguard, the Tutor, the Werewolf, and the Vampire. I give it Six Stars!"

—**Virginia Henley,** *New York Times* Best Selling Author

"*Secrets, Volume 6* is the best of *Secrets* yet. ...four of the most erotic stories in one volume than this reader has yet to see anywhere else. ... These stories are full of erotica at its best and you'll definitely want to keep it handy for lots of re-reading!"

— *Affaire de Coeur* Magazine

Reviews from Secrets Volume 7

Winner of the Venus Book Club
Best Book of the Year

"...sensual, sexy, steamy fun. A perfect read!"
—**Virginia Henley,** *New York Times* Best Selling Author

"Intensely provocative and disarmingly romantic, Secrets Volume 7 is a romance reader's paradise that will take you beyond your wildest dreams!"

— *Ballston Book House* Review

"Erotic romance is at the sensual core of Red Sage's latest collection of short, red hot novels, *Secrets, Volume 7.*"

— *Writers Club Romance Group* on AOL

Reviews from Secrets Volume 8

Winner of the Venus Book Club
Best Book of the Year

"*Secrets Volume 8* is simply sensational!"
—**Virginia Henley,** *New York Times* Best Selling Author

"*Secrets Volume 8* is an amazing compilation of sexy stories discovering a wide range of subjects, all designed to titillate the senses."

— **Lani Roberts**, *Affaire de Coeur*

"All four tales are well written and fun to read because even the sexiest scenes are not written for shock value, but interwoven smoothly and realistically into the plots. This quartet contains strong storylines and solid lead characters, but then again what else would one expect from the no longer *Secrets* anthologies."

—Harriet Klausner

"Once again, Red Sage Publishing takes you on a journey of sexual delight, teasing and pleasing the reader with a bit of something to appeal to everyone."

—Michelle Houston, Courtesy Sensual Romance

"In this sizzling volume, four authors offer short stories in four different sub-genres: contemporary, paranormal, historical, and futuristic. These ladies' assignments are to dazzle, tantalize, amaze, and entice. Your assignment, as the reader, is to sit back and enjoy. Just have a fan and some ice water at your side."

—Amy Cunningham

Satisfy Your Desire for More... with Secrets!

Did you miss any of the other volumes of the sexy **Secrets** *series? At the back of this book is an order form for all the available volumes. Order your* **Secrets** *today! See our order form at the back of this book or visit Walden Books.*

Kimberly Dean
Kathryn Anne Dubois
Bonnie Hamre
Lisa Marie Rice

Volume 9

Secrets

Satisfy your desire for more.

SECRETS Volume 9
This is an original publication of Red Sage Publishing and each individual story
herein has never before appeared in print. These stories are a collection of
fiction and any similarity to actual persons or events is purely coincidental.

Red Sage Publishing, Inc.
P.O. Box 4844
Seminole, FL 33775
727-391-3847
www.redsagepub.com

SECRETS Volume 9
A Red Sage Publishing book
All Rights Reserved/December 2003
Copyright © 2003 by Red Sage Publishing, Inc.

ISBN 0-9648942-9-7

Published by arrangement with the authors and copyright holders of the
individual works as follows:

WANTED
Copyright © 2003 by Kimberly Dean

WILD FOR YOU
Copyright © 2003 by Kathryn Anne Dubois

FLIGHTS OF FANTASY
Copyright © 2003 by Bonnie Hamre

SECLUDED
Copyright © 2003 by Lisa Marie Rice

Photographs:
Cover © 2003 by Tara Kearney; email: jodesign2@yahoo.com
Setback cover © 2000 by Greg P. Willis; email: GgnYbr@aol.com

Printed in the U.S.A.

Layout and book typesetting by:

Quill & Mouse Studios, Inc.
2165 Sunnydale Boulevard, Suite E
Clearwater, FL 33765
www.quillandmouse.com

Contents

Wild For You

by Kathryn Anne Dubois

To My Reader:

Ever fantasize about being kidnapped and held captive by a modern day Tarzan? I have. Which is why I had so much fun writing this story. An implausible premise some might say? You bet. Which only doubled the fantasy for me as I hope it does for you. Enjoy!

Chapter One

Georgie wasn't lost, technically speaking. At least not completely. According to her protractor or compass or whatever it was, she was three miles north and maybe a little west of their camp with just a few fifty foot cliffs, rapidly rushing creeks, and thundering waterfalls between her and civilization and ultimate safety. She gave a little snort.

Hardly either. No more did she want to return to that malaria infested scorching patch of dirt that the professor called a village than she wanted to be hiking circles in this steaming overgrowth of vegetation that sported banana leaves longer than her body. Course, she *could* use them for clothes should she be stranded into the next millennium.

She cursed the professor. If he hadn't tried to hunt her down she never would have slipped away. But she refused to haul another water jug up that steep hill just so the village women could cook gluey stew they'd all have to choke down. What else could she do but hide out?

And she doubled-cursed him for earlier insisting she wear this Salvation Army scrap of a sundress that the chief had presented to her with such pride—a threadbare cotton floral too short, even for her small frame, to keep her legs from getting scratched up as she hacked her way through brush and tangled vines. Its spaghetti straps bared her shoulders and much of her breasts to the unrelenting heat of the sun and overgrown jungle so that now she burned and itched all over her fair skin. She could only imagine the multitude of parasites that lived in the oozing bark and wet moss.

But she wasn't desperate. Not yet. She kicked aside a rotting log and watched a swarm of insects cloud the air. True desperation was twelve lousy credits away from graduating and parents who threatened to cut you off and take away your red metallic Miata until you do. *This* nightmare she could handle, if this little internship gained her the promised credits and freedom.

A college degree by her 21st birthday had meant access to her two million dollar trust find and independence from her fire-breathing parents. She was 26 now and still working on it. Her parents thought *they'd* lost patience? What about her? Imprisoned in academia during her prime was not exactly her dream either. She should have been honing her underdeveloped sailing skills and nurturing her love of nature—at least the nature that included a smooth Grenade on a hot sandy beach.

The darkness hovered lower, whether from the sun setting or from traveling deeper into the jungle, she couldn't be sure, but either way, it wasn't a good sign.

The hair on the back of her neck prickled. She glanced up at the canopy of trees above, aware that the tiny dots of light peeking through the ceiling of vegetation were growing dimmer. She wasn't frightened. Just concerned. She'd find a cave to sleep in, hopefully a nice studio whose lone tiger had taken off on a little jaunt.

She crawled through what looked like an opening to somewhere and ran smack into a pair of hairy feet with nails long overdue for a manicure. For one paralyzing moment she looked up into the small beady eyes of the largest Silverback gorilla she had ever seen. Only gorilla she had ever seen. But before she allowed terror to strike, she remembered the professor describing the species' lack of aggression and innate gentleness.

The huge-skulled beast reared up on two legs and let loose a roaring growl that rivaled King Kong's best. Then it beat its chest with a fury, its dagger-like teeth glinting in its ugly face. *So much for the esteemed professor.*

She did an about face without daring to look back to see if her furry friend followed and made a run for her life. After she had run for what seemed like the distance of three laps around Central Park and was sure he wasn't chasing her, she dropped herself down by a rubber tree in a thick part of the forest and applauded her skillful escape. But not for long, because the darkness was growing and the eerie silence of the day was slowly being replaced by the sound of creatures. And they seemed to be coming closer by the minute.

She gave a quick glance around. Nothing. She was starting to rethink the cave idea when she was yanked up from behind by her ponytail and dragged out into a small clearing.

Pain shot through her as she grabbed frantically at her scalp and twisted to see if her attacker was animal or human. But before she could catch her breath, she was whipped around to face her aggressor. A band of hunters, three native men with rifles in hand and ammunition and knives strapped to their chests, stood before her while the fourth one hauled her to her feet. He thrust her into the pack. They jostled her, clicking their tongues and laughing. She blanched at the feel of sweaty palms sliding down her bare arms.

When she pushed back at them, she was scooped up from behind around her waist, one thick arm trapping her. She dug her nails into hairy skin and kicked out her legs, but the man held her tight. The others surrounded her, chuckling and stroking her face, trying to flip her dress up, and terrifying her as she imagined what they would do next.

No doubt they were poachers, because a pile of satchels, filled with the scent of blood, rested nearby.

The professor had bemoaned the profitable illegal trade in gorilla meat and warned his adoring student groupies of bands of outlaws roaming the jungle. She wished she had paid more attention, like that kiss-up graduate student, Kristy, who hung on his every word.

The men's toothless grins widened when one poked a stubby finger at her nipple, raised against her sweat soaked dress. She thrashed and kicked, cringing at the feel of him.

But then abruptly they released her and stepped back when a small figure emerged from between the trees and stood before them. His wide safari hat did nothing to disguise his weak-jawed face and his white legs looked like bamboo shoots under his baggy shorts. A leer split across his face the instant he saw her.

"Well…" he murmured. "What's this?" His thick nasally voice made her skin crawl. Her heart pounded in her chest as her eyes darted around seeking an escape. But while she could probably take this little runt, the numbers were not in her favor. She took a cautious step back, but before she could get her bearings, he signaled to the men. Instantly, they surrounded her and dragged her to a large tree.

"Get off of me!" She scratched down at a face, drawing blood and an angry bellow from one attacker, but it didn't stop him and the rest of them from smashing her back against the tree and tying her arms around the trunk.

Then they fanned out as one, facing the perimeter of the clearing and stepping a few feet into the jungle, as though guarding against intruders.

Alone now with the white man, she watched as he took a few deliberate steps toward her, at the same time he reached slowly into a side strap of his shorts. He whipped out a long gleaming blade. Its shiny metal glinted even in the growing darkness. Her heart leaped in her throat. Did he plan to slice her like he did the animals he hunted? For what purpose? Unless he was plain crazy.

"My…" He lifted a blonde curl from her neck with the tip of his knife and smiled. "I haven't seen skin this creamy in a long time."

Her heart raced as he trailed the knife along her neck clear down to her collarbone and then took the cold metal tip and pricked at the peaks of her nipples through the worn fabric of her dress. A paralyzing fear gripped her unlike any she'd ever felt. Her mother's oft-recited complaint came back to haunt her. "The child has no fear. Just once she needs the living daylights scared out of her, then maybe she'll listen." As right as her mother probably was, Georgie was sure this was not what her mother had in mind.

"You're such a pretty little thing. I don't know where to look first, your lovely face or your luscious tits." She shuddered beneath his twisted smile.

In one swift movement, he grabbed the front of her dress and sliced down to her waist, popping every button. He drew aside the fabric and feasted his eyes on her, letting out a low chuckle. "You are too beautiful. I've surely died and gone to heaven." He lifted her skirt and tried to hook his fingers under the elastic of her panties.

With perfect aim, she kneed him in the groin and watched in relief as he doubled over. A hefty whoosh left his lungs as he struggled to stay on his feet.

"You little bitch," he growled, grabbing her skirt. He brandished the knife and made menacing slicing gestures with the blade into the space between them. He was furious now and out of control. He lunged for her.

A scream froze in her throat. With alarming dexterity, he slipped the knife under her panties and ripped through them, sending them to fall at her ankles. Then he unzipped his shorts. She writhed in confusion as he fumbled with his limp penis. What did he plan to do with that?

After her precision slam, he should be out of commission for some time, but the rage in his faded blue eyes and his shaking body told her he'd rape her with his knife if needed. She fixed her eyes on the polished blade, willing her brain to move fast and figure an escape.

He prodded her thigh with the sharp tip of steel. "Open up!" he spat. With his initial shock aside, the raw pain must have surfaced because he grabbed his balls now and moaned.

"My father is Minister of the Interior," she warned, hoping such a position existed. She yanked against the leather line at her wrists.

For a half second the man faltered and then grinned wickedly. "Minister of the Interior?" He gave a cynical laugh.

Behind him, a bush shook and then a dull thud sounded, but he was too intent on her to notice. She hoped against reason that this little band of thieves was being followed by the authorities and had just been tracked down. She listened for more sounds but only silence followed.

"What's he gonna say when I fuck his daughter?" He pushed up her skirt and gawked at the golden tuft of hair between her legs. Another tree shook, followed by a gentle whishing sound, metal slicing flesh. She dared to hope.

"You wouldn't be the first man to fuck me," she quipped, saying anything that would keep him distracted from what was going on behind him. She only prayed it was good. His sickly eyes clouded with lust.

"Open yourself for me," he rasped.

Oh, God. The thought of spreading herself for this creep made her want to vomit.

"Do it," he shouted.

Behind him, a half-naked male dropped out of the sky, landing with a grace that belied his muscled bulk. Without making a sound, he lassoed his forearm around the white man's neck. His eyes met hers and held as the hunter dropped his knife to claw at the thick arm suffocating him.

The poacher's skin turned a satisfying shade of blue and spittle formed at the corners of his mouth while he stared at her without seeing, bug-eyed. Her gaze flicked between her attacker and her rescuer. Her rescuer's gaze remained steady. A crack of bone signaled a crushed windpipe and then, with a flick of his elbow, the man snapped the hunter's pale white neck. He dropped the body at his feet.

She stared, open-mouthed, as the loin-clad barbarian dragged aside the crumpled figure and dumped him into the trees.

Her heart pounded.

She had never seen someone killed right before her eyes, or seen anyone die for that matter. Her eyes followed the movements of her rescuer, this disturbingly solid violent man she was now alone with as she contemplated what would happen next.

He towered well above six feet and with his long dark hair in a wild tumble to his shoulders, he looked like a throwback to a medieval warlord. All he lacked was a good set of chain mail to replace the primitive loincloth that draped his muscled thighs. He, too, brandished a long sword-like knife and with those boulder-like shoulders and biceps as thick as tree trunks, she knew one well-executed swipe could slice her in half.

Her eyes widened when he came to stand before her, legs braced apart and hands on hips, sweaty muscles flexing. He shoved his knife into a leather pouch strapped to his thigh watching her closely as he did, his gray eyes intense. This bronze-chested savage was obviously wild and dangerous, primitive, a terrifying specimen of masculine power and... gorgeous. She swallowed.

His eyes followed the movement of her throat, traveled over her hair and then settled on her face. He gave a little frown and then took a hesitant step forward and raised his hand.

She startled, causing him to drop his hand abruptly and step back. He grumbled something under his breath.

"I'm sorry," she said, finding her voice. "I... I should thank you." His eyes followed her lips as she spoke. "You saved my life."

His thick lashes blinked and the little creases in his forehead smoothed out. After a moment he cocked his head and then took a hesitant step forward before he stopped again, as though gauging her reaction. She would stay still for now, until she figured out what he intended to do with her. A glistening layer of moisture skimmed his chest and clung to a tight patch of dark hair. He smelled of rain and fresh male sweat.

He eased a fraction closer and hesitated. Then he tipped her chin up with one finger and studied her, turning her face to one side and then the other before he ran his fingertips over her cheek with the softest touch. He dipped his head to her throat and moved in closer. Warm fingers slid along the curve of her neck. Then he breathed deep against her skin. He was smelling her.

The thought drew a pull of sexual awareness from her that took her by surprise.

He straightened a bit and cupped her face.

Behind him the trees wobbled and then thrashed. She glimpsed a blur of fur and claws. "Oh my God," she screamed. "Untie me!"

King Kong had returned.

Her rescuer glanced at their intruder and grunted, gesturing abruptly with his hand. She held her breath.

But Kong just ambled forward and plopped himself down to lean against a nearby tree. Her rescuer nodded and then returned his gaze to her.

Then it occurred to her. He had to be the legendary wild man of the jungle. Local legends echoed through the mountains of a creature not of their race who sliced and diced poachers with a vengeance, the reward for his capture rivaling the price the underground market paid for the largest catch of primate heads. Even the government was eager to rid the country of him with tourist revenue already taking a plunge.

As she stared at Kong she felt the press of fingers along her neck again. Tarzan was sliding his fingers down her throat and murmuring something unintelligible. His fingers came to rest on her rapid pulse. After her horrible ordeal, his touch was warm and surprisingly soothing. He leaned his big body in closer and she wondered if he would try to smell her again, but he continued to stroke her skin as though fascinated with its feel, his eyes following the deliberate path of his caress. Her blood pumped hot as his fingers continued a slow travel down, over her collarbone and then along the top swell of her breasts. His fingertips lingered on the sensitive skin between her breasts.

She glanced down. In her struggle with her captor, her dress had partially covered her breasts again, the opening edges catching on each nipple.

His brows knit together in a puzzled crease as he studied the sweat-soaked fabric that clung to her skin. Her nipples grew instantly taut under the worn cotton.

He frowned and then cupped her breast.

She gave a startled cry, struggling against her restraints. His expression grew more bewildered as he blatantly continued to cradle her, despite her protests, with both palms. He gave a grunt and grumbled.

She tipped her chin. So, she had small breasts, big deal. At least they were real. But his insult to her feminine pride was soon softened when his persistent feeling and fondling drew a warm sexual heat from her. Still, she squirmed and pulled on her restraints.

"Are you going to release me?"

His eyes glinted with interest, but he finally dropped his hands. Up this close the rough shadow of his jaw smelled deliciously of shaving cologne. She gave herself a mental shake at the crazy thought.

He turned to Kong and mumbled something indiscernible. Then he began to pace, casting her sideways glances as he did.

King Kong watched, his clumsy head cocked in curiosity. "What are you looking at?" she snapped.

He bared his teeth and let out a roar.

Oh God. She held her breath. The angry beast pumped up his chest and leaned forward on his thick arms as though ready to jump her. His small dark eyes gleamed bright under his wide forehead. She didn't dare move or speak. From out of the corner of her eye, Tarzan stopped his pacing and lifted a lazy hand to the animal. Immediately, the ferocious monster relaxed.

She sighed with relief. But still, she had to get him to untie her.

"Please... Tarzan. Untie my hands." She motioned to her back and pulled.

But he wasn't paying any attention to what she said. He was sweeping his eyes over the corkscrew knot of her curls that fell to her shoulders. He reached up and pulled gently on the tips of her curls and watched with fascination how they bounced back. He drew in a soft breath.

The air grew thick between them.

He lifted pensive eyes to hers and brushed his thumb along her bottom lip, his expression a mixture of pleasure and confusion.

She dropped her gaze and one look at his groin settled any confusion on her part. The rough leather loincloth grew right before her eyes. And it looked like his size there matched the rest of his body.

He stepped back and looked over at King Kong. After a moment of what she'd swear was male commiseration, they *both* stared at her. She straightened her shoulders and stared back. *For Heaven's sake, you'd think they'd never seen a woman.*

Her eyes widened. She watched them, her heart hammering. *My God. They hadn't.* She would bet her Tarzan had never seen a woman. The shock of it was more than she could comprehend.

His hands flew to the top of her dress. "What are you doing?" she gasped. With a quick hand, he drew aside the fabric, fully exposing her small white breasts. She struggled against her restraints, burning with embarrassment as his eyes eagerly traced over the small swell of her cleavage and settled on her nipples. The smoky gray of his eyes lightened and he seemed truly fascinated.

He mumbled something, his voice low, and then smoothed his palms along the soft curves. She drew in a shocked breath and was mortified by how quickly she warmed to his sensuous caress.

His subsiding erection reversed direction.

She squirmed against his hands. "You can't just do whatever you—oh..." She stifled a groan when he pinched her nipples between his fingers, sending fire to her groin. Her nipples tightened to hard points. His eyes lit with interest.

Then he mercifully stopped.

Noticing her panties lying at his feet, he bent to pick up the scrap of lace. He drew the silky fabric to his face and breathed deep. He liked her scent, because there was no mistaking the full erection that was forming under the skimpy leather draping him. He turned his hot gaze back to her and stuffed her panties in his waistband. Then he dropped to his knees and threw up her skirt.

She gasped.

His eyes widened and he stared for several long moments.

Then he quickly opened the last of her buttons and let her dress fall open.

He gave a small sigh, then moved his palms over the swell of her belly and ran his fingers through the springy golden coils. She silently moaned.

He brushed with the lightest touch, smoothing aside the soft tangle of hair with his thumbs to see what was hidden beneath. He leaned closer, studying her. She blushed scarlet when his nostrils flared, sending shivers up her spine.

"You've got to stop this—"

He brushed one thumb down between her lips. She bit back a groan and squirmed. He locked his hands onto her hips and looked up at her with those intense eyes and grumbled. A warning? Was he telling her that she had better stay still or he wouldn't release her?

He grumbled again and cocked his head as though expecting an answer.

"Okay, okay. But then you better untie me."

He seemed satisfied and returned to his inspection.

With gentle fingers, he smoothed both thumbs down her swollen lips, separating her, slicking the pads through every pink layer. His eyes widened.

It was torture not to squirm, but no man had ever examined her this closely. She swelled full and hot, restless under his penetrating gaze. He slipped around her moist folds with the tips of his fingers, stimulating her in a way he couldn't have known. Despite that she tried to ignore his stroking, she grew wetter. And then he found her center. She watched his eyes light up as his finger slipped up into her, disappearing up to his first knuckle.

He looked up at her a moment and then pressed forward. She closed her eyes with the feel of him sinking into her, not wanting him to see how he pleasured her. But when she opened her eyes he was staring at her flushed face. He slowly withdrew his finger and then licked it.

He growled.

And then everything happened at once.

He licked her sex, one burning swipe with the tip of his tongue drawing a groan of pleasure from her that she couldn't stop.

She was horrified and automatically glanced around.

King Kong still languished against the tree trunk, one finger scratching his forehead.

A deep moan escaped her throat. He licked her again and again, curling his tongue around her swollen lips like a wet flame igniting her flesh. A moan tore from her throat.

But when he dipped his tongue in to taste her, she nearly expired.

"Tarzan, please," she choked.

He growled and slid his tongue up as far as he could, sliding his palms around to cup her bottom and holding her still. She groaned and ground against him, hardly recognizing the soft needy sounds coming from her. This was crazy.

When he stopped a moment, she drew in a stunned breath and throbbed with the sudden loss of his heat.

King Kong decided at that moment to rear his hideous head. His nostrils flared and then he twisted his neck and lifted his face to the breeze. A low growl rumbled deep in his throat. Another warning growl? It had better be, to interrupt this.

In the time it took to catch her breath, Tarzan leaped to his feet, untied her wrists, and lifted her like she was a sack of feathers and tossed her over his shoulder.

Chapter Two

"What are you doing?" Georgie screeched, giving a frantic tug of her hem over her bare bottom.

He ducked under some low lying banana trees and soon they were heading farther up into the mountains with no sign of stopping. King Kong took up the lead, pausing regularly to see if Tarzan followed. Did this wild man think he could just keep her? And what if he truly had never seen a woman? But she decided he must have some concept of mating, having lived so closely among the animals, so recognizing her as his mate would be an easy stretch.

If her stodgy professor knew how close she was to this legendary anomaly he would expire. No anthropologist had gotten close to the elusive and sought after subject believed to be one of three children lost in the wild at a very young age. He had rejected all human contact and was considered homicidal, predictably deranged due to his lack of civilizing contact, expected to have been reduced to a dangerous predator of his own species.

It was a staggering thought. Yet, she was completely unafraid. She sighed. She supposed her mother was right.

After what seemed like two or more miles of heavy hiking through twisted and tangled brush and rocks, her mountain man showed no sign of fatigue. Finally, they hit a sizeable clearing. While he paused along a wide granite cliff, she twisted to peer over his shoulder. Below her, far below, rested an emerald green valley and all around stood steep jagged cliffs.

Without warning, Tarzan dumped her on her feet and stalked over to a large tree. When he yanked on a thick vine, it uncoiled like a rope and pooled at his feet. He wrapped it around his waist and grunted at her, motioning her to come.

She looked on in puzzlement. Where was King Kong? He motioned again, this time with impatience. Down below, movement caught her eye.

Her gaze lit on their furry friend making his way down the sharp cliff towards the valley. From the looks of things, he was already half way down the one-hundred foot drop.

Too late, it dawned on her what Tarzan had planned. With purposeful strides, he came at her and plucked her up, this time settling her on his hip.

"Oh no you *don't*." She pushed against his rock-hard chest. "No way you're dragging me down there, you... lunatic."

He frowned and hugged her to his chest. Before she could level another protest he leaped off the edge.

"Oh, my God!" She closed her eyes and prayed to all the gods to help her. He bounced and then leaped, repeating the motion several times with horrifying speed. She climbed up his chest and wrapped her arms around the thick trunk of his neck and screamed while he continued his plunging descent in graceful arcs, her wild thrashing not enough to even break his rhythm. It was long moments before she got the courage to open her eyes. A mistake.

They were free-falling into a lush green canopy of trees just below them. She clung tighter, half burying her face in his neck with one eye open. Through the tops of the trees they sailed and then landed with a thud along a thick moss covered bank.

When he released her abruptly, she landed on her bottom on a soft mound of grass. She blinked up at him as he uncoiled the ropey vine from around his waist. Then she took in the unbelievable sight that greeted her.

A huge circle of mist rose between a wide oval of cliffs and the scent of sweet foliage filled the air. Tiny purple and pink buttercup-like flowers trailed along overhanging vines and twisted around dangling tree branches that stretched over the pool's edge and kissed its bubbling surface.

The gentle chirp of birds hovered around the edges of the quickly gathering darkness. Upon closer look, she spotted tiny creatures hidden among the branches, the whites of their eyes gleaming through a split in the leafy trees.

She drew in an awed breath and forgot for one moment that she was the captive of a dangerous, unpredictable, primitive being. She looked up at her abductor to find him gazing down at her with alarming intensity. He dropped down in front of her and touched her cheek. With a small nod he motioned to the pool. Then he leaped up and tugged on his corded belt. A minute later his knife dropped, along with his loincloth.

He was fully erect... completely, unabashedly aroused and growing thicker with each passing second.

"Oh, my…."

He crouched in front of her. She swallowed a gasp. She shouldn't look, but he was beautiful, the entire pulsing, veined length of him … *considerable* length of him. While she tried to tear her gaze away, he stroked his hand down his full girth as though presenting his treasure to her hungry eyes. He tipped her chin up and motioned for her to turn around.

"What?" she breathed, reluctant to take her eyes off him but realizing that perhaps he'd like some privacy. She turned on her knees in a slow daze. Not a moment later, he tossed up her skirt and anchored his hands onto her hips. "Oh my God, no," she choked. He caressed her bottom with his palm and then drew her backside against him. He let out a low moan. "Stop!"

He rubbed his penis between her bottom cheeks and groaned, exerting gentle pressure on her back to keep her bent over. The hot tip of his cock probed her swollen lips before she wrestled her bottom away from him and turned to face front. "My God, you're a menace," she gasped, with as much indignation as she could muster, but there was no mistaking the heavy pulse of arousal throbbing between her legs.

He tipped his head and frowned.

"You can't just grab me up when you want and…and do what you will. Even animals have some kind of mating ritual or something, don't they?"

He was studying her lips and intermittently letting his eyes rove over her face. At least he paid attention, which was more than she could say for most males. He touched a finger to her lips, running it gently along the bottom curve. With a small nod, he encouraged her to continue while he cupped her chin as though trying to decipher how she formed the words.

"Maybe I could teach you to talk?" she said, and then chided herself at the ridiculous notion. He stroked his thumb along her jaw, drawing her closer, so close the rich scent of his skin taunted her, a mingling of musk and leaves after a good rain. He was so large and starkly masculine. She dropped her eyes. And he was still erect.

She scrambled to her feet. He followed her and then snagged her waist, pressing her against him. His eyes closed with the contact, his heat throbbing thick between them. She stifled a low moan as a rush of pleasure slicked between her legs and up her spine to tighten her nipples. He slid against her, the pressure against her tiny nub unbearable. They groaned in unison. *This was madness.*

With a quick hand he unfastened her few intact buttons and pushed her dress off her shoulders.

"No." She clutched the dress closed and stepped back a pace.

He gave an impatient grunt and ran one hand down his face in a gesture so entirely male that she almost smiled. Then he settled his warm gaze on her again and threaded his fingers through the sides of her hair, sifting the strands with an unhurried touch. She encircled his wrist, feeling the heavy beat of his blood, wonderfully warm and alive. She could lose herself in this man. *Where did that come from?*

She gave him a gentle push. "We need to get some things straight," she said, clasping her dress closed and smoothing down the front. "I don't know what your plans are. But I'm not sticking around, so just keep your distance."

He might not understand her words but he understood her intent. He backed up and frowned and then began pacing, his arousal subsiding slowly with his frustration.

He could simply take her, like that horrible poacher intended to, she'd have no way of stopping him, yet he didn't and his restraint touched a tender chord in her and drew a bit of sympathy at the thought that he was probably a virgin. He had to be. He must be dying to finally experience what he'd seen every other species enjoy. Picturing his rough hands sliding all over her body and his weight pinning her under him was deeply arousing.

He gave her a disgruntled glare before motioning again to the bubbling surface of the water. The darkness grew thicker. Soon they'd be unable to see each other anyway, she reasoned, and the clean water was so inviting to her sticky body.

"You first," she motioned, still holding her dress closed while he stood before her stark naked.

To her surprise, he gave an annoyed shrug and slid over the bank. Her eyes followed his tight backside and thighs. Even his back was riveting, hard and muscled.

She gave a naïve look around, as though someone would actually see her, and then dropped her dress on the bank and followed him to a wide ledge of rock across the pool.

The soothing warmth hit her first, so different from the heat of the day. But it would be more wonderful if the darkness had not almost completely settled, for now she grew eerily wary with the quickly encroaching nighttime and the thought of animals lurking.

He emerged from the water and stood waist deep by the granite slab, not even glancing in her direction. She peeked around, aware of the creatures surrounding them and wondering where Kong was and all those like him. They might not be quite as friendly. Were there alligators in this water or snakes? Her notes from that environmental science class would come in handy at a time like this. Of course, she never actually *took* any notes.

When she reached him, she swam around to his back, staying neck deep in the water and moving close to him for protection. He was so close she could feel the heat of his body, but he paid no attention to her. A large array of scented soap and shampoo littered the rock, no doubt the spoils from his tirades on the poachers. A cold chill stole up her spine at the thought of all the people he must have killed. Still, she pressed closer to him as it grew too dark to even see her hands. The strange sounds of the creatures encircling them grew more distinct in the silence as the darkness descended.

He grabbed a bar of soap, sudsing his hands and running them down his ample chest and then along his biceps. He smelled delicious. She had wondered about the traces of his dark beard and decided the evidence that he shaved was a sure indication that he had some connection with civilization.

A splash sounded behind her. She turned abruptly, just in time to see the shadowy outline of two huge animals slide into the water a few feet away. She screamed and scurried around Tarzan to take a diving leap into his arms and crawled up his body in a fury. She wrapped her arms around his neck in a fierce lock and held on for dear life.

"Something's behind us," she screeched. "Get us out of here!"

He let out a low groan but didn't even turn, just held her close, encircling her in his huge arms and rubbing his nose along her neck, breathing in her scent. A low murmur rumbled in his throat. He nipped her tender skin with his teeth and moaned.

"Tarzan!" she squealed, peeking behind her at the sea monsters. He hitched her higher and wrapped her legs around his waist. *Oh God. He was erect again.* The hot feel of him between her legs sent her into a swoon, threatening to dispel her concerns over the beasts behind her. He reached between her legs and probed with the blunt tip of his cock, pressing between her sex lips, pushing for an entrance that she knew instinctively was too tight.

She stiffened and tried to scamper down but he held her tight, nipping her earlobe and pressing onward. The full feel of him stretching her was heaven, but when she looked behind her, her furry friends were standing on their hind legs watching them closely.

She startled. With the help of a full moon that appeared suddenly from behind the clouds, her eyes focused on King Kong and what looked like a girlfriend. She pounded on Tarzan to put her down, pushing with conviction against the granite feel of his chest until he finally lifted her off him and dropped her unceremoniously into the water where she landed with a splash.

She came up sputtering a curse, but he was too busy leveling a disgruntled glare at his friends to notice. Then he turned his back on all three of them and continued his washing with frustrated swipes, grumbling something inaudible.

"Go away," she snapped at her four-legged intruders. "We were here first."

The female cocked her head and scratched. Then with an audible grunt, she turned and trudged away. King Kong tramped behind her. She watched them until they reached the edge of the water, where they started to scramble up, but the sight of Kong's girlfriend turning her bottom to him must have proved too much. To Georgie's fascination, Kong dipped down between his mate's legs and sniffed her. Then he licked her, his long pink tongue teasing her with gentle swipes.

Georgie was riveted. Kong's girlfriend squirmed and moaned in obvious pleasure. Then Kong mounted her, biting her neck and shoulders as he did so, drawing high pitched cries from her that didn't sound like pain. He plunged into her, turning her cries to a shallow keening. Georgie felt her face flush at their pleasure.

From behind her Tarzan's massive arms encircled her. She sucked in a breath as his rough hands slid along her breast and then smoothed over her belly to slide between her legs. He separated her with slippery fingers that stroked between her folds, making her tingle, leaving a hot path of pleasure wherever he touched. And he was so adept, oddly gentle, under all that strength.

How did he know what to do? He teased, exploring between her legs and squeezing her nipples to hard points.

He moaned deep in his throat and pressed full against her bottom, his hard warmth engulfing her. She clutched at his wrist, intending to push him away but the ache between her legs made her press against his hand. He growled into her ear and slid one thick finger up through her hot folds, the sweet pleasure of it causing her to dissolve into a long shudder against his chest. His breath hitched and, encouraged, he continued to gently thrust with two fingers.

His breath came fast and heavy when he imitated the gesture by pumping his cock against her bottom in rhythm with his fingers, easing her further forward so she lay on her belly along the rock. He bit gently along her shoulders, murmuring and completely covering her while he pressed his weight to keep her still. He drew her one knee up, opening her further to him. She muffled a groan and grew unbelievably restless. How could she deny him, deny them both?

She struggled to clear her head. Of course she could deny him, she'd never had trouble fighting off bumbling frat boys who made a game of trying to get in her pants. She might be wild and incorrigible but she wasn't stupid. She'd decided long ago that she wouldn't jeopardize her vibrant health for a quick lay with a stranger. And he was a stranger by all accounts.

He licked her neck, running his tongue up along the curve of her throat and sliding his cock between the swell of her buttocks. He was so patient, and obviously delighted with what he'd found. And she had no doubt he knew what to do, regardless of his lack of experience. Yet he waited, for a signal from her. Was there no concept of rape in the jungle?

On instinct and pure lust, she raised her knees, tilting her bottom up in silent invitation. It was all he needed.

He slid his fingers out and replaced it with the blunt head of his cock, hot and throbbing with arousal. She waited, breathless, for the thick feel of him filling her. His fingers played with her lips, spreading them, and sliding her wetness and the soap everywhere as though he knew it would ease his passage. Then she felt the unbelievable pressure as he shoved his full length into her, slipping in easily because she was so wet, and releasing a deep grunt of satisfaction as he impaled her to the hilt.

Oh, God, he was buried up to her waist, completely filling her. He let loose a guttural moan and twisted inside her, throbbing thickly, his hands in a lock on her hips. Every nerve in her tight passage was lit to bursting. A few deep thrusts and she would surrender, but he was so aroused and this was so new to him that she feared he wouldn't last through even a few shallow thrusts. Still, she couldn't resist wriggling her fanny in encouragement. To her surprise he growled and tightened his hold on her hips, keeping her still. Didn't he know he was supposed to move?

"Tarzan," she cried. "Please, I'm burning up." She squirmed her bottom against him, encouraging him to thrust, but he growled louder and then slapped her bottom.

"What the?" she gasped. The shock of it got her immediate attention. She stopped squirming and stayed still, but rather than decrease her ardor, his little spank fueled her desire beyond rational proportions.

He began to move slowly, too slow for her. She bucked against him and in response he landed another firm spank on her fanny and growled and then another.

"Oh, my God!" Heat swelled her groin, hardening her clit to tortuous proportions. She thrust against him. He withdrew and smoothed his hands over her bottom, murmuring low, before plunging back into her. He cursed in words she didn't understand. When his thrusts grew more violent, her clit burned and then throbbed out a pleasuring rhythm that was so sweet she thought she would die. Her entire body contracted tight into itself and then finally let loose with warm bursts of pleasure that spread through her whole body as she came with a force beyond imagining.

Her every nerve stayed lit to extreme sensitivity. When he drove deep into her and held her tight, her arousal spiked once again with the tight stretching of her sex lips. She couldn't believe it. She slid an anxious finger over her clit and then he moved forcefully again, stretching and plundering her, his body tense and rock hard.

He growled and wrapped his arms around her, covering her with his full weight so she lay prostrate along the hard surface of the rock as he hitched as far as he could fit and then finally released his seed. She came again with the thrill of feeling him pump deep inside her.

A slow meltdown followed.

It was unbelievable. While she was hardly a virgin, her few experiences hadn't brought her anywhere close to this kind of bliss. After some time she felt his weight lift. Then he turned her over to lie flat on the rock. He stood between her legs, looking down into her face with an intensity that was terrifying.

She wondered what he must be thinking. He nudged her legs apart and ran one finger along her wet and swollen folds. He licked his lips. She drew him to her clitoris, still hard and sensitive, and guided him to circle the rough pad of his finger around the edges and then down it's length. She moaned and throbbed in response, shocked to feel herself grow aroused and ready for more. When she spread herself wider, he sucked in a harsh breath and swelled to thickness again. She didn't think that was possible but the telltale pearly drop of his readiness soon gleamed in the soft moonlight as he continued his exploration.

He moved to turn her over.

"No," she whispered, grasping his wrists and urging him forward. She lifted her knees and arched her hips.

He immediately understood and clasped his penis, guiding the tip between her sex lips and pushing. This time, as he slid in deep, he held her eyes with his as long as he could, the whites of his heavy lids gleaming in the darkness, his raw pleasure palpable. Then his lids closed on a soft murmur and he eased himself down along her body, pressing skin to skin, his lips buried in her neck.

He lay still for some time, as though savoring the sensation while she skimmed her nails down the broad expanse of his back. The moon shimmered above them, a glittering beacon in the hovering darkness.

Little pinpoints of light peaked out from the surrounding vegetation and, a little disconcerted, she remembered her audience. Small harmless creatures, what did it matter? Then, like with the sudden flick of a switch, a stream of light cut through the overhead cover and illuminated their little cocoon. A full moon sliced a brilliant path from the sky to the slick granite slab where they lay entwined.

She peeked behind her. He reared up on his elbows and looked where they joined, his eyes aflame. He thrust deep, impaling her to her full depths. "Oh, my God." She shuddered. "You feel wonderful…" He grunted and watched himself pull out almost entirely only to thrust once again, this time faster, his breathing accelerating and his thick muscled body shaking with his pleasure. That she could bring such a powerful man to his knees with pleasure awed her.

He ducked and bit her nipples and then licked along her breasts. But soon he threw back his neck and let out a tortured moan. He thrust faster, his urgency building.

Her body thrummed with sensation, every pleasure point strung to bursting. Within minutes, she was spiraling once again over the edge. For a short moment, she lost consciousness, shuddering with the sweet hot pleasure swamping her and the wonderful strong feel of him pumping his need into her once more in hot thick spurts. She swore she could feel the warm living liquid squirt hot against her womb.

He lowered himself onto her and groaned, his skin slick with sweat and hot, his muscles twitching. She collapsed under him, limp with exhaustion and held him close.

The next thing she remembered, she was awakening under his crushing weight. They must have both slept, for how long she couldn't imagine, and would probably still be sleeping if his body hadn't hindered her breathing. His breathing was deep and smooth and his smell so male. It seemed his body was everywhere, powerfully containing her movements. But she felt no fear. Only a contented safety in his arms.

What in the world was she thinking?

She gave him a hard shove. "Wake up!"

He grunted and rolled over to lay prostrate on the smooth slate of rock, looking as breathless as she felt.

"No one would believe this," she muttered to herself before slipping off the rock to wash up. "I don't believe it."

Chapter Three

A gentle morning mist filtered through the quiet valley deep in the jungle. The curious family of gorillas gazed at the grassy shelter, high up in the trees and waited, curious as to their new visitor.

As the warm rays of the sun peeked through the forest's top canopy and played along Georgie's cheeks, she slid with a yawning stretch against the cool crisp sheets and breathed in the sweet smell of honeysuckle. She lingered on the scent, momentarily confused as to its source, but stubbornly refusing to fully awaken. She pushed any uncertainty to the back of her mind, so reluctant was she to start the day and have to face the relentless dry dust of the village. She burrowed back into the pillows and shut her eyes tight against an image of the professor's boring drone as he described tribal custom. This morning, for the first time in the weeks since her arrival, she actually felt refreshed, having finally gotten a full night's sleep. Even the hard lumps of the grass and plywood mattress seemed a distant nightmare.

Why was that?

Without opening her eyes, she patted the soft pillowed mound beneath her. *What the?* Her eyes popped wide. When she rolled over, her face slapped into muscled chest, covered with a light sheen of summer sweat, bringing visions of last night flooding back in sharp focus along with all the smells and sensations...the wonderful feel of him. She breathed in a tantalizing breath of his rich scent, remembering his taste. She groaned.

She gazed up at the hard line of his jaw, relaxed in sleepy repose. Last night she'd succumbed to him three times. No, four. He was insatiable and so eager... fascinated with her.

The honeysuckle soap that he'd slathered all over her body still clung to her skin and scented the sheets. She glanced at her surroundings. A sheer mosquito net walled the space where they slept, the fabric tenting into a high peak that nestled among a thick cluster of trees. No. She let out a startled gasp. She was *in* the trees. She scampered up on her knees. They were high up. A roped ladder dangled from a split in the netting and plunged a good forty feet to the ground. A roped walkway spanned between the trees to another mosquito tented shelter. A jungle suite in the trees. It had its charm.

The sheet fell away. She was naked. She glanced down at him. He was, too. Gloriously tanned and golden. It was so dark last night. She looked her fill now, letting her eyes travel along the acre of muscle that spanned his chest and taking in the dark mat of wiry hair sprinkled along the ridges. The hand that lay on his chest was large but finely boned, rough, yet with long tapered fingers. She remembered those hands last night, exploring and satisfying his bone deep curiosity. She flushed crimson at the knowledge he had of her.

She didn't even know his name. *He* didn't even know his name. A wave of sympathy mollified her. She ran a thick strand of his hair through her fingers, recalling how his wild mane draped her when he entered her, the waves framing a face dark with passion, his eyes liquid with ecstasy. With her fingertip, she traced the long chord of muscle running from beneath his jaw to his collarbone. The texture of his skin was rough with beard growth. Then her eyes involuntarily dropped to his groin.

Even in his relaxed state, he looked powerfully male. He had needed very little time between climaxes. And she knew after last night's initiation, he could never go back to his celibate life.

She put that thought aside and looked again at her surroundings. On top of a small wooden stand sat a basin and along the wall, pegs made from broken off tree branches held scraps of cloth, small cups, her panties, some—. Her panties?

She scurried off the bed, taking the sheet to wrap around her and snatched the torn lace off the hook. She sighed in frustration. They were useless now. Where was her dress? She spotted it draped over a small tree stump.

She dropped the sheet and hastily donned it, securing the front buttons on the bottom and clutching the top closed, looking about at the same time for something that would hold it, when she felt him watching her. She met his gaze with a stern look, intending to start this day off right. Regardless of last night, she was going back to the village. He couldn't keep her here, a prisoner, to do what he wanted with her. And she couldn't leave without his help or she'd be lost in the jungle forever.

But the warm glow in his eyes as he studied her with his head propped in his hand and stretched completely naked along the bed melted her. Her eyes flicked to his groin, swelling quickly under her blatant admiration.

"Oh no you don't." She lifted her palms and backed up. "You're taking me back today, now." Her eyes dropped again to his erection, full and thick and then back to his face. She had to be imagining the amused glint in his eyes. He held a hand out, beckoning her to the bed.

"No," she said. "I know you understand me, even if you don't understand the words."

His hand stroked down his aroused length.

"Stop that," she demanded as she watched him. A warm drum of arousal filled her, heating her skin with alarming speed. Her nipples tightened and ached. Maybe just once more before she left?

He inched back from the edge of the bed and patted with his beautiful and oh so clever hand the place beside him.

She sighed in frustration. "What am I going to do with you?" she murmured while she went to him as if in a trance.

In the seconds it took him to strip off her dress and ease her down beside him, his lips were everywhere, tasting and licking and teasing her beyond belief. His moans of pleasure as he savored every inch of her body had her shuddering in his arms. He was so adept.

He had learned quickly the magic of her small pearly bud that heated and swelled her sex lips, opening her to him and making her burn, beg him. He was so focused on her pleasure.

His lips brushed down over her belly to lick at the tops of her legs. He spread her, running his tongue along the smooth skin of her inner thighs, first one and then skimming over her burning center as he moved to the other. She arched her hips with the gentle touch.

"Please," she breathed.

She felt the tip of his tongue sweep over her in a light caress, probing gently, separating her layers, teasing her. She dug her fingers into his hair and urged him further, but he held her at bay, murmuring something inaudible as he drew back and looked at her.

She was starkly aware of the morning light baring all her treasures to his hungry eyes, but she was too aroused to care. He touched her clitoris lightly with the tip of his tongue and then withdrew and watched as it contracted and throbbed.

"Stop it," she wailed, popping him on the head. He licked her, one quick thick swipe up through her lips and over her clitoris and then withdrew again. She groaned and thrashed. "You're just doing this to torture me." He slipped his thumb into her, but withdrew on her sigh of pleasure. She pounded on his shoulders. She couldn't believe it when he released a low warm chuckle. The brute knew exactly what he was doing.

Before she could beat him again, he crawled up her body and laid on top of her, nudging her legs wider, his expression no longer playful. She loved the hard, heavy feel of him, his muscled weight pinning her, and the scent of his skin, masculine and clean, the feel of him warm under her fingers. She clutched his shoulders as he reared up on his elbows and gazed down at her. The seriousness of his expression took her by surprise as well as the tenderness in his eyes.

She skimmed her fingers along the strong set of his jaw. He closed his eyes at her touch and then thrust deep, bringing a cry of surprise from her that turned into a moan of pure pleasure. He bit back a groan and shuddered, his strong face dissolving into an agony of bliss. He collapsed on top of her and buried his lips in her neck, holding her still, but spreading her wide with his knees and hitching deeper. She was burning up. She bucked against him, urging him to move.

"I need to feel you," she whispered. "Please."

He withdrew and thrust but then held her still again, his breathing labored, his lips still buried in her neck. When she squirmed, he moved, but this time with a slow sensuous, rhythmic thrusting that drove her crazy. The heat and thick feel of him filling her was heaven, the friction of his thrusting lighting every nerve. She clutched at him, digging her nails deep into his flesh and whimpered, begging for more.

He growled and thrust faster until the frenzied heat of it was too much for her. Every nerve cried out for release. "I can't, I…" she sobbed, not understanding what was happening to her. She would die if this lasted much longer.

He held her close and plundered her until she surrendered to his strength and warmth and exploded in his arms. His release followed right behind.

It was a long time before he lifted his face and with gentle fingers, smoothed the wet curls from her forehead. He murmured sounds but no words formed and the warm timbre of his voice stirred her in an entirely feminine way. She wanted to know what he felt, what he was thinking. It frustrated her that he couldn't tell her. She touched a finger to his lips. He closed his eyes and sighed and then rolled off her and lay on his back, looking up at the leafed canopy above. Deep furrows creased his brow.

On impulse, she ran her fingers along the lines, smoothing away the wrinkles with a comforting hand. He turned and looked at her, circling her wrist, his eyes filled with a longing that overwhelmed her and an intensity that she could too easily drown in. She drew away gingerly and began searching for her dress. Spying it on the floor beside her, she tipped on her side and reached for it. A warm palm settled on her bare bottom.

She groaned. "No," she said, snatching at his hand. He drew her against him, cradling her bottom against his rising erection.

"I have to go," she cried, giving his hand a firm yank. She jumped off the bed and shoved her arms through the straps of her dress and buttoned it quickly. Clutching the front closed, she eyed him with a sternness that she didn't feel. "You've got to get me back," she told him and motioned off in the distance, pointing down the ladder and beyond the trees. "Take me now," she said with little conviction. His eyes shone with a devilish gleam. "It'll take us all day and I don't want to be trapped in the jungle at dark."

He watched her speak, easing off the bed as she did.

"Good." She sighed, her eyes traveling involuntarily down his body when he stood. She told herself to look away, but she knew she wasn't likely to be rewarded with a look at such a virile specimen in the near future, probably in her lifetime. He pulled the leather loincloth off the hook and wrapped it around his ample bulge. Her eyes lingered on his bronze chest and followed the dark shadow of hair that ran up his neck. His beard was heavy this morning and his hair lay in an awry tumble to his shoulders. He looked fierce, but she knew better. His gentleness with her tugged viciously at her heart.

She stifled a small whimper and glanced away.

He smiled and took her hand, guiding her to the small table that held a large water bottle and a basin. Toothbrushes and hairbrushes hung neatly on hooks, surrounding it. Even mint toothpaste lay alongside the basin. He poured water from the bottle into the galvanized bowl and splashed his face. Then he drew her over to stand in front of him to do the same.

Although she still felt wonderfully clean from the hot tub last night, the heat of the jungle was already rising and the cool water refreshed her. She pulled back her curls and dabbed apricot scrub along her cheeks. She could feel him leave her side. When she glanced around, he had moved to a shelf along the wall.

He was shaving, using a small mirror that was anchored along a tree trunk. He skimmed down over his jaw and along his neck, his biceps rippling as he shook off the soap and rinsed the razor.

She had no brothers, no siblings at all, and the little experience she'd had with men didn't include this intimacy. Watching such a personal male ritual was oddly arousing. He glanced over when he dried off with a towel. His hair was tied back with leather into a thick ponytail and as he came toward her, she could smell the fresh scent of mint on his breath. He touched her cheek, smoothing along the soft skin and then took her fingers and laid them along his hard jaw. Then he smiled. A warm, drawing smile that melted her insides and told her that he, too, enjoyed their differences. For such a primitive man, one who had little contact with humans and none with females, he was marvelously perceptive.

He fingered the front of her dress, but she quickly stepped back further and clutched it closed. His smile widened. He released a small chuckle as he grabbed a leather cord off a branch hook and picked up a small pocketknife from the table and flicked it open.

"Stay back, Tarzan. I'm warning you." *Or what?* She'd deck him?

With a casual hand, he laced the leather through one button hole and then cut tiny holes along the other side of the dress so he could lace the cord through. He crisscrossed it over her bodice, pulling it snug, and then twisted the laces at the top into a small knot.

"Thank you," she said, giving him a warm smile.

He cupped her chin and drew his thumb along her jaw line, drawing her closer as though to kiss her. But of course he wouldn't know what a kiss was, would he? Even after all they'd done, they'd never kissed. It was tempting to show him, so tempting, but that would only lead to much more and she needed to leave here, not linger. He brushed his lips along her cheek, then his nose, breathing deeply. All she needed was to turn her lips to his and press.

Before she could give in to temptation, she ducked her head and walked around him to the top of the roped stairs.

He shook his head and gestured to their mouths and then their stomachs. She reluctantly agreed. She *was* hungry and had been since she'd come to these ends of the earth. But she longed for penne pasta with sun dried tomatoes and *Ben & Jerry's* New York Chocolate Chunk Fudge, not the gluing stew she feared he would feed her.

He took her hand and guided her through the roped bridge that connected to the other trees. The small room he brought her to had grass mats and a low table. After he settled her on a mat, he produced a small lime-looking fruit that he sliced in two, pressing half to his lips. He drank in the juice. Then he offered her the other half. The sweet juice had a delicious tang and she sucked eagerly, suddenly aware of her thirst and hunger.

Before long, he had enticed her with more. Some fruits she recognized, like the bananas and mangos, but others were unknown – all were delicious. When she approved each new taste with a smile, he smiled back in satisfaction. He watched her mouth as he fed her, running his fingertips along her bottom lip more than once and then licking the sweet nectar from his fingertip. How he would enjoy a kiss! When she licked her lips, his eyes grew stormy and he watched every move.

She shook off the tempting thought of a kiss and waved away his offer of what looked like fried banana slices with guava dip. "I'm full," she said, patting her tummy and wiping her lips with a cloth napkin made out of rough cotton.

Were his civilized ways traces of his life before his disappearance or were they due to his observing poachers and others who had wandered into his territory? Since he'd only seen men, she doubted the latter. If she were smart, she'd stay a while and study him, take notes to share with the professor, really impress him. It didn't appear that she'd starve here. He certainly wasn't.

Her eyes lit on a sizeable wooden box. His treasures? Silver items stolen from camps? Or maybe just extra supplies. Everything necessary for survival seemed to be hanging all around them.

Seeing her studying the box, he walked over and crouched before it but then hesitated. When he looked at her, his eyes were troubled, as though he questioned whether he could trust her. He lifted it a crack and peered in. Then he opened it wide and stepped back. With a nod and a small motion of his hand, he offered her a look.

She dropped to her knees and searched its contents. A leather wallet lay on top. She flipped through it. Credit cards, a few dollars, a drivers license from Boston—a Professor Stanton. She wondered if he was still alive. She wanted to believe he only killed poachers, those who harmed innocent creatures. Several gold chains and a watch lay across a few pieces of folded cloth, heavy denim and some leather. A small red shiny object in the bottom caught her eye. When she picked it up, she realized it was a *Lego*. Or rather, several *Lego* pieces fit together to make a car. All the wheels were intact and a little *Lego* man sat atop. Even the steering wheel remained.

She drew in a breath. A remnant of his past? If he was a small child when he was lost, perhaps this was in his pocket when he had wandered off? Her heart picked up beats. She riffled through the box in earnest. Rings, belts, lots of precious metals, no doubt scavenged from the poachers, a few more wallets with identifying information that meant nothing to her. Then she picked up coveralls that might fit a three-year-old. Blue denim shorts with the label carrying the unmistakable name of *OshKosh B'Gosh*. This had to be what he was wearing when lost! It startled her to see this ghost from his past. She fingered the cloth and looked back at him, trying to see the boy in his rough masculine features. He watched her closely with obvious apprehension. She poked in the pockets—nothing. A few more unimportant items and then her fingers brushed paper.

Sitting at the bottom was a small child's book, old and weathered, its bright colors dulled to whiteness. It looked so fragile, she feared picking it up. With great care she lifted it and then sat back on her heels.

He looked over her shoulder and peered down at the book on her lap.

"Richard Scarry," she breathed, stunned. "It's *The Please and Thank You* Book." She smoothed her fingertips along its surface and then carefully turned to her favorite part— "Pig Will and Pig Won't." She smiled in recognition at the familiar words she'd ceaselessly begged her mother to read and that she had listened to with such pleasure. As young as she was, probably two, she had memorized parts and would fill in as her mother recited the lines.

Now, she read the words aloud that told the story of Mother pig who was trying to teach her little pigs to be helpful. Tarzan was sprawled behind her and had settled his chin on her shoulder.

"Mother Pig had two little pigs—Pig Will and Pig Won't. Whenever she asked them to do something, Pig Will said, 'I will.' But Pig Won't said—"

"I won't."

Tarzan's voice startled her. Not the rich timbre of it, because he had grumbled what sounded like curses to her several times and then later murmured soft endearments that she didn't understand. But this time his words had perfect diction.

"What did you say?" she asked, although she had heard him perfectly. She turned fully to him. He looked as perplexed as she felt, as though he hadn't understood himself why he'd said it.

She was anxious to read on. The pigs were asked by Daddy to play more quietly and of course that kiss-up, Pig Will, chanted again "I will." She read on with a smirk, relishing Pig Won't's part. "But Pig Won't said—"

"I won't."

She drew in a soft breath. There it was again, clear and unmistakable.

She set the book down with care and turned to kneel before him, searching his face for some recognition that he understood. But he was frowning. Cupping his face with her hands she said, "You were a Pig Won't too, weren't you?"

He blinked his long lashes and reached up to encircle her wrists, listening to her closely. "That's why you wandered away from your parents. You never listened either."

He ran his thumbs along the smooth skin of her inside wrists and stroked, never taking his eyes off her. A small part of her understood him. She pictured a small hellion of a boy, defying his parents at every turn and then lost, hopelessly separated from those same parents, never to see them again.

This was no savage beast. This was an intelligent strong-willed boy that had grown into a strong man who had somehow survived, separated from his world for far too long.

Well, no more. She would bring him back! But first she'd teach him what he already knew and of which he just needed to be reminded. His English was perfect, she was sure, but buried deep in the recesses of his mind.

She'd start her introduction back to civilization with a kiss.

Chapter Four

"Would you like to kiss me?" she asked.

He frowned.

"Kiss," she said clearly, slowly, exaggerating the *s* sound and showing how her lips formed the word. She touched his lips with her fingertips and then touched hers. "Kiss," she repeated. His eyes lit with interest.

She ran her finger along her bottom lip as she said the word again. "Kiss." Then she touched his, nodding her head, urging him to imitate her.

After a moment's hesitation, his voice came on a whisper. "Kiss," he said. She smiled in approval.

"Kiss," he said a little louder.

"Okay," she said. Leaning forward, she pressed her mouth to his.

His eyes widened as he watched their lips meet. Then she drew back. "Kiss," she explained.

He swallowed. "Kiss," he repeated, his voice rough. He framed her face with his hands and drew her toward him. *He caught on quick!*

When their lips met this time, his softened and his eyes closed. She pressed and brushed along his, taking the lead, allowing their breath to mingle. She settled her palms on his chest and felt the pounding of his heart. But other than his lips softening under hers, he was still, content to learn what she was doing.

She licked his bottom lip and he groaned, instinctively parting his mouth and holding her face more firmly. She touched his tongue with the tip of hers and then withdrew a fraction, teasing, getting him to lean forward, searching for more. His tongue chased hers, playing and exploring until he would no longer be teased.

He delved deep, exploding with urgency, his mouth restless, moving over hers and drawing her closer, demanding more. He picked her up and settled her on his lap, stroking his tongue with hers. He tasted of mint and warmth and the forest, and he was wet, wonderfully wet and slick, then rough and smooth at the same time.

She soon lost herself in his plunging thrusts and the feel of him grow-ing bone hard beneath her as he enveloped her in arms that felt like bands of steel. But rather than panic, she melted into his heat, turning soft and yielding. Her loins felt liquid and marvelously loose.

He licked along her lips and then plunged again. Who was teaching whom? She supposed some things were pure instinct.

Their tongues tangled together in a heated dance so sensual her body ignited and burned. He nipped her lips, pulling with his teeth and sucking her bottom lip gently. For only a kiss, it was unbearably erotic. Then his hands were under her skirt, cupping her bare bottom and lifting her. His finger slid into her slippery wet heat. He lifted her easily and slid her down onto him so that he impaled her completely. She thrilled at the full feel of him and breathed a deep sigh of satisfaction.

Her eyes flew open. He was doing it again. Capturing her, mesmeriz-ing her, so she couldn't think straight. Before she could protest, he lifted her and thrust hard several times before he exploded inside her. The power of his climax shook her, and the fierce tension lines in his face that sud-denly gave way to an expression of extreme pleasure only served to in-crease her fright. She had to get away from him.

But when she pushed against him, he reached between her legs with his thumb and stroked the hard knot of her pleasure to excruciating taut-ness until she was blind with it and begging for release.

He pinched her clitoris, and she exploded with primal moans that had her shaking in his arms. She lay limp against his chest where he cradled her, sifting his long fingers through her hair.

She wanted to cry. She'd never make it out of here.

She settled into the safety of his arms, still impaled by him, and let him soothe her, soothe away all the conflicts facing her. She loved the timbre of his voice. Even if she couldn't understand the words he mur-mured, she felt his calm wrap around her like a warm blanket. How was she to leave him now?

He would just have to come with her. After she taught him the words he had forgotten and brought back memories of his past life. But what if he wouldn't come?

They read the book several more times, each time with him repeating the "I won't" parts and learning a few more words as she pointed out the boat, TV, and car, and even the ice cream in the story.

How he would love ice cream! A group of little animals ate chocolate ice cream with Pig Will. She had frowned as the rest of the story came back to her. Pig Will got to have ice cream with all the other "hard workers" but since Pig Won't had stubbornly refused to help, he'd been left home, missing out on both the work *and* the treat. She smiled despite herself, wondering how many such treats her stubborn Tarzan, like her, had missed out on.

Suddenly, it occurred to her to look inside the book jacket for a name. When she found the shaded square with *My name is* and looked at the line beneath it, she sighed with disappointment. The letters where his name would have been had long since faded. She held the book up to the light, hoping for a miracle. She got it.

Although the other letters were too faded, the first one was clearly an M. "Michael," she murmured. "Matthew, Mark." She held it closer, then farther. "Maybe Martin or Mitch—"

"Mark," he said, clear as a bell.

She held her breath and turned to him. "Mark?" she repeated.

He frowned and kneaded his temples with his forefingers and then gave a shrug and looked away, thoughtful. She wanted to shake him, but instead she forced herself to be patient. When his gaze finally returned, his eyes shone with conviction and then he placed his palm against his chest. He patted it. "Mark."

To her horror, she let out a small sob and leaped into his arms. "Mark," she called him, raining kisses over his face. He smiled with pleasure.

"Mark," he repeated and she kissed him all over again and yet again when he repeated it. Soon, she wasn't sure if his name really was Mark or he just wanted kisses for saying it. But she felt deliriously happy just knowing his name.

She patted her own chest. "Georgie," she said.

His eyes fixed on her breasts. "Georgie," he said and fondled her breast.

She slapped his hand away. "No, *I'm* Georgie," she scolded, "and you're Mark," she said, pointing to him. She repeated the gesture.

He studied her quietly for so long that she wasn't sure he understood. Then he slid his fingers along her jaw. "Georgie," he said, his voice low and with a reverence that moved her. He kissed her chastely on the lips, tenderly, and she filled with an emotion she didn't recognize. But at that moment, she felt a bond grow between them that she feared could not be broken.

The next month was filled with lessons. But not all were for him. While he caught on to the language with a speed that astounded her, she was less quick to learn and adapt to the wilds of the jungle.

Cooking was a luxury because finding dry timber of any kind was near impossible. Since she had refused to eat anything raw that moved—although *he* felt no such aversion and feasted on a variety of food sources that made her gag just watching him—this left her with only fruits, vegetables, and nuts. The fruit slid down easily but the vegetables were a chore. She relished the crunch and chew of a multitude of seeds and nuts, however, for she missed sinking her teeth into a nice chicken breast or tender fish fillet, and she found she craved the oil taste in the nuts. But with such a small variety of food available to her, she worried that she'd lose the few pounds of fat she had and then she'd *really* look like a boy.

She had frowned a bit at her pique over the food. She knew she was spoiled—a little—having never wanted for anything in her life, other than more of everything that she already had. She wasn't greedy, her father had often said in her defense, just spirited. But she ruefully admitted now that even her father had lost patience with her these last couple of years. With that thought in mind, she determined to appreciate what food they had and not think about what they didn't.

Less easy to adapt to were the thousands—millions—of insects and other creepy crawlers. Flies, beetles, and stinging insects, and ants and spiders of every variety buzzed around the multitude of hanging herbs and flowers, eating and pollinating with a fury. She knew they were hungry, too, and just doing their job, but she found them almost impossible to ignore. It was weeks before she learned to casually flick a spider off her arm rather than screech with revulsion and leap off the forest floor.

Mark was always bemused by her outbursts. Everything she did seemed to bemuse and fascinate him. Just for entertainment he'd sometimes plant little bugs on her shoulders to tease her. But the game he enjoyed best was planting spiders on her thigh so he could rescue her by playfully slipping his hand up her skirt and saving her from the creature. Even more he enjoyed how quickly her skin heated and the way in which she eagerly rewarded him for his bravery.

And if she'd had any lingering doubt about his potential for violence it dissipated under his gentle protectiveness toward her.

Georgie and Mark had been hiking for some time and he was patiently pointing out all the creatures of the rain forest. She supplied him with the names she knew, or at least the most likely family of species they belonged to, but she was far from an expert, despite that several units in her earth science class had covered the rainforest. She mentally calculated the number of those classes she had missed and could have kicked herself. But that class met on Mondays. What was she to do after a long weekend on the ski slopes? Certainly not show up for a class at the ungodly hour of 10:00 am.

He had already hesitatingly introduced her to his gorilla friends. And she didn't know who was more scared of whom. They stayed safely at a distance that first week. When Mark would swim across the hot spring or go over to their marked territory to meet with them, he always communicated exclusively with the large Silverback that she'd encountered that first day and who was the obvious leader of the clan. The two spoke in grunts and gestures. It saddened Georgie to think that perhaps they understood each other better than Mark understood her.

She grew grim. If it was the last thing she did, she would change that.

By the end of the fourth week, she knew which snakes to avoid and what a deadly scorpion looked like, and that, although the various conglomerates of lizards might be ugly, they were harmless—at least to everything but the insects. She even learned to sense when a jaguar was prowling the area. The forest would grow deadly quiet as all the smaller animals burrowed underground or deep into trees. She and Mark had stayed high up in his treehouse those few times and waited silently, he with his knife poised in one hand and a hatchet in the other, and she shaking like a leaf.

He understood her terror afterwards and gathered her into his strong arms until she calmed. And when he held her, she truly believed he was stronger, far superior to the jaguar, and could protect her from anything.

As they moved along now, with the steamy heat of the forest rising around her ankles and the sunlight like glass crystals shimmering through the canopy above, she thought she had never seen anything so beautiful. Soft blushes of pastels and purples smudged the emerald green leaves and vines that dangled all around. The rich clean scent of rainwater that sparkled and dripped from the ends of every leaf smelled so fresh and gently rinsed away the day's dust and pollen.

She breathed in the sweet fragrance, content to follow Mark deeper into the jungle, watching the flexing muscles of his backside and corded thighs as he stepped over logs and branches.

He stopped suddenly and put out his arm in a silencing gesture. "Stop," he ordered. "Listen." He grew very still.

Had he not sounded so urgent, she would have enjoyed the ease with which he used his new language skills but he tensed, his jaw rigid as he lifted his face to listen.

Then she heard it. Could almost smell them. Humans.

Her heart stopped. Male voices. One English speaking. Mark swung into action. In one swift movement, he scooped her up and hitched her onto his hip, darting around tree trunks and limbs until he found a thick oak. Before she realized what was happening, he climbed the trunk with a few strong strides and settled in the crook of a high branch, settling her onto his lap. He pressed a finger to her lips and held her close.

Not a moment later, two men passed below them, one clumsily swiping aside the twisting branches of the understory vegetation as he followed behind his native guide.

"Are you sure you're not lost?" the white man grumbled. "My mission is to find the girl, not get lost myself."

Georgie's breath stopped. The accent was New York. She must be the girl he was looking for.

"Her parents will pay me a small fortune to find her but will pay nothing if I don't—"

"Maybe in valley," the native grunted, pointing ahead.

"But what about that wild man who supposedly lives in the valley? What if we meet up with him?"

The native man scowled. "Kill wild man. Get big money from government. We both rich."

Georgie gasped and snuggled in closer to Mark. How could she have forgotten about her parents? Of course they'd be looking for her and must be worried sick. But one of these men wouldn't hesitate to kill Mark in the process of finding her.

The white man wiped his forehead and neck with a madras scarf. "Jesus, this is like a sauna. How much farther?"

"Few miles." The native man swung a leather pouch to his mouth and gulped.

Georgie wanted to leap from the tree as her brain filled with visions of home and her little red Miata, Thai food, her CDs. What she would give to listen to her *Diskman* while running along the Long Island shore.

The white man tipped up his canteen and drank greedily before saying. "If she's with the wild man, I hope she's still alive."

They moved on, with the native man moving gracefully through the thick foliage and the white man stumbling after him, their pace slow enough that she knew Mark could easily get them back to the valley before the two reached it. But then what?

Chapter Five

"What?" she breathed.

Mark's face darkened. "No," he roared, his body vibrating with fury. He advanced on her with powerful strides and swept her into his arms.

"Put me down," she demanded, pounding against him with little effect until he dropped her onto the bed.

If the investigator her parents had hired had made it to the valley with his guide, they'd yet to see them, and Georgie and Mark had returned hours ago. But the valley was huge, and most likely the pair was rooting around deep at the other end. It could take hours to cross the valley on foot if you didn't know the terrain and dark was falling quickly. Hopefully, the investigator wouldn't give up and would resume his search tomorrow.

She had been trying to explain to Mark about her parent's worry over her and that she had to talk with the investigator, that she couldn't stay. She didn't know how much he understood, but *she* understood that he didn't like what he heard. But she didn't know why.

"Mark," she tried to patiently explain while she lay sprawled out on the bed, watching his agitated pacing. "There are only two of them, and you have guns." She pointed to the abundant supply hanging off the walls. "They have more to fear than you do. They'll take me without harming you or the animals."

"No," he said, coming toward her. He dropped to sit beside her on the bed and leaned over her, trapping her between his arms and pinning her to the mattress. "You are mine now!" he growled, his eyes fierce.

Her eyes grew huge. She didn't know which stunned her more. The fact that it was the first time he had communicated with more than one word, having strung several words together to form a complete sentence, or the fact that he thought he owned her.

"You … you can't keep me," she stuttered.

He leaned in nose to nose. "Yes," he hissed, his eyes smoldering. "You are mine!"

She strangled a gasp of panic. His eyes blazed with vehemence and his fortitude terrified her. He *could* keep her here. She'd have no way of escaping him. And he could easily kill anyone who tried to take her. She was sure that he *would* kill anyone who tried.

His pupils dilated and his eyes blackened with restrained rage. She held her breath. She would *not* be a prisoner. *But now didn't seem the right time to tell him.*

She smoothed her palms over the muscles of his chest, tense and rigid now with the effort to control himself. The hard muscles flexed and then relaxed under her tentative touch. She flicked her nail over his nipple and he let out a soft moan. She licked the tiny flat nub, amazed again that he would be so sensitive. He tasted salty with sweat and smelled like the forest and him, tangy and fresh and male.

She spoke to him soothingly, knowing he wouldn't understand more than half of it. "You can come with me. We'll find your parents. I'll introduce you to all the delights of civilization." He eased down beside her, gathering her into his arms and trailing his lips along her forehead as she continued to lick his chest and neck. He was so warm and solid. They were meant to be together.

He unlaced her bodice and played with her nipples, his large palms completely covering her breasts. "Will you come with me, Mark?" she purred.

"No," he said, his voice low and sure.

Her lips stilled and she sat up. "Mark?" She tried to look him in the eye, but he had locked onto her breasts while attempting to slip his hand under her skirt. He palmed her thighs. "Look at me, Mark." She pushed at his shoulders. "We're going back where we *both* belong. You are *human*. You're coming with me."

He eased his finger up through her hot folds where, already, she ached for him, yet he had barely touched her. A tingling shiver snaked through her. She grabbed onto his wrist. "Mark, you—"

He shoved in deep and then looked at her, impaling her with his gaze. His thumb, wet from his probing, grazed her clitoris. Pure pleasure stripped through her. "*You* stay with *me!*" he breathed.

She strangled on a protest as he pressed with his thumb, taking away her strength and reducing her to liquid. Her eyes rolled up into her head, and he stroked with greater pressure and thrust deep within her. She moaned and struggled against the urge to let him take her. He'd take her surrender as acquiescence. But as she sat crossed legged on the bed, fully exposed, as he relentlessly plunged her, she felt helpless to resist him. The front buttons of her dress were splayed open and she was spread wide for him, wider by his searching fingers. The juices of her arousal coated his fingers as he skillfully stroked her. He bit gently on her nipples and she exploded, in long shuddering groans that held her captive in his arms. The same way he planned to hold her captive in his treehouse.

He stripped off his loincloth and laid her across the bed. Taking his engorged cock in hand, he positioned himself between her legs. But while her body still wanted him, she would not let him win. Would not let him think she had succumbed to him and would stay.

She pushed hard against his chest and bucked her hips.

He frowned and held her hips, but as he drew back to guide himself, she kicked up with her knee, just missing her target. She scratched at his face. For one shocked moment he stilled, but then he grabbed her wrists with a vengeance.

"No," she screamed at him. "You can't force me. You can't keep me. Let me go!" She tried to bite his neck.

He growled deep in his throat and then clamped her wrists together above her head. The next moment she felt a leather cord tight around them, binding her hands together. He leaped off the bed and pulled on the cord. Her back arched as she was pulled upward. "What are you doing?" she shrieked. "You can't tie me up." But he did, pulling hard on the cord and yanking it around the tree at the head of the bed. She kicked wildly, her body bouncing off the bed. "Let me go, you beast." She pulled on her restraints.

He came around to the front of the bed. He was still fully aroused. She kicked at him, wishing she could make contact. His eyes smoldered and heated. Taking his eyes off her for just a moment, he grabbed up one of his knives and came at her. With one swift movement he sliced the straps off her sundress and ripped it out from under her.

He dropped her cut sundress onto the floor, leaving her naked as he feasted his eyes on her.

He stroked down his thick length. The small pearly drop of his seed glistened on the angry head of his penis. When her eyes dropped to the smooth wet skin, his cock pulsed and throbbed under her gaze. He was beautiful and so powerful but at this moment she despised his strength.

"I hate you," she choked, furious at her own helplessness.

He blinked and then went stone still.

She kicked again, a useless gesture that would accomplish nothing if he was intent on taking her, dominating her, showing her that she was his. It was blatantly apparent that that was exactly what he planned on doing.

He made the mistake of coming slowly around to the side of the bed, the tension lines in his forehead softening, telling her that he had let his guard down. As he went to ease down beside her, she kneed sideways and got him right in the groin.

A bellow ripped from his throat and he grabbed himself as he buckled over. His breath came in deep gasps. She had gotten him good.

While he crouched on the floor, she yanked and struggled against her bonds, hoping against the odds of him being careless in his knot tying this time. But her wrists held firm. She panicked now. What would he do when he recovered?

She glanced down beside her and watched him struggle to his feet. He stumbled over to the washbasin and splashed water along his face and neck and then dried himself, his back to her. The tight muscles on his bare buttocks flexed and tensed. His shoulders heaved in a long-suffering sigh.

Maybe he'd think twice about keeping her here now.

He dropped the towel onto the stool and turned slowly to face her. It wasn't surprising that he wasn't erect anymore, but he didn't look permanently damaged either, she decided with relief. His face relaxed as he studied her. She didn't dare utter a word as his eyes grazed down her body and then up again. She struggled defiantly with her bonds, but all that did was thrust her breasts up even farther. She felt boldly exposed and burned at her vulnerable position.

She could tell by his softened expression as he continued to study her that he would untie her. Relief filled her. She would be free and then she'd convince him to go with her. She hadn't meant to hurt or upset him. He just needed to know that she was in charge. If he would just listen to her, he'd soon see that everything would be all right.

He snapped another leather chord off a branch. She blinked in confusion as he approached her with slow deliberate steps.

"What… what are you going to do now?" she breathed. He slapped the chord against his thigh. "Mark?" She looked up into his black eyes, glittering now like polished marble. She swallowed. "You're not… you're not going to…" her voice trailed off as her eyes dropped to his hand, flexing against his thigh. His penis was throbbing to life.

When he pounced on her, it took her a moment to realize that he was tying her legs. After he clamped her ankles together, he then looped each ankle separately until she was bound to the bed, spread-eagled before him. "You're despicable," she railed at him. "A barbarian!"

He smiled in satisfaction as he looked down at her from where he stood at the foot of the bed, his gaze fixated between her legs. His erection rose to full glory.

She gasped. "Only a brute would take advantage of a helpless female."

He gave a snort.

With slow deliberate movements, he eased down onto the foot of the bed, hot eyes glittering and raking over every inch of her body as he kneeled between her legs. She burned, feeling so starkly exposed, helpless against his barefaced dominance of her.

But not complete dominance! She had her spirit.

She'd be damned if she'd allow herself to respond to him, no matter how clever his hands—

"Oh!" She let out a soft breath.

With the lightest touch, he scraped his nails down her breasts and over her nipples, causing them to pucker traitorously.

A knowing smile curved his conceited mouth.

She bit back an angry retort, determined not to give him the satisfaction of any response at all. She turned her face aside and closed her eyes, her mouth set in a determined line and forcing her thoughts elsewhere.

His warm palms settled on her thighs.

She wanted to go home. She'd think of that and all that she'd lost. Thoughts rose up and overwhelmed her with a terrible longing. It wasn't horrible here, with him, it was just that she didn't belong. She missed her life, her car, her apartment.

She choked back a sob. She missed her mother. Her mother had promised to look after her flowers and collect her mail, to pay overdue credit cards so Georgie could start new when she returned after her successful internship.

More like aborted internship. Not halfway into her time and she had been lost, rescued, and now kidnapped.

She would not stay here!

The powerful feel of him settling between her legs drew her head up. His teeth nipped her chin and tugged the delicate skin. She kept still, even when his warm tongue laved where he had bitten her. He cupped her bottom, drawing her hips up to meet him. She went rigid under his touch. He probed, but got no answering moan from her.

Not until he slid a finger between her bottom cheeks and stroked. Instantly, she heated and squirmed. He growled in his throat and slid his thick shaft between her legs and then thrust deep, taking her breath away.

One long finger probed her backside and sunk, completely impaling her tight entrance. The low moan she struggled to suppress came tumbling out.

A few deep thrusts at both ends and she was shuddering and convulsing uncontrollably in his arms. He held her close and pumped greedily into her.

When it was over, she burst into tears.

Given her complete abandon with him, now he would never let her leave.

He turned her face to look at him. "Georgie?" he murmured, catching a tear with his thumb.

"Leave me alone! I hate you." She glared at him.

His face stilled and then tightened with rage. The next moment, he bounded off the bed.

"Untie me."

"No!" He whipped around, his eyes blazing with fury. "You will run. I won't let you."

"I won't."

"You will." His fists clenched. "You will stay. You will listen. You are mine!"

"*You* are a brute, a savage brute, a barbarian, a… a monster. I hate you. I *will* run. And you'll *not* catch—"

He all but leaped over the edge of the treehouse and slid down the roped ladder.

"Where are you going?" she shouted. "You can't leave me here. Mark!" She thrashed against the ropes, frightfully aware of how quickly the darkness was descending. A faint rustle of leaves in the breeze was the only answering sound.

"Mark," she sobbed. "I'm sorry." Though his eyes had been dark with anger she had seen the hurt, too. She didn't hate him. She shouldn't have said it. A heavy weight crushed down onto her heart. *She just wanted to go home.*

When next she awoke, it was morning. He hadn't come back and she had cried herself into an exhausted sleep and now her chest ached and her wrists and ankles stung from her struggles.

But when she opened her eyes, he was with her, sitting beside her, his brow creased with tension.

She sat up, startled to find herself tucked safely into crisp sheets, her bonds no longer holding her down and him offering her a cup from his large hands.

"Drink," he said.

She covered his hands and drank greedily, spilling the sweet cold nectar down her chin and over her breasts. She couldn't get enough.

When she was finished, he licked the drops off her lips and chin and then tried to clean her breasts but she pushed him away, remembering his vow not to let her leave.

His eyes filled with regret and he sighed.

"Food?" he suggested.

"Take me home."

He ran a hand down his face and rose wearily. When he came back, he handed her a damp cloth. She ran the refreshing coolness of it along her face and throat.

He offered up her tattered dress, the straps neatly repaired now with needle and thread.

He touched her jaw, a tentative touch that nearly broke her heart. "Stay." His voice was rough with suppressed emotion, his jaw tense, but it was the gentle plea in his eyes, raw with feeling, that almost drove her to answer that she would.

She loved him. The knowledge of it shocked her to the core. She didn't think she could ever love anyone, not like this, with this soul wrenching torture. This overpowering, all consuming, crazy love that she'd read about and that drove lovers to sacrifice everyth—

She stopped on that thought. What sacrifice? She wasn't willing to do it. She wasn't going to sacrifice anything for him. She wanted it all – *her* life, *her* home, and she wanted him with *her*.

Even in love she was selfish.

It shouldn't have surprised her.

For the first time, she fully accepted her nature. She was self-centered, immature. A Pig Won't who always got what she wanted and gave up nothing in return.

Why didn't he realize that in the long run he was much better off in civilization, with his own kind? He was young, intelligent, and strong.

And she loved him. Or did she? Not enough if her plan was to wear him down until he agreed to come with her regardless that she truly believed he was better off. And what if he did come with her simply because she selfishly insisted? She supposed he wouldn't then *be* the fierce, independent, strong-willed King of the Jungle with whom she'd fallen in love.

They were hopelessly doomed. She couldn't stay and she couldn't make him come.

She closed her eyes, fighting back tears. When she opened them she spoke with deliberate slowness, making sure he understood every word. "I can't stay," she told him. "I want you to come with me, but I know this is *your* home." She made a gesture that took in the contents of the room and the jungle beyond. "I won't make you come. But please, take me home." While she meant every word, she also couldn't imagine being without him.

His hand dropped and he looked away.

When he returned his gaze, his eyes were sad. "We go. I take you back," he said and then rose from the bed.

"We?"

"First eat." He yanked the mosquito net aside and strode down the roped bridge.

"Mark, do you mean that you're going, too?"

He didn't answer and she was too afraid to press him, fearful that if she badgered him he might change his mind.

On shaky legs, she stood and followed him, hopeful for the first time that he might be considering going with her.

Chapter Six

As he swung through the branches, she clawed up his chest and hung on with a tenacity of someone who feared for her life. She knew it had to be a quicker way out of the valley as they soared from cliff to cliff, but she wouldn't have minded the slow route either.

She tried to convince him, but he said little and apparently ignored her pleas. The same way he ignored her explanations about what he could expect if he came with her. But he never once said that he wasn't coming with her.

When they cleared the valley and were heading steadily downhill to the edge of the rainforest, she outlined once again her plans for them, explaining more than she knew he could understand but wanting to tell him everything.

Dr. Cahill would want to claim him, interview him endlessly and examine him, but the professor was harmless, she assured him, annoying but harmless. No doubt the villagers would fear him and be in awe of his size and reputation. He was a legend, she explained, and had been for some time. But while the authorities no doubt had their own plans for him, the professor, here at the invitation of the highest government officials in concert with New York University, one of the most prestigious universities in the world, would see that he remained in his custody.

Georgie could tell by Mark's responses that, while he might have missed some words, he understood the main gist of what she was telling him. Like any person learning a language, he understood far more than he could yet speak.

When they reached a clearing high up the hill and could see the small cluster of grass huts as dots below, they stopped to rest. A feeling of relief consumed her. If someone had told her a month ago that she'd be weak with joy to see those twig shacks teetering on a clump of dirt, she'd have thought them crazy. But that was when she'd had more than two miserable months to go. Now, she'd be going home. Surely she wouldn't be expected to finish out her internship after her horrific experience. They'd hand her a college diploma on a silver platter.

Strong warm hands encircled her from behind and slid up over her breasts. Within moments she was wet for him and he knew it. His searching fingers spread her sex lips and probed, his voice groaning at the feel of her arousal.

"Mark," she breathed. He nuzzled her neck and pinched her nipples while his finger still played between her legs. He was rutting behind her and soon she felt the smooth tip of his cock, hot against her thighs. He slid into her quickly, easily, filling her, and the pleasure she felt with him, the desire, was like the first time. She would never get enough of him.

The wet friction of their mating and his clever hands burning a path wherever he touched had her crying out for him.

He clutched her hips and pounded into her. Just when she thought she couldn't stand anymore, he stopped and pushed his thumb into her tight bottom hole, filling her completely.

She burst apart, giving herself over to the flood of ecstasy enwrapping her, and then she felt him empty his seed in long pulsing throbs. The guttural groan that tore from his lips sounded like a cry of pain.

He held her tight for long moments afterwards, her bottom snug against his groin and his lips buried in her hair. Perched on all fours as she was with him covering her, she felt oddly at one with nature as though their act of love blended with the beauty surrounding them.

Too soon he lifted her to standing and turned her to face him.

His expression was somber as he bent slowly, reverently, and pressed his lips to hers. He lingered, his breath warm on her skin, his scent of leather and rain filling her pores as he brushed gently along her lips. He drew back, his eyes clouded with sorrow.

In that instant, she knew what he had planned.

"No." She grabbed onto the corded rope circling his waist. "You're coming *with* me."

He unwrapped her fingers and dropped her hands roughly, stepping away. "Go," he growled and leaped up onto a boulder at his back. She scurried forward, trying to reach him, her arms flailing. "No," she choked, tears stinging her eyes.

"Go," he hissed. "Go home!"

Then he was gone. She watched as his dark mane and the bronze glow of his skin peeked through the trees while he traveled up and away from her, making his way so fast that he seemed a fleeting aberration until he finally disappeared.

She was too stunned to move.

The air left her lungs and all feeling drained from her body. She stood like a stone, looking in the direction he had gone, unable to believe that he'd left her.

But while he hadn't contradicted her when she explained how it would be, he also had never agreed with her and a small part of her knew this could happen.

Was she never to see him again? The thought seemed impossible. She could never go back to the way things were, not after what they'd shared. Once she was safely home, she'd find a way for them to be together.

But then she thought about how easily he had just left her. It broke her heart to think she'd meant so little to him that he could leave her without saying goodbye.

"What do you mean, you can't take us to him?" Professor Cahill balked incredulously, taking off his gold-rimmed glasses and pinching his nose for the umpteenth time. "Okay." He shoved his glasses back on and dug one hand into his scalp. "You were with him for one month. He must have formed some connection with you. Right?"

Her face burned at how connected they had been.

"I see." He ducked his head and began pacing. "Maybe he'll come for you."

"He won't," she said forlornly. "I tried to get him to come with me, begged him."

"Yes, well." The professor cleared his throat and dragged his glasses off again. He wiped an arm across his forehead. "I guess it depends on how… connected you were, doesn't it?" He plopped down onto the rock next to her. "I mean, a man like that, isolated for so long happens upon a young woman… and one that looks like you, well…"

"Looks like *me*?" She stared at him. "I'm hardly a double for Marilyn Monroe."

"So?" He frowned and slapped his knees as he stood. "That's it. We wait. He won't be able to stay away from you for long. And when he comes for you, the trap will be set."

"Trap?" She jumped up.

"Metaphorically speaking of course." He looked uncomfortable. "We know he doesn't want to re-enter society, yet we know that's what he needs. So, in a sense it is a trap, but a humane one." He took her hand and gave it a fatherly pat. "He'll thank us one day, believe me, no matter what his initial reaction."

Georgie had tried to warn Mark of the professor's trap, but had failed miserably and now Mark, or Marcus Richard Steadman as he was believed to be, was literally in chains in a tent, by order of the Tribal Chief.

From the time Georgie had returned, the local agents had lied, the top government officials hedged, and the University apologized while Georgie's parents, locked out of the country, threatened to sue everyone. Upon Mark's capture, his parents had been found and they, too, were kept from him. Now Georgie was under house arrest—in this case, grass hut arrest—until everything was sorted out.

For two tortuous weeks she had worried that he would come to her at the same time that she yearned for him to. Then when he didn't, she cursed him bitterly, bemoaning how callously he had left her while her heart had ached for him every minute. Meanwhile, her parents petitioned the government, the embassy, and the University for her release, but no one was sending her anywhere, not while she purportedly knew the whereabouts of the legendary beast and was telling them nothing.

In order to pressure her to give up information, the University had vowed to protect him and the government promised to turn him over to his mother country after they questioned him, but Georgie trusted no one. Not even her esteemed professor.

While he waited to trap Mark, he had hounded her relentlessly for details of Mark's life and how he had responded when they first met, but Georgie feared the professor wasn't interested in Mark as a human being as much as for his potential to make the professor famous. He was not happy that Georgie refused to tell him anymore than the government which amounted to zero.

And then Mark *had* come for her, just as the professor had predicted.

She had managed to slip away again to one of her many hiding places, as she had done all week, hoping to warn Mark should he come for her. What she didn't know was that she was being closely followed the entire time. On that day, Mark had been lying in wait and caught her.

"Mark!" She hadn't know whether to warn him about a possible trap now that he had finally come or to hug him tight to her and never let him go.

He swung her into his arms and carried her over to a soft bed of moss.

"Make love," he growled, slipping a hand under her skirt.

"No," she gasped, tugging at his warm palm as he cupped her mound. "Oh," she strangled a moan. "I don't mean no exactly, but we can't do this now. Mark, listen to me."

Instead he knelt back on his heels and lifted a leather pack from off his back. He opened it to reveal its contents. Included among one gun and other valuables were the little blue coveralls and the Pig Will book.

He cupped her chin. "I go home with you." His eyes filled with warmth.

At first she was too stunned to respond, hoping it was really true that he was leaving the only home he knew to be with her. That he could leave his animal friends whom he trusted and amongst whom he had grown into the strong man that he was and enter a life of which he remembered nothing hardly seemed possible. But why else would he have brought the small treasures that linked him to his past if not to come back to civilization with her, to his human family that awaited?

At that moment she realized how much he must love her and how unworthy she was of his sacrifice.

She choked back a sob.

And then all hell broke loose.

Mark was lassoed and chained, his leather pack swooped up by the guards, while she was muzzled behind him and dragged away before he could see what was happening. While they kept her tied and gagged to a tree in the bushes, she watched him fight and claw against the band of men who struggled to shackle his arms and legs, while his eyes searched for her, but she had disappeared.

He had sensed betrayal, his eyes shone with it, and the raw emotion in his face haunted her then as it continued to torture her now.

But Georgie couldn't have known, as she did now, that the villagers, eager for the reward money, were laying in wait for him to come to her.

Now, he must think she had abandoned him, maybe even tricked him and was responsible for turning him over to the villagers before fleeing.

She had to get to him now and tell him that she hadn't betrayed him, that she loved him, and that she'd never hurt him.

Although in some ways, she had, by not staying with him but instead forcing him to come to her. She hadn't been willing to sacrifice her life to stay with him as he had been willing to do for her.

She kicked at the wooden tray of food and sent it flying across the hut. The guard peeked in, poking his rifle through the low arch that served as the front entrance. He lifted the curtain aside with the barrel and grunted when he saw the mess she'd made. "You eat. You too skinny, anyhow. Legs look like chicken."

"Shut up, you stubby little weasel."

He grinned wide, the gold on what teeth he had left glistening in the sun. He stepped into the hut, hitched his jean shorts higher, and then patted his protruding gut. "No stubby. Big and strong."

She snorted. He was five feet two if he was lucky. But she was getting nowhere with him. If she planned on getting to Mark, she had better try a new strategy. Nearly three full days had passed since he'd been captured.

While the tribal elders fought with the local officials, guarding their catch until they saw the money, the rest of the villagers regarded their prize with eager curiosity and gave Mark no privacy, but at least they weren't hurting him. A few times a day they took him out to walk and stretch, albeit in his chains and other roped restraints. Mark looked so big next to this small tribe of people, truly fierce. She understood their fascination with him and their fear. But so far, he had not been alone.

At night when the tent was illumined with a lantern, she could see that he was fed, although still tied. An older woman performed this duty, the same woman who washed his face with care and readied his bed at night. Still, Mark was never alone.

The professor was no better than the villagers.

He hounded Mark, bombarding him with questions and then mystified when Mark wouldn't answer him. When the professor complained to Georgie, he was then furious with her because she wouldn't help him either and leveled veiled threats at her about needing his internship to graduate.

Georgie wanted to scream with frustration. If she openly attempted to go to him they would banish her to the other end of the village, and she might never have a chance to get to him. So she waited for him to be alone at night, so she could slip out while the guards slept and talk to him. But now she watched as another group of young girls passed by, giggling and whispering, heading toward Mark's tent.

This had been going on since yesterday. And they grew bolder today. They flirted and cajoled the guards, distracting them at their posts while each girl took her turn slipping into Mark's tent. Georgie burned to know what they did in there. Her only consolation was that the taboo against losing your virginity before marriage was very strong in this tribe to the point where a girl could ruin her chances of ever marrying. She took comfort in the knowledge that they were innocents and probably just curious about the legendary Wild Man.

She watched the young girls now. One dangled across the lap of a young guard near the tent entrance. He was slipping his hand up her thigh and she was swatting him playfully, but ineffectually. It seemed his hand slipped up farther each time. Georgie frowned. Perhaps not so innocent after all.

Another girl leaned against a thick oak tree while another guard pressed her against the trunk with his hand … digging in her neckline? He was squeezing one breast and grinning stupidly. The girl hardly looked shocked.

Georgie wanted to scream out, sure now that they were experimenting with Mark, too, but if she did, they'd move her farther from his tent.

She gritted her teeth. Would no one let Mark alone? She needed to call to him. Let him know that she was captive, too, and that she loved him, and that somehow they needed to make it out of here together. *Especially since he was being regularly entertained by the girls of the village.*

"Let's make a deal, Professor." Georgie leaned forward slyly. "For every question I answer about Mark, you answer one for me."

His eyes lit up. "Deal. What do you want to know?"

"Okay," she said. "For starters, I want to know what the parade of girls are doing in his tent?"

When darkness had descended last night, the train of young girls blessedly stopped, but then grown women, *married* women, took up the slack, each one slipping the guards some bribe to get in Mark's tent. Just when the two guarding his entrance would nod off in sleep, and there was a lull in traffic, another woman would show up.

They couldn't be doing what she thought, could they? If the guards outside had not been talking and laughing the whole time, she might have been able to hear.

Professor Cahill cleared his throat. "I think it's pretty obvious what the girls are visiting him for. Of course, I can't be sure, but I don't think it's hard to figure out."

"What about your stupid lecture on the power of taboos in a small village?" Georgie snapped. "They're virgins, remember?"

"Well, yes, but there are *virgins* and then there are *virgins*."

"What in the world does that mean?"

The professor puffed up. "That's the best I can do—"

"Well it's pitiful. And you'll get the same from me unless you find out."

Georgie almost wished she hadn't given the professor hope that she would cooperate if he helped her, because the result was two sizeable mirrors rigged up in a tree in back of her hut, one that angled toward Mark's side window, with the other at a right angle to it so it reflected what the first mirror caught. And it caught plenty.

At first she was just so happy to see his face. Although his hair was unrestrained, giving him that Wildman look that the villagers must have loved, he was clean and seemed comfortable resting against a large cushioned mat. His restraints were not pulled so tight that he didn't have some freedom of movement. And the older woman who tended him even smiled as she fed and cared for him.

Now and then the professor or the chief would come in and talk to him, but Mark's face always turned to stone during these times, and he refused to even acknowledge them. While the tribal chief railed at him to tell him how many people he had killed, the professor spoke to him in the simplest English and very slowly as one would to a child.

Mark ignored them both, although Georgie could tell that he understood most of what was said.

It was only when the young girls came for their little visits that Mark perked up.

It broke her heart to see the eagerness with which he responded to them. But she had no one to blame but herself.

Mark had loved her enough to let her leave, and she was too self-centered to realize just how hard that must have been for him. Instead she had screamed that she hated him.

And now he thought she had betrayed him.

Why wouldn't he turn to these lovely young girls for comfort?

For the first time Georgie realized just how much she had lost. And it terrified her that she might have lost him for good.

Chapter Seven

Mark's latest young guest dropped down before him, all shyness and innocence, her long black lashes fluttering and her pert breasts thrust high. She gazed at him with adoring eyes. No wonder in all these days he hadn't once attempted an escape.

Georgie gritted her teeth as she watched the girl coyly toy with her dress strap, letting it slip off her shoulder until her bodice trim hung enticingly off her nipple.

Mark's eyes, level with her breasts, lit up.

Georgie's heart sank.

When the girl nudged closer, Mark stripped her to the waist and cradled her dark golden breasts. Why didn't his stupid captors shorten the chains of his restraints? He suckled her greedily, going from one breast to the next, as though he couldn't get enough of her, causing her to moan and writhe. Within minutes his hands were exploring under her skirt. The girl's gasps of pleasure infuriated Georgie, but not as much as when he tossed up her skirt and licked between her legs. The girl collapsed onto her back, her legs spread before Mark while he anchored his hands onto her hips and continued to torture her.

Georgie forgot her fury for a minute, fascinated with the rosy flush to the girl's breasts and the way her nipples tightened to sharp points until she came with a shuddering groan. Georgie was breathless.

Mark lifted his face and stroked soothingly along her inner thighs. He slipped his finger between her wet folds and then drew it out and licked it.

Georgie's jaw clenched so hard she thought her teeth would snap. Tonight, come hell or high water, she'd get a message to him. He had to know she was here and that... she loved him and *they* were meant to be together, before it was too late.

She sank down onto the dirt floor of her hut and sighed in frustration. How could she blame him for taking what pleasures were offered?

She had abandoned him, or so he thought, forgotten him.

She choked back tears. Nothing was working out as it should. Where were the officials who would return him to his country? Georgie bent her head between her knees and ran her fingers through her scalp, clear down to the tips of her tangled curls. She couldn't blame Mark for being human… for being a man.

She rose gingerly and looked out her window again to see him reflected in the mirrors, eyes closed and neck thrown back, the corded muscles pulled tight. His friend's face was buried in his lap now and for a virgin she was doing pretty well.

He was thrusting his hips up and holding the girl's head, his fingers buried in her tight curls and groaning.

Georgie groaned herself at the look of the girls wet lips running the length of him, her tongue circling playfully along balls pulled up tight in arousal.

A thunderous roar broke their concentration and made them look toward the hut entrance. Georgie wondered what they saw.

The girl scurried around behind Mark, clutching him, her head peering above his shoulder as Mark sat there fully erect and wet from her mouth. The girl's eyes widened in fright. Mark blinked nervously.

A man loomed before them, shouting words that Georgie didn't understand. Behind Mark, the girl was arighting her dress. The man came around and grabbed her by the arm, dragging her to him. She looked as though she were pleading for mercy. Her father? Older brother? Georgie heard her call him the tribal word for Uncle.

The next moment Georgie watched in shock as the uncle dropped to a seat and draped the girl over his knee. He tossed up her skirt, yanked down her panties, and spanked her in full view of Mark and now Georgie.

Mark's eyes blinked wide and his subsiding erection returned full force. Georgie groaned at her own arousal at the wicked sight. What was wrong with her that she found it so stimulating?

She felt her sex grow heavy and full. Her skin flushed with warmth.

Apparently, she and Mark weren't the only ones who found it arousing. The girl's cries turned suspiciously to moans the redder her rounded bottom grew. The uncle paused to smooth his palm over the delicate curves before spanking her again with zeal.

Georgie shouldn't look, but she couldn't take her eyes off the licentious scene. And what about Mark? He was riveted.

The uncle interrupted his spanking to slide his hand between her mounds. He dipped one finger between her lips and then slid the finger up to play with her bottom hole. The girl wriggled beneath him, no longer even trying to escape. Georgie watched with curiosity. Mark leaned forward. The uncle slid the wet finger around the tiny opening, probing gently, and then sunk deep. Georgie sucked in a breath. The uncle thrust with his long finger, slowly at first and then faster. Georgie thought she would expire. She didn't know this was done. Mark looked as surprised as she and he was fully erect.

But it was what happened next that sent her beyond shock.

The uncle lifted her up and placed her on all fours, tilting her bottom up to him and then he shoved his pants down and stroked her backside with his erect penis. He slipped between her globes and probed. Georgie's breath stopped. He plunged between her bottom and the girl groaned deep and shuddered. It was obvious she was no virgin to this practice.

A few pumps and the uncle was growling out his release.

Mark fell back against the propped pillows and swallowed. His own release followed. Georgie watched, mesmerized, as he closed his eyes and then exploded into the air in powerful jets, his strong body shuddering with each pump. Her own body went liquid with desire.

Georgie dissolved onto the grass mat beside her and sobbed.

On the fifth day, Georgie didn't have to wonder what that little suck-up, Kristy, was doing heading towards Mark's tent.

When the professor stomped out of her hut earlier today for the upteenth time this week, Georgie figured he had given up, which was smart since Georgie had no intention of telling him a thing. She'd gotten her information and wanted to know nothing more. She'd already regretted knowing what she knew. Not even the professor's guarantee that she'd fail her internship and not graduate if she didn't cooperate got her attention.

So, it looked now that he'd found another route to Mark. Tall, lithe Kristy, with breasts the size of overgrown cantaloupes. Georgie wanted to rip every last red hair out of her head, with tweezers, one by one.

Even the guards at the entrance went bug eyed when she showed up at midnight, sheer dress clinging to every curve, her nipples tight and clearly outlined against the silky cloth. Her braless breasts swayed and bounced as she sauntered up to them. She didn't have to offer a bribe. Just bending low and asking politely to enter Mark's tent got her what she wanted and got the guards a full view of her cleavage. She hugged herself, feigning chill, puckering the fabric so they could look down her dress and ogle her nipples.

Georgie sneered in disgust. What some people wouldn't do to get ahead. Professor Cahill's star student was no doubt expecting a nice fellowship to result from her... cooperation.

Georgie groaned in dismay as Kristy ducked into his tent. Please Mark, don't play into her game. Pay no attention to her or her obscene breasts. Georgie knew Kristy intended on exploiting Mark for her own gain. She couldn't love him like Georgie did.

Georgie went to the back of her hut and studied the mirror. She could only see Mark. He scowled mildly. Maybe he knew Kristy was connected with Professor Cahill. Good, he wouldn't give her a thing.

Before long Kristy dropped to her knees and joined him on the cushions. He still eyed her warily, so different from the way he treated the village girls, as though he knew the girls were innocently experimenting, whereas with Kristy he sensed something different. Georgie should have realized he'd trust his instincts on this one. Kristy twirled a lazy finger through his hair and was talking to him softly, too low for Georgie to hear, but the look on her face told Georgie the message was seductive. Georgie was relieved to see that Mark kept silent.

More than a little piqued, Kristy frowned and then rose to her knees. She knelt before him and in one quick sweep slipped her dress to her waist. Her melon-shaped breasts came bouncing out.

Mark's mouth dropped. Kristy giggled at his response while he sat there stupefied, his eyes locked onto her monstrous boobs. Don't fall for it, Mark, Georgie soundlessly pleaded.

He buried his face in her cleavage.

She groaned in frustration. Men! They were so weak.

Chapter Eight

Georgie laid on her bed and stared up at the ceiling in her room, exhausted, the newspaper dropped onto the carpet beside her, and sure that she had no more tears left to shed.

A light knock sounded on her bedroom door.

"Honey, are you all right?" Her mother's soft voice threatened another eruption of tears. "Can I come in?"

Georgie wiped her eyes with the back of her hands and propped herself on her elbows. "Come in, Mom."

Her mother slipped through the door and set a silver tray of cocoa and sugar cookies on her bedside table.

"I thought these might make you feel better," her mother said.

Georgie knew her mother was only trying to help, but the only thing that would make Georgie feel better was being wrapped in Mark's powerful arms. But her mother had been wonderful since her return, so Georgie simply thanked her.

Spotting the abandoned newspaper, her mother picked it up. "So, this is him," her mother murmured. "He's certainly a handsome young man."

Georgie shrugged. "Maybe. But more important, look how gullible he is. I can't believe he would make such a spectacle of himself, trapezing around with that… slut, Kristy."

"But you said he's been kept in hiding. No one is allowed near him, including reporters."

"Well, apparently, *she's* allowed near him. The professor's pet. From the looks of her draping her arm through his, they've been around each other plenty."

"Says here, he's recently emerged from his seclusion—"

"But with *her*, Mom. Don't you get it?" Georgie accepted the cocoa her mother offered and took a comforting sip. "I just don't understand how he can't see through her. Why, even the university can't be trusted to consider his best interests. They just see him as a means to more grants." Georgie sighed in frustration. "Why aren't his parents *protecting* him?"

"I'm sure they are, honey."

"Protecting him from *me*, you mean."

It had been eight months, eight long torturous months, and not one word from him. The authorities had spirited him out of the village during the night, drugging the guards while the rest of the village slept, and whisking him safely to the embassy where he was flown immediately to Chicago, his home. He had never even known Georgie was in a hut close by. The next day, they came for her.

Her first month back home she had tried every way conceivable to see him, talk to him. She had no way of knowing if he knew. The team responsible for his re-entry into society chanted the same refrain each time she tried. "His parents have given strict orders that he is to have no contact with anyone until they deem him ready. They'll call when that happens."

But it had been eight months now, and then she saw that awful picture in the newspaper. He was dressed in a tux, his hair still long but stylishly restrained, making him look primitively male in his crisp white shirt. And Kristy's dress was tighter than ever. They were attending a fundraiser for the University of Chicago. Georgie bet Kristy wheedled a fellowship out of them in exchange for bringing Mark.

Her mother smoothed a tangle of hair from off Georgie's cheek. "That reporter called again. The one from the Enquirer."

Georgie growled and swung her legs over the side of the bed. "Don't those guys ever give up?" She grabbed her jeans off the bedpost and shoved her legs in. When she zipped them, she was relieved to feel them finally fit. Most of the bony angles of her body had smoothed back into curves under the watchful eye of the family cook.

"They've upped their offer," Georgie's mother said, eyeing her closely. "They're up to two million."

"I don't care if it's two billion, Mom, they're not getting a word out of me. I would never exploit him like that."

Her mother turned to the serving tray. "Well, I just thought you might have reconsidered," she murmured, as she poured herself chocolate from the carafe, "since the University rejected your final appeal and sided with Professor Cahill about not graduating you this semester."

"I can pick up the final 12 credits in the next semester… or two."

"Of course you can, honey." Her mother gave her a small smile and blew gently on her cocoa.

Georgie slumped down onto the bed.

Her mother laid a gentle hand on Georgie's shoulder. "What is it, honey?"

Georgie fought back tears. "The truth is, Mom, I love him. But it's time I face the fact that he doesn't love me."

"You don't know that until you talk to him—"

"He doesn't want to see me. And he's had plenty of opportunity. Sometimes I think I love him so much that I would do anything to get him back. But then I see how happy he looks in that photo, and I remind myself that he's made no attempt to contact me despite all my efforts and I realize... that whatever our time together meant to me, that it didn't mean the same to him."

Georgie pulled herself to her feet and walked over to her dresser mirror. Her mother came up behind her and placed her hands on her shoulders. She covered her mother's hands with hers. "It's possible, Mom, that he wants to put his past behind him so he can successfully adapt to his new life. If I really love him, I'll let him do that. Even if it means losing him forever."

Her mother turned Georgie into her arms. "Maybe he just needs some time, honey, to realize what he really wants." Her mother stroked a gentle hand down her back.

"I don't know, Mom. But I've got to stop this incessant crying over him. It's time that I grew up."

Chapter Nine

Marked wiped his brow. *Jesus, he was nervous.*

The long winding drive off the main road to Georgie's parents' shore house was interminable and yet not long enough. He ached to see her, but still hadn't figured out what to say, despite having gone over and over it in his head.

He had learned she was raised in wealth, been educated in the best schools, and that her family occupied a place within the highest social strata of New York Society and had for generations.

Mark ran a finger under his neck collar and tugged. He had nothing to offer her. While his parents, both college professors, promised to do everything to catch him up after a lifetime of isolation, it would still be years before he finished his formal education. In any career he'd be pathetically behind his peers and as far as social graces went, hell, he didn't think he'd ever fit into high society.

He should tell the driver to turn right around. What made him think she even wanted him? While his parents and the team they'd hired had been bombarded with calls and letters when he first emerged from the jungle, all requests were dismissed and no records kept. They had no way of knowing at the time how important Georgie was to him. He made himself believe that she had tried and failed to contact him from the moment they were separated. But now he wasn't so sure.

Then he remembered her total abandon with him in the jungle. He was behind in his experience with women, too, but he'd still bet Georgie had never given herself to anyone the way she had with him.

His jaw tightened. For the first time he thought of the possibility that she could be with another man. He ground his teeth. If that were the case… they'd just see how long *that* lasted.

The limo driver hit a small rut in the sandy road. Up ahead a large weathered cedar house with white shutters perched high, overlooking the ocean. Its large wraparound porch faced the side lawn and drive.

He reached instinctively and touched the driver's shoulder and asked him to stop.

Georgie was rocking in a large wicker chair, one leg draped over its arm, a sandal dangling from her foot. He watched as she ran an idle hand through her honey colored curls. He wanted to feel those curls sift through his fingers.

"Shall I leave you here, Sir? Maybe you'd like to walk the rest of the way?"

Mark glanced at the driver. If he was seventy, he was young. Mark wondered if he'd been with the family since Georgie was little.

It had surprised Mark when he had called Georgie's house and her mother had been so accommodating. While the entire world knew *of* him, Georgie's mother would have grilled her daughter about what happened between them during that long month in the jungle. He just hoped Georgie hadn't told her *everything*.

He was surprised when she offered to send a car to Kennedy Airport to pick him up and take him to Georgie. He shrugged. Apparently, Georgie *hadn't* told her everything.

He looked at the chauffeur. "What do you think I should do, Denton?"

The man turned to look at him fully and smiled. "No one ever knows what to do where Georgie is concerned." He gave a chuckle. "But why don't you go on up by yourself from here."

Mark sighed and then nodded. "Well, here goes."

"Good luck, lad."

Mark closed the door of the limo and brushed down the crease in his khakis. He undid his white button-down shirt to the second opening to give himself some air and rolled the sleeves up his forearms. Then he laughed. Preparing to wrestle a tiger was easier than this.

Then he envisioned wrestling his fierce tigress to the grass and he found himself smiling.

He hiked around the corner and then advanced up the hill. Before he reached the top, he heard the car engine start and then saw it head back down the hill. Georgie heard it too, because she had risen, and with her hand shielding her eyes from the sun, watched the family chauffer back down the drive.

He was no more than 50 feet away when she turned and spotted him. He stopped in his tracks. Her eyes clouded in confusion and then she sprang off the porch, kicking off her shoes, and dashed toward him. Her long hair blew out behind her and her sundress clung to her as she ran.

His heart turned over at her happiness at seeing him. "Mark," she cried, half-laughing and half-crying, and running like the wind. The she jumped into his arms. The sweet scent of her skin washed over him, so familiar and comforting.

He held her so close he thought he'd snap her slender frame.

She buried her lips in his neck. "Oh my God. I can't believe it's you. I've missed you so much." She sobbed hard, clutching him to her. "I can't believe you're really here."

He was speechless, so filled with love for her and desire that he could barely breathe.

She pulled back and cupped his face in her palms and rained kisses all over him. "They wouldn't let me see you or talk to you." She stroked along his jaw. "Did they hurt you?" She stepped back and took in his full length. "God, you are so beautiful." She flew back into his arms. "I was terrified that I'd never see you again," she moaned, wrapping her arms around his neck.

She thinks I'm beautiful.

"I was so afraid you didn't want to see me ever again. That you'd left your old life behind and me with it." She hugged him close and brushed her mouth along his jaw.

How could she think he'd never want to see her again?

"Mark?" She stopped abruptly and looked into his face. "Say something."

He swallowed. He hadn't expected this. He should just cut to the chase and tell her that he loved her.

"What have they done to you?"

Done to me? He blinked.

Her eyes narrowed. "It was that slut, Kristy, who did this to you, wasn't it?"

Kristy? He raised both brows. *This could get interesting.*

"You were speaking in sentences in the jungle, maybe not complex sentences, but you could communicate." She grabbed both his hands and clutched them to her heart, her eyes filled with sympathy. The next instant she was pounding his chest. "How could you be so stupid to not have seen past those watermelon breasts."

He smothered a laugh.

She pushed at him. "Oh, I could scream." She whirled away and ran a frustrated hand through the crown of her soft curls. The sundress she wore billowed in the breeze around her shapely legs. *He didn't feel like talking anyway.*

Then she drew up close and wrapped her arms around his neck. "I'm sorry, Mark." She stroked his cheek. "I don't know what's happened, but none of it matters now." She choked on a sob. "We'll go back to the jungle and start all over again. And we won't leave until you're ready, no matter how long it takes." Her eyes filled with tears.

She was willing to live in the jungle for him? Indefinitely?

"We were doing so well together, Mark. We were both learning things everyday, together. We can do that again. I promise. And I'll never leave you, no matter what."

He was dumfounded and so filled with emotion he was paralyzed to respond. She had to be in love with him. There was no explanation for what she promised, other than that she loved him.

"Just give me a nod." She traced her finger along his lips. "To show me you understand even just a little."

He nodded. And then before he could form a sentence, she pressed herself against him.

He filled with arousal and grabbed her waist. A deep growl rose up from his throat.

She gave him a sultry smile. "I'll make you forget Kristy."

Why would she think he'd be interested in Kristy? Then he thought of the photo Kristy had grabbed with him before he could shrug out of her grasp while he was on the steps of the university.

Georgie stood on tip-toes and pressed her lips to his. He groaned and exploded with an urgency suppressed too long and just waiting to be released when he saw her again. He delved into the soft recesses of her mouth and plundered her, tasting her with a hunger that bordered on painful.

They collapsed together onto the soft bed of grass and he covered her, laying himself along her length. She yielded to him, offering herself with little groans and whimpers. "Oh God. I've waited so long for you to hold me again. I love you, Mark. I love you so much."

He stilled, now too *stunned* to speak.

She drew his face up. "I know you don't understand me, yet, but soon you will." She kissed him with agonizing sweetness. "I want you inside me, now."

He plucked her buttons open and bared her to his eyes. He swelled full and hard. He'd never be able to get enough of her. She was so smooth against his rough hands as he lifted her breasts to his lips. He licked hungrily along the soft swells, taking special care to taste her swollen nipples, so large and ripe looking against the smallness of her breasts, the contrast so powerfully erotic. He had dreamed about these nipples for long months. "I wish you could talk to me," she sighed, arching to his lips. "Anything. Even just my name."

She was going to kill him when she discovered he could talk. He'd keep her delirious. He suckled her with enthusiasm, feeling his own groin throb in response to her soft contented moans. He forced himself to slow down despite his driving need to take her, hard and fast and completely.

"I shouldn't have worried about Kristy," she purred, yielding to his lips and giving him greater access to her breasts. He slid his hand up her thigh and slipped his fingers under the elastic of her panties. "Oh…" Her breath came out in a whoosh. He met with delicious wet warmth when he slid two fingers up through her. She moaned in his ear and raised her knees up, sighing with pleasure. "It's obvious you couldn't have liked those huge D-cup breasts bouncing around, anyway."

He bit her nipples. "Actually," he murmured, "they were more like double-D's."

She gasped. "What?" She slapped his back.

"I said they were more like—"

"I heard you… you, you—" She gave him a furious push, struggling mightily against his heavy bulk. He accommodated her temper tantrum by tumbling off her and onto his back. He suppressed a chuckle. Life would never be dull with Georgie.

She kneeled beside him and railed at him. "How could you let me go on like that?" She punched his chest. "Oh, I could just—"

He plucked her up and brought her down on top of him. "I've missed you," he whispered. He slid his hand up her skirt and over her bottom, stroking the warm smooth curves, rewarded by her soft moans. "And I love you."

Her breath caught. "You love me?" She propped her hands on his chest and her eyes widened in wonder.

"Yes," he said, his voice husky. "I love you, Georgie."

"Oh, Mark." She collapsed against his chest. "I was so worried. But I kept hoping, so sure that we were meant to be together."

"Georgie, look at me." He lifted her up to face him. "You have to understand something. I have nothing to offer you."

"What do you mean? You said you loved me?"

"I do. And I always will. But look at me. My life has only just begun. It'll be years before I catch up. If I ever do."

She cradled his face. "None of that matters, Mark. We have a whole lifetime to catch up. We can do it together." She looked sheepish. "Besides," – she gave him a small grin – "you don't really know how behind *I* am, and that you're the one who helped me to grow up. If it weren't for you I wouldn't have realized what's really important. I would still be the spoiled little rich girl that you met."

"Georgie…" He stroked along her cheek.

"So you see, Mark, we need each other."

He nodded. "I see." He kissed her tenderly. "I love you, Georgie."

"And I love you."

"I need you now," he breathed. He unzipped his pants and shoved them down over his hips. His penis came springing out as she straddled him.

With one good yank, he ripped the delicate lace between her legs in half.

"Oh my God, Mark."

His penis slipped around her wet swollen folds, torturing him, until he found heaven and slipped in deep.

She shuddered on a long moan. "My God, how could I have forgotten what a wild man you are," she groaned and rode him thrust for thrust. "This is one thing you have to promise will never change."

He thrust up hard and held her hips. Then he gave her a teasing smile. "If you don't stop talking, I'll have to tie you up."

"You wouldn't!"

"Strip off that dress."

Her eyes shone as she lifted her dress over her head and tossed it onto the grass. She sat astride him, fully impaled and naked and beautiful. He fought back the punishing release that threatened to overtake him.

"It's a good thing you've decided to listen to me, because if you don't, I'll have to spa—"

"Mark!" She slapped at him.

He chuckled and then thrust up hard several more times until she tightened around him and then cried out his name. He felt her explode all around him. He followed moments later with his own thunderous release.

Then he held her in a tender embrace he intended never to end.

About the Author:

Kathryn Anne Dubois lives the demanding life of a mother of five, wife of 30+ years, and a public school art teacher. What better reason to escape into the delicious fantasy world of writing erotic romance.

Visit Kathryn's website at www.KathrynAnneDubois.com.

Wanted

❧❀❧

by Kimberly Dean

To My Reader:

The thrill of the chase awaits. Enjoy!

Chapter One

The blue sedan was still there.

Danielle glanced nervously at the lights in her rearview mirror. It was two car lengths back, seemingly inconspicuous, but still…

"Damn it, Reno," she whispered. Her hunger disappeared, and she stuffed her Twix bar into its wrapper. Without looking, she tossed the chocolate bar onto the passenger seat.

Taking a deep breath, she tried to settle her nerves. If he wanted to get caught up in a high-speed chase, she'd be happy to oblige him. Of course, the rattletrap she was driving couldn't do more than sixty. No doubt, he had a high-powered engine concealed under the modest exterior of that car. Still, she wouldn't give up easily. He should know that by now.

Her gaze flicked again towards the mirror. The car had moved over one lane.

"Clever," she muttered. "You're trying to confuse me, make me doubt myself. Well, it's not working, Bub."

She knew that most of the world would consider her paranoid, but it wasn't paranoia if somebody really was chasing you. Over the past months, she'd learned to trust her instincts. And right now, they were screaming that it was no coincidence that the blue sedan had kept pace with her for the past ten miles.

"You're smart, Reno. I'll give you that."

He'd kept her on her toes for months now. He was always out there, somewhere, watching in the shadows, waiting to make his move.

The blue car suddenly signaled and took the off-ramp. Danielle was so surprised, she blinked twice to make sure she wasn't seeing things. Finally, she gave a sigh of relief.

"You are paranoid, you twit." Shaking her head, she reached for her candy bar. She bit off a piece of chocolate and tried to slow her racing heart. "You're paranoid, and you're tired."

She eased up on the accelerator and glanced down at the dash.

"Oh, good heavens. Some high-speed chase that would have been." She was nearly out of gas. With luck, she might have barely enough fumes to get to the next town.

"Dani, Dani, Dani. You know better than that. Always keep your tank full of gas. Always." Tiredly, she rubbed a hand across her forehead. A stupid mistake like that could cost her everything.

Shaking her head, she began to watch the passing highway signs. It was getting late, and it was time to find someplace to hole up for the night. Suddenly overwhelmed by exhaustion, she leaned her head back against the headrest.

"Well, you've made it through another day on the FBI Most Wanted list without getting caught," she congratulated herself.

A grim smile pulled at her lips. So far, she'd managed to elude Special Agent Jeff Reno. For half a year, he'd been on her trail and, for half a year, she'd been able to slip out of his reach just when he thought he had her.

That had to piss him off to no end.

"Serves him right," she said.

Sometimes, she'd escaped by mere inches. She remembered the time that she'd been washing dishes at that rundown diner in Tuscaloosa. She'd been talking to the cook when he'd strode into the place looking all tall, dark, and delicious. For a solid minute, she'd been caught frozen as she'd stared at him. She'd only snapped out of it when Old Mabeline had stepped up to the counter to wait on him. The woman's wide form had allowed her to make a break for the door without him seeing.

Sometimes she wondered what he'd do if he caught her…

"Stop it," she told herself, even though she knew better.

These dangerous little fantasies about him were sneaking up on her more and more. She didn't know why out of all the agents in the Federal Bureau of Investigation, she'd had to get the one who could make her toes curl. It had been a sick twist of fate, but she had to deal with it. It was just getting harder every day. She found herself thinking of him at the most inopportune times. His dark eyes, his sleek brown hair, his yummy tight ass…

"I said 'Stop it!'"

She shoved another bite of chocolate into her mouth and began to gnaw on it. Jeff Reno might look like something that just stepped out of *GQ Magazine*, but he suspected her of committing a horrible crime.

Treason.

"I'm not a traitor! How many times do I have to tell you that?" she said out loud. The words echoed throughout the small car.

The mere thought that she might sell government secrets was ludicrous. Why would she jeopardize all her hard work like that?

Half a year ago, she'd had a great life. She'd had an awesome job as a computer programmer for a defense contractor. The project she'd been working on was top-secret, and she'd loved the challenge. She knew she didn't fit the usual computer nerd stereotype, but she'd been extremely good at what she did. Sometimes she thought that she understood computer code better than she understood English. After all the blood and sweat she'd put into that project, there was no way that she could have sold it for her own gain.

It would have been like selling her soul.

But somebody had sold out—and Reno suspected her.

Damn his cute, tight ass! Because of him, she no longer had her awesome job. Because of him, she was on the run to avoid treason charges. She no longer had a home, and she hadn't seen her family and friends for months. Sometimes, she didn't even know where she was going to get her next meal.

She took another harsh bite out of the candy bar and noticed her fingernails. They were totally unrecognizable as the perfectly manicured set she'd had before she'd gone on the lam. Her gaze dropped from her fingers to the steering wheel and she remembered her Corvette. She'd been forced to sell it at a used car dealership for cash.

"That's something I'll never forgive you for," she said with an edge to her voice. "I don't care how tight your ass is."

The exit came upon her suddenly, and she had to pull hard on the wheel of the little two-door to make the off-ramp. The sign read Conrad, Population 16,201. It would have to do.

Driving slowly down Main Street, Dani considered her options. Her mind went to the meager supply of money in her purse. She had enough for a motel, but it was time to get another job. Not only was her cash supply low, she also needed a new car. She'd been driving this junker for too long.

"By now, he probably knows not only the make, model, and license plate number, but also the fact that it pulls to the left." She didn't know where he got his information, but it was uncanny what that man knew.

A flashing, pink neon sign caught her eye, and she turned into the parking lot of the Waterbury Inn. The place looked cheap, but clean.

Would it be too much to hope for hot water?

She reached into the back seat and grabbed a brown wig and a pair of plain, metal-rimmed glasses before she headed to the registration desk.

Twenty-three dollars later, she found herself in Room One with a nice view of the busy street.

Sighing, Danielle carefully set her laptop down on the table next to the window before tossing her bag onto the bed. Just once, she'd like to treat herself to a nice hotel. Just once. Muttering under her breath, she grabbed her toiletry bag and headed for the shower.

Special Agent Jeff Reno sat on the bed in his hotel room with his back propped up against the pillows. His hair was still wet from his shower, and he'd only bothered to put on his jeans. Taking another swig from his bottle of beer, he glared at his laptop.

"Come on, Dani," he growled. He was tired and ready to catch a few Z's.

She'd spotted him; he was sure of it. He'd kept his distance from her when they'd been on the road, but somehow, she'd noticed him. She was getting eerily good at knowing when he was near.

He could have caught her this time, but he hadn't wanted her to get hurt. She would have run and too many car chases ended in crashes.

He didn't want their little hide-and-seek game to end like that.

"Not after this long," he said as he wiped a droplet of water off the beer bottle. After all she'd put him through, it was going to have to be something special when he caught her—something very special indeed.

He trailed his thumb down the gentle curve of the dark bottle, but his thoughts were on softer, more rounded curves.

"Damn," he said as he ran a hand through his wet hair.

There were much better things to do with that body of hers than to wrap it around a tree. That was why he'd taken the exit into Gilroy. It had killed him to let her out of his sight, but she'd taught him a modicum of patience over the past few months. Tomorrow would be soon enough to catch up with her. He could wait one more night.

"One long, never-ending night from the looks of it."

The bulge behind the zipper of his jeans was going to make sure of that. Hell, his dick was like a divining rod when it came to her. It acted like this whenever she was within a ten-mile radius.

"Damn it, where are you?" he barked. He inspected his instant messages again. It was past time that she checked in.

With a curse, he flopped back against the headboard and stared at the ceiling. He'd been trained on how to avoid personal involvement in cases, but he'd gotten into the habit of chatting with her at the end of every day. Now, he couldn't sleep if he didn't know she was safe for the night.

It was still strange how their cyber relationship had evolved. The first time she'd emailed him, he'd nearly fallen off his chair. It had been soon after her escape. He didn't know how she'd gotten his email address, but she'd sent a scathing message protesting her innocence. He'd had his technicians try to trace the connection, but she'd woven such a tangled, knotted web they hadn't been able to unravel it before she'd signed off.

Now, he knew better than to even try. She knew computers better than his entire staff combined. Instead, he'd started talking with her. One conversation had turned into two and then ten. Now they chatted daily. Although he told himself that he looked forward to their talks for professional reasons, inside he knew better.

"Come on, babe." He glanced at the clock on the bedside stand. She wasn't still driving, was she? God, he didn't want to get back on the road to follow her. Was she planning on driving through the night? If she were, that would put a lot of distance between them.

"No, she'll be stopping soon," he said, trying to convince himself. Dropping the tail had been an inspiration on his part. The action had gone against the grain. She'd never believe that he'd just give up and let her go. By now, the blue sedan was a distant memory.

"Her guard will be down. Tomorrow will be the day." He glanced down at his crotch. "It's got to be the day."

Tilting his head back, he gave another pull on the longneck. Hell. He was going to have to drink the rest of the six-pack to get rid of the hard-on he was nursing. Reaching down, he carefully adjusted himself into a more comfortable position inside his jeans.

This sucked. He was edgy, irritable, and horny as hell. For too long now, she'd been leading him around by the nose – or more aptly, by the dick. The problem was that although his brain knew that she was a fugitive from justice and it was his job to bring her in, his libido tended to forget. From the first moment he'd set eyes on her, he'd wanted the lady in his bed.

He could still remember that day. He and his partner, Charley Squires, had intercepted disturbing information that Quadrangle Computing's top-secret code was up for grabs on the black market. They'd had little time to act. Plans had rapidly been set into motion and, without giving notice, they'd walked in and closed the company down.

Phone service had been stopped, doors had been blockaded, and records had been seized. Combining their intelligence with the information they gathered on-site, they'd narrowed the trail down to one suspect—a Ms. Danielle Carver.

From that point, things had moved quickly. Reno closed his eyes and, suddenly, he was back in that moment.

"Bring this Carver woman in," he told her boss. "I want to question her."

The manager threw him a nervous look, but picked up the phone. When a blonde head popped up over the cubicle wall, Reno didn't pay much attention. As the woman started moving in the direction of the office, though, he began to watch more closely. When she finally came into full view, his entire body went on red alert.

"You've got to be kidding me," he said. He'd been suspecting some-body… geekier.

The short, balding man smiled knowingly. "Her IQ is probably twice yours," he replied smugly.

Reno's eyes narrowed. "*That* should be illegal."

Just watching the way she walked made his mouth water. She had a smooth, effortless gait that swiveled her hips in a manner that wasn't overtly sexual, but packed a punch nonetheless. When she entered the room, her understated perfume traveled across the air, and he broke out in a cold sweat.

He didn't like his reaction. He didn't like it one bit. The crimes he suspected her of committing were serious. The code she was writing was for the Air Force's newest fighter planes. If she planned to sell it, she was willing to jeopardize American lives.

He didn't care how hot she was—the entire idea left him cold.

"Ms. Carver," he said icily. "Please take a seat."

"What's this about?" she asked.

She settled into the chair in front of the desk and looked at him uneasily. Caught in the stare of those clear, startlingly blue eyes, he forgot what he'd been about to say.

All he could do was look at her.

She was wearing close-fitting jeans that showed off her shapely ass. The way they cupped her buttocks made the palms of his hands itch. Her hair was pulled up into one of those plastic clips. Some of the ends had slipped loose, and the mussed look made him ache.

He wanted to see her hair down. He wanted to touch it. He wanted to feel it brushing against his hips as she lowered her mouth to his dick.

"Damn," Reno breathed. He shifted restlessly on the bed as the vivid memory overtook him. Thinking of her like this wasn't helping his un-comfortable condition at all. Still, he couldn't stop himself from remembering the most important part of that picture.

The sweater.

She'd been wearing one of those little, cropped sweaters that were so popular these days. The material had been stretched across her full breasts, and a good two inches of her midriff had been exposed. He'd gotten so hard looking at her tight, smooth skin that he'd quickly had to make sure that his suit jacket hid the bulge in his pants.

"The birth of the divining rod," he noted.

The memory of her tight stomach still made his jaw clench. Back then, he'd had to fight the urge to drop to his knees and kiss and lick every single exposed inch of skin. He'd wanted to drop his tongue into her sexy, little belly button and feel her quiver against his face.

With a curse, Reno sprang off the bed and began to pace around the room. "If you hadn't let yourself be so affected that day, you wouldn't be in this situation right now!"

He still blamed himself for her escape. He'd gone soft on her. There was no other excuse for it.

Once his frazzled brain had finally kicked into gear, he'd begun to ask her questions. *Pointed, delving questions.* Her skin had taken on an unmistakable green tinge as she'd slowly comprehended what was happening. When she'd clapped a hand over her mouth and rushed to the restroom, he'd let her go.

"I had to," he told himself for the millionth time. "She was sick."

Damn it, he'd followed procedure. He'd sent a female agent to accompany her, but apparently the woman also had a weak stomach. When Dani had gotten sick, the agent had gone into the next stall and puked right along with her. When the agent had recovered, their suspect had been gone.

That had been six months ago, and he was still trying to catch up with her.

Reno stalked around the room. Frustration had his nerves stretched tight. He was tired of this cat-and-mouse game. It had gone on for way too long. Something was bound to snap soon.

The way things were going, that something might be him.

He swiveled on the ball of his foot and glared at the computer. "Damn it, Dani. Come on!"

Back in her hotel room, Dani stared at her laptop as she damp-dried her hair with a towel. Shivering, she pulled the belt of her robe more tightly around her. The water in the shower had been tepid at best. She knew the robe was too thick and bulky to tote around with her, but she doggedly kept it nonetheless. It was her one comfort, her one indulgence.

She tossed the towel over the back of a wooden chair and sat down crossed-legged on another. She tucked the flaps of the robe around her legs until they began to feel warmer and, at last, felt like she could concentrate. She hit the power button on her computer and waited for the machine to boot up.

Was he still awake? She hoped so. She couldn't relax without talking to him. If he was online, he couldn't be out there tracking her. Besides, that blue car still had her worried.

Quickly, she began typing. By now, the process was old hat. She waited as the connection was routed through various servers across the country. She wasn't stupid. Every time she chatted with Reno, she hooked up differently, always making sure she put in enough twists and turns to discourage a trace. The first time she'd done it, she must have sent the call across three different countries.

She still wasn't quite sure why she'd taken that risk. The shock of being accused of something so horrendous had surely had something to do with it. She'd just been so angry, she'd had to yell at somebody. The Fed had been the obvious choice. Of course, he hadn't believed her, but gradually, their chats had become more and more frequent.

In a weird, philosophical sort of way, their cyber relationship made sense. Over the past six months, she'd lost contact with everybody she knew. She'd made acquaintances along her travels, but she could never tell anybody what was truly happening in her life. She never stayed in one place long, so she hadn't been able to make friends. Who knew what she was going through better than her hunter?

He knew the struggles she fought. He knew how much she missed her life. So, even though she knew that he was her enemy, she relied on the connection they had. Their relationship kept her sane.

A message was waiting for her when she entered the system.

"You're late," it said.

"You're grouchy," she responded.

She waited for him to notice that she was there.

"You've kept me up past my bedtime," he typed more quickly than she expected.

He *was* grouchy.

Something about the response made her inner alarm start to sound.

Was his mood due to the fact she was late or because he'd been driving a pesky blue car?

"Were you chasing me tonight?" she asked carefully. He might not be able to trace her computer connection, but he was very good at tracking her down the old-fashioned way. If it had been him and she said anything about cars or the interstate, he'd know he was on the right trail and be back on the road in ten seconds flat.

"I'm always chasing you, sweetheart. You know I'm coming for you."

Dani shivered involuntarily. Her body, so relaxed after its recent shower, immediately tensed.

Was he that close?

Cautiously, she peeked out the window. Blinking lights from the strip club across the street greeted her. Was he out there, hiding in the shadows?

An unexpected gust of wind shook the tree outside the window, and she let out a startled shriek. The curtain dropped back into place, and she pulled her robe more tightly around her waist. "You don't scare me," she typed stubbornly.

"Liar."

The hairs on the back of her neck stood up. He did scare her - but in more ways than he could possibly know. She shifted uneasily in her seat. For the longest time she'd tried to deny her feelings, telling herself it was a Stockholm Syndrome of sorts, but her attraction to him refused to go away. It only seemed to grow, and that was more frightening than any-thing. "Is that a threat?" she asked.

"No, it's a fact. I'm not going away, baby. One day soon, you're going to have to deal with me."

"I've been dealing with your stupid treason charge for six months."

He didn't reply, and she began to wonder if she'd lost the connection.

"That's not what I'm talking about," he finally typed. "You're going to have to deal with me. With us."

"I don't understand."

"I think you do."

She swallowed hard. "There is no *us*. You're the predator, and I'm the prey. That doesn't make this a relationship."

"No? Then why are we both starting to wonder what will happen when I lay my hands on you?"

Dani froze with her fingers poised over the keyboard. He couldn't mean-. She had to be misinterpreting him. Still... "You'd get fired for something like that, Reno," she typed experimentally.

"At this point, do you think I really care?"

There was no misinterpreting that declaration.

Dani stared at the screen and shivered at the promise—because that's what it was. He couldn't have been more blatant.

She'd always felt the sexual danger that he presented, but neither of them had ever dared to mention it before. She'd certainly never thought he'd follow through on it. After all, he was Mr. Fed, and she was an embarrassing blotch on his record. He was supposed to be chasing her because she was wanted – not because he wanted her.

Suddenly, her blood began to pulse hotly through her veins. "Leave me alone, Reno," she ordered.

"Are you sure that's what you want?"

Her stomach flipped. He couldn't know. She pulled her hands away from the keyboard as if they'd been burned.

She'd thought that she'd hidden her feelings well. If he knew… Oh God, this made him a thousand times more dangerous. She held no misconceptions when it came to him. He was out there to do a job, and he wouldn't hesitate to use her feelings against her if he thought it would help him accomplish his goals. "What I *want* is my freedom," she typed with clumsy fingers.

"Turn yourself in, Dani. You know you can't keep running forever."

"I can try."

"You won't succeed. Run and I'll chase. Eventually, I'll catch you."

Her gaze flicked once again to the window, and she couldn't help but scoot her chair further away. She didn't know what made her more nervous, the "chasing" or the "catching".

"Why won't you believe me? Haven't we gotten to know each other? You should know by now that I'm innocent."

"Baby, we've been over this. The evidence says otherwise."

"The evidence is wrong."

"Then show me what's right."

Dani slumped back against the wooden chair, and her heart tumbled. They'd had this discussion a million times. She was innocent until proven guilty, but the evidence wasn't helping her cause. She'd wracked her brain for months now trying to find a way to refute it.

"I can't."

Reno stared at the simple admission on the computer screen. Tiredly, he leaned back against the headboard. He'd like nothing more than to believe her, but the evidence against her was overwhelming. "We might be able to come up with something if we worked together," he typed. "Just meet with me."

The answer came back almost instantaneously. "Nice try, GQ, but I'm not falling for it."

He cursed. Just when he thought they'd been getting somewhere... Irritated by his warring emotions, he reached over and grabbed his beer from the bedside table. He drained the bottle and slammed it back down. "Did you eat today?"

When he got no response, he tossed the empty bottle into the trashcan and sat upright. "Danielle, you've got to eat."

"I did."

"What, exactly?"

This was yet another argument they had on a regular basis. Due to her lifestyle, she'd fallen into the bad habit of grabbing food wherever she could get it. He knew her constant motion had kicked her metabolism into high gear, but it wasn't healthy. Nothing about the lifestyle they led was healthy.

"I had an apple for breakfast and a turkey sandwich for lunch," she wrote.

"Dinner?"

"A candy bar. Okay?"

"No, damn it, that's not okay. You've got to eat better."

"I was in a hurry."

That was right. She'd been hurrying away from a blue car on the interstate. "Slow down next time and get a good meal," he typed grouchily.

"If I slow down, you might catch up with me."

He gritted his teeth. "Would that be such a bad thing?"

There was a long pause before she answered. "What's gotten into you?" she finally asked.

You have. Reno rubbed his gritty eyes. She'd gotten into his blood.

Suddenly, he'd had enough. He was tired of talking to her through a machine. He wanted to hear her voice. He wanted to see her in person. He wanted to touch her.

And damn it, he was going to have her. There had to be a way.

He ran a hand through his hair and tried to get his tired brain to function. Maybe there was a deal they could strike – one that would keep her out of prison. For all he knew, there could be mitigating circumstances. Maybe she'd been coerced into selling the software, or maybe she'd been an unwitting accomplice. That could be the reason she was running; she'd fallen into something bad and didn't know how else to get out of it.

She wasn't a hardcore criminal; he knew that.

His hands dropped limply to his sides. If only she'd confide in him… If she'd meet him halfway, they could stop this insanity.

"I'm tired, Dani. It's been six months. For half of a year, I haven't had much more of a life than you have. I spend all my time thinking about you, chasing you, and having these stupid email conversations. It's gone on long enough."

"Then let me go."

"No way, baby. You're mine."

Knowing she was so close was driving him mad. If he made it through the night with his sanity intact, it would be a miracle. Six months was a long time, but the game was nearing its end. He could feel it. Soon. Soon, he'd have her just where he wanted her.

"This is ridiculous," she said. "I'm going to sign off now."

"Running again?"

"Goodnight, Reno!"

A muscle in his jaw worked, but he knew that he'd pushed the issue hard enough for tonight. She just needed to get used to the fact that when he caught her, he wasn't going to immediately turn her over for prosecution.

No, that wasn't how this was going to play out. He had questions. Lots of questions… Like why did all the evidence point to her? Why had she run? And how were they going to get her out of this mess? He was willing to put in a lot of hot, dark hours with her until he got his answers.

His fingertips caressed the keyboard. "Sweet dreams, baby," he typed.

Danielle unplugged her computer from the phone jack and hopped out of the chair as if it were a hot seat. Her heart pounded in her veins, and she felt little, electric sparks shoot deep into her belly. Quickly, she checked the lock on the motel room door.

The sudden move caused her robe to gape open, and she snatched the lapels back together. She was naked underneath the soft terrycloth. She glanced around the room nervously.

He was coming for her.

She'd always known that he was hunting her. She'd even known that one day he might catch her. She just hadn't known what he intended to do if that ever happened.

Now she knew.

She pulled the robe together at her throat, but her nipples poked up like twin tent poles beneath the fabric.

Now she knew.

Chapter Two

In the end, it took Reno three days to find her. Three, indescribably long days. By the time the call came in, he was in a near panic fearing that he'd made a huge mistake in letting her go.

"Damn local boys," he muttered as he drove down the interstate.

He'd expected them to track her down more quickly. Strangers couldn't hide very easily in small towns and an unfamiliar car would ordinarily attract attention. Somehow, though, the Conrad Police Department hadn't been able to spot her for almost half a week.

Conrad!

He still couldn't believe it. For three days, he'd been cooling his heels in Gilroy, and she'd been hiding in the next town down the road.

He took the exit and drove slowly down Main Street. Her car had been spotted behind a cheap motel called the Waterbury Inn. The neon sign wasn't hard to find; the pink was almost blinding. It forced him to squint as he scanned the parking lot, but he didn't see her car. Turning at the stoplight, he drove along slowly until he found the dark alley that ran behind the place.

There it was.

He pulled into the alley and parallel parked behind her car, effectively blocking her exit. He made a tsking sound as he quietly got out of his sedan. She'd made a mistake pulling in so close to that tree.

"Come out, come out, baby," he whispered. "I'm ready to play."

The gravel crunched loudly beneath his feet, so he moved onto the soft grass. He didn't want to spook her now. Carefully, he rounded the building and looked into the window of Room 1. The lights were off, but the pink neon let him see through the slit between the window shades.

She wasn't there.

But her bag was. It sat, ready to go, on the edge of the bed. She couldn't be far.

Most likely, she was making some cash. He turned around and looked over the area. If she hadn't taken her car, she must have walked. Right across the street was another neon sign, this one blue and screaming "Grinders." A strip club. His eyebrows lowered.

"Maybe."

Down the street was an all night diner.

"More likely," he said. He started down the street.

Ten minutes later, he was back at the strip club.

He looked over the place with a practiced eye. Damn it. What the hell had she gotten herself into this time? This was no "gentlemen's club." It was a sleazy, down low, hump and pump. His blood pressure went up ten points just imagining her working inside.

Putting his palm firmly on the wooden door, he pushed his way into the nightclub—and froze where he stood. A blonde bombshell stood on stage with her back turned to the audience.

It was her.

Lust hit Reno in the gut like a two-by-four. It was Danielle, all right, and all she was wearing was an impossibly high pair of stiletto heels and a tight, little G-string. His gaze was pulled to the spot where the thong disappeared into the crevice between her buttocks, and he forgot to breathe.

Somebody bumped against him as they made their way out the door, and he stepped to the side. Air rushed into his lungs, but he couldn't take his eyes off of her. She was absolutely mesmerizing. He watched in fascination as her sleek hips rocked to and fro, muscles clenching and releasing to the beat of the music.

Her long, blonde hair swung from side to side, brushing suggestively across her back. The need to have her turn around so he could see the rest of her was so strong, he almost called her name. The only thing that stopped him was his clenched throat.

"Good God," he choked.

The music faded away too soon, and he took an unconscious step forward when she looked over her shoulder and threw the audience a wink. Wolf whistles permeated the air, and the noise broke him from his trance. Still, he watched as she strutted off the stage and disappeared behind the curtain.

"The case," he muttered to himself. He had to keep in mind why he was here.

A hard smile pressed at his lips when he remembered their discussion from a few nights ago. Tonight. Tonight, he had her.

With purpose, he made his way to the bar. After a moment, he got the bartender's attention. He waved the guy over and slapped a hundred dollar bill onto the counter. "I'd like to make a special request."

Fifteen minutes later, Dani stood outside the door leading to the private back room. A three hundred-pound bouncer stood quietly nearby, waiting for her to gather her nerve. She looked at him and pressed a hand against her stomach to try to stop the butterflies.

"Don't worry," he said. "I'll be right here if you need me."

She smiled at him weakly.

She really didn't know if she could do this. Dancing on stage was one thing, but did she have the guts to put on a private show?

She still couldn't believe that she was stripping for a living! It had all happened so fast. She'd started out waitressing. That decision alone had been a big one. Going topless had been intimidating, but simple economics had taken the decision out of her hands. She'd known that she'd make better tips at the strip club than at the diner down the street.

Still, her waitressing job had only lasted for about three hours. She'd been ready to quit when the manager had pulled her aside and asked her if she'd consider filling in for a dancer who'd called in sick. At the time, she'd wanted so badly to get away from the bar floor that she'd said "yes" without really thinking about it. Her butt had already been pinched more times than she could count and her "titties," as the boys liked to call them, were sore from being grabbed by mauling hands.

The thought of getting up on stage had been daunting, but it had to be better than waiting on tables. Dancers made more money and were further away from wandering hands. She was already topless, so what difference did it make?

"This is just one more step," she told herself quietly. "You managed to do that. You can do this."

It hadn't been easy, though. She'd only received a few bits of advice from the other girls before she'd been thrust upon the stage. Once there, she'd frozen like a deer in the headlights. Every eye in the room had been on her, and the hoots and whistles had been deafening. Pure fear had made her turn to run, but something inside her had made her stop.

She still didn't know why, but suddenly, she'd been tempted.

Experimentally, she'd started moving her hips to the beat of the music. The roar inside the club had gotten louder and the sound had filled her with a sense of power unlike any she'd ever known. Slowly, she'd begun to take off her clothes. With every stitch of material that hit the floor, her crowd's appreciation had increased.

It had been such a freeing experience. For months, she'd felt trapped. The FBI had been tracking her down, running her life, and making her hide. On stage, she'd been out in the open, but she was the one in control. She was the boss. Innately, she'd known that she held the attention of a roomful of men in the palm of her hand. With a twitch of her hips, she could have had them all begging.

When she'd bared her breasts, a groan of masculine approval had swept through the crowd, and she'd been hooked. The power she'd yielded with her body had made her head swim. The men wanted her, but they couldn't have her.

It was like the game she was playing with Reno. He could chase her all he wanted, but he couldn't catch her. Like him, they could look, but they couldn't touch.

"Neither can this guy. You can drive him crazy, but he can't do anything about it."

The teasing was the best part. And wasn't that exactly what she'd be doing if she went into that room? Her belly clenched, and she looked at the closed door.

Her mother would die of mortification if she ever found out what she was doing, and her dad would probably try to kill every man who looked at her. Still, Dani couldn't help it. Deep inside, a naughty part of her loved to strip.

But this? Could she do this?

Apparently, her last dance had inspired some guy from the audience to request a one-on-one show—a lap dance, to be precise. She'd had to ask what that was. When she'd found out, she'd turned white as a sheet, but inside, she'd been more than a little excited about the prospect. She knew that as long as he wasn't allowed to touch her, she could let herself enjoy it.

"And it will put even more money into your pocket," she said out loud to bolster her nerve. That, really, was the deciding factor.

With a deep breath, she nodded to the bouncer. He opened the door for her, and she walked into the room. The lights were off, and she stopped in the doorway to let her eyes adjust to the poor lighting. She reached for the switch, but the bouncer stopped her.

"He paid extra for you to keep it dark."

One of her eyebrows rose as she considered the request. Hesitantly, she turned around to look across the room. The man was already sitting in the chair. She could see his boots and his jeans in the dim light cast by the moon. A sliver of light slanted across the room from the window above his shoulder, but she couldn't see his face. That suited her just fine.

Quietly, she shut the door and waited until she could see enough so that she wouldn't make a fool of herself. As her eyes adjusted, she realized that the moonlight was enough. The shadowy haze was cool and seductive. The undistinguishable figure remained silent and a little thrill shot down her spine.

With his face hidden in darkness, he could be anybody.

A powerful surge of wanting hit her when she realized she could pretend it was Reno.

"Hey there, big boy," she said in her sexiest voice. "I'm Candy."

Her stiletto heels clipped across the floor as she made her way to the stereo. She'd been told that the music had already been chosen, so she hit the play button. A sultry melody started floating across the room, and she let herself be drawn into its captivating tone. Slowly, she closed the glass case.

She turned on her spiked heel and walked across the room so she could stand in the lone sliver of light. Stopping mid-floor, she spread her legs into a wide stance and simply looked at the shadowy figure. Dark pleasure unfurled in her stomach when she saw the toe of his boot twitch unintentionally.

The motion told her a lot. It told her that she was the one in control.

"Tell me what you like," she said. "I'm here to please you."

With deliberate movements, she began to gradually sway with the rhythm of the song until her hips began to bump and grind suggestively.

"Only you," she crooned as she let her hands skim her hips.

Reno's Adam's apple lodged in his throat as he watched her. He'd meant to lure her into the room and then surprise her. Now, he couldn't have moved if he'd tried.

Oh God, she was good.

Too good. He shifted his weight in the chair. What the hell did she think she was doing, flaunting herself in front of a stranger like this?

His teeth clenched as her hands skimmed temptingly over her body, teasing him because he knew he wasn't allowed the same liberties. When her hands stopped at her waist and balled up the material of her blouse, his job, treason charges, and the rest of the world were forgotten.

"What should I take off first?" she asked.

Reno knew he shouldn't talk. She might recognize his voice. "The top," he said hoarsely.

Would she do it?

She slowly lifted the hem out of the waistband of her short skirt, and his fingers bit into the arms of the padded chair when he saw her smooth flesh. She took her time toying with the material, pulling it and twisting it until he thought he'd go mad. She finally lifted it over her head. She tossed the garment carelessly aside, and his gaze lasered in on her flat belly.

Her body was tight, and her skin was smooth. She rolled her hips, and a distressed sound left his throat. "The skirt."

She hesitated when she heard him, but then her hips started grinding again. Her hands moved down. She fought with the zipper, and eventually the material plopped onto the floor.

For a moment, Reno forgot to breathe. He'd never thought she'd actually follow through.

"Get over here," he whispered hoarsely. He wanted her in his lap. Or under him. Or on all fours.

Her movements stilled, and she stood frozen in the middle of the room.

Good, he thought. So it wasn't so easy after all. "I paid for a lap dance, baby," he said, testing her.

His fingers nearly ripped holes in the upholstery when she took timid steps towards him. She stopped only a foot away, and his knuckles turned white as he forced himself to stay put. It was either destroy the furniture or grab her.

He couldn't touch her, so he let his gaze wander where it wished. It wished for everything. In the pale moonlight, she had to be the sexiest thing he'd ever seen. The stilettos lifted her heels high off the ground, making her legs look incredible. Sheer, black hose covered those long legs up to her thighs, where a skimpy garter belt met them. Under that garter belt, she was wearing an even tinier black G-string. It was so tiny, it would hardly have been worth mentioning if it hadn't barred his gaze from the most private part of her. He couldn't help it; his gaze zeroed in on that spot between her legs.

Somehow she sensed his attention. Her hands moved and, suddenly, the tiny triangle was hidden from his sight. The self-conscious gesture made him feel better, but she made no move to stop things.

Just how far was she willing to go? His hungry gaze settled on her breasts as they nearly spilt out of the lace bra. Uncontrollably, his hips shifted on the chair. "Take it off," he said, the words escaping before he could catch them.

Dani took a step backwards when she felt the man's lust buffet her. Somehow the balance of power had shifted. She didn't like it. "Take what off?" she asked nervously.

"The bra."

A moment of fear gripped her when she realized what she was about to do. *Think of Reno*, she told herself. She'd love to get him in a situation like this. She'd love to make him sweat, knowing that he couldn't do anything to her.

The man wasn't allowed to touch. If he got off by ordering her around, she could do that for him. He still couldn't touch.

The thought comforted her, and a slight smile crossed her lips. She stepped back up to him, so close that her knees brushed against the denim of his jeans. Again, the reins of control were in her hands.

Reaching behind herself, she found the clasp of her bra. With a slight tug, it came undone. The material loosened around her, and she wiggled her shoulders. She bent forwards slightly so that the bra slipped off her body and down her arms.

She heard his sharp intake of breath and immediately felt proud of her body. When the lace confection reached her hand, she twirled it about her finger and boldly dropped it in his lap. He snatched up the material as if it burned, but she could tell that his eyes were centered solely on her.

The attention was flattering.

It was also a turn on.

Dani couldn't help it; she was becoming aroused. She didn't know if that was supposed to happen, but all her muscles had gone warm and loose. Her breasts felt heavy, and she could feel the moisture gathering between her legs.

"Now what?" she asked silkily.

Reno's eyes narrowed. There was something about the throaty tone of her voice. He let his gaze drop slowly. It immediately got stuck on her tits. They were full, more than a handful, but still so ripe. They lifted proudly off her chest, with the nipples charging perkily into the air. He swallowed hard and let the visual journey continue. There was an even rise and fall to her stomach with every breath she took, but her thighs were pressed together almost rigidly. As he watched, she rubbed them against each other.

She was aroused. The knowledge hit him in the gut like a sledgehammer.

Godammit, she was getting into this!

He stared at her hard through the pale moonlight, and the air between them practically crackled. There was no doubt about it. Her nipples were tightening as she stood there. She was reacting, all right, but what was she reacting to—the act or him?

He had to find out.

"Get rid of the stockings," he said roughly. "*Now*."

She wavered for a split second. Then her eyes closed and she took a deep breath. Her breasts lifted and the reckless half of him nearly went crazy.

When she opened her eyes again, they were filled with determination. He groaned when her stiletto heel landed on the arm of the chair next to his clenched fist. *God, he wanted to touch her.*

"Slow," he ordered. "Keep it slow."

Her long, nylon-clad leg was propped right up at eye level. He watched in fascination as her fingers fumbled with the strap of her garter until the black hose loosened. His fingers itched to help her when she reached for the back catch, but it soon gave way with a silent pop. He started breathing harder when she began to roll the silk down her leg, past her knee, and towards her toes. When she pointed the heel of the shoe at him, he grabbed it and threw it across the room. She flinched, but the thin hose soon followed, and he fought to stay in the chair.

Dani's heart pounded as she moved to the other leg. She couldn't believe she was doing this. A man she couldn't even see was sitting in front of her, hidden in the shadows, watching her do something extremely intimate. She was baring her body to a total stranger.

Her nipples tightened almost painfully at the thought, and a shiver ran down her spine. She'd never been so sexually excited in her life.

Finally, she pushed the garter belt down over her hips and stood in front of him wearing nothing but the G-string. She tried to look through the shadows, but she couldn't see him. She preferred it that way.

If she couldn't see him, she could stay lost in her fantasy.

She could pretend she was teasing Reno mercilessly, punishing him for all he'd put her through over the past half-year. And she *was* tormenting this man… She could tell by the way he shifted uncomfortably in the cushioned leather chair.

She swallowed hard and tried to gather her nerve. It was time to make him suffer even more. She was supposed to get up on that chair with him. As he'd said, this was a *lap* dance.

"Is there room on that chair for me?"

She took a cautious step towards him. He drew his knees together so she had room to straddle him, and her heart leapt into her throat. Warily, she put one knee onto the cushion beside his hip. She could feel his heat. His desire lashed at her like hot flames. It intimidated the hell out of her, but she lifted herself fully onto the chair and settled across his lap. His thighs bunched up beneath her, and her pussy clenched.

Reno watched her come at him, totally stunned. There was a far away look in her eyes as she climbed onto the chair with him, but she knew exactly what she was doing. And she wanted to do it!

He made himself stay glued to the seat. Her breasts bounced lightly as she settled into position, and he clenched his teeth together hard. Her shyness was gone, and in its place was thick arousal. It melted over him like warm syrup. He was no longer some hazy, hidden figure to her. He was flesh and blood.

She was reacting to *him*.

His cock surged against the zipper of his jeans. He didn't know what was going on in that complicated head of hers, but by God, he deserved this. She'd put him through hell over the past six months, but now she was sitting all but naked in his lap. He deserved a little slice of heaven.

"Start moving," he growled.

She flinched, but slowly began to sway to the music. His fingers pulled the leather to its ripping point as he watched her body undulate. Good Lord, she was incredible. Her breasts were inches away from his face, and he was dying to kiss them.

He forced his gaze to move up to her face. Her gaze flickered around the room as if she didn't know where to focus. She looked as if she was either scared or uncertain as to how to proceed.

He wanted to believe it was a little of both. She'd only been working here three days. She sure as hell better not have danced like this for anybody else. The mere thought of her sitting on somebody else's lap made him see red.

What was she doing here anyway? She was better than this. Why had she lowered herself to using her body to make money? Didn't she know what kind of lowlifes frequented places like this?

"Look at me," he whispered harshly when her eyes closed. "You're dancing for me."

The sudden order surprised Dani, and she jerked back from the voice that was so close to her. The motion made her breasts jiggle, and she was suddenly embarrassed of her nudity. The widespread position of her legs made her feel vulnerable, and she bit her lower lip as she fought back the uneasiness.

She kept moving, but the fantasy she'd clung to disappeared. This was her job; she had to remember that. She was getting paid to help this guy get off.

"Like this?" she asked shakily.

Reno. *Think of Reno*, she told herself.

Her eyelids became heavy as the rhythm of the music floated through her veins. She began to rock her hips in time with the beat and lifted her hands over her head. Sensuously, she brought them down and covered her breasts. She'd learned that men liked it when she did that on stage. They liked it when she touched herself. Intentionally, she lifted the twin globes and flicked her thumbs over the already-taut nipples. Her eyes popped open when she felt him move.

"You can't touch me," she said, stopping mid-motion.

"I'm not," he whispered as his hand reached for the butterfly clip in her hair. "This doesn't count."

With a quick pinch, the clamp on her hair was loosened. Dani felt her hair drop down across her shoulders, and she shivered. That was supposed to have been her move. Instead of enticing him, though, she felt her own muscles go weak.

She froze as the man softly began to comb her hair with the teeth of the hair clip. She didn't know what to do. Technically, he wasn't touching her; the plastic was. He dragged the clip softly across her scalp, massaging it lightly, and she closed her eyes.

"Oooh," she sighed. Some of the tenseness in her muscles relaxed as shivers of delight ran down her spine. He combed her hair diligently, but carefully avoided any contact between their bodies.

He was following the rules. She didn't need to call the bouncer.

"Keep dancing," he whispered.

The sensual haze drifted over her again, and she obeyed. She began to rock softly, and she gasped when he mirrored the movements with his own hips. The motion was blatantly sexual. The moonlight cast enough glow that she could see his huge erection as he pushed it towards her.

"God, baby. Yeah, just like that," he said.

"Yes," she agreed. "Just like this."

Every muscle in Reno's body was taut. She was killing him with this little teaser dance. It was all he could do not to rip that G-string off of her and thrust up into her. He knew she'd be hot and wet. He could tell from the way she was breathing that she was as excited as he was. The pulse at the base of her throat was pounding wildly.

He wanted to see her get even wilder. Watching her reactions closely, he settled the teeth of the hair clip against her shoulder. She looked down hastily, but didn't stop the gyrations of her body. Carefully, he dragged the clip over her chest down to her quivering breast. Thin white lines scored her flesh, but he made sure that the pressure was light and arousing, not painful. When he finally made it down to the pretty red tip, he heard her whimper in anticipation.

"Easy," he crooned. He flicked the delicate nub with the plastic teeth of the comb, and she nearly came out of his lap.

He almost reached out to pull her back down, but she stayed of her own accord. His hand lifted again, and she reached out to grab the arms of the chair. She stared at the moonlight coming through the window as he brushed the plastic back and forth. At last, she cried out in pleasure. He moved to her other breast, and she bit down hard on her lower lip. He watched it turn white as he tortured her responsive flesh.

"More?" he asked.

She gasped when she saw him pinch the clamp, opening it like jaws. "No!" she breathed.

He ignored her and directed the teeth towards her nipple. Her eyes widened as the clamp approached her quivering breast. She was shaking, but she didn't move away. Carefully, he let the butterfly clip close. It caught the rosy nub in its teeth, and she let out a short scream.

She cut it off quickly and looked worriedly towards the door.

Satisfaction settled deep in Reno's chest. She didn't want to call the bouncer any more than he did.

When she looked at him again, her eyes were cautious. He opened the clamp and let it close in a soft bite. She turned her head to the side as her body bucked.

"Oh God!" she moaned. "It's too much."

A muscle worked in Reno's jaw. "Looks like it's just right to me."

Her hips were rocking wildly against him. He doubted if she knew it, but she was rubbing hard against his erection, nearly causing him to explode. He nipped her breast playfully, drawing out her torment until he couldn't take any more himself. Finally, he pulled the butterfly clip away from her nipple and aimed it lower.

"You didn't finish undressing," he said in a low voice. "This has got to go."

She squirmed as the plastic slid down her stomach and over to her hip. When he slipped the teeth around the strap of her G-string and began to pull it downwards, she froze.

"I want it off," he said firmly.

Slowly, she shifted her hips to help him. He pulled the G-string down as far as he could with her legs spread so widely. The straps pulled tightly, digging into her thighs, but he'd uncovered what he wanted to see. He let out a curse, and her breath hitched when the air from his words touched her abraded nipples. With a sound of desperation, she grabbed hold of the chair behind his head.

"A true blonde," he said. He hadn't expected anything less.

Suddenly, looking at her wasn't enough; he had to touch. He wanted her to take her pleasure from him, not some toy. He tossed the hair clip aside and reached his hand between her legs.

Dani reared back when the man's fingers began prodding against her most sensitive flesh. "You're not supposed to—! Oooooo…"

She couldn't stop him. *She didn't want to stop him.* One of his thick fingers had found her opening and was burrowing into her. He pushed it deep, and with a groan, she let her head drop back.

She couldn't fight him when he leaned forward and took one of her nipples into his mouth. Somewhere, somehow, the balance of power had shifted. He had her irrevocably under his control, but she didn't care. She reveled in her submission.

He flicked his tongue across the rosy tip, and she quaked against him. He'd worked her so hard, his mouth felt like fire when he latched on. He began to suckle intently, pushing the nub hard against the roof of his mouth.

Her neck arched and stars danced behind her eyes. He wasn't being gentle. He wasn't even trying.

She moaned in delight and finally let herself touch him. She wove one hand through his silky hair and held his head against her as he sucked greedily. She gripped his shoulder as the hand between her legs became more insistent.

"Please," she begged. It had been so long.

He shoved another thick finger into her and found her clit with his thumb. She flinched at the intimate touch, but he wouldn't let her get away. His fingers plunged into her and his calloused thumb rubbed relentlessly. He worked her until she was trembling wildly in his arms.

She was close, so close. She rocked hard against his hand and pushed herself against his teasing thumb.

"Dani," he groaned.

Danielle froze. The glimmering haze left her with a lurch and sent her crashing back to earth. Her name. He knew her name!

"No!" she cried.

Her muscles clenched, but then exploded into motion. Frantically, she began pulling away from him. "No! Not you!"

It was a trap! *It was Reno!*

Her fists pounded against his shoulders, but he stopped her by simply wrapping one arm around her waist and pulling her flush against his chest.

"You want it," he bit out as he wormed his fingers inside of her.

She gasped at the way his fingers rasped against her sensitive flesh, but reached down and pushed at his forearm. "Let me go!"

"Never."

Suddenly, she remembered the bouncer.

"Help!" she screamed at the top of her lungs. "Get him off of me!"

The door to the hallway sprang open and slammed against the wall. The guard who'd been standing outside rushed in and flicked on the light, illuminating the lewd picture they made. His face darkened when he saw her naked in the arms of the man who wasn't supposed to touch her. "Get your hands off of her," he growled.

Reno looked at the three hundred pound behemoth and then back to Dani. Her face was flushed and accusations of betrayal flashed in her eyes. His expression tightened, but there was nothing he could do with the bouncer headed his way.

Quickly, he removed his hand from between her legs and pulled up her G-string. He didn't want anybody else seeing her that way. As soon as he let her go, she hopped off his lap and began scrambling for her clothes. Out of the corner of his eye, he saw her grab her skirt, but then it was time to defend himself. He ducked just as a right cross whizzed past his ear.

Dani knew she didn't have much time. Her blood pounded in her ears as she leaned down to pick up her blouse. How could he do this to her? How could she not have known it was him?

Because she was wishing it was him?

Her hands shook as she pulled the shirt over her head. She was about to look for her shoes when she heard the scuffle break out behind her.

She could do without the shoes.

She ignored the astonished looks of the patrons as she ran barefoot to the bar. The manager looked at her in surprise, but she didn't give him time to ask questions. "Give me my money!"

He didn't move.

"Now!" she yelled.

He opened the cash register, and she grabbed the wad of bills he held out to her. She headed out the door at full speed.

"Damn you! *Damn you!*" she cried.

Her hands shook as she reached for the keys in the pocket of her skirt. She couldn't believe that she'd been fantasizing about him the entire time he'd been touching, squeezing, and suckling at her. A low sound left the back of her throat. He'd certainly been true to his word. Not only had he laid his hands on her, he'd left her wanting and aching, with her body craving completion.

"You rotten bastard," she said through clenched teeth.

Rocks bit into her feet as she ran across the street to the Waterbury Inn, but she didn't even feel the pain. She hurried to her room and cursed when her hands shook so badly, she couldn't get the key into the lock.

"Come on!" she cried. Finally, the key slid home, and she pushed her way inside. As always, her bag was packed and ready to go. She grabbed it and her purse before tossing the room key onto the table by the window. Skidding to a stop, she reached for her laptop before making a mad dash to her car.

It was parked behind the motel, hidden in a dark alleyway. She'd moved it every day to try to make sure the police wouldn't notice it. Apparently, her little trick hadn't worked. She rounded the corner, but came up straight when she saw a familiar blue sedan parked behind her.

"I knew it," she hissed. It had been him on the interstate.

She glared at the car. He'd used it to block her in! He'd pulled right up on her butt, barely leaving her any room to maneuver. But barely wasn't the same as none.

Determinedly, she hopped into her car and tossed her belongings into the back seat. She jammed her key into the ignition, and the little car roared faithfully to life. Looking in the mirror, she threw the transmission into reverse and hit the gas.

Bam!

The crunch of fenders wasn't nearly loud enough. She shifted into drive and cranked hard on the steering wheel. She pulled forward until she was inches from the old tree. Then, it was back into reverse and *Wham!* The crunch of a headlight made her smile.

"There," she said without humor. "That's better."

It took valuable minutes to complete the twelve-point turn, but by the time she cleared the tree, his front end was sufficiently mangled to satisfy her. She inched by the old oak, and gravel flew when she hit the gas. He'd come too close this time. She'd made a mistake in not trusting her gut, but she was listening to it now. It was time to run.

She took the turn onto the street almost on two wheels and gunned the accelerator as she headed for the interstate. She needed to get out of Conrad and out of the state. Maybe it was even time she left the country.

By the time Reno emerged from the fight in the back room, Dani was long gone.

"Shit!" he said as he looked down the hall. He slapped the doorjamb and immediately reached for his aching side.

He'd received a black eye and some bruised ribs, but he'd left the bouncer moaning on the floor. He knew that the cavalry would soon be coming to the man's rescue so he turned to the back door. Gingerly, he made his way around the bar and across the street.

She couldn't have gotten far. He'd made sure of that. His footsteps quickened when he saw the light in her motel room was on.

"Dani," he called as he knocked on the door. "Let me in. We have to talk."

He looked in the window when she didn't answer, but he didn't see her. His eyebrows lowered; he doubted she was in the bathroom. He held his side as he turned around. She must be on foot.

Which way would she have gone?

It was impossible to tell, but he knew he'd make better time on her if he drove. He reached into his pocket for his keys and headed to the alley. His footsteps skidded to a stop, though, when he saw his battered car. "Fuck!"

Her car was nowhere to be seen.

"Son of a bitch!" he roared as he hurried to his car.

The front end looked like a crushed aluminum can. Worse, glass covered the ground. She'd made sure to smash both his headlights. Impulsively, he kicked the crushed bumper, but had to step back quickly when it fell off completely.

"Ah, hell," he said as he reached for his ribs. That had been a smooth move.

He let out another curse as he planted his hands on the hood of the car and hung his head. She was gone, and he was hurting. Not only were his ribs sore, he still had a steel-hard erection.

"Idiot," he said as he slapped the hood.

Could he have been any more stupid? She'd done it again. She'd slipped out of his reach just when he'd been certain he'd had her. Only, this time, he'd helped her escape.

"What the hell kind of agent are you? Just when did it become more important to screw her than to arrest her?"

His professionalism had flown right out the window the moment she'd walked into that dark room. He hadn't thought once about her supposed crimes or his job to apprehend her. All he'd been able to think about was getting between her legs. He'd just wanted to grab her and screw her until she was too tired to run from him anymore.

Yeah, that had worked.

Shaking his head, he reached into his pocket for his cell phone. The car was probably still drivable, but without headlights, he couldn't chance it. He needed to find a repair shop quick, or better yet, a rental agency. He'd have to let the Conrad boys follow her and catch up to them.

"Ah, Dani," he sighed. He lowered the phone. He couldn't send anyone after her. She wasn't safe to be driving right now as it was. He wasn't going to put some overeager highway patrolman on her tail.

He ran a hand through his hair. Hell, he'd really done it tonight.

Only he wasn't fully to blame. She was the one who'd crawled right onto his lap.

He pushed himself away from the car and started pacing. What had she been thinking, anyway? He thought he understood the reason why she'd begun stripping. It was a good way to make fast money. He just didn't like how much she obviously enjoyed her new occupation. She'd been squirming around on his lap like a cat in heat. For all she'd known, he could have been any neighborhood pervert, yet she'd let him touch her and masturbate her almost to the point of orgasm.

A garbage can suddenly stood in his way. He let his foot fly and it clattered down the alleyway. "Only it wasn't a stranger, it was me."

Cautiously, he rubbed his sore chest. She'd responded to him. Nobody and nothing would ever make him believe otherwise. She might not have known who was touching her, but she'd definitely been attracted to the man in that chair.

"We're good together," he said in wonder. Real good. So good, he hadn't cared about his job or his reputation. All he'd cared about was her.

He stopped pacing and leaned against the back wall of the motel. Damn. He'd been close for months, but he'd just officially gone over the edge. To hell with the rules; he was emotionally involved.

And she was still out there running for her life.

With a heavy sigh, he tipped his head back and looked at the stars. It had taken only minutes for them to return to where they'd started; he was chasing and she was running. Only now, things were different.

Things had suddenly gotten very personal.

Chapter Three

Dani drove until nearly four o'clock in the morning. She would have kept going, but her eyelids finally got so heavy, she had to pull over to avoid falling asleep at the wheel. The rest stop was filled with semis, but she found a spot near a streetlight. Making sure all the doors were locked, she closed her eyes and fell into a disturbed sleep.

The early morning movements of the truck drivers woke her a few hours later. Sleepily, she made her way to the women's restroom, where she splashed cold water on her face, changed her clothes, and brushed the knots out of her hair. On the way back to her car, she grabbed a cup of coffee from a vending machine and tried to wake up.

For the next two days all she did was drive, drive, drive—and then drive some more. The road became a blur as the miles passed, but she only stopped when it was absolutely necessary. By the third day, she ran out of fuel. Her car tank was full, but she was just too exhausted to run anymore.

Giving in to her fatigue, she found another cheap motel room in another no-name town. Her body was on autopilot as she walked into the room, but she was torn between the bed and the shower. Two days of sponge baths in gas station restrooms tipped the scales. Her clothes hit the floor as she made her way to the bathroom.

"It's warm," she said in tired surprise when she ran her hand experimentally under the shower nozzle.

Her head dipped as she stepped under the spray of water. It eased the stiffness in her muscles and soothed out the kinks in her shoulders. For the first time in days, her body relaxed—but so did her mind. She'd been running on adrenaline for so long, she hadn't allowed herself to slow down to stop or think. With the warm water sliding down her curves, she couldn't stay numb anymore.

Her body still ached for him.

"Damn you, Reno," she said. Turning, she leaned back against the shower wall.

The water caressed her breasts and followed the lines of her body down to that sensitive area between her legs. Her hands clenched into fists and her eyes closed. He'd done this to her.

Pictures and sensations flew through her brain. She couldn't believe she'd reacted so strongly to what she'd believed was a complete stranger. For God's sake, she'd been so aroused, she'd thrown caution to the wind and slinked right onto his lap. She hadn't even given a thought as to the danger. All she'd cared about was that it felt good.

Why? Why had she done that? It was so unlike her.

Unless, of course, she was thinking of Reno. She took a deep breath. Did it matter what had tripped her trigger? The man in her fantasies and the man in the chair were one and the same.

With a shaky hand, she pushed her wet hair out of her face.

He'd told her he wanted to lay his hands on her, but he'd done a lot more than that. He'd stroked her, prodded at her, squeezed her... She bit her lower lip and turned her face away from the spray.

He'd been as into it as she had.

She'd heard it in his sighs and groans. She'd felt the urgency in his touch, and there was no way he could have faked that bulge in his jeans.

"Oh, God," she said softly.

He'd told her that she'd have to deal with what was between them. She'd just never dreamed it could be something so powerful. It had rocked them both. She'd been right in his grasp, but he hadn't made a move to arrest her. He'd been intent on screwing her brains out. The realization made her knees go a little weak. She knew how important his job was to him. For him to ignore it to satisfy his own wants and needs was staggering.

But he'd also promised he'd bring her in.

Her eyelids snapped open and the erotic memories fizzled. When had he ever let anything stand in the way of his job?

"Never," she whispered.

She knew him better than anyone, and his commitment to his job was something that was ingrained in his very DNA. He believed in truth and justice and would do almost anything to uphold them.

Almost anything.

"It was a trap," she said numbly. Her hands fell to her sides. "It just got out of hand."

She turned and grabbed the soap. She rolled it between her hands and began scrubbing her body fiercely. "I knew he'd use it against me," she said past the lump in her throat.

Her hands worked her hair into a lather. This new power he held over her was unnerving. Now that he'd found her Achilles heel, he was going to keep poking at it until it gave way.

Even realizing his intentions, she didn't know how long she'd be able to resist. The pull she felt for him was strong, and she was so very tired. It would be so easy to give up and let him have her. At least she'd find some pleasure and happiness before he locked the door and threw away the key.

"No!" she cried out. She turned off the water abruptly and whipped back the shower curtain. "I'm not going to make it that easy for you."

Her skin turned red as she rubbed it briskly with a towel. She wrapped herself in her robe and went to find her laptop. He'd changed his tactics, so would she. "You need a strategy," she said as she massaged her aching temples.

She couldn't keep running blindly. He was too close. She had to find a new set of wheels and put some direction behind her moves. She wouldn't feel safe until she'd put more distance between them.

With determination steeling her spine, she logged onto the Internet and pulled up a map of the state. Looking at her options, she realized that Longmont was within an hour's drive. It was a town of over seventy thousand people. She could easily sell her car there. An idea came to mind, and she called up another web site. "Aha," she said when she found what she needed. "Go Greyhound!"

He'd be expecting her to get another car. If she hopped on a bus instead, she might be able to lose him—at least for a while. She hadn't used a bus before.

"It's a plan, at least." A weak plan, probably, but her brain was still fuzzy. It would have to do.

She started to shut down her computer, but the temptation to check her email account was too strong. She hadn't spoken to anyone in over two days, and Reno wasn't the only person who sent her messages. Her parents also knew they could get in touch with her there. Convincing herself that she needed to keep in contact, she began the rigmarole of logging onto her account.

When she plugged in her password, though, she immediately saw that there weren't any messages from her family. Her in-box, however, was filled with messages from Reno.

Her hand jerked back from the mouse. "You snake!"

He had balls.

She squirmed uncomfortably on the chair. It was best if she didn't go there.

Curiosity got the best of her, though. She couldn't help but reach for the mouse and begin paging through each and every message. The more she read, the more upset she got. Apparently, Mr. Fed wanted to know where she was and if she was okay.

He was acting like he cared.

Her chair tumbled over when she abruptly stood. "Don't you dare do this to me," she hissed.

She couldn't take mind games. His messages sounded so honest, so concerned.

"No," she whispered. Before she could do something she'd regret, she reached out and closed the connection. With shaking hands, she shut down the system and yanked the power cord out of the wall.

She needed to get moving. Now. She'd planned to stay the night here, but she couldn't waste that much time. He was closing in from every angle. Hurrying, she dried her hair, got dressed, and packed up her belongings. She looked longingly at the bed, but she couldn't risk it. She'd have to sleep on the bus.

Reno unlocked the motel room door and stepped inside. He knew within seconds that Dani had been there. He could sense her. Slowly, he wandered around the room. According to the manager, a woman matching her description had checked in yesterday afternoon – only to leave less than an hour later.

"Why didn't you stay, baby?" he asked quietly. "Why waste good money like that?"

She was behaving erratically, and it made him uneasy. He'd pushed her too hard. Now, she was scrambling around acting on impulse. It wasn't like her.

If only he'd been able to keep his hands off her.

"Yeah, right," he muttered under his breath. He'd come to terms with what had happened between them.

It was clear that she hadn't.

He put his hand flat on the bathroom door, and it swung open with a creak. His gaze went immediately to the sink. The salesman at the used car lot had described her as a brunette. He leaned his shoulder against the doorframe. She'd be just as sultry with dark hair, but he was kind of attached to her soft, blonde tresses. He'd never forget the way they had spilled over her shoulders when he'd taken her hair clip.

"Come on, now," he told himself as he pushed away from the door. "Get it together."

The car. It was what had brought him here. He'd just about thought he'd lost her when the VIN number popped up on a trace. She'd sold it at a used lot in Longmont, and he'd backtracked her movements to this motel through the license plate. He'd thought he might find a clue as to her where-abouts here, but looking around the room, he could see that was hopeless.

Where was she, and how was she moving? It was like she'd vanished into thin air. The used car salesman said she'd just sold him her car and walked away.

"Smart," he muttered. "Mix things up."

Wearily, he sat down on the bed and tried to think. She'd checked in here, changed her appearance, and left to sell her car. Where would she go from there? He had no doubt that she was still on the move. Mobility had been the key to her survival.

"Godammit, you'd better not be hitching, Danielle."

The thought curdled his stomach. She was desperate, but she wouldn't put herself in danger like that. Would she?

"A bus," he said, the answer popping on in his head like a spotlight. It was so obvious. He should have figured it out before, but his brain was fried. He hadn't slept much at all since he'd limped out of that strip bar.

The idea brought a bit of energy with it, and he pushed himself off the bed and headed to his car. He retrieved his laptop and brought it back inside. Sure enough, Longmont was a stop on the Greyhound line. A quick scan of the available destinations, though, made his shoulders droop. She could be anywhere by now.

"Ah, crap," he sighed. He got up to pace the room. Which way would she have gone?

He'd only made it halfway across the room when he heard a beep. Every nerve in his body jumped at the sound, and he swiveled on his heel to look at the computer.

"What the hell?" He hadn't received any messages for days.

It was probably a note from Charley, but he hurried across the room and pounced on the laptop just the same. Relief flooded his system when he saw Dani's email address. His eyes quickly scanned her message, but the light feeling in his chest soon became a dead weight.

"I hate you."

A knife turned in his stomach. He'd been out of his mind with worry for days, and she had the nerve to send him a message like that? "It didn't feel like hate when you were shoving your nipple into my mouth," he typed quickly.

Danielle's jaw dropped at the sudden, unexpected response. She hadn't thought he'd still be watching his email. She hopped out of her chair and took three good-sized steps backward. He wasn't supposed to have been watching.

She stared across the room, but the cursor blinked at her relentlessly. She'd just gotten sick of cleaning out her in-box. He'd overloaded it, and she couldn't stand to read another heartfelt message from him. Her defenses weren't that strong.

And now he was sending her a note like that? Impulse carried her back across the room. Leaning over the table, she typed, "I was just doing my job. You're the one who crossed the line."

The accusation made Reno even angrier. "I thought your job was to dance, not to let men paw you."

"I thought it was your job to arrest me, not to rape me."

He almost sent the laptop flying through the window. "That wasn't even close to rape, and you know it! You were getting off, letting a strange man touch you."

"It wasn't a stranger. It was you!"

"But you didn't know that," he fired back.

The computer blinked at him, and he waited for her response. It was a long time in coming, and he felt some of his anger begin to fade. "You didn't know it was me, did you, Danielle?" he asked.

"No."

Something about her closed-mouth response made him stop. She hadn't known who was sitting in the shadows; she couldn't have. If she'd known he was in that room, she would have run in the other direction.

He was onto something, though; he could feel it. He took a deep breath and tried to remember the situation detachedly. She'd been timid when she'd first entered the room, but she'd gradually grown bolder the closer she'd gotten to him. And she hadn't been shy at all when she'd climbed onto the chair, closed her eyes, and begun rocking her hips against him.

A jolt caught him unexpectedly. She'd *closed her eyes.*

His heart started thudding in his chest. It was like she'd been lost in some kind of fantasy.

"Were you pretending you were dancing for me?" He stared at the question for a long time before hitting the send key.

The cursor didn't move.

Bingo! Reno slapped his palm onto the table. A smile settled on his face, and he couldn't stop grinning. *She'd been dancing for him.* Satisfaction took root deep in his chest. "Where are you, babe?" he typed quickly. "Tell me, and I'll come find you. We can finish what we started."

"You're not getting within a hundred miles of me ever again," she wrote in capital letters.

His mood wasn't about to be dampened. "Come on, sweetheart. Give me a chance."

"Don't 'sweetheart' me. Why should I ever trust you after that little stunt you pulled?"

"You're the one who decided to take off all your clothes in front of me. I can't help it that I'm a red-blooded, American male."

"You'll understand, then, why I don't trust you."

Touché, Reno thought. A grin still lit his face as he settled down into the chair, turning it backwards so he could straddle it. Things were suddenly getting very, very interesting. "Did you take care of yourself?"

"I always take care of myself," she snapped. "Nobody else is looking out for me."

Reno laughed out loud. "I'm asking if you let yourself have an orgasm."

"You have no right to ask that!"

He'd never seen her send so many typos. Obviously, he'd hit a nerve. He decided to push it a little further. "I have every right since I'm the guy who took you ninety percent of the way there before he was forced to stop."

"Shut up!"

"Hell, I'll admit I did it. I jacked off in the shower that night. Baby, you were so hot, not even the cold water could cool me off. I had to resort to some soap and my own hand, but I was thinking of you the entire time."

Just the visual image of Reno in the shower was enough to make Dani's insides melt. She remembered the size of his erection, and she almost crumbled to the floor. "Don't tell me things like that!"

"Why not? Because they excite you?"

"Just stop."

"Do it, Danielle. I would have gone mad days ago if I hadn't done something. Stop torturing yourself. Let yourself go."

She ran a hand through her disheveled hair. The conversation alone was making her hot.

"Call me, and I'll talk you through it," he typed.

Her jaw dropped. "No!"

"No, what? No, you won't finger yourself, or no, you won't call?"

"You'd trace it."

"Ah."

Dani dropped her head into her hands. He'd tricked her. She could practically hear him chuckling in her ear.

"I promise it will just be you and me, babe."

"No," she typed again. She'd never call him. She'd have to be an idiot to do that, but still...

She pulled back and wrapped her arms around her stomach. She'd given in to the temptation of emailing him. It would take so little to get her to pick up the phone. The way he talked to her was as sexy as anything. And she was still so uncomfortable. Just one stray thought, and she was right back in that chair. She glanced at the phone next to the bed, and pressed her legs together hard. Would it be so wrong to try to find some relief?

Yes! her brain screamed. Forget call tracing, what about Caller ID? The name of her new motel might be displayed before he even picked up the phone. Even if it wasn't, she couldn't make herself that vulnerable to him. There was no telling what she might say in the throes of passion. He was smooth enough that she might betray herself even as her hand was moving between her legs.

"All right, then," he wrote. "Don't call. Just lay back on that big, soft bed and pretend I'm there with you."

Her hands dropped to her sides, and she stared at the words. There was nothing she could say.

"Close your eyes and put your hands on those gorgeous breasts of yours," he typed. "Rub them in circles until the nipples press hard against your palms. When they're ready, pinch them a little, pretending it's me with the hair clip - or my fingers, you decide which."

Danielle bit her lower lip when she felt her body respond to the memory.

"Remember how my fingers felt inside of you? You can do that yourself, sweetheart. You might have to use three instead of two, because my hands are a lot bigger than yours."

Her eyelids grew heavy, and she gripped the tail ends of her robe belt tightly.

"Play with yourself, baby. Do whatever feels good. Let yourself experience what you should have felt with me."

She couldn't take any more. He was trying to lure her in, and she could feel herself drifting. With shaking fingers, she quickly logged off the system and shut down the computer.

She couldn't turn off her feelings, though.

Her body was positively humming. Her muscles felt as hot and tight as they'd been the other night when she'd been on his lap. She tried pacing about the room, but nothing seemed to help. She just couldn't get his suggestive words out of her head.

"You shouldn't," she said.

But she had to.

Finally, she gave up and took a hesitant step towards the bed. Nobody would ever know. Nobody was here to see her.

He'd know, though. He'd know what she'd done.

Instead of worrying her, instead of making her fear she'd given him the edge, the thought made the blood rush even more swiftly through her veins. She reached for the tie of her robe. The terrycloth fell onto the floor as she climbed onto the bed. She closed her eyes, and Reno's face was emblazoned on the back of her eyelids.

She could remember vividly how he'd looked when the bouncer had turned on the lights. His face had been fierce with passion. He'd been ravenous for her. He'd wanted her.

Slowly, she lay back and reached for her breasts.

Reno finally headed back to the home office. He'd lost track of Danielle completely and was just wasting his time driving down miles of open road. He didn't feel good about chasing her anymore, anyway. Now that she felt vulnerable to him, she'd only run harder and that would put her in even more danger. The idea put him in a bad mood, and it only got worse when he walked in the door and found Charley waiting for him.

Although the case had been frustrating, his partner seemed to take delight in hearing how she managed to foil him at nearly every turn. This time, Reno didn't feel much like talking.

"A strip club, huh?" Charley asked. He shifted his weight in his specially designed, ergonomic chair. "Did you get to see her dance?"

"Some," Reno said shortly.

Charley's eyebrows rose, making his chubby face look even rounder. "That good?"

"She was all right."

He laughed out loud. "Looks like she knocked you right off your rocker. How did you say she escaped again?"

"The bouncer got in the way," Reno growled. He turned towards the coffee machine and poured himself a cup. "She ran out while the guy busted my ribs and gave me this black eye."

"I heard that you did worse to him."

Reno threw a glare over his shoulder. "He was aiding and abetting a fugitive."

Charley chuckled at the flimsy excuse and rubbed his hands over his expansive belly. "And the fact that he cut her dance short had nothing to do with it."

"You think this is funny?" Reno asked harshly. Coffee spilled out of his cup as he turned sharply. He could think of a lot of words to describe the hell this case had put him through, but "funny" wasn't one of them.

"No, I think it's humbling," Charley said seriously. "The FBI has put significant resources into catching this woman, but she's managed to thwart our efforts using only ingenuity and sheer guts. You've got to admit she's one of the smartest and slipperiest suspects we've ever come up against."

"What did you expect? She's got an IQ like Einstein."

"True."

Reno sipped some of the strong brew. "The stubbornness of a mule," he added.

"Mm hm."

"And the tenacity of a Komodo dragon."

"I'd say." Charley tipped his head to the side. "Looks like she's got something else, too."

Reno looked over the rim of the Styrofoam cup. "What's that?"

"You. By the balls."

Reno's jaw tensed. "Watch it."

Charley rocked forward and caught his partner's arm when he tried to walk past him. He voice dropped low, but it carried a sense of urgency. "I have watched, Jeff, and until now I've kept quiet. But no more. You've been chasing that hot piece of ass until you can't see straight, and now she's using it to her advantage."

Reno jerked his arm away.

"Hey, don't give me that. My sixteen-year-old looked at me the same way when I took away the keys to the car." Charley leaned forward in his chair. "He had the hots for a blonde, too, if I remember correctly."

Reno concentrated on taking slow, deep breaths. "This is none of your business," he said.

"Uh, yeah. I think it is. I need to know my partner's head is in the game – the one that sits on the top of his shoulders, that is."

Reno's muscles hardened, and his temper flared. "If you've got issues with the way I'm doing my job, just say so."

Charley slapped his hands on the armrests of his chair. "I am saying so, and I'm not the only one. People are starting to talk – like about how maybe you don't want to catch her. It's never taken you this long to bring in a fugitive before."

"Yeah, well, she's different."

"How? She's still a criminal, for God's sake."

"Who says?"

Charley's mouth dropped open. "Uh, I thought we did," he said sarcastically.

"Well, what if we've been wrong?"

Charley leaned back slowly in his chair and gave his partner a good once over. "Man, you've got it bad."

Reno started to deny it, but found that the words wouldn't come out. Warily, he looked over his shoulder to see if anybody else was listening to their conversation. "Yeah, I do," he admitted, "But it's not getting in the way of our investigation."

"Bullshit."

Reno's teeth ground together. They never should have gotten on this subject, but now that they had, he might as well lay it all on the line. "Think about it, Charley. She doesn't fit the profile. Why would she sell the software? She didn't need the money. Hell, she drove a Corvette. We've gone over her background with a fine-toothed comb, but we haven't been able to find any political affiliations. So why? Why would she do it? Where's the motive?"

Charley's face turned red. "Don't do this. Don't start dreaming up holes in our evidence. It's solid. Hell, you were instrumental in building the case against her."

"Yeah, well maybe that case is built on quicksand."

Charley's eyes rounded. "Okay, now you're freaking me out."

Reno ran a hand through his hair. The pressure inside his chest was almost ready to explode, but he couldn't describe it to his partner. Something about this whole mess was off. Way off.

"Maybe it's time you took a break from the case," Charley finally said. "You've been going non-stop for too long. Go get some rest. Let someone else take over."

"I can't."

"Why not?"

"Because she didn't do it." The words came out of Reno's mouth so easily, they stunned even him.

She didn't do it, he realized. And it wasn't wishful thinking on his part; it was the truth. That was why she'd kept in touch with him even as she was running. She could have gone underground before now and stayed there, but she hadn't. She was scared, but she was still fighting to clear her name. He'd just been too bull-headed to listen to her.

He reached up and ran a hand over the lax muscles in his face. How could he not have seen it? He'd fought his attraction to her for so long, it had made him blind to something right in front of his nose.

"I have to help her," he whispered under his breath.

"Oh, God," Charley said, flinging his arms into the air.

Reno quickly pulled up another chair. He sat down next to his partner and looked him in the eye. "We've missed something, Charley. Something big."

Squires gave him a hard look – one that had broken down many a suspect in the interrogation room. "You're my partner," he finally said, "But I need something more than that. Just wanting it to be true won't make it so."

"It's not a wish. I know it in my gut."

"In your gut or in your cock?"

"My gut."

Charley rubbed his chin. He knew what the evidence indicated, but he was also an old-timer. You didn't ignore an agent's instincts.

Reno saw him wavering and pressed on. "Everything seems a little too set and dried to me."

His partner nodded slowly. "I've noticed that, too. It's like somebody placed a line of bread crumbs right to her door."

"Why didn't you say something sooner? It's been six months."

Charley's hands came up defensively. "Hey, evidence is evidence. I can't help it if it's all just a little too clean."

Reno rubbed his forehead. He needed to slow down and think. Dani needed him. He had to do this right. "Okay, so we agree that maybe we haven't got all the facts. We need to go through everything again, piece by piece."

Charley smiled, knowing how against the grain that was for his partner. He was the detail man of the team, but Reno preferred action. "You're serious? You're going to sit at a desk while she's out there waiting for you?"

Reno's fingers bit into the Styrofoam. She wasn't waiting for him. She was running from him. "She's gone underground. I'm hoping that if we do our homework now, I might have some good news to tell her when she comes up for air."

"She must really be something," Charley said, shaking his head. He pressed his toe against the floor and spun back to his computer. "All right, I'll pull up the files again."

The knots in Reno's stomach eased. "Thanks, buddy. You won't regret it."

"I'd better not."

Reno pushed himself to his feet. He wasn't going back out on the road, but he couldn't sit behind his desk all day. Waiting for the phone to ring would drive him crazy. Kind of like waiting for an email…

"I'm going to take one of the tech guys over to Quadrangle." He tossed his empty cup into the garbage and headed to the door. "We're going to take that place apart piece by piece."

It turned out that Mr. Hanson, Dani's former boss, was more than willing to work with the FBI to find additional evidence on the case. The man still believed in her innocence, and to prove so, he gave them his best man to help in the investigation. For the next week, Reno and his computer guru consulted with Arnold Pfizer, the man who'd taken over Dani's job.

The geeky little man was more what Reno had expected in the position. He was short and thin with horned-rimmed glasses, a pocket protector, and allergies. Plenty of allergies. The guy spent more time reaching for the box of tissues next to the monitor than the keyboard. Somehow, though, he just didn't look right sitting at Danielle's desk.

He was competent, though. Whenever the tech or Reno had questions about the password protection system, the back-up system, or the security procedures, Pfizer was there to answer them. As a team, they looked for any weakness in Quad's system. Painstakingly, they searched for anything that would have allowed somebody other than Dani access to the code that had been intercepted.

Unfortunately, although they looked in every nook and cranny, their investigation turned up nothing new. The person who had tried to sell the code had definitely used Danielle's account to access the information. The FBI tech was certain.

Reno was dejected when he returned to headquarters a week later. He'd put everything he had into looking at the finer points. Things just hadn't panned out like he'd wanted. When he walked into the office, Charley shook his head. He hadn't found anything either.

Reno slumped into a chair. "Shit," he sighed.

"This is getting us nowhere," Charley agreed. "We need to find her and bring her in."

The fax machine started to whine, and Reno looked at it tiredly. Leaning onto the back legs of his chair, he reached over and grabbed the paper the machine spat out. The front legs came down hard when he got a good look at the information. "We've got her," he said. "She's working as a maid at a hotel in Vailport."

"How did you find her?" Charley asked, even as he snatched the piece of paper out of his partner's hand.

Reno was already reaching for his things. "Before I left Longmont, I checked the Greyhound stops north to the border. I figured it wouldn't hurt to send her wanted poster to all the motels and hotels along the route. That's one thing about her M.O. that hasn't changed. Dani's all about comfort."

"Yeah, yeah. What hotel?" Charley asked as he scanned the fax.

"The Roquefort," Reno said with a hard smile. "The manager's been watching her closely. Apparently, she's making herself at home in the empty rooms. He's not too happy about that."

"She's made a mistake," Charley said, his eyes rounding.

"Give me that address," Reno said grimly. He grabbed the info and his partner didn't try to stop him as he headed to the door.

This time was it. There was a certainty in Reno's gut that hadn't been there before. This time he was going to catch her; and this time, he wasn't letting go.

Chapter Four

It had been a long day. Danielle tiredly let herself into her hotel room, peeled away the tape she'd put over the lock, and shut the door. She turned the deadbolt and, drained of energy, leaned back against it.

She looked at the expansive room. She'd wanted to stay in luxurious surroundings like this for the past six months. After endless nights of lumpy pillows and cold showers, she'd craved some of the finer comforts. She just hadn't thought she'd have to work so hard to get them.

Be careful what you wish, she thought.

She pushed herself away from the door and headed towards the bathroom, removing her maid's uniform as she walked. She'd made enough hospital corners today to please even her grandmother. She hadn't realized what slobs some people were until she'd taken this job. How could they make such a mess when they stayed for such a short time?

"Pigs," she muttered.

A hot shower sounded so inviting. She turned the water on full blast and ran her hand through the mist. It almost made all the work worthwhile. Almost. She stepped into the tub, pulled the shower curtain closed, and bent her head under the pelting spray.

"Ahhh," she sighed.

This latest job of hers paid next to nothing, but she knew opportunity when she saw it. The hotel paid cash, and their hiring practices were questionable because she hadn't had to fill out a W-4 form or show any type of identification for employment. That suited her fine. So did the free room and board she received—although the hotel wasn't exactly aware of the arrangement. She'd been using her master key to let herself into empty rooms at night.

She rolled her shoulders to loosen up the knots and reached for the soap. She could remember the good old days when she could tell people that her name was Danielle Carver. She remembered when she could pay for a nice hotel room like this with a credit card.

"I remember having a life," she said miserably.

She slicked back her hair from her face and felt tears press at her eyes. This was so unfair. Not long ago, she'd been a happy, productive member of the community. How had she been reduced to cleaning toilets and sneaking into empty rooms for shelter?

The doldrums settled upon her, and she couldn't shake them. She turned off the water and dried off with one of the hotel's big, fluffy towels. Not even laundry softener managed to cheer her up. She wrapped herself in her robe and dried her hair, but the lonely feeling remained.

She desperately wanted somebody to talk to.

She shuffled out of the steaming bathroom and looked longingly at her laptop. She'd had no contact with Reno since their last, heated email conversation. Things were too edgy and complicated now. Getting physical at the strip club had changed everything. She wished they could go back to the way they were—not the running and chasing part, but the camaraderie. She'd never been so lonesome in her life. She'd even be happy to hear him criticize her eating habits.

She ran her finger along the edge of the sleek, black screen. Could he still be waiting to hear from her? The rules of their relationship had changed, but was he still there?

The pang in her stomach was hard to ignore. Without him, she felt stranded. He'd been her one true constant. This total isolation was beginning to make her desperate—desperate enough to consider his offer to work with her. What if he'd meant it? Her instincts screamed at her that it was a trick, but that lonely, aching part deep inside of her reminded her that he'd never lied to her.

He'd had his chance to arrest her, but he hadn't.

Ignoring everything that was telling her not to, she began to set up the system. The procedure was so habitual, she disconnected the phone and plugged her modem into the wall without even noticing. She pulled out a chair and settled down onto the plump cushions.

"Looking for me?"

She jolted at the sound of a voice right behind her. In one fluid motion, she shot out of the chair and spun around.

"Reno!" He was standing just inside the door connecting to the next room. Her heart stopped for a split second and then took off at triple speed.

No, this couldn't be happening! She'd been so careful.

With morbid fascination, she watched as he closed the door behind him and locked it with a decisive click. The sound set her into action, and she poised herself on the balls of her feet, ready to take flight. "How did you find me?" she asked.

"I have my ways." He took a quick, nonchalant look around the room. "Moving up in the world, aren't you, Danielle?"

Sweat broke out on her palms. She'd been in tight jams before, but this was different. She hadn't seen this coming. She was so unprepared. Nervously, she clutched her robe together and looked for an escape route. "I'll scream," she warned.

He gave a soft chuckle and began to walk slowly towards her. "That won't work this time, sweetheart. Your manager is the person who turned you in, and you're the one who chose a room on a nearly empty floor."

He was bigger than she remembered and more intimidating. She took a cautious step backwards, but bumped into the table behind her.

He ran a hand across the cream colored wall at his side. "That's the thing about these expensive hotels. The walls are a lot thicker than the places you've been living in lately."

Dani's breath shortened, and she looked frantically towards the phone. It was unplugged. A desperate laugh left her lips. Who was she going to call anyway? He was the law.

He moved again, and her head snapped back towards him. His dark gaze settled on her, full of determination. She tried to back up, but the table pressed solidly against the back of her thighs, telling her she had nowhere to go.

"Time's up, baby," he said softly.

Without warning, she charged for the bed. If she could get past it, she had a slim chance.

"Hey," he called.

She managed to get one foot up on the mattress before his hand wrapped around her ankle and gave a solid tug. She fell hard, but the plush mattress cushioned her fall.

"Let me go," she cried as she flipped onto her back. She kicked outwards and he took a cautious step backwards. She lashed out again and squirmed towards the far edge of the bed. She still had a shot.

Reno had seen the way she'd eyed the door, but he wasn't about to let her get to it. He was trained in hand-to-hand combat, but he didn't want to hurt her. He blocked another kick and lunged at her before she could get in position to throw another blow.

"Stop it, Dani," he said, breathing hard. "The game's over."

He leveraged himself over her, using his body weight to pin her torso to the bed. It only infuriated her. A flurry of punches came at him, and one managed to clip him across the chin. It didn't have much force to it, but it irritated the hell out of him. There'd already been enough violence between them. His black eye was still fading.

He grabbed her wrists and pressed them solidly to the bed. "Assaulting an officer? Honey, you're better than that."

Her next attack plan shown clearly in her eyes, and he quickly wrapped his legs around hers. "That's it," he growled.

He pulled her hands over her head and caught them in one of his as he reached behind him for his cuffs. She heard the jingle of metal just before he waved the shiny links over her face.

Her eyes went round, and her body heaved beneath him. "No!" she pleaded.

He was in no mood to compromise. The way her body was working beneath him, he had no doubt she'd send her claws at his face if he let her go. He looped the restraint over one delicate wrist, and clicked the handcuff into place.

"I'm innocent!" she cried out. "This isn't right. You can't do this."

"Watch me."

She began to struggle more violently, but he caught her under the armpits. Her eyes flashed towards the headboard when she saw his intent. "Don't you dare!"

"It's for your own good," he growled. "You need to settle down or one of us is going to get hurt—but I'll be damned if it's going to be you."

He tugged her resisting body into position and looped the handcuffs around a slat in the headboard. She fought him as he pulled her other wrist upwards, but he easily locked the metal bracelet into place.

"No!" she screamed when she heard the click of metal against metal. That one, little sound signaled the end of her freedom.

She went a little wild underneath him, and Reno couldn't help his reaction. He felt for her, but his body had other ideas. Letting go of her wrists, he pushed himself up onto his haunches and looked down at her. "Take it easy."

He cupped her cheek gently, and her fiery blue gaze seared him.

Lord, she was magnificent. Her blonde hair spilled across the dark bedspread, making the strands seem like sunshine. Her curves were swamped in an over-sized, white robe, but he knew what the terrycloth was hiding. She was the embodiment of pure, hot adrenaline.

She fought like a tigress, and a growl left her lips. She bucked her body, trying to dislodge him, but barely lifted him an inch. A hard smile crossed his face. Leaning down close to her, he whispered, "Gotcha."

Dani closed her eyes as she felt the bitter taste of defeat. It settled in her chest, blocking out any hopes for her future. She wouldn't be slipping out of his clutches this time. No, she'd just drawn a "Go Directly to Jail" card.

She almost cried out from the frustration. She was trapped. It didn't matter how she twisted her wrists or pulled against the metal. He had her.

She opened her eyes and found him looking down at her. His dark brown eyes were deep and fathomless, but she detected a hint of some emotion... sympathy? Did he feel sorry for her? "Please take them off."

He let out a low laugh. "Not on your life."

Watching her closely, he shifted his weight. All of a sudden, she became vividly aware of the bulge behind the zipper of his jeans. It nudged purposefully against her mound until it settled in the niche at the top of her legs.

Danielle sucked in a harsh breath.

The position was full of intent.

Slowly, he reached for the tie of her robe.

She watched, her muscles tense, as he methodically undid the knot at her waist. There was nothing she could do when his fingers sank into the soft material and parted the robe. Her body was bared to his gaze, and she'd never felt so exposed – not even at the club.

"Bastard," she hissed.

She watched anxiously as a muscle ticked in his jaw. Her nipples tingled, and she bit her lip in embarrassment. Slowly, deliberately, he reached out and settled his hands firmly over her uplifted breasts. The intimate contact made her back arch and the air catch in her lungs.

"Were you going to try to email me?" he asked in a hoarse voice.

Dani hardly heard the question. He'd begun to mold and shape her with his big, strong hands, and her pulse was pounding in her ears. She felt so helpless. Here, all the lights were on, and she knew exactly who was touching her.

She squirmed under his fondling, but it was impossible to move more than a centimeter with her hands chained above her head and his heavy weight pinning her hips. She'd never been more vulnerable in her life, and her most feared enemy had her body at his mercy.

She flinched when he leaned down close. He ran his tongue softly over her earlobe. "I've missed you, Danielle," he whispered.

The words rumbled into her ear, and she felt her pussy clench. He began to roll her nipples between his forefingers and thumbs, and the combined pleasure and pain was intense. Too intense. She pulled hard against the handcuffs and tried to roll away from him.

He didn't ease up. "I think you missed me, too."

She looked up at her persecutor through hazy eyes. He knew exactly what he was doing to her—and he knew that it was working. "Like a rash," she said defiantly. A lie.

"Liar," he said with a chuckle. "Your body missed me."

To prove his point he let his hands wander. He sat back again and began to stroke her. His hands left her breasts to massage her shoulders. His fingers caressed her underarms, tickled her nipples, and swept down her stomach. Playfully, he tugged at the triangle of hair between her legs, and she couldn't stop herself from crying out.

He combed the hair covering her mound. "I'm glad you're still blonde. I had reports that you'd gone brunette."

His hand pushed more firmly at the crevice between her legs, and Dani's toes curled. She couldn't escape his touch. He could do anything he wanted to her. And God help her, she wanted to let him.

"Oh," she groaned.

He leaned down towards her chest, and she waited in breathless anticipation. After all his attention with his hands, her nipples were swollen and craving his hot mouth. She whimpered when his teeth grazed her sensitive flesh.

"You're so responsive," he said. He licked her and teased her before finally opening his mouth and suckling her.

Dani closed her eyes and gave in to the hot waves of pleasure that coursed through her belly.

"That's better. Just like the night at the strip club," he crooned. He moved to the other breast and laved the nipple with his rough tongue. "Did you touch yourself after we talked, sweetheart?"

Crimson color flooded her face as she remembered what she'd done at his encouragement. She turned her head and pressed her face against her arm.

"I knew you did. I was with you. Could you feel me?"

She had. In her mind, it had been him touching and caressing her. Her skin had burned under his attentions, but it had been nothing like this. "You can't do this," she panted. "If you do, I'll tell your superiors and you'll be fired before you can say 'sexual harassment'."

Reno lifted his head and shot her a hard look. Inside, his guts were churning. Her smooth skin was driving him crazy, but she was still fighting the combustible attraction between them.

Fine, he thought. He'd just turn up the heat a little higher and see if she could still ignore it.

Slowly, he lifted his weight off of her and onto his elbows. He slid further down her body but kept his gaze locked with hers. "My superiors are very thorough in their questioning. You'll have to be very specific when you tell them what I did."

Her head lifted sharply off the pillow.

"For instance, you'll have to tell them that I did this."

She gasped in surprise when he experimentally let his lips rub across her skin. Her belly quivered, and he let out a groan as he gave in to his own private fantasy. Opening his mouth, he began to kiss and nibble his way across her abdomen. Little choked sounds erupted from her throat, and she began to squirm with arousal. When he licked her skin and softly bit her flat stomach, she let out a sharp cry.

"And they'll want to know about this," he growled.

Reno felt himself getting light-headed. She tasted as good as she looked. He wrapped his arms around her writhing body and held her still for his mouth. Giving into temptation, he dipped his tongue into her belly button. She shuddered, giving him the reaction that he'd wanted for so long, and he felt his own control slipping.

"And you'll definitely have to tell them about this," he rumbled.

Frantically, she tried to kick him, but she had no angle or leverage. He caught her legs and opened them. She cried out when his hands slipped under her buttocks and lifted her hips off of the mattress.

"I'll have your job," she said between short, hitched breaths.

"You'll have me."

Within seconds, he had her immobilized with her hands chained above her head and her thighs draped across his shoulders. His fingers bit into her waist as his head nudged deeper between her spread legs.

Why was she still fighting him? Why wouldn't she surrender to what they both wanted the most? "Stop running, Dani," he said.

She wriggled in his hands, but he held her still for his mouth. He let his tongue rake across her swollen, pink lips, and she jerked. He heard her panting cries and zeroed in for an intimate kiss.

"Let yourself enjoy it," he said. "You know you want to."

He licked, stroked, and sucked until her body was rocking with sensation. He could feel her heated muscles contracting. Still, she fought the orgasm—fought the inevitable. He refused to let her deny herself pleasure. His tongue prodded at her, and she sobbed when it pushed inside.

"Reno," she gasped.

"Do you want me, Dani?" he said against her skin.

He could feel her beginning to come undone. Deliberately, he moved his attentions up to her apex and firmly licked the tight bud of nerves.

Her back arched, and her muscles went tight.

"Dani?" His tongue prodded her clit, and the caress seemed to push her over the edge.

"Yes!" she said in a strangled voice.

He pushed his face hard against her bucking hips and gave her what she needed. Her body heaved, and the climax held her in its grip for a long, long time before letting her go. When it did, she went limp in his arms. His own body was surging, but he lowered her hips gently to the mattress before reaching for his zipper.

Danielle was vaguely aware of Reno leaving the bed. She heard something hit the floor and, groggily, looked over towards him. Her eyes widened with surprise. He was stripping uninhibitedly in the harsh light of the room, and her gaze was drawn to the obvious.

He was hung like a horse.

She'd felt his erection against her, but she'd underestimated his length and thickness. She looked at him unabashedly. For such a big man, he was all muscle. Dark hair covered his chest in an inverted V, and her nipples tingled in anticipation. The same dark hair circled the base of his prick.

She felt a flutter of feminine fear when she saw that his balls were drawn up tight. He was aroused to near the bursting point and she knew that within seconds, she'd be taking that big cock deep inside of her. He walked towards the bed, and her fingers wrapped around the headboard tightly.

"Reno, please." She drew her knees together instinctively and rolled away from him. "It's been a long time for me."

"Me, too," he rasped. He crawled onto the bed and grabbed her thighs. He rolled her onto her back and pushed her knees towards her chest before she could try any more evasive maneuvers. "Stop running from me, damn it. Surrender."

"I can't," she breathed.

The muscles in his jaw tensed. He positioned himself, and her heart thudded against her ribs when she felt the broad head of his cock find her slick opening. Without giving her any time to prepare, he thrust hard and true, driving himself deeply into her.

Dani cried out at the sudden penetration. He felt huge inside her. The pressure was enormous, spreading her, opening her. His weight pressed her knees back against her chest, forcing her to take him deeply. She felt every thick inch of him as he took advantage of her vulnerable position.

"Ah, ah," she panted.

She bit her lip and waited for the pain, but felt nothing but pleasure when he began to move.

"There you go, babe," Reno crooned. He rocked gently back and forth, trying to give her time to adjust. His hands moved on her ass until he held her at just the right angle for his thrusts. Leaning forward, he spread the vee of her legs wider and let the rough hairs on his chest scratch at her sensitive nipples. A feeling of triumph surged through him when she groaned.

She turned her head away in defeat, but accepted his slow, deliberate, deep thrusts. Soon, his needs had him plunging harder and faster. Beads of sweat popped up on his forehead, and her fingers turned white around the headboard. Out of the corner of his eye, he saw her toes point like a ballet dancer's.

"God, you're tight," he said on a rough breath.

She was gripping him in a hot, snug vice. It felt so good, he was worried he wouldn't last.

He didn't want it to end so soon. He'd waited for so long. He wanted to tie her to him, bind her in a way that would make her never want to run again.

"Fuck!" he said. He lowered his head and let his hips ram against her.

"Ah, Reno," she cried. "Oh, oh, oh!"

He tried to kiss her. She turned her head away, so he dropped his head into the gentle slope of her neck. His grunts and groans echoed in her ear as he screwed her into the mattress.

The bed rocked with their motions, and the headboard banged against the wall with every thrust. The handcuffs jingled and her cries blended with his curses, until suddenly, he crested.

Mindless with pleasure, Reno clenched her to him. His fingers bit into her slick buttocks, and somewhere in the back of his mind, he felt her fly over the edge with him.

After an eternity, he collapsed upon her in exhaustion. Their skin clung to each other, and they both struggled to catch their breath. Reno waited for his heart to slow. When his faculties returned, he lifted his head out of the crook of her shoulder. He smoothed her hair out of her face and looked down at her. "Okay?"

Dani nodded because her throat was clenched too tightly for her to speak. Why did it have to be this way with him? Why did it have to be Reno? She saw his lips begin to move towards hers, and she managed to choke out, "Don't."

If he kissed her, she'd fall totally, irrevocably, in love with him—and then it would be over for her.

His jaw tightened when she resisted, but he kissed her forehead instead. Suddenly, he seemed to remember her bindings. He leveraged himself up, and she felt his softened cock twitch inside her. His hands settled on her shoulders, and he began to massage her tight muscles.

"I think we can take these off now," he said as he ran his hands up to her wrists.

She flinched when he started to pull out of her. She gave him up with as much difficulty as she'd taken him, and he seemed to realize that. He moved slowly, watching her face every second. She felt empty when he was gone.

He bent down to retrieve his jeans. Her eyes lit up when she saw the keys in his hand, but he shook his head slowly. "Don't get too excited. You're not going anywhere."

Her heart sank as he took one of her wrists in his hands and unlocked the handcuff. She pulled her hand down from over her head, but he caught it. His thumb ran softly over the bruise that was already forming and a frown lowered his brow. He lifted her sore wrist to his lips and gave it a soft kiss. He quickly removed the other cuff and gave that wrist the same attention.

Danielle watched anxiously as he strode naked towards the door to the room. She couldn't read what was going on inside his head. He'd done what he'd promised to do to her, but what were his plans now? Was he going to call his partner? Was he going to drive her down to the local police station?

Her heart began to pound again, but this time from fear, not arousal. When the light went out, she became even more skittish. He moved to the bathroom next, and soon, all that was left on was the bedside lamp. Was he getting ready to leave? "Please don't turn me in, Reno," she blurted.

He looked at her sharply. "Oh, babe," he sighed. "Don't worry about that. We'll work it out tomorrow."

Dani's chest tightened. But how? How did he plan to work things out?

"Let's just enjoy tonight," he said gruffly. "Come on, stand up."

Her insides tangled. She wanted desperately to believe him. It was just too much to hope for. He might be feeling magnanimous now, but she knew how sex could cloud issues. When his brain cleared, he'd remember his job and his duty. Her legs shook as she got off the bed and drew the robe around her.

"Don't you think it's a little late to play shy?" he said.

She rubbed her sore wrists. "What are you going to do with me?" she asked quietly.

"Fuck you," he answered simply as he pulled down the covers.

"But we already…"

His smile turned wolfish. "It's been six months for me, too, baby."

Her face flushed. "But the… arrest."

"All that can wait." He began pushing the robe off her shoulders. She tried to stop him, but he simply brushed her hands aside. Soon she was naked like he wanted. "I can't."

Her arrest could wait. His intentions hadn't changed at all.

"What if I told you I don't want you?" she snapped.

His smile broadened. "Then I'd say you're damn good at faking it."

Dani gasped when he caught her about the waist. He pulled her to him and lifted her like a feather. Her legs wrapped around his waist as if it was the most natural thing in the world, and her arms went around his neck. Without ceremony, he pushed his thick cock into her. The fullness made her back arch.

"Damn good," he growled as he licked her turgid nipple.

Her fingers bit into the muscles of his shoulders.

"Relax, baby," he said. "Let me take care of you. Let me make everything all right."

He began to pump in and out of her, and her resistance melted. God, she wanted to let herself sink into that fantasy. She wanted to trust him. She wanted to believe he'd protect her.

She wanted to believe that he loved her as much as she loved him.

Her eyes closed in surrender. She knew she shouldn't let this happen. He was her hunter. He'd been chasing her forever – but she reveled in finally being caught.

"Reno," she sighed as her fingernails raked down his back.

Tonight, she'd give in to all the wants and needs that had been building inside her for months. Tonight, she'd love him like she wanted to, but tomorrow…

Tomorrow, she was going to go down fighting.

Chapter Five

Sunlight streaming through the window woke Reno the next morning. He didn't know what time it was, but he could have slept for another four to five hours *easy*. With a groan, he pressed his face into the pillow.

God, what a night. He and Dani had gone at it until almost dawn. He hadn't been able to get enough of her, and once she'd let go... Man, he'd had a wildcat on his hands. Hard and fast. Slow and easy. It hadn't mattered how, as long as he'd been inside her.

He reached out to pull her warm body closer, but his head jerked up when his hand touched cool sheets. She wasn't there.

He surged upright. The move nearly separated his shoulder. His head snapped towards the headboard, and a flurry of curses flew from his lips.

She'd handcuffed him to the bed.

"Shit!"

He twisted his wrist and tried to pull his hand through the cuff, but it held tight.

"Damn it!" She'd turned the tables on him *again*.

His temper snapped. Had last night meant nothing to her? He'd thought they'd made a connection.

He tugged hard on the headboard. It held solid. He wrapped his fist around the spindle he was chained to and yanked it so hard, the bed bucked. As he'd been so quick to tell her, though, The Roquefort was a nice hotel. That meant good furniture.

Twisting about, he tried to push with his feet for more leverage, but that didn't work either. Kicking was useless. He didn't have the flexibility.

"Ah, hell." Finally, out of breath, he gave up.

His breath pumped in and out of his lungs. She'd gotten away again. This time, though, it hurt like hell.

He sank back against the pillows and stared hard at the ceiling. She was still running—running from him. Only now, he felt like his heart had been ripped out of his chest.

Opening his eyes, he looked around the room. A bitter laugh left his lips when he saw the mirror. How sweet of her to leave him a note. The word "key" was written in lipstick with an arrow pointing downwards to the dresser.

He laughed again and, suddenly, the humor of the situation got to him. "You are going to pay for this, baby. Big time."

There was nothing he could do but make himself comfortable, but it was an hour before he heard somebody in the hallway. Embarrassing as it was, he called out for help. A little maid responded, and her dark eyes got huge when she discovered his predicament. Reno didn't know who was more embarrassed when she picked up the key and timidly approached him.

He didn't have time to explain, though. As soon as she turned him loose, he grabbed the sheet from off the bed and made a beeline to the bathroom. He heard her giggling behind him and his face, along with most of the rest of his body, turned red with embarrassment.

If that wasn't bad enough, it took another half-hour to explain the situation to the irate hotel manager. He'd had to lie through his teeth. Reno was so frustrated and embarrassed; by the time he got out of there he had a pounding headache. He walked out to the parking lot, but his mind was on other things—like his pride, his reputation, and his weakness for a hot-blooded, but cold-hearted blonde. He reached into the pocket of his jeans for his keys and stopped in his tracks.

"Fuck!" She'd taken them, too.

His head snapped up and he looked for his car. He couldn't have been more surprised to find it still parked in the space where he'd left it.

Even more shocking, Danielle sat on the hood.

A band of steel circled Reno's chest, and suddenly, he found it hard to breathe. She was huddled into a ball with her feet propped up on the bumper. Her elbows were settled upon her knees, and her face was buried in her hands. She looked so sad and alone his heart squeezed.

He didn't say a word as he approached her. She heard his footsteps, though, and glanced up quickly. When she saw that it was him, she hurriedly wiped the tears from her face. She swallowed hard and watched him with wary eyes.

The tears were what did it. He walked straight up to her, reached out, cupped the back of her head, and kissed her.

They'd done a lot of things last night, but this was the one intimacy she'd denied him.

Her lips trembled under his. He changed the angle of his mouth and the contact deepened. With a groan, she leaned her head back. Her fingers dug into the leather of his bomber jacket, and he wrapped his arms tightly around her.

At last, she surrendered.

The band around his chest loosened, and he swept her off the hood of the car and into his arms. Her fingers dove into his hair, and their tongues rasped as they learned each other's taste.

When they finally broke apart, they were both breathless. "Baby," he said hoarsely. "You've got to stop running."

Dani found she couldn't look at him. Nerves had her stomach churning. She was putting a lot on the line. No, not a lot. *Everything.* "Were you telling the truth when you offered to work with me to prove my innocence?"

"Yes," he said without hesitation. "I should have made that clear last night."

Her heart lodged in her throat, and her voice went tight. "I didn't do it. I swear. I wouldn't do something like that."

A muscle in his jaw worked, and he cupped her face with both hands. "I know."

"Really?" Dani asked, tears pressing at her eyes.

"Really."

She jumped so hard against him, she almost knocked him over. She buried her face against his neck and hugged him tightly. Her air worked in her lungs, but she tried not to get too excited. Her name hadn't been cleared yet.

But he'd said he believed her, and that was worth almost as much.

"Okay, now. Stop that," he muttered. His hands swept up and down her back. "I'm not good with tears."

She let out a long breath. His hand ran over the top of her head, and she sagged against him.

He kissed her temple. "How long have you been sitting here? Have you eaten yet?"

She shook her head.

He sighed and looked at her sternly, but gave her a quick hug. "That's the first thing we need to do. Come on, we'll find someplace that serves a big breakfast. Then we'll talk."

She pulled back and wiped the moisture from her cheeks. She gestured towards the hotel. "The restaurant here is pretty good."

"No way."

She looked up at him, and her eyes rounded. Special Agent Jeff Reno's face had gone bright red.

He rolled his shoulders self-consciously. "After what you did to me, I can't ever show my face in that hotel again."

Dani couldn't help it. A smile pulled at her lips, and for the first time in months, she broke out into laughter. "Was your face really the problem?"

He looked sheepish. "One of your maid friends got the surprise of her life."

She covered her mouth with her hand to hide her smile, but her eyes lit up with laughter. "There's another restaurant down the street."

He reached out and caught her by the hair. "You know I'm going to make you pay."

It didn't sound like much of a threat. "Promise?"

"Promise." He leaned down and kissed her again. "Let's go. I'm starving. We burned off a lot of calories last night."

She gave him back the keys to his car and they walked down the street together. When his hand slipped around hers, she looked down quickly. He gave her fingers a squeeze, and the last bit of tension in her shoulders eased.

He had no idea how hard it had been for her to turn herself in. She'd been so nervous when she'd slipped out of bed and retrieved the handcuffs. She'd been sure that he was going to wake up and grab her. Her entire body had been shaking with nerves when she'd found his car keys in his pocket. She'd hurried out to the parking lot and used the remote to locate his car. She could have escaped. It would have been easy – if only she could have turned the key.

She just hadn't been able to do it. She was too tired. Tired of running. Tired of hiding. Tired of being alone.

Last night… What they'd done… It had been shockingly intimate. All the emotions and desires they'd suppressed for months had come to the surface. Reno had taken control of her body, but once she'd given herself to him, he'd taken incredible care with her. She'd let herself go with him, and it all came down to one thing.

Trust.

She'd put her body in his hands. Now, she'd put her future.

She hoped he wouldn't let her down.

Reno made Dani eat every bite of her of her bacon and eggs before he let her talk. When she put down her fork, he pointed to the blueberry muffin sitting on a side plate.

"Oh, I can't. I'm about to burst," she complained. She sank back against the back of the booth and wrapped her arms around her stomach.

"Fine, we'll save it for you to eat later." With a wave of his hand, he sent a waitress scurrying for a doggy bag.

Danielle rolled her eyes. "What is it with you and my diet?"

He shrugged. "You've always brought out the protective side of me."

"Always?"

"From day one." He took a sip of his coffee. "You should have seen my reaction when I walked into that strip joint and saw all those men panting over you."

She looked at him through the veil of her eyelashes, and a trace of a blush graced her cheekbones. "You saw me on stage?"

"You're kind of hard to miss—especially when all you're wearing is butt floss and fuck me pumps."

Her blush reddened, and she looked out the window. "I liked that job."

"You *liked* it?"

She shifted in her seat.

"You got off on it," he said slowly.

She didn't answer.

"What was it, the attention?" He looked at her closely and shook his head. "No, it was the power. You liked being in control."

"Can you blame me?" Her gaze leveled with his, and her chin came up. "I haven't had control over my life for half a year."

"But you kind of liked that, too. You liked being under my thumb." His gaze heated. "In fact, you'll take my thumb any way you can get it."

"Reno," she hissed. "Keep your voice down."

He chuckled. "It's the truth."

She ran a hand through her tussled hair. "All I know is that working at Grinders sure beat cleaning kennels. I certainly made a lot more money. Do you know that I made as much stripping as I did writing computer code?"

He set down his coffee cup slowly. "I thought that Quad paid good money."

She shrugged. "They do, but a computer programmer doesn't make tips."

"No bills in your G-string for a good line of C++?"

She chuckled. "Not in that manner of speaking."

Reno sat back in his seat. It was time to get into it. He couldn't let this liaison go on for long. He needed to clear her name before anyone at HQ found out that he'd made love to her. "So money could have been a strong motivation for whoever accessed that code," he said.

She went still. "Are you sure we can talk about it here?"

"Here's as good of a place as any."

"I've thought a lot about it," she finally said. "Whoever took that code did it for either money or political reasons. There are countries out there that would pay a lot for that application."

She wasn't telling him anything he didn't already know, but he listened carefully to see if she recalled anything he might have missed. "Explain it to me again," he said. "Tell me exactly what the code is intended to do."

He could see she was tense. Her restless hands picked up a paper napkin and began smoothing it on the tabletop.

"Fighter planes are governed by a system called fly-by-wire," she said. "That means that the controls such as the ailerons, the elevator, and the rudder are governed electronically—not with the old-fashioned hydraulic and cable systems."

He nodded his head in understanding, and she looked quickly around the restaurant to make sure that nobody else was listening to their conversation. With that one, unconscious gesture, Reno knew she was innocent.

He'd believed it before, but now, he knew it with a certainty. Relief filled his chest. Suddenly, his interest was upped a hundred-fold. Now he *had* to prove her innocence—for himself as much as for her. His job was to jail the criminals, not the victims.

Her voice lowered. "The code that Quadrangle Computing is writing will double the speed with which the commands are relayed to the control surfaces. I mean, it's already fast. It's imperceptible to humans, but there is room for improvement. Once that code is installed on our fighter planes, they'll be some of the most maneuverable birds in the air."

"They'll be able to respond to the pilots' commands that much faster."

"Exactly. That split second could be the difference between life and death."

Reno sat back in his seat and looked at her closely. "There are armies out there who would kill for that advantage."

"I know." She tossed her napkin on her plate and looked him square in the eye. "That's why the project was top-secret. That's why I've never talked about it with anybody outside the company. Until you, of course."

He leaned forward and set his elbows on the table. "Dani, the section of code that Charley and I intercepted was one that you had written."

"I know."

His eyebrows rose. "What do you mean, 'you know'?"

"Why else would the FBI send their bloodhounds after me?"

"A bloodhound? Do I look like a bloodhound to you?"

"I've always thought of you more as a wolf."

He leered at her. "Don't distract me," he warned.

He ran a hand over his chin. "Whoever slipped that code outside of the company intended for you to take the blame. It had to have been somebody who had the opportunity and the motive. Who don't you trust at Quad?"

She sighed heavily. "I hate even thinking about this."

He nodded. "I know you considered your co-workers friends, but try to take a step back and look at it. Had anyone been acting strangely? Was there anything unusual that caught your attention?"

"Don't you think I would have told you long ago if I had?"

"Think back," he said patiently. "This person couldn't sell their own work because they knew that the trail would lead straight back to them. They needed to put the focus on someone else—namely you. Why?"

She ran a hand through her hair. "I don't know. I can't think of anyone who would want to hurt me like that."

"Do you have any enemies?"

"No. Everybody at Quadrangle gets along really well. We have our occasional arguments, but the hard feelings never last. Everybody knows how stressful the job is."

"Is anybody jealous of you?"

She gave him a blank look. "Well, I couldn't answer that. I can't read minds."

"I can." He reached out and caught her hand. "Danielle, have you ever looked at the people you work with? Really looked at them? You're like a square peg in a round hole."

Her forehead furrowed as she looked at him in confusion.

He pressed his palm against hers and intertwined their fingers. "Sweetheart, to be blunt, you work with a bunch of geeks."

At that, she laughed. "Maybe, but they're very talented geeks."

"I won't deny that, but those talented, high paid geeks were probably unpopular losers in school." He let his gaze run over her body. "A sexpot like you would turn their world upside-down. Hell, Arnold Pfizer probably gets a boner every time you talk to him."

"He has asked me out a couple of times."

"Did you go?"

She let out a very unladylike snort.

"I hope you didn't respond like that."

She looked at him and finally realized how serious he was. "I was nice about it. He didn't say anything."

"He wouldn't. It would be too embarrassing." Reno ran his thumb up and down the side of hers. "That doesn't mean he wants you any less. Baby, I don't think you understand the effect you have on men. A never-ending hard-on can really piss a guy off."

"I'm not a tease."

"Of course, you are."

"I—"

"It's not intentional," he said, interrupting her, "But with that blonde hair, those amazing tits, that tart little ass… It would be pure hell for a guy like Arnold to sit next to you every day. You might have been working hard, but I guarantee you that he was trying to figure out a way to get into your pants."

Her gaze dropped. "But if he liked me, why would he want to hurt me?"

"Because he couldn't get past your chastity belt."

She shook her head. "This is all supposition."

"Could he have gotten into your account? I've seen the security system, but he's the one who showed it to me."

She shook her head quickly. "Absolutely not. He'd have to have my… *password.*"

Reno leaned forward. "What?"

She pushed her hair back and licked her lips uncertainly. "His account went down one day, and he had a deadline to meet. I let him use mine."

"So he did have your password."

"He had it for one day, several months before you and Charley showed up at our door. I changed it as soon as I got back into the system." Her words slowed.

Reno looked at her closely. He could practically see the gears turning in her head. "Dani?"

Her face was solemn when she finally looked at him. "He might have put in a temporary back door. That way, he could have gone back later, gotten what he needed, and erased his tracks."

Reno stood and held out his hand to help her out of the booth. "Let's get out of here. We've got a lot of work to do."

Chapter Six

Reno pulled his cell phone out as soon as he'd paid the bill. He had an idea, but he needed help. He dialed Charley's number as they walked down the street and waited impatiently for his partner to pick up the line. "Charley? It's Reno."

"Hey, partner. It's about time you called. What happened? Did she get away again?"

"No, she turned herself in."

There was the sound of a chair squeaking. "You're kidding me."

Reno glanced at Dani. Tension radiated from her like a nuclear bomb. "She claims she's innocent, and I believe her. Listen, Charley, we need you to do something for us."

"*Us?*"

"Us." Reno refused to elaborate. "You know that fence that we picked up on this case? I need you to ask him a few more questions."

Charley gave an uncharacteristic grumble. "Like what? We questioned him to death before we locked him away. He doesn't know anything that he hasn't already told us."

"We might not have been asking the right questions. I want to know more about the voice at the other end of the line."

Charley's grumble got a little louder. "He couldn't tell if it was male or female. The person whispered. Remember?"

The fence who'd sold the code to the FBI hadn't been very helpful when it came to identifying the source inside Quadrangle Computing. He'd never seen the person. He claimed that all their interactions had been conducted over the phone and through a post office box.

"I remember. I'm the one who questioned him," Reno said. Charley was patient as a saint when dealing with information and data. His fuse just tended to get short when the human element was involved. "We need to ask him one more thing."

"All right, all right. What do you want to know?"

"I want to know if the source had allergies. Was there ever a sneeze? Was he or she hacking all the time? Did he have to stop to blow his nose?"

"I'm not following you."

"Arnold Pfizer," Reno said. Just the guy's name was enough to make his stomach sour. "Dani said that he hit on her a couple of times, and she blew him off. It might be the motive we've been looking for."

"Pfizer? Isn't that the guy you worked with last week?"

"The one and only."

"Holy cow." Charley paused for a second. "I see where you're going with this. Don't worry. I'm on it."

Reno hung up and stuffed the phone into his back pocket. He looked at Danielle, who was waiting anxiously. "He's going to work on it and get back to us," he told her.

Dani put a hand on her stomach. The butterflies inside felt like they were riding a roller coaster. She couldn't ever remember being so nervous in her entire life. There was just too much riding on this wild assumption. Arnold had never been anything but nice to her. Were they grasping at straws, trying to pin this crime on him?

"Relax," Reno said. He put his arm around her shoulders. "Making yourself sick isn't going to help. Believe me."

"I just don't want to accuse him of something he didn't do," she said.

"I understand. How do you think I feel about what I've done to you?"

She relaxed against him. "I don't know if I can take this."

He softly kissed her temple. "It will be over soon."

It was going to take more than words to make her feel better. She knew more than anyone how quickly things could go wrong. She turned so she could see his face. "What if we're jumping the gun? If your partner doesn't find anything, we'll be right back where we started."

"No, we won't." They'd reached his car and he opened the passenger side door for her. "For one thing, I won't have to chase you anymore."

Dani paled and took a step back. "I thought you believed me."

He caught her by the arm. "Easy, baby. Have a little faith. I meant that I'm not going to let you go. I didn't say I was going to let you take the fall for this."

His dark gaze leveled with hers. "If this thing with Pfizer doesn't pan out, we'll just start over. Together. No more running. Got it?"

The knot in her chest eased when she saw the emotion in his eyes. He didn't even try to hide his feelings from her. "Got it," she said past the lump in her throat.

She blinked back the tears that threatened to fall. He was going to protect her. She'd taken a huge risk this morning, but he was making good on her trust. She could rely on him, lean on him if she needed to. A lightness that she hadn't felt for a very long time suddenly filled her chest. It was relief—with more than a tinge of hope.

His hands slipped down to her rear, and he pulled her flush against him. Her eyes widened when she felt a familiar ridge press against her abdomen. "What do you say we go work off some of this nervous energy?" he said.

His head swooped down, and the kiss he gave her was potent. It had her knees buckling and her hands clutching at his jacket for support. At last, she had to come up for air. "How long do you think it will be before Charley calls back?"

His eyes lit up, and he started bundling her into the car. "Hours."

Soon, they were checked into another hotel. Danielle followed Reno into the room and found herself quickly caught in his strong arms. He pushed her up against the door as he shut it.

Her eyes drifted closed as he pushed her jacket off her shoulders and began tugging on her shirt. His wicked tongue danced along the side of her neck, and goosebumps made her shiver.

"I want you so bad," he growled against her neck. "I was ready for you this morning, but you weren't there."

His hips rubbed against her, and she let her hands trail down his back. "Reno," she sighed.

His hands spanned her waist, and his fingers set up an insistent massage. "The bed. Now."

Dani looked over his shoulder. She hadn't even taken a look at the room. She saw the bed, but a flame lit inside her belly when she saw an easy chair in the corner. "Wait," she said.

He drew back to look at her.

She took his hand and stepped around him. He looked at her in confusion, but comprehension hit when he saw where she was leading. "This time, we're going to do things my way," she whispered.

His eyes burned with fire. "I'm all yours, sweetheart."

Her belly clenched in delicious anticipation. He was going to let her take control.

Determinedly, she tugged him to the easy chair. He turned, but caught her by the waist again. He started to pull her down with him as he sat, but she stopped him with her hands on his chest. "My way," she repeated.

She let her hands drift down to the front of his Levis, and he jerked under her touch. "Whoa, be careful there, babe."

She smiled and slowly rubbed her hand over his fly. "Don't worry, big boy. You're in good hands."

He cursed under his breath, and the sound emboldened her. She gave him a firm squeeze and he went right up on his toes. When she thought he could take no more, she dropped down to his feet to remove his socks and shoes. Slowly, she rose back up and looked into his deep brown eyes. "Had it really been six months?" she asked.

He nodded towards the bulge that was trying to get out of his pants. "In case you haven't noticed, baby. I've got a thing for you."

Without breaking his gaze, she reached for his belt buckle. She pulled the belt out of its loops, but her hands began to shake when she reached for the fastening of his jeans.

"Want some help?" he asked.

"Take off your shirt."

"Anything I can do," he said. He grabbed the t-shirt, pulled it over his head, and sent it flying.

Dani swallowed hard. God, she loved his body. Her nerves settled, and she let herself lean into him. She kissed his chest close to his heart and felt it pound under her lips.

He was excited.

So was she.

She let her fingers explore the hard muscles of his abdomen, and the beat of his heart took off under her tongue.

"Baby," he growled. His fingers dove into her hair and pulled her head up for a harsh kiss.

His teeth scraped against her lips when she tugged at his zipper. She nipped him right back as she caught his jeans and pushed them downwards. His briefs went along with them, and every muscle in his body went rigid.

Including the muscles of his cock.

It bumped insistently against her belly, and Dani felt her body grow warm. She reached for him blindly and wrapped her fingers around his hardness. He shuddered against her and exhaled sharply into her mouth.

"Into the chair," she said.

"Danielle," he warned.

He wasn't in the mood for teasing.

Neither was she.

He fell back when she pushed lightly against his chest. When he reached for her, she caught his hands and pressed them against the arms of the chair.

"Oh, God. No. You can't expect me not to—"

"I thought you wanted me to pay."

With a groan, he dropped his head back against the chair. "Lord help me."

His cock stood upright like a fat flagpole. Dani touched him again, and his hips bucked. Her eyes widened. His size was impressive, and she remembered how completely he'd filled her. How had she managed to take him at all?

Inquisitively, she dipped her fingers lower and cradled one of the puckered sacs at the base of his cock. She ran her thumb lightly over him and a guttural sound broke through his lips.

"Get down there," Reno said in a rough voice. "You're supposed to be paying—not me."

Reno thought he was going to have a coronary for sure. His heart was pounding faster than it had ever pounded in his life, and sweat had broken out on his brow. Even the balls of his feet were sensitive. He rubbed them against the carpeting, trying to find some relief.

He watched as Dani dropped to her knees in front of him. He spread his legs for her, and she crawled closer. Her gaze was on his pulsing cock. She slowly bent her head, and his hand left the arm of the chair of its own volition. His fingers sank into her blonde tresses and pushed her head gently downwards.

"Suck me, baby."

She dipped her head low and placed a kiss near the base of his prick. Her hair draped across his lap, and his hips shifted.

"Oh yeah. That's it," he said. It was even better than in his dreams.

She let her tongue glide up his cock until she found its head. She licked him, and his hand clamped down harder on her skull. She opened her mouth and began sucking lightly.

"Holy mother of… Shit!"

Both of Reno's hands dug into her hair, and his hips came off the chair. She whimpered when he pressed himself deep into her throat. Harsh, wild words passed his lips, but he held her against him, not letting her go.

She sucked harder, and his vision started to blacken. His hips began to pump, and her head began to bob. It was good, but he liked her hot, tight pussy even better. With a growl, he slipped his hands under her armpits and pulled her upright.

"Reno!" Dani gasped.

She missed the taste of him, but when he started to rip at her clothes, she knew he was out of control. She groaned when he pushed her t-shirt upwards and began to wildly kiss and lick her stomach. Her knees buckled, and she grasped his shoulders for support. His teeth raked across her skin, and she bit back a cry. Suddenly, she, too, was at a fever pitch.

"Do you want me, Danielle?" he asked.

"Yes," she groaned.

"How?"

"Inside me. Deep inside me."

He clapped his hand over her mound and squeezed. "Here?"

She ground herself against his palm. "Yes!"

Together, they tore at her clothes. He pulled at her jeans and pushed them down her hips. She kicked them off and felt his hands go to her panties. Her trembling hands tried to free herself of her t-shirt and bra. As soon as she felt the cups loosen around her breasts, he was there, ready to take her offering.

"Tell me you never danced for another man like that," he growled. "Tell me!"

"You were my first," she panted.

His mouth fastened on her nipple, and his hands closed around her waist. Naked, he pulled her onto the chair with him. She spread her legs wide to straddle his hips. He thrust, but she rocked away from him.

"Let me," she whispered. She caught his cock in her hand and felt him pulsing under her fingertips. Her pussy almost cried in wanting. She swiveled her hips and guided him to her.

The head of his cock slipped inside, and Dani felt as if she might melt from pure pleasure. She pushed down and slowly took him, inch by inch. Her breath hitched, and he quickly looked at her face.

"You're swollen," he whispered.

"Last night…" she said weakly.

He'd used her well last night, and he was big. It hurt a little, but the hurt was good.

He understood. Bending his head, he licked at her nipple.

Danielle felt her juices start to coat him. She bit her lip, and let the muscles in her thighs relax. Gravity impaled her on his cock.

It was hot, so hot. The pressure inside her was nearly overwhelming.

Wanting to feel more of it, she raised her hips and began a mindless, pounding rhythm.

"Dani!"

"Ohhhhh," she moaned.

His pelvic bone bumped against hers with every thrust. She caught the chair behind his head and began to ride him more roughly.

"Fuck!"

Reno was sure the top of his head was about to come right off. He wrapped his arms around her shuddering body and pulled her close. Their lips tangled in a hot, breathless kiss, and they strained to reach completion.

He knew the sounds of their lovemaking; the sighs, the moans, and the cries had to be reaching the hallway, but he didn't give a damn. He'd finally caught her. He'd caught Danielle Carver, and she was *his*.

With a powerful surge, he thrust upwards. Both their hips lifted into the air, and he felt her squirm helplessly. Two more pushes, and she went taut as a bow. Her pussy squeezed him tightly, and he called out her name as he came inside of her.

With an expulsion of air, they collapsed onto the chair. She melted over him like warm butter, and he held her with limp arms. Exhausted, he leaned his head back against the cushion of the chair and gave a final groan. Closing his eyes, he waited for the room to stop spinning.

"Dani?" he said, not bothering to open his eyes.

"Hm?"

"Were you about to email me yesterday when I found you?" His proprietary instincts were skyrocketing. He'd just placed his stamp on her, but he wanted more. He wanted the whole package.

"Yes," she murmured as she burrowed closer to his neck.

He wanted to see her face. He gently pulled her head back. "Why?"

She licked her lips and cautiously looked into his eyes. "Because you're all I've got, Reno. I was so lonely without you."

His heart skipped a beat and then began to thud. His gaze ran over the delicate features of her face. He felt her curves pressed solidly against him and the part of him that was still inside of her began to stir. "You've got me, babe. I almost went out of my mind this morning when I woke up, and you were gone. Don't ever do that again."

"Oh, Reno. I didn't know."

"Well, now you do," he said gruffly.

Standing abruptly, he carried her towards the bed. "And I'm going to make sure you never forget it."

Hours later, they were awakened from a sound sleep by the ringing of his cell phone. Before the second ring, Reno was alert and moving. He rolled out of bed and dove for his jeans. "Yeah?" he answered.

"Reno, it's Charley."

"Charley! Give me some good news, partner. Did you find anything?" Dani sat up on the bed and pulled the sheet up to her chest.

"We hit the motherload, my friend."

A jolt of excitement hit Reno square in the chest. "Tell me everything."

"Your hunch paid off big time," Charley said happily. "When we asked the fence about the allergy thing, he said that the source had been a regular sneezing machine. We took his statement along with some other evidence to a judge and got a search warrant for Pfizer's home."

"What happened?" Dani asked.

Reno nodded at her. Her eyes rounded with shock, and he quickly climbed back onto the bed with her.

"What did you find?" he said into the phone as he nibbled on her neck.

"What didn't we find?" Charley said. "Somehow, that little weasel found a way around the security checks at Quad. He'd brought home disks, documents—even hardware."

Reno's head came up quickly as a thought hit him. "Have you got him in custody?"

"That's the best part. When we showed up at his office and slipped the stuff under his nose, he fainted. Honest to God, he fell right out of the chair. When he came to, he starting singing like a bird."

"He confessed?"

"Oh yeah."

Dani's fingers bit into his arms.

Reno put his hand over the mouthpiece. "They got him."

Her face drained of color. She covered her face with her hands, and her body began to shake. He wrapped his arm around her, but tried to concentrate. "Did he say why he did it?"

Charley cleared his throat. "Well, I don't know if you want to tell your lady this or not. Ah hell, Jeff. When we searched his house, we found all kinds of pictures of Danielle. This guy was obsessed. My guess is that she rejected him somehow, and he snapped."

Reno's teeth ground together. "He's never going to get near her again. You hear me, Charley? *Never.*"

"I don't think he'll have a chance. With the evidence we've got against him, he's going to be put away for a long, long time."

"Good. Otherwise, I'd have to go after him myself."

"I didn't hear that," Charley said tactfully.

Reno took a deep breath. "Right. You're right. Thanks, partner. I owe you."

"You don't owe me anything. Just treat her right. She deserves it."

Reno looked down at Dani, but her face was buried against his chest. He kissed the top of her shiny head. "Yes, she does."

He hung up the phone and tossed it on the floor. He hooked his finger under her chin and lifted it. Her face was still white, but the shaking had stopped.

Dani was dying for answers, but all Reno seemed to want to do was look at her. She caught his shoulders and shook him. "Well? What did he have to say?"

"Pfizer confessed. They found all kinds of proprietary information from Quadrangle Computing in his own home."

Her eyes went wide. "In his home? But how did he get it out of the building? And why did he frame *me*?"

"He was a nut, sweetheart."

"But…"

"No 'buts'," Reno said sharply. "He's crazy, and that's all there is to it."

Dani couldn't believe it. The Arnold she knew was so unlike the man he was describing. How could she not have seen it?

"We've got him, and the case is closed. It's over, baby. It's finally over."

Danielle froze when she realized what that meant. Everything inside her went still, but she didn't want to hope too much. Her hopes had been crushed too many times. "Does this mean that I'm a free woman again?" she asked hesitantly.

"Free as a bird," he said with a smile.

Her breaths went short. "No more cheap motels? No more rundown diners?"

"And no more strip joints," he said sternly.

Danielle let out of whoop of joy. She threw her arms around him. She'd never thought this would ever happen. She'd thought that she'd be running for the rest of her life. To have everything fall into place so perfectly stunned her.

She had her life back.

Only her life wasn't there for her to go back to anymore.

"What's wrong, sweetheart?" Reno asked. He gently pushed back a strand of her hair and hooked it behind her ear.

"What am I supposed to do now?" she asked. Her fingers dug into the muscles of his back. She'd never thought about what would happen if she ever did manage to clear her name.

"What do you mean?"

"I don't have a place to live. I don't have a job. I don't even have a car," she said in a near panic.

He pulled her down with him so they were lying face-to-face. "First of all, I happen to know of a company who just lost a computer programmer. Quad would certainly be glad to have you back. Your manager believed in your innocence the entire time, and now, he probably feels pretty guilty about trusting Pfizer. He'll hire you back so fast, it will make your head spin."

She wasn't so sure.

"Secondly, you might not have a car, but I do," he said. "There's a red Corvette that's been sitting in my garage for about four months."

Dani blinked and pushed herself up onto an elbow so she could look down at him. "My car? *You bought my car?*"

His smile was devilish. "I was only about a day behind you when you sold it at that used car lot. The guy gave me a sweet deal that I couldn't pass up. It's a hot car and, besides, it had something that no other car in the world has."

"What was that?" she asked as she poked him in the shoulder.

"It smelled like you," he said with a growl. She shrieked when he zeroed in on her neck. He pulled her back down next to him and kissed his way up to her ear. "I could smell your perfume when I took the test drive."

Dani moaned softly when she felt his tongue delve into the soft recesses of her ear. "That still leaves me without a place to live. I'm sure that the lease on my apartment expired months ago without me paying rent."

"I know a place," he said.

"Where?"

"With me."

Her heart flipped. She felt his hands tighten against her waist and, for a moment, she was uncertain. When she saw the vulnerable look in his eyes, though, everything made sense. "Okay," she breathed.

"Okay?"

A smile suddenly lit up her face. "It's time you paid for all the hell you put me through, Agent Reno."

His eyebrows rose. "That's *Special* Agent Reno."

Dani screeched when she found herself suddenly thrown off balance. She gripped his body tightly as he rolled on top of her.

"And I always get my man," he growled. "Or in this case, woman."

His head lowered, and she lifted her lips for his kiss. As his weight settled more heavily upon her, she knew that she was trapped. She'd been caught by the long arm of the law, but for the first time in ages, the thought didn't send her into a total panic.

She trailed her fingernails down his back to his hips. "I guess that means I'm off your wanted list."

"You're joking, right?" He thrust heavily into her and groaned. "Baby, you're the most wanted woman I know."

About the Author:

Kimberly Dean is very excited to be joining Red Sage. When not slaving over a keyboard, she enjoys reading, sports, movies, and loud rock-n-roll.

Secluded

by Lisa Marie Rice

To My Reader:

Nicholas Lee walks on the dark side and always walks alone. By choice and by necessity. Anyone Nicholas loves would be destroyed by his enemies. Luckily he's never loved anyone—until now. When Nicholas loses his heart to beautiful, gentle Isabelle Summersby, he will allow himself only a week with her. One week of bliss and then they must part. Any longer and Isabelle will die. But what if Isabelle wants more?

Dear Reader, impossible loves have always tugged at my heartstrings. I hope the story of Nicholas and Isabelle will tug at yours.

Chapter One

"I want your daughter."

Nicholas Lee kept his voice low but the man sitting across from him heard and turned pale.

Thunder rumbled in the distance. Four heartbeats later, a blinding bolt of lightning lit the darkened study with a violent phosphorescent glare. Richard Summerby IV started. "I—I beg your pardon?" he stammered.

Ah, Nicholas thought. The perfect manners of the upper crust. Good thing he himself didn't have any manners at all.

Summerby had the pale refined looks only generations of wealth and privilege could bestow, and the dissipated features of the soft and the weak. For all that he'd been born rich, he'd managed to whore and gamble it all away. He was a whisper from total ruin and Nicholas would have been happy to push him over the edge if it weren't for the fact that Summerby had something he wanted very, very badly.

Nicholas studied the storm raging outside the big beveled window panes then brought his gaze back to Summerby. He smiled and the man paled further. Good. Nicholas needed for him to be afraid.

"I said I want your daughter," Nicholas repeated, his voice hard. "For a few weeks. And you will make sure I get her."

"This is—this is crazy." Summerby gave a half laugh. It strangled when Nicholas remained silent. "You can't have my daughter. Why, you're nothing more than a—a gangster."

"No, I'm not." Nicholas lifted his eyebrows. "Not any more, anyway."

He let his eyes roam thoughtfully around Summerby's elegant study. Original Chubb watercolors, Georgian furniture, an Aubusson carpet. And the paler spots on the dirty off-white walls where paintings had been taken down and sold, the Chippendale desk which needed restoring, the empty shelves where first editions had been auctioned off. The house itself would be the next to go. "Though I do keep my hand in some…

ventures. For example, I just bought Morris Caneman's business."

Nicholas smiled as Summerby jerked in shock and made a choking sound in his throat. Now the man was beginning to understand just what kind of trouble he was in. "Caneman's creditors are mine now, Summerby. You owe Caneman three million dollars you don't have. Owing Caneman three million dollars is bad. Owing me three million dollars is much, *much* worse."

Summerby had broken out in a sweat. Lightning flashed again, followed a second later by a clap of thunder so loud its echo boomed in the room. Outside the study windows, the branches of the massive oak on the front lawn dipped and swayed, whipped into a frenzy by the rising wind.

"I'll be very clear." Nicholas speared Summerby with his gaze. "I might be persuaded to forgive the debt and save you from ruin. You might even get to keep the house. I understand it's been in your family for four generations. But you have to do something for me."

"What—" Summerby's voice came out as a croak. He wet his lips and tried again. "What would it take for you to do that? And what do you want with my daughter?"

"Sex," Nicholas said. "For a few weeks. After which you get your life back again." Summerby's eyes rounded and he made a strangled sound. Nicholas watched him coldly. "This is the way it's going to be, Summerby. Your daughter, Isabelle, should be here in a few minutes. She always visits you on Thursday afternoon. You will introduce me to Isabelle as an old family friend and as a man you've done business with for years. You will be perfectly natural and at ease. For all she knows, I am an old friend of her father's. And then for the next few weeks, you will cease all contact with her. If Isabelle contacts you, you'll avoid her. You will, above all, say nothing about me, my past, my... business dealings. Otherwise I call in my debt and you lose everything you have. This magnificent house, your Yacht Club membership, the mistress in Fairview Heights. The lot. I will strip you of every possession you own and I will leave you a broken man. Is that clear?"

Summerby's head nodded jerkily.

"Oh, something else," Nicholas said smoothly. "You will never ask your daughter for money again. I know all about you, Summerby." Nicholas didn't even try to hide his contempt. "You dumped your first wife and let her and your daughter go hungry while you lived it up with your second wife, who's now about to take you to the cleaners because you cheated on her. When your first wife became ill, you cut off all contact. Isabelle nearly killed herself putting herself through college while paying her mother's medical bills. And now that she's earning decent money with the TV show, you crop up with the daddy act and start asking for 'loans', which you never pay back. It's despicable and it's going to stop right now, is that clear?"

Summerby made a strangling noise in the back of his throat.

"Pops?"

Both men turned their heads at the soft voice. Nicholas's muscles tightened as Isabelle Summerby walked into the room, carrying the essence of springtime into the dark winter afternoon.

Nicholas rose from his chair, out of deference to a lady, and because he knew from experience that if he stood up to his full height while she was close to him, he might make her feel overpowered. If he stood while she walked towards him, he would give her time to adjust.

His size and obvious strength intimidated a lot of people and he used that fact often. There were plenty of people in this world he wanted to intimidate, to frighten, but not Isabelle. Never Isabelle.

Nicholas eyed her hungrily as she crossed the room, grace in every line of her slender body. This was the closest he'd ever been to her and every step she took seemed to echo in every beat of his heart.

He never missed her show on TV. He'd watched the recordings over and over again until he knew the programs by heart. She'd given a talk two weeks ago on new mysteries and he'd stood at the back of the packed hall and watched her. Watched her charming the crowd with her gentle humor, touching their hearts with her understanding of human nature. Making him yearn for what couldn't be.

He couldn't count the nights he'd sat in his car outside her bedroom window, waiting for the odd glimpse before she shuttered her windows for the night.

But this was the first time he'd been within touching distance. His heart thundered.

He'd seen her first on TV. One dark, rainy night when he'd let the despair seep into his soul, nursing it together with half a bottle of Glenfiddich. Reading had helped for a while, staving off the loneliness and heartsickness, but the book had ended, as did everything. *Deep in the Beast*. He could have sworn the author had had a direct line into his soul. He'd turned the book over and studied the author's picture. Lamont Serrin. A young black man with dreadlocks and small, scholar's glasses perched on his nose. Dark, piercing, all-seeing eyes and a poet's mouth.

It was as if Serrin had spoken for Nicholas, had lived Nicholas's child-hood and written about it. The shock of reading his deepest thoughts had still echoed when Nicholas turned on his TV and stopped, frozen. It was Lamont Serrin, talking. But what had him springing to his feet to come closer to the wide screen was the woman Serrin was talking to.

Beautiful, yes, but then most women on TV were good-looking. It went with the territory. But this woman had an old-fashioned beauty, a romantic beauty, tinged with sadness. The expression on her heart-shaped face was intent as she spoke with the young black man, speaking some-how to Nicholas, too. She was reading his mind, his heart. All his life Nicholas had felt alone. He was used to it, used to feeling on his own. And in one night, two strangers reached out to him, one a beautiful woman. Isabelle Summerby.

He watched her program religiously after that and made it his busi-ness to find out everything about her. Finding things out about people, legally, illegally, was just one of his many money-making talents.

The more he found out about Isabelle, the more obsessed he became. Through his sources he discovered her history, her likes, her dislikes. Her courage, her steadfastness, her loyalty. Her intelligence, her gentleness.

Isabelle was standing in front of her father's desk, ash-blonde eye-brows drawn together in a frown. Her eyes were a pale, silvery blue, flash-ing likc lightning as she looked uncertainly from her father to him.

"Pops? Are you all right?" Summerby started, a bead of sweat trail-ing down his cheek. Nicholas watched coldly as Summerby battled with himself. But Summerby had a great incentive to play the part. Three million of them. Summerby straightened. He passed a hand over his pale blond hair.

"Isabelle..." His voice became smooth, unctuous. "How nice to see you, my dear."

Isabelle looked at him, then at Nicholas. "Am I interrupting anything?"

"Not at all, not at all." Summerby managed to sound jovial. "We've finished our business anyway. My dear, I'd like to introduce you to a very good friend and old business partner of mine, Nicholas Lee."

Isabelle smiled gently, extending her hand. "Mr. Lee. Pleased to meet you."

"The pleasure is mine." Nicholas smiled back, though smiles had never come easily to him. He folded her hand in his. Her hand was slen-der and long-fingered, bare of rings. Her skin was amazingly soft and he felt an electric shock run through his body at her touch. He had become semi-aroused just watching her walk across the room and now his entire body was signaling acute pleasure. Her perfume, a subtle cloud of meadow flowers, enveloped him.

She looked at him curiously. He was mesmerized by the silvery sheen of her eyes. Her look was feminine curiosity mingled with a desire he suspected she wasn't aware of. He was. He was used to that look of sexual speculation in a woman's eyes, as if the woman could tell that he was a man who liked his sex long and hard and often.

Isabelle's pupils expanded and her nostrils flared. The female animal in her smelled the scent of a dominant male. She stood stock still for a moment, and Nicholas could feel panic and excitement war in her. Her hand trembled. Her soft lips were slightly open and the sound of her sharp intake of breath was loud in the silent room.

His eyes narrowed as he honed in on her mouth, open and moist, the mouth that would receive his tongue, his cock. He wanted that mouth violently. Now.

He wanted to sink to his knees with her in his arms. He wanted to lay her out on his bed, naked and wet and shaking with desire, and take her with his mouth, his hands… He wanted to penetrate her, body and soul, over and over again until she lay limp in his arms, completely his. He wanted to tug at her breast like a child while his fingers stretched her sex before he mounted her. He was big and he didn't want to hurt her. He would always make sure she was ready for him.

Through the silk, he could make out the shape of her breast and it was perfect, for his mouth and for his hands. Perfect.

She would fit him perfectly in every way.

Almost shaking with the effort it took him, he released her hand, subtly pulling his long dark jacket to disguise the full erection touching her had given him.

She was outlined against the darkness of the window, grace and light and woman in pale peach silk. She stared for a moment longer than was polite, then turned to her father. "I'll be at the Southside center tonight."

Southside. Nicholas froze. Southside was the most dangerous part of town.

"Bye, Pops." Isabelle leaned over gracefully and kissed her father on the forehead. She turned her head. "Goodbye, Mr. Lee. It was nice meeting you."

Nicholas bent his head solemnly and watched her walk across the room. Her hair fell like a sheaf of wheat between narrow shoulder blades.

He could just imagine burying his face in the soft, fragrant mass. She was slender but womanly, hips flaring from a small waist, begging for his touch. The second time he took her would be from behind, plunging into her warm sheath, hearing her moans as he used his knowing fingers on her.

Mine, he thought. *You're going to be mine, Isabelle.*

Chapter Two

Nicholas Lee. Her father knew Nicholas Lee.

At the Southside Center after her lecture, Isabelle started stuffing her briefcase with the books and slides she'd used in the adult literacy lecture. A book fell off the edge of her desk and the sound echoed eerily in the empty hall.

Nicholas Lee. The man was as mysterious as he was notorious. His name was never in the newspapers. He never attended parties and was never seen around town. And yet everyone knew about him. Though immensely rich, no one really knew where the money came from.

Gun-running, Isabelle suspected. Smuggling, maybe. Not drugs. The one indisputable fact about Nicholas Lee everyone knew was that he hated drugs with a passion.

He was a man who was beyond the bounds of society, essentially an outlaw. How on earth could her father know such a man? Be friends with him? There were a lot of things she didn't know about her father. She'd only recently re-established relations with him after her mother's death.

Nicholas Lee had a reputation as a very dangerous man to know. Not a man to cross, not a man you'd want as your enemy. Dark rumors swirled about his name.

But maybe he wasn't so dangerous, after all, if he was her father's friend.

Very dangerous to women, though, she imagined. Certainly dangerous to *her* peace of mind. She hadn't been able to shake him from her thoughts. She could still see him, in her mind's eye. Long black hair, black eyes, dark blade-like features, black linen jacket, black silk shirt, black fine wool trousers. He was immense—powerful and dark with an almost palpable aura of menace around him. He also had seemed superbly fit. For all his bulk, he had moved with the grace of a panther.

A small sound at the back of the hall made her lift her head suspiciously.

The Southside Center was in a rough part of town. Of course, she took precautions. She had pepper spray in her purse, on top of the various items there, within easy grabbing distance. She always walked close to the walls, away from the street side of the sidewalk. Her car was parked only two blocks away. Five minutes after leaving the center, she'd be inside her locked car, on her way home.

Still, it would have been nice to have someone waiting for her, to walk her safely back to her car. Someone who cared, someone to watch over her.

In the large, dark auditorium, something shifted in her heart.

Isabelle's hands stilled. This was totally unlike her. She'd had a lover or two and dated. Not much, but enough to know that she wasn't missing much by not having a man in her life. She was used to solitude. After her father had abandoned them, she'd watched her mother descend into a frightening depression and then into illness. She'd learned early on the price you paid for love and trust and it had never seemed worthwhile up… up until now. What was changing? Why was she even thinking of a man to protect her? She'd been on her own for as long as she could re-member and had learned the hard way to look after herself. Not to count on anyone else. Men were weak, anyway.

Most men.

A sudden vision of Nicholas Lee, standing silently in her father's study, flashed before her eyes. He hadn't seemed weak at all. He had looked exactly like the kind of man who would protect to the death what was his.

Stop that, Isabelle told herself. She knew nothing about Nicholas Lee, except that he had a reputation as a dangerous man. In the rare moments when she had fantasized about falling in love, she'd imagined someone gentle and tender. Certainly not someone like Nicholas Lee, a man who walked in darkness.

She was the last person in the large auditorium. As always, the jani-tor, an elderly black man, showed up at a side door. He motioned to her and she waved back. For a moment, Isabelle thought she saw a large, dark figure behind him and her heart leapt. But a second later, no one was there.

For a moment, she thought she'd seen Nicholas Lee. It seemed that she was having trouble dismissing the mysterious and oh-so-attractive Mr. Lee from her mind. She shook herself and tried to concentrate on her surroundings. Maybe once she got home safely and sat in her favorite chair with a cup of tea, she could let herself go and wonder about the man who'd made such a strong impact on her senses. But not now. Walking out on the streets of Southside while woolgathering was as good a way to commit suicide as any she knew.

Two women had been carjacked in Southside last month. She kept her cellphone in her jacket pocket, switched on, with 911 on speed dial.

Isabelle walked across the dark auditorium, the sound of her high heels echoing sharply in the large space. She frowned. She should have worn lower heels, but she had had so little time to change, she'd forgotten.

She opened the heavy steel doors of the auditorium and gave a gasp, shrinking back instinctively as a bright bolt of lightning cut through the bruised-looking sky, followed immediately by a clap of thunder so loud she felt as if her eardrums would burst. The rain was coming down so hard it looked more like a waterfall than a shower, pellets of water bouncing waist-high off the cracked sidewalks. She sighed and set off, holding her briefcase over her head.

If she'd spent less time in the center mooning over Nicholas Lee, she'd be halfway home by now. She skittered in her high heels down the street, trying to avoid the major puddles, but was soaked within a minute. The roar of the rain sounded in her ears and she could barely see. At least the weather should keep the low lifes away. She hoped.

She ducked her head down lower and tried to pick up speed. Another minute and she'd reach her car ...

Isabelle staggered at the sharp blow to her head. It took her completely by surprise and almost knocked her off her feet. She thudded into the brick wall she'd been following by touch more than by sight. A heavy body slammed into her.

She couldn't seem to catch her breath, her bearings. Her ears rang and she couldn't focus her eyes. It was all so sudden, she didn't have a chance to react. Suddenly she was surrounded by men with sharp, angry faces. She blinked blood out of her eyes as one of the men tore her purse out of her hands. He opened it. With a laugh, he tossed out the pepper spray. Instinctively, Isabelle reached for the spray bouncing away and received another hard slap which made her head bounce off the wall and her ears ring.

Fumbling, her fingers numb, she tried to get to the cellphone in the jacket pocket, but her fingers tangled with his and he pulled it out and threw it to the ground.

Dazed, Isabelle stared at the little plastic rectangle in its bright blue holster in a puddle of muddy water. Whimpering, she stretched her hand down towards the phone and received a powerful punch to the stomach.

She sagged weakly. The man's body tightly pressed against hers was the only thing holding her upright. She tried to pull away, but there was only the hard brick wall against her back.

"Who ya thinkin' a callin', huh?" he breathed into her ear. His breath was horrid—hot and fetid with the smell of liquor and cigarettes. "The cops?" He snickered. "No cops down here, lady."

A chorus of coarse male voices echoed him. "Yeah man, tell her!"

It was all happening so fast. Isabelle had no time to catch her breath, to fight back. Hard hands grabbed her and threw her to the ground. The rough concrete of the sidewalk scraped her legs and hands. Her head bounced hard and she gritted her teeth not to lose consciousness.

The man curled his hand around her necklace and tugged hard. Again, harder. It was a thick gold chain. If he ripped it off her, he'd break her neck.

Isabelle tried to scream but, like in nightmares, only a strangled cry came out. Vomit tickled the back of her throat. She tried to kick the man in the groin, but missed. He slapped her, hard.

"Bitch!" he hissed. "You'll pay for—"

He stopped, an almost comical look on his face. Isabelle was so battered it took her several seconds to notice the gaping hole in his forehead, like a monstrous third eye. The man started toppling forward, the heavy rain washing away the blood as fast as it could spurt from his head.

Horrified, she rolled away before he could fall on top of her. Sobbing, she turned to see another body lying on the pavement, the rain turning bright red next to it, gradually fading into pink as the water sluiced away from the body.

One of her assailants lifted a gun, but never got a chance to shoot it. It was kicked out of his hand by a tall, dark, powerful figure, who then whirled and, almost faster than Isabelle's eye could follow, felled him with another kick, so powerful the sound of the booted foot meeting flesh carried over the din of the rain.

Her rescuer looked up, powerful chest lifting in a deep breath. She recognized him with a surge of emotion. Nicholas Lee. Their gazes met and held as he moved towards her.

"Look out!" Isabelle's voice didn't carry above the roar of the rain, but something in her face must have warned him. Another powerful whirl, a sickening thud, and the last of her assailants went down like a bull in the slaughter-house.

He didn't even look to see where the man had fallen. A second later, he was at her side, kneeling in the rain.

"Isabelle," he said. His voice was so deep it seemed to reverberate through her. That single word released her from her frozen terror. With a choked cry, she leaned forward into his open arms.

She barely knew him, but the violence of the attack had blown away her usual caution. At the deepest level of her being, she sensed that there was safety and shelter in this man's arms.

"Shh, it's okay. You're safe now. No one's going to hurt you. You're safe, I've got you." Murmuring comforting words over and over in that deep compelling voice, he slid his arms under her legs and back and stood up in a smooth, fluid motion.

Isabelle's head ached and the terror of the past few minutes still rushed through her. Her arms clasped his neck and she shivered, edging closer to him in her terror.

She turned her head into his neck and inhaled, and somehow the smell of him—intensely male, yes, but worlds away from the raw feral smell of her attackers—calmed her on some deep, primitive level.

He walked swiftly, carrying her as if she weighed nothing. Her ears rang, every muscle in her body hurt and her heart was still racing with the horror of the attack. But being in his arms soothed her.

His even strides, the power she sensed in his arms, the strong planes of his face—all reassured her. She didn't know him, not really, but in some unknown way she sensed she'd been waiting for him.

"You came for me," she murmured, barely aware of what she was saying.

"Yes, Isabelle," he said, his deep voice tender. "I came for you."

Chapter Three

Nicholas placed Isabelle gently in the passenger seat of his car and reached behind to the back seat where he kept a blanket. Spreading it over her, he tucked the edges around her shaking body, then hurried to the driver's side of the car.

He was drenched. It didn't matter for himself but Isabelle was injured and in shock. The cold and wet weren't doing her any good and she risked pneumonia.

He turned on the engine and revved it up, then turned the heat on, full blast. Isabelle needed medical care as soon as possible, but she also needed to get warm. Her teeth were clacking and he could almost feel the air around her vibrate with her intense shivers.

With one last look at her, Nicholas put the car in gear and sped off. He was a good driver and rarely exceeded the speed limit, but now he rocketed through town, taking the curves dangerously fast, blessing his reflexes and the makers of the Lexus.

He knew these streets well. He should. He'd grown up on Southside, until he'd been able to claw his way up and out.

Paying careful attention to where he drove, to changing the gears and keeping the powerful car fast and steady in the high winds and driving rain, he tried not to dwell for even a second on the rage that pulsed inside him or he'd be lost. He couldn't lose control. Not now. Isabelle needed him.

That thought alone kept his rage from overpowering him. Just thinking about those thugs attacking her almost sent him out of control.

He hadn't even intended for her to see him. He'd hung out in the back of the auditorium and had followed at a distance, just to see she got home safely. In those few minutes, she'd been attacked.

His hands tightened on the steering wheel until the dark skin of his knuckles turned white. Until he took his last, dying breath, he'd never forget the sight of Isabelle being beaten.

Taking another sharp corner, Nicholas exited Southside onto Herbert Boulevard.

"Where—where are we going?" Isabelle asked.

He looked sharply at her. Her tremors had abated somewhat, but her face was colorless, even her lips. She clutched the blanket tightly around her, the pale hand emerging from the soft folds of the blanket trembling.

"I'm taking you to St. Luke's. It's the closest hospital."

"No!" Isabelle's voice was anguished and her eyes widened in panic. "Please." She reached out with her pale, slender hand and touched him. "Please, *please* don't take me to St. Luke's. I'd rather die!"

Nicholas took one hand off the steering wheel and enfolded her hand in his. It was icy cold. "I have to." Surely she was in shock. "You need medical attention, Isabelle. You're probably concussed. You were beaten. What if you're bleeding internally? A doctor's got to see you. If there's nothing wrong, you'll just check out tomorrow."

She shook her head. "No." Her voice was low and stark. "Please, Nicholas, *please* don't take me to St. Luke's."

At any other moment, he would have been pleased to hear her say his name so naturally, as if they'd known each other for a long time, but he was too puzzled by her behavior to linger over the thought.

Isabelle took in a deep breath, as if to steady herself. "St. Luke's is where my mother died. I spent the better part of two years there. Please don't make me go to St. Luke's," she said quietly.

"Okay." He gently disengaged her hand to turn the steering wheel to the right. "Then I'll take you to Wallington Memorial. It's only a few miles further than St. Luke's would be."

"No." Isabelle whispered the word. As if exhausted by her pleas, she leaned her head back against the headrest and closed her eyes. "No hospitals. I've had enough of hospitals to last me a lifetime. No doctors, no needles, no prodding. I beg of you. Please. I couldn't stand it." A tear slipped out, falling down an alabaster cheek. *"Please."*

"Isabelle..." He didn't know how to resist her. It would have been easier if she'd ranted and railed. But that forlorn whisper and that single tear did him in. It simply wasn't in him to deny her anything. "You might be concussed."

"If I'm concussed, there's nothing anyone can do."

"Or wounded."

"No." She drew in a deep breath. "I'm scared and shocked and I have cuts and scrapes but nothing serious. I want to go home. God, I want to go home. Can't you just drive me home? The address is 1165 Rosewell Avenue." She turned her head against the headrest towards him and opened her eyes. They glowed silver in the pale light of the dashboard. "Please take me home." Her voice had sunk to a whisper.

She bit her bottom lip and closed her eyes again, as if she couldn't bear to watch him make his decision to hospitalize her.

He was helpless. "Okay. I'll take you home." His voice came out harsh and low. "But here's the deal. You do exactly as I say. I'll stay the night and at the first sign of something wrong, I'm bundling you up and taking you to the nearest medical center. Is that understood?"

"Yes." Her voice held a world of relief, as if his words hadn't been harsh, as if he'd given her a reprieve. When she closed her eyes again, he pulled out his cellphone and called his assistant, Kevin. He spoke quietly.

The rainstorm didn't abate in the twenty minutes it took him to drive to her house. He drove straight there, but Isabelle was too shocked to notice that he knew the way without direction. Pulling into the driveway, he threw the car into park and slanted a glance at Isabelle.

The worst of her trembling was over but there was such a look of desolation on her face his heart clenched. "Get your keys out and ready," he said quietly.

"Keys." She blinked and stared at him blankly. Her eyes widened suddenly. "My purse!" she exclaimed. "They—"

"Here. Your cellphone's in there, too. I picked it up." He handed her the purse. It was muddy and scratched, but he was fairly sure everything was still in there. The bastards hadn't had time to rifle through it.

"Oh." She bent her platinum head over the purse and pulled her hand out, holding a set of keys with a silver key chain in the shape of a dolphin. She placed it in his outstretched hand. "I seem to have a lot of things to thank you for."

Taking the keys, he kept his eyes on hers while lifting her hand to his mouth. "My pleasure."

Though wind howled outside and rain beat a tattoo on the roof and hood, utter silence reigned in the car. She stared at him, eyes wide, gentle mouth slightly opened.

Slowly, he ran his thumb over her soft knuckles and heard her trembling sigh.

He let her hand slip away and exited the car. Opening the passenger door, he wrapped her in the blanket and lifted her out.

In a few moments, he had her in the building and at her door on the second floor. He let her slide down gently next to the overstuffed soft green couch in the living room, and held her hand as she gingerly sat down.

"Where's the bathroom?" he asked.

"Second door to the right."

He went into the bathroom and ran hot water into the tub.

Nicholas was used to taking in a situation quickly, to focusing on two, even three things at once. Keen senses had helped him rise out of Southside quickly and make a million dollars before he was twenty, though he didn't want to remember how. While depositing Isabelle gently on the couch, he was observing her living quarters.

The apartment building was carefully calibrated to appeal to people whose tastes were elegant and genteel, but whose pocketbook didn't stretch to luxury.

The stairwell had been spacious, with low risers on the stairs and a graceful mahogany balustrade, but there was no elevator. The rooms were high-ceilinged and good material had gone into their construction, but they were small. The kitchen and bathroom were standard issue—no fancy additions such as ice makers and jacuzzis.

He knew that Isabelle had finished college with student loans pending and massive debts due to her mother's medical expenses. Her grandmother had died then and left Isabelle a house which she'd sold to help pay off her debts. The few good pieces in Isabelle's apartment were clearly hcirlooms, thc others cheap department store knock offs which Isabelle brightened with throw rugs and pillows.

She had started to earn decent money from the TV show, but there still wasn't much to spare after the medical payments.

Nicholas vowed that when their affair ended, as it had to end, he would leave Isabelle financially set for life.

She would never have money problems again.

And he would never see her again.

Isabelle watched warily as Nicholas Lee walked back to where she huddled on the sofa. Nervously, she clutched the blanket more tightly about her shoulders.

She'd just survived an encounter with four terrifying men and here was another one, right in her living room, coming closer. His powerful body moved fluidly, gracefully. She'd seen for herself how dangerous he was. If she lived to be a hundred, she'd never forget how quickly and violently he'd overwhelmed four street punks. He was a violent man.

A violent man who'd also saved her life, she reminded herself.

Nicholas stopped in front of her and hunkered down until he could look her in the eyes. He lifted her chin with a long finger. "How are you feeling?" Isabelle pulled in a breath. "Better," she said softly.

He watched her so intently it was as if he were walking inside her head.

"Your pupils are the same size." He reached out and put two fingers on her pulse. "Your pulse is a little fast – 90 to a minute – but that's only to be expected after what you've been through. You don't have a temperature." He tilted her head and carefully touched the abraded skin on her cheekbones. Gently, Nicholas pulled her hands and then her arms from the blanket to examine them. "Nothing needs stitches. Let me feel your head." Probing gently, he felt through her scalp, stopping when she winced. "You've got two small lumps, but the skin isn't broken. All in all, you're lucky the damage wasn't worse."

"I'm lucky you arrived when you did," she said.

He shrugged. "Come on," he said softly, and pulled her to her feet. Once she was up, he lifted her in his arms.

"Where are you taking me?" she asked, startled.

"You need a hot bath and something hot to eat, in that order."

He carried her into the bathroom, all steamed up from her bath water. Isabelle realized that he'd deliberately left the door closed so the steam would cloud the air and had dumped half a bottle of bath foam into the tub. The steam and the bubbles would afford her some privacy in the tub.

"Take your clothes off and get in." The words were stark, impersonal, but a muscle was jumping in his jaw.

Isabelle froze. She didn't know this man, not in any real sense of the term. How could she strip with him in the room? The idea of being naked in his presence made her shiver.

"Go ahead." He turned and spoke with his back to her. "I put some shampoo on the rim. Can you wash your hair yourself?"

Isabelle hesitated. "Yes."

"Then get in while it's still warm."

She looked at that immensely broad back. She'd seen him in action. She'd felt his strength as he carried her. He could do anything he wanted with her. She looked with longing at the frothy tub, steam rising in wispy tendrils, then back to him. Shivering with nerves, she clutched her torn and tattered clothes.

He seemed to understand. "Go ahead, Isabelle." His voice was low and steady. "I'll wait until you get in. I just want to make sure the hot water doesn't make you feel faint." His head bowed. "Go on. I won't hurt you. I could never hurt you."

Something about his deep low voice, the bent head, the stillness of his wide shoulders reassured her. Stripping quickly, she eased into the hot water of the tub and sighed. The unease she felt at being naked with him was overridden by the relief of the warm water seeping into her sore muscles.

"Can I turn around?"

The silvery foam covered everything below her neck. "Okay."

Their gazes met. He didn't drop his eyes, didn't try to catch a glimpse of her body beneath the foam and water, but she was acutely aware of her nakedness. Her breasts ached, the warm water seemed to burn between her thighs. There was complete silence, except for the silvery sound of the bath water as she shifted.

He broke the silence. "You'll need something to put on."

"My bedroom is the first door on the left. There's a chest of drawers. My nightgowns are in the second drawer."

Without a word, he disappeared soundlessly through the door. Isabelle would have liked to have breathed a sigh of relief now that he'd gone. But while he'd been in the room she'd felt… safe. Scared, anxious and even – now that he was gone she could admit it to herself – aroused; but also safe from the outside world. Safe and cared for.

Isabelle slipped further down in the warm, fragrant water. When was the last time she'd had someone to take care of her? When was the last time she could actually just… let go? She couldn't even remember. She'd spent most of her life caring for her depressed mother, particularly in the last years of illness. Even her father seemed so childish and needy. Certainly not someone she could count on.

She was being ridiculous. Nicholas Lee was a stranger. He was a man shrouded in mystery, a man whose name was whispered. An underworld kingpin. Why should she imagine that Nicholas Lee would be a man she could count on? Because her father knew him? Because he'd been able to dispatch a bunch of street punks with ridiculous ease? Because his dark eyes seemed to penetrate her mind? Because his shoulders were so broad, his hands so strong, his touch so gentle?

Because he was so impossibly attractive and her body reacted with pulse-pounding desire?

There were no answers.

Her head tilted back, resting on the rim of the bathtub. Her eyes drifted shut.

Nicholas answered the doorbell.

"Here you go, boss." Tall, as blond as Nicholas was dark, Kevin Morris stood outside Isabelle's door with a large insulated case. He hadn't had much time since Nicholas had called him on the cellphone, but Nicholas knew that Kevin would come through for him. He always did.

Nicholas had caught Kevin trying to lift his wallet twelve years before. He'd been about to break the kid's wrist and toss him to the police when Kevin had fainted on him. From hunger.

Turned out what he thought was a hardened street punk was a fifteen year old boy who'd run away from a brutal foster home and had been living on the streets for two months. Turned out he'd been suffering from malnutrition. Turned out he still had raw wounds from the beatings he'd taken. He had burn marks all along his arms from where cigarettes had been put out on his skin.

Nicholas had been there, knew what that kind of abuse was like.

He'd taken the boy home, fed him and straightened him out. He'd hired tutors so Kevin could get his high school equivalency and had offered Kevin a room, clean clothes and daily meals in exchange for household chores.

Like most of his instincts, this one had been rock solid. Kevin had taken to education like a cactus soaks up water in the desert. And like a cactus, Kevin had blossomed. The tutors could barely keep up with him.

He'd shown an unusual affinity for computers and numbers and was finishing an advanced degree in accounting while working as Nicholas's right hand man.

Kevin was the one man in the world Nicholas trusted. And Kevin had shown over and over again that he was worthy of that trust.

Nicholas took the heavy, warm case. "Thanks, Kevin. Be on standby for the next few days."

"Right, boss." Kevin nodded and left.

Nicholas put the case in the kitchen. In Isabelle's bedroom, he pulled open the second drawer and rummaged. The nightgown he found was made of thick, soft white cotton and buttoned up to the neck. A nightgown more suited to a grandmother than to a desirable young woman.

He was going to buy Isabelle negligées in pale rose silk and in every other color of the rainbow that did justice to her delicate beauty, but for the moment he knew she'd feel better in a nightgown designed for comfort, not seduction.

He walked back into the bathroom and stopped to look at her. Isabelle was dozing, her head tilted back over the rim of the bathtub, her long slender neck exposed. He could see delicate collarbones, the slight swell of her breasts, and one narrow knee rising out of the foam.

"Isabelle." He shook her shoulder gently. Her skin felt like satin and he gritted his teeth. "Don't fall asleep." He still wasn't entirely certain she wasn't concussed.

Her eyes opened slowly and he saw the exact moment when the memories returned. He didn't want her dwelling on them a moment more than necessary.

"Here," he said, and opened a large bath towel. She hesitated, and with one last quicksilver glance at him, she rose and stepped out of the tub and into the towel.

A silken lock of pale blonde hair had fallen down from her topknot. It spilled over her shoulder and down her breast. The last pale soft curl fell over her soft full breast to circle her nipple, like a frame offering him her succulent breast. Both nipples were full and pink. Her nipples were erect because she'd gone from the hot bath to the relative coolness of the air in the bathroom. But he'd also seen her shudder at his look. She wasn't aware of it, but she was aroused.

Not as much as he was.

He stifled a groan as he held the large bath towel open and enveloped her in it. Her breasts brushed his chest and he had to work to keep his hands gentle.

He was painfully aroused. Nicholas marveled at that bitch-goddess, fate. Six hours after meeting Isabelle in person, she was in his arms—and he couldn't act on what his entire body was clamoring for.

He was as far from making love to her as if she were on the dark side of the moon.

Every muscle was rigid with the desire to bear her to the floor and mount her immediately, slide into her warm, welcoming sheath, feeling those long, pale, slim legs hugging his waist, full breasts crushed against his chest...

He stepped back, grateful that he'd kept his jacket on. "Can you make it to the kitchen?" he asked, his voice low.

At her murmured yes, he made his escape.

By the time she entered the kitchen in her granny nightgown, he'd found her dishes and cutlery and was filling a bowl with soup.

She stood framed in the doorway, pale hair drying in tendrils about her face, eyes wide and shadowed.

His body clenched with desire to take her and wipe the sadness from her face. He wanted her to think only of the pleasure he could give her, feel only his body in hers.

Not now, he vowed to himself. But soon. Soon.

"Sit down and eat. You'll feel better." He pulled out a chair.

Isabelle stood for a moment, looking at him. She studied his face so intently he swore she would have seen into his soul, if he'd had one. "You're being very... nice to me. Why is that? I hardly know you."

"Don't worry about that now. Eat something."

Isabelle continued scrutinizing his face. Finally, she moved forward slowly and sat down. After a long moment, she picked up the spoon and dipped it into the rich-smelling brew. He'd asked Kevin to have the cook send whatever he'd been cooking for dinner and he had—a thick cream of tomato soup.

Nicholas uncorked the bottle Kevin had taken from his cellar and poured a glass for Isabelle and one for himself. He glanced at the label and smiled at Kevin's excellent taste.

There was total silence, broken only by Isabelle's spoon lightly glancing off the rim of the bowl and the soft sounds as they sipped the wine.

By the time she'd finished the soup and the glass of wine, a little color had come back into her face. She was far from over the shock of the attack but the healing, however long it would take, had begun.

She hung her head, a few strands of drying blonde hair falling forward over her breast. She still held the spoon in her hand. It clanged tinnily against the china bowl as her hand started trembling.

Nicholas picked her up and carried her into the living room. He sat down on the lone armchair with her in his arms. Threading his hands through her hair, careful of her injuries, he held her tightly as she turned her face into his neck and burst into tears.

They were the tears of a strong woman who didn't cry easily. At first, she resisted, holding herself stiffly, shaking with the effort to keep the tears at bay.

Nicholas brushed pale strands away from her face and leaned down. He kissed her ear, then whispered into it. "Let go." He shifted her in his arms to hold her more closely. "I'll be here to catch you."

Isabelle shook once, a deep tremor and then the tears started coming, quickly, silently. Nicholas cupped the back of her head and gave her his warmth and his strength. They were hers for the asking.

He remembered Isabelle in the bathtub. The delicacy of her, the satin softness of her alabaster skin. And the bruises on her arms, the finger marks on the side of her face and neck. Nicholas clenched his fists, wishing he could kill the bastards all over again.

If he hadn't been there… but he had. He expelled his breath in a long, controlled stream to rid his body of tension. If there was one thing life had taught him, it was to look forward, not back. 'What if' didn't exist. Only the here and now existed.

And here and now was Isabelle who needed tending.

Gradually, Isabelle's breathing slowed. He glanced down to see the tears drying on her cheeks, long lashes lowered, so thick they cast shadows over the delicate cheekbones. She was slumped bonelessly against him, half-lying in his arms. She felt delicate and soft and… right. Long after she'd fallen into a deep sleep, Nicholas sat and held her, one hand cradling her head, the other around her back, holding her tightly.

He sat with her in his arms while the sky outside her living room window turned pewter, then slate, then black. The rain stopped and stars shone coldly down as the wind pushed the clouds away and still he held her. She was deep in the sleep of exhaustion. At the most primitive level, she knew he would keep her safe and her mind had just shut down completely to give the body rest.

Around ten, the rain started again, drumming against the windowpanes. Somewhere in the house the thermostat kicked in.

Nicholas rose easily from the armchair with Isabelle in his arms. He carried her into the bedroom, gritting his teeth as she turned instinctively towards him in her sleep. She felt so soft and light and right in his arms. The temptation to simply sink to the floor with her, pull up her nightgown, spread her legs and thrust into her was almost overwhelming. He shook with a tangle of lust and love. He would be taking care of his lust very soon. The love was something he couldn't allow to happen.

He placed one knee on the mattress and lowered Isabelle to the bed. She sighed and moved her legs restlessly. She was frowning. Was she reliving the attack in her dreams?

Nicholas sank down on the bed behind her and put his arms around her. He put his nose in her soft hair and inhaled deeply. She smelled of shampoo and bubble bath, of woman and the lavender sachet he'd found in her dresser drawer.

This was exactly where he'd planned to be this evening—in bed with Isabelle in his arms. Her house or his—it wouldn't have mattered. He'd intended to 'bump' into her after her father's introduction and invite her out to dinner. He was used to the dance of seduction; they'd have ended up in bed together, he knew how to make sure of that. Nicholas lifted the corner of his mouth in a half-smile. Of course, the plan was for Isabelle to be awake and participating.

She stirred, her breast fitting perfectly in his hand, her soft bottom rubbing up against him. Nicholas bit his lip and resisted the urge to slide her nightgown up, lift her leg over his hip and slide into her. Instead, he held still as blood rushed to his cock. He couldn't remember the last time he'd been this full, this hard. He was hard as stone. Nicholas tortured himself again by pressing his cock against her and clenched his teeth to stop from groaning aloud.

He wasn't a masochist but this was the best way he knew to torment himself. Isabelle settled back against him.

He shouldn't be this needy. He certainly wasn't deprived. He had sex as often as he wanted. Just the other night he'd fucked an attractive woman five times and in the time it took to leave her apartment and go down in the elevator, he'd forgotten her name. He'd felt cold and dry and empty, the fleeting pleasure of orgasm already forgotten. This was happening more and more often lately. He could fuck for hours and feel nothing.

It was in the elevator that he finally decided he needed Isabelle. For just a while. She'd been his far off star, the woman who inhabited his dreams, the last thing he thought of before drifting off to sleep, the first thought in the morning. She was his obsession and he realized that he needed to live his obsession just once before dying.

He cupped her breast gently and moved his groin against her and grew, impossibly, even harder.

It was hell.

It was heaven.

Chapter Four

Isabelle awoke slowly, grudgingly from the depths of a deep sleep. Dimly, she was aware of a dull, far-away noise and it took her a few moments to realize that it was the patter of rain outside the window. A steady rain, not like—suddenly she stiffened as yesterday came back to her in a rush. The thunderstorm, the wild men attacking her, Nicholas Lee's rescue.

In a way, he was still rescuing her.

As if he knew that waking up alone after the terrors of yesterday would frighten her all over again, she had slept clasped in his arms. He was behind her, his big body enveloping her, wide shoulders bracketing hers. She was lying on one of his brawny arms, the other was around her waist.

She was warm and felt utterly enclosed and protected. She realized that she'd come awake slowly, as if her subconscious didn't want to face the coming day, and that at each stage of her awakening, she'd been subconsciously aware of his protection.

She also remembered that he'd shaken her awake a number of times during the night, to see if she was concussed.

Yesterday had been shocking and horrible, but it had only lasted a minute or two before Nicholas had rescued her. Since then she had been tenderly handled, even pampered.

Isabelle had faced many hard things in her life, including a mother dying slowly and horribly of cancer, and she had faced them completely alone. She possessed a core of strength deep inside her, which would allow her to recover from this ordeal, too.

Being with Nicholas had helped. She couldn't ever remember not being alone to face a problem.

She had wept her heart out on Nicholas Lee's shoulder last night while he had held her tightly, one big hand covering the back of her head, his other arm around her waist in an embrace of total protection. While she'd cried, a hard knot of tension and fear, not only from the attack but from other, older sorrows, had begun to dissipate.

She stretched slightly... and froze at the feel of the enormous erection against her backside.

"Don't panic." The deep voice was wry. Those huge arms tightened briefly, then he slid his left arm out from under her. "I've been like that all night and I haven't attacked you yet."

Isabelle turned over and blinked to find his face so close to hers. She hadn't dared in her father's study, but now she took the time to peruse him.

He'd lifted himself up to prop his head on his left hand. Though she knew he couldn't have had much sleep, he looked exactly as he had yesterday—strong and tireless and intense. His hair had come free from the long ponytail he wore tied at his nape and his straight black hair brushed past wide shoulders to spill incongruously over her pale pink frilly pillow slip. His hair was thick and had the sheen of health, so black there were blue highlights. Her hands itched to touch it.

Suddenly, she remembered his erection, and what he'd said.

"All *night*?" she asked huskily before she could stop herself. Her eyes widened and she could feel a fiery blush bloom on her face.

"All night," he confirmed soberly. A corner of his mouth lifted and she was fascinated by the changes in his face. It was such a strong face, the features clean and sharp. That half smile made him even more wildly attractive. She was suddenly aware of her heart thumping in her chest.

"Ouch," she whispered.

"You better believe 'ouch'." He reached out and brushed away a few strands of her hair. His hand was large, easily double the size of hers, lean and strong. The raised veins of an athlete coursed along them, along his muscular forearms and up the huge biceps.

Everything about this man was outsize. Leaning on his side, his shoulders were so broad he blocked her view of the window on the opposite wall. He was bare-chested and the sight of the large, hard slabs of muscle made her stare. A mat of thick black hairs covered his chest, narrowing to a broad stripe over his flat stomach. Luckily for her heart rate, the sheet covered the rest. She'd had enough excitement for the year.

He studied her soberly and seemed pleased with his perusal. "You're looking better. Are you up for some breakfast?"

Isabelle wrenched her mind away from what the sheet might be covering. The memory of what she'd felt with her bottom—a long, thick column as hard as steel—made her blush even harder. "Yes, I—" She stopped and frowned. "Actually, I don't think there's much to eat in the house. I've been too busy lately to do much shopping."

"I suspect your house just grew some espresso beans and croissants."

She smiled. Since she'd been a small child alone in the house with a severely depressed woman, no one had ever prepared breakfast for her. "Is that right? Would this be from the same tree that grew cream of tomato soup and Merlot?"

He inclined his big head. "The very same. Stay here." He bent and kissed her lightly on the lips and rolled out of bed, his movements powerful and graceful. He was out the door before she had time to react.

He'd kissed her. In her father's study she must have wondered how his kisses would taste, because her first thought was — *so that's what it's like.*

It had been the merest breath of a kiss, his firm lips just brushing hers, and she had felt it to her toes.

It took her a moment to calm her senses and by that time, the rich smell of excellent coffee had wafted into the bedroom and she discovered, to her surprise, that she was hungry.

Minutes later, he walked into the bedroom carrying a tray with a steaming cup of coffee and a plate with two croissants.

Isabelle sat up, plumping pillows at her back. Nicholas set the tray on her bedside table and sat on the edge of the bed. He unfolded a large linen napkin with a snap, placed it over her lap and handed her a cup. It was bone china with a delicate rose print.

Isabelle fingered the napkin. "Does that tree grow linen napkins and—" she ran her hand around the rim of the cup, "Rosenthal china?"

"Limoges," he said. "Absolutely. And that same tree is going to grow some lunch in a few hours."

She sipped the excellent coffee and sighed in pleasure. "It will probably be delicious, judging by this coffee, but I'll have to pass, I'm afraid. I've got a luncheon date for noon."

"No, you don't." Nicholas's deep voice was calm as he cut a bite of the croissant and lifted it into her mouth. Startled, she bit into the warm flaky pastry and nearly moaned at the buttery taste. She chewed, swallowed and frowned. "What do you mean—"

"Open up," he ordered, and delicately held another bite before her mouth. She opened it to ask what he meant about her luncheon date and he tipped the morsel in. She chewed quickly and swallowed. "What—"

"You had an appointment with Nancy Ruger at the Blue Lagoon. I called her up an hour ago and cancelled the date. She'll get back to you."

Isabelle sat up straighter. "How on earth—"

"Easy. Your organizer is right next to the phone. You very efficiently put your appointments and the phone numbers on each day. I've cancelled all your appointments for the next three days."

"How dare you do that!"

His eyes glittered. "You'd better believe I dare. You need peace and quiet. The last thing you need is to go skittering around town in this weather." He gestured out the window at the gray, sullen sky and steady rainfall. "All I did was make sure you'll have the opportunity to get the rest you need. You need rest, Isabelle. One way or another I'm going to make sure that you get it." His voice was calm. That and his measured movements reassured her on a level deeper than words.

And he was right.

She hadn't been looking forward to the lunch with Nancy Ruger, a colleague from the station. If truth be told, she wasn't looking forward to her other upcoming appointments, either. She was tired and ached all over and the idea of taking it easy for a few days was immensely appealing.

Somehow, Nicholas Lee knew that. She should be angry at him. He'd been high-handed in rearranging her life and he certainly hadn't apologized for changing her schedule. But the knowledge that he'd forced her to do something she should have had the good sense to do for herself pulled the punch of her anger.

He was watching her closely, his expression so intense the skin was pulled tightly over his broad, high cheekbones. She couldn't begin to read the meaning of all that intensity, except for the fact that it was focused tightly on her.

Amazingly, even in the full light of day, the irises of his eyes were almost the same color as the pupils. She'd never seen such black eyes before. Most dark eyes had color in them—it just didn't show up except in sunlight. Nicholas Lee's eyes were as black as midnight.

His skin was dark, too, a strong olive with no ruddy undertones. She couldn't tell if he was deeply tanned or whether it was his natural skin tone. Maybe he had some Native American blood in him, which would explain the thick, straight black hair and his coloring.

She was staring at him. To cover her embarrassment, she took another sip of coffee.

"Is the coffee good?" he asked softly.

He had an unusual timbre to his voice. It was deep and rich, with bass undertones that set up an answering vibration in the pit of her stomach.

She nodded her head jerkily.

"Let me find out for myself."

Before she could understand his intention, he leaned forward and put his mouth over hers, slanting to open her lips. This time it was a real kiss and she shivered as his tongue met hers, sliding over it, exploring her mouth. He bit lightly at her bottom lip, licked it, then licked into her mouth. She couldn't open her eyes, she couldn't move. All she could do was open her mouth helplessly to his as his lips and tongue gave her a honeyed pleasure. She heard a soft noise and realized, dimly, that she was moaning deep in her throat. She shook and her hands clenched in the covers. His tongue swirled deep and withdrew. His mouth lifted, settled, then lifted again. He pulled back and gazed at her. Her eyelids felt heavy; it took great effort to open them. She stared back at him, numbly.

"God, yes, it's good," he whispered, and covered her mouth again.

This time she participated fully in the kiss, opening her mouth under his, raising her hands to rest them on the iron slabs of muscle on his shoulders. When his tongue met hers again, she dug her nails into his shoulders. There was no give to his skin at all. He was pure steel.

She breathed in deeply, her nose next to his cheek and drew in a heady odor of soap and male musk. His eyes were closed and she saw that he had thick, blunt black lashes.

She couldn't see anything more because her own eyes drifted closed. It was as if all her senses were concentrated on her mouth and she couldn't drum up enough energy to keep her eyes open.

With each beat of her heart, with each stroke of his tongue, she slid further down in the bed. Because she couldn't stay upright. Because his hard body was pressing down on hers.

He groaned and, dimly, she realized he was as affected as she was. He was hard everywhere she touched—the muscles along his shoulders, his biceps, the penis she could feel digging into her thigh.

She should draw away, but his mouth was too delicious, stroking heat into her, his taste too heady. She drifted dreamily, drugged with sexual heat as he explored her mouth.

He withdrew the barest breath away and she sighed in disappointment, but he immediately placed his lips on her jawbone and nipped lightly.

She jerked with surprise, with pleasure. Her breathing speeded up as his mouth moved to her ear, where he traced the delicate whorls with his tongue.

His thick hair fell like a cloud around them, encircling them in a private black embrace.

She felt cool air on her breasts and looked down. He'd unbuttoned her nightgown and spread the wings wide.

He lifted his head and she shivered at the heat in his eyes. Arousal had turned his harsh features even starker, his normally dusky skin flushed with blood. His hand was gently stroking her breast, his thumb slowly circling her nipple.

Before the sluggish thought formed in her mind—*I should protest*—he'd bent his head to her breast and she gasped as he took the tip into his mouth.

He cupped her breast, suckling strongly, and the sensation was so intense it was like a white hot wire drawing her towards his mouth. This wasn't a gentle suckling, like a child's, but a grown man's tugging with such strength she thought she would faint from the overwhelming sensations.

Isabelle looked down and found herself aroused by the contrast of his black head on her breast. His hand looked darker, even more powerful, against her white skin.

Isabelle let her head fall back as he moved to her other breast. The rain had stopped, as if the world had hushed to make way for the sounds they were making—her soft pants, his harsh groans, the erotic pulling of his mouth at her breast.

She was too wrapped in a sensual haze to protest when a strong hand stroked her leg. First her calf, his hand so large it easily met around it, then the back of her knee, then slowly, slowly up the inside of her thigh. He was using his teeth and tongue on her nipple, tugging sharply, and she was on fire.

At the first gentle hint of his hand, her shaking thighs fell apart.

He pressed his large, warm palm over her mound and she sighed with pleasure.

Nicholas lifted his head. "Look at me, Isabelle," he said softly. She lifted heavy lids to meet his eyes burning into hers. The air felt cool on her breasts, still wet from his mouth. He was breathing heavily, his chest expanding like a bellows. His body gave off waves of heat and hers felt as if a furnace burned just beneath her skin.

A large, blunt finger circled her flesh, stroking the folds. He couldn't help but feel her arousal, feel her hot wetness and she saw satisfaction in his lowered lids, in the flush of red over his cheekbones. His mouth was wet, lips slightly swollen from her kisses. He unfolded her as gently as a flower, petal by petal and her womb clenched.

He pushed a large finger into her heated center, barely at the entrance, and her hips arched to take more of him.

"That's it," his low, deep voice crooned. "That's it, open for me, love."

He moved his finger deeper and circled her clitoris with his thumb. He slowly withdrew his finger and slipped a second finger in. She gave a high cry and her thighs trembled.

"God, you feel so hot and tight, love. Like a virgin. You haven't had a man in you for some time, have you?"

She couldn't breath. She was burning up. He slid the two fingers gently in and out and then slowly separated them. She whimpered.

"Isabelle? How long has it been since you've had a cock here?" He thrust his fingers hard and she writhed. His fingers felt as large as a penis. Her whole body was trembling.

"Not—" she licked her lips. "Not since college."

"Good," he murmured, increasing the rhythm of his strokes. "My cock will be here soon. When you're ready. In the meantime, you're going to get used to my hands and my mouth on you. You'll come over and over again before I take you, and you'll be ready."

He circled her clitoris again, hard, and Isabelle exploded. She clenched helplessly around his fingers as his mouth ground into hers. Her fingers dug into his biceps as he continued stroking, harder and harder as she climaxed. She cried out, but his mouth covered her moans as she kept clenching around his fingers.

He knew just how to touch her, just how hard and how soft, to keep her on the edge, in helpless spasms of pleasure so blinding it was almost painful.

She finally subsided, exhausted, and lay back in his arms. He withdrew his fingers and touched her nipples, wetting them with her juices. He bent and licked them and she jerked. She couldn't possibly be feeling desire again, but she was.

Isabelle had never lost control of herself this way, hadn't known she could. It was exhilarating and frightening. She still shook with the intensity of her release. Her eyes closed and her hands fell to her sides. She could still feel the echoes of her orgasm in her lower body.

Nicholas kissed her closed lids. "Sleep now, love," he said in his black magic voice and she surrendered, sliding into darkness.

Chapter Five

"What do you want from me?"

Nicholas looked up from the book he'd taken from Isabelle's book-shelves.

He'd been pleased, but not surprised, to note that her tastes matched his. Her bookcase could have been his. He chose a book he'd read many times, noting from its well-worn look that she must have read it over and over again, too.

Isabelle stood in the doorway of the bedroom, eyeing him warily, too tense, too taut to move into the living room where he sat on the couch.

She held herself stiffly, arms crossed over her waist. Her face was expressionless, as if she were holding herself against him, determined not to give in to him in any way.

He'd let her sleep the morning and the afternoon away, knowing she needed it, both for the rest it would give her body and because her mind needed down time to process the violence yesterday.

Kevin had stopped by again leaving supplies and Nicholas could heat her up a late lunch or early dinner at any time.

"What do I want with you?" he repeated, putting the book down, rais-ing his eyes to hers. She stood there, the woman who haunted his dreams, rumpled, delicate, fragile. He had never been vulnerable to anyone or anything but he knew in the deepest recesses of his heart that she could bring him to his knees. "I want to fuck you," he said calmly.

She winced.

Nicholas used the crudest expression to hide what he wanted to say with all his heart. *I want to love you. I want you to love me back. I want to court you, I want you to be mine forever.*

He'd come up from the dregs, from a rat-infested tenement and a drug addict mother who sold her body for a fix. But though he'd been born in poverty, he'd also been born strong and smart and ruthless. He'd used all the strength, power and cunning nature had invested him with to build an empire. He was rich and powerful beyond even the dreams of most men. He could have anything in the world, satisfy any appetite, save one.

He couldn't have Isabelle for a lifetime. A week or two at the most was all that fate would give him.

He got up and slowly walked towards her. He didn't take his eyes off hers. "I want to fuck you so hard and so often you'll forget what it's like not to have me inside you. I want to make you scream with pleasure, over and over again. I want to fuck you so much your body will be molded to mine, your cunt shaped to my cock, your skin smelling of me. I want you to forget where you end and I begin."

He stopped in front of her. Her eyes were huge as she scrutinized his face, as though trying to see what was behind his hard words.

He reached out to untie the knot of her bathrobe and slid it off her shoulders. It fell softly to the floor in heavy folds. Isabelle drew in a sharp breath, the sound loud in the silent room, but she didn't stop him.

In a moment, Nicholas had the buttons of her nightgown undone to the waist. He lifted his hands to her shoulders and opened the nightgown. It slid, caught for a moment on her hips, then slithered to the floor to lie around her feet.

He wanted her more than he wanted his next breath and she wanted him back, just as much.

A lifetime of sex had taught him all about female desire. Isabelle didn't move, barely breathed, but she wanted him. Her cheekbones were flushed, the pupils of her eyes were so dilated only a shimmering silvery band rimmed the black. Her nipples were deep pink and hard. He reached out with one finger to touch her.

He loved the contrast of his skin against hers. Countless times he'd read descriptions of a woman's skin, but words paled against the reality of hers. It was incredibly fine-grained, as smooth as a child's and the palest ivory in color.

With the lightest of touches, he followed her slender collarbones, the swell of her breast, the smooth pink aureole a shade lighter than the nipple, down to the full, womanly underside. She was so finely made; he ground his teeth together so hard they ached at the thought of those bastards who had attacked her.

Her breasts were amazingly large for so slender a woman—heavy, firm and high with nipples turned a deep rose with arousal. He smoothed his hand down over her other breast and cupped it, loving the full weight of it in his hand. He bent to take her nipple into his mouth.

She liked it when he pulled hard at her. She might not even have known that she liked his mouth on her that way. He remembered her soft gasp of surprise when he'd first taken her breast in his mouth.

She didn't have much sexual experience, that was clear. His fingers had barely fit inside her and she had seemed stunned, almost frightened, at her body's response. And yet, her response to him had been strong and immediate.

There was so much he wanted to show her. He knew, from his experience with an endless number of sex partners, that when he finally took her completely, they would fit like a lock with a key. She was made for him, for his hands and his mouth and his cock.

Nicholas slowly sank to one knee and gently urged her thighs apart with his hands. She had silky, pale blonde hair between her thighs, soft pink flesh peeking temptingly through. He couldn't resist the temptation and leaned forward.

"Oh!" Isabelle swayed and Nicholas clamped two hard hands on her hips as she tried to pull away.

"Not yet," he said huskily. "I need to know what you taste like here."

Like seashells, like a rose, like the dawn.

He moved his mouth gently on her, his tongue feeling the soft folds of flesh open up as he explored her sheath as thoroughly as he had explored her mouth.

He lost himself in her flesh, delighting in her soft textures, in the smell of her. For minutes, they stood there, his hands holding her up as he delved deeply into her. Suddenly, Isabelle gave a sharp cry and her hands clasped his head. She trembled violently and erupted in the sharp contractions of orgasm.

Nicholas stood up swiftly, catching her in his arms, and carried her to the sofa.

Much as he wanted her naked in his arms, she might be cold, so he wrapped her in the soft teal blue blanket which had been draped over the sofa. Isabelle still trembled. She turned her face into his neck, as if she wanted to hide from him.

Nicholas settled her comfortably in his embrace and lifted her chin with a finger. Her eyes were closed. The color that had tinged her face with arousal had fled and now she was pale. He waited patiently until she opened her eyes and looked at him.

"Let me tell you the way it should be in a perfect world, Isabelle," he told her quietly. "This is our story. One night, when I'm depressed and have had too much to drink, I watch your program on TV. You're a beautiful, intelligent woman, with a fascinating take on life. I like the way you think. I like the way you look. You love books. I love books. I get someone to introduce us and then I ask you out. I take you to a nice restaurant and to a jazz club afterwards. We have fun. We're very attracted to each other. Maybe you're a little lonely, too, looking for someone. We click on a number of levels. I take you home and kiss you goodnight. It's a good kiss, a solid kiss. Both of us would like to take it further, but it's too early yet. We both know this is something serious, something worth taking slowly."

Nicholas bent to give her a gentle kiss on the cheek, his lips lingering over the smooth skin. When he lifted his head, he looked her straight in the eye.

"I've had a lot of sex in my life, Isabelle. I need it often and I've never had any trouble getting as much as I want." She was watching him carefully, intently. Her eyes, that stunning mixture of silver and blue, never left his. He shrugged. "Ordinarily, an hour after I've taken a woman out to dinner, I'm in bed with her. Then we have a hot affair for a week or two at the most. Sometimes less."

For a moment, Nicholas rested the back of his head against the sofa and closed his eyes. Hearing himself describe his own life depressed him. He'd had all the sex he'd ever wanted but it had never been enough to fill this gnawing emptiness inside him.

For so long he'd refused to acknowledge his loneliness, the desire for a connection. Connections were for other people. All his life he'd thought of himself as utterly apart from the rest of humankind. He'd been born that way and, he thought, he'd die that way.

And all along, like a powerful underground river, his need for love had flowed until it had found the right place to come up into the light.

Right now, he felt closer to Isabelle than he'd ever felt to any other woman. And he hadn't even been inside her yet.

It couldn't last. The connection had to be severed and his river had to dry up. But first, he was going to give himself a taste of what others thought of as their birthright—a chance at love.

Nicholas opened his eyes at the feel of Isabelle's hand against his cheek. Her gaze was soft.

"That sounds like a lonely way to live," she said gently.

He covered her hand with his, then turned her hand around to lace his fingers through hers. He brought the back of her hand to his lips.

"Very lonely," he agreed. "Still, you can't miss what you don't know. Only... in this perfect world, I realize what I'm missing and it's in my grasp. I find you and I'm not going to let you go. I take you out every night. I accompany you to your conferences and lectures. I call you several times a day to find out how you are. I meet your friends and colleagues and I make it clear to everyone that I'm staking my claim to you. Like now, in this other world it's mid-December when I start courting you and on Christmas Day, I give you a diamond and sapphire ring and ask you to do me the honor of becoming my wife. We marry on New Year's Eve and we finally make love for the first time that night, as fireworks explode all around us."

Nicholas looked at her lying in his arms. Gently, he opened the edges of the blanket a little, as if opening a present. Her skin shimmered like a pearl in its shell. "It is well worth waiting for," he whispered.

He closed his eyes for a moment and ran his hands down her body, knowing her now by touch as well as by sight. He fondled her breasts, ran his hand over her flat belly and stroked his fingers into the notch between her legs.

"I fill you with my seed so often that you get pregnant right away. Every night we make love and every day I watch your body change as you carry my child. Late in your pregnancy, I start taking you from behind, very gently, and you feel both me and our child moving in your body." His fingers delved deeper, loving the way she grew soft and wet for him.

Isabelle arched, legs falling apart to ease his way. He stroked her, listening carefully to the way her breathing speeded up, watching her eyes flutter.

"When our baby is born, I watch you nurse him and sometimes I feed at your breast, too, and you climax. Then you hold us both in your arms and the three of us are together, connected by love."

Isabelle gave a sharp cry and convulsed, contracting strongly around his fingers. His heart pounded as he turned his head to kiss her fiercely.

She clung to him and moved her bottom in his lap. He knew she could feel how aroused he was.

Nicholas lifted his head and looked down at her for a long time, letting her see his pain and regret.

"But," he said finally, harshly, "that's not the way it's going to be. This isn't a perfect world, Isabelle, and I haven't lived a perfect life. I've been forced to do things I regret and I've made powerful enemies, chief among them Luis Mendoza."

"But—" Isabelle blinked, clearly trying to emerge from a sensual haze. "But he's a criminal, a gangster!"

"Yes, he is," Nicholas agreed calmly. "And I'm not. Or at least, not any more. We had… dealings when I was starting out."

"He's a drug smuggler." Isabelle looked at him soberly. "That's what the newspapers say."

"And a murderer," Nicholas agreed. He wasn't about to whitewash his background but he didn't want her confusing them. "I've never touched drugs, Isabelle, and I've never killed anyone. Other than that … I did what I had to do to survive. By the time I figured out what a psychopath Mendoza was, I had moved on. I didn't want anything more to do with him. But our paths have crossed and tangled enough times to make us rivals. I've bested him often and he hates my guts. He wouldn't hesitate to hurt someone who means a lot to me. That hasn't been a problem up until now."

Nicholas hesitated, aware with every cell of his body of what he was going to say. Aware he'd never said it before. Aware that he meant every word.

"No one has ever mattered to me before, Isabelle. I don't have any family. I have household staff but I rarely see them and they have orders to stay out of my way. I have sex partners but I don't have love affairs. So I've never showed a soft underbelly to anyone. I've never been in any way vulnerable to Mendoza because no one has ever meant anything to me. But now—now someone does."

Isabelle smiled and her hand tightened on his arm. "Oh, Nicholas."

"Wait," he said harshly. "There's more. That rosy scenario, the one where I court you and marry you and live with you? That's for another world, not this one. In this one, if I were to marry you, I'd be signing your death sentence. You'd be a living target every day and I would go insane trying to keep you safe."

Nicholas closed his eyes and the image of a broken and bleeding Isabelle swam against his closed eyelids. He shuddered. He opened them again and stared down at her.

"About the only way I could survive in any kind of shape would be to keep you locked up. Literally. Twenty four /seven. Never let you out. And even then I wouldn't feel a hundred percent secure, because Mendoza could bribe a member of my staff to kill you, or poison the water mains leading to the house or blow up the place with a bazooka. He'd find some way to destroy you to get to me."

She was watching him closely, as glowing and as beautiful as moonlight in his arms. He tightened his grip.

"You say your… relationship with Mendoza was a long time ago?" she asked.

Nicholas nodded.

"Don't you think he might have… forgotten?"

"No. Mendoza's not the kind of man who forgets. He wants to put his hands on my businesses. Not that he'd be able to run them. To be frank, he's not the sharpest tool in the woodshed, but he makes up in ferocity what he lacks in smarts. He's just a crazy murdering son of a bitch."

Isabelle listened quietly, silver eyes watching him carefully. "Surely you're smarter than he is."

Nicholas's jaw worked. "Oh, yeah, I'm much smarter than he is. That's not the problem. You don't need a genius I.Q. to pull the trigger on an AK-47. You don't need to be smart to plant Semtex in a car and have it blow up at the turn of a key. All you have to be is relentless and ruthless. And you better believe that is exactly what Mendoza is. The instant he realizes you mean something to me, you're a walking dead woman." He closed his eyes briefly, then opened them again. They were black and hot. "I wouldn't be able to stand it."

Isabelle's face was colorless. He knew she was smart. She didn't doubt his words and he knew she could easily imagine the situation. She didn't even try to conjure up rosy scenarios, and he respected her for that. But her next words shocked him to the core.

"What if I were willing to accept the risk?" she asked quietly.

"No!" Every muscle in his body rejected the notion. He tightened his arms. "There's no question of that. I won't gamble with your safety. We have to accept the situation as it is, Isabelle. And the situation is that we can have a hot affair for a while—ten days, two weeks. No one will blink at that. So that's what we'll do. And on New Year's day we'll go our separate ways." Nicholas drew in a deep, shuddering breath. "We'll never see each other again. I'll make sure of it. But I'll also keep an eye on you. Watch over you. I'll leave you a way to get word to me and if you ever need my help, you'll have it, no questions asked. You have my word."

He didn't say that he'd make sure she would never want for anything again. Isabelle would reject the notion. But it soothed the ache in his heart to know that he could do this for her.

He'd rather give her a husband and children, but he'd learned long ago that pining after what was impossible led to heartache and nothing more.

"So, that's the way it is in the real world." He deliberately made his voice hard. "We can only be together for a short time. I want you to move in with me until the end of the year. I'll accompany you to the station and your book presentations and out to dinner and to concerts. We'll go wherever you want to go. We'll do whatever you want to do. We'll have as much sex as two people can have and still remain standing. We'll spend New Year's Eve making love. And on New Year's Day we say goodbye. That's what I can offer you. That's *all* I can offer you. Will you accept?"

Nicholas could almost feel the intensity of Isabelle's gaze. Her eyes moved slowly, giving off glittering silvery shards of light with each movement, looking deeply into his. Her gaze roamed over every inch of his face, as if to measure his resolution.

Nicholas was used to hiding his feelings. Until Isabelle, he'd have denied having any feelings at all.

So now he showed Isabelle the smooth, hard facade of his resolve. She mustn't have any illusions. They would be fatal. To her and to his sanity.

He had to keep her safe. He was guilty of many things in his lifetime, but bringing harm to Isabelle would never be one of them.

"What will it be, love. Yes or no?"

Suddenly, Isabelle expelled her breath and softened in his arms. She brought a hand to his cheek and a silvery tear slipped out and coursed down a smooth, ivory cheek. She held his gaze with hers and he could read everything of her character in it.

Strength, courage, understanding.

She tried to smile but it was a weak effort, and it broke his heart.

"Yes," she whispered and lifted her mouth to his.

Chapter Six

"Are you ready?" Nicholas asked quietly two days later, his hand on Isabelle's front door. "I want us to make it home before it starts snowing again."

Isabelle glanced up at Nicholas standing in the darkened foyer. His face was in shadow but she didn't need light to see him. Those strong features were etched in her memory forever. Everything about him was imprinted on her consciousness, on her senses, on her skin, and would be until the day she died.

She was leaving the house for the first time since the attack. Nicholas had insisted that she needed the time to recover and he'd been right. She finally felt fully herself again.

He'd stayed by her side constantly. Three times a day, a tall blond man named Kevin delivered box after box of marvels: books, magazines, videotapes, exquisitely prepared food and a selection of the finest wines. Nicholas had insisted on feeding her himself. She'd almost forgotten what it was to feed herself, to bathe herself, to dress herself. For the first time in her life she'd had someone to take care of her.

She'd been utterly pampered and loved from head to toe, over and over again. He'd used only his hands and mouth while telling her, in excruciating detail, just how he would take her completely once they were in his house. She shivered at the memory.

He glanced at her out of midnight eyes. "Cold, love?" he rumbled. "Maybe I can do something about that."

He reached down to one of the magic boxes Kevin had delivered and pulled up the sealing tape. He unfolded the flaps and pulled out something soft and blue. A flick of his hand and it billowed out—a rich silvery blue cashmere coat by Valentino. He held it up. "Here, try it on."

Stunned, Isabelle shrugged into it, her fingers lingering over the lushly soft material. It came to mid-calf and enveloped her in soft folds of warmth.

"Nicholas," she breathed. She brushed her hand down a sleeve. She'd never had anything as fine as this in her whole life. "Oh, I can't possibly—"

"Now, love." Nicholas started buttoning the coat up. "I hope you're not going to say something silly like you can't accept it. Not when I sent poor Kevin all over town yesterday looking for exactly the right coat. And then I had to listen to him complaining bitterly that shopping for a woman isn't in his job description. He told me in no uncertain terms that I owe him, big time. So, after all of that, you're not going to refuse it, are you?"

Isabelle smiled up at him and sighed. She pulled the collar of her coat around her neck, her fingers lingering over the soft material. "I guess I can't. But it's a very… extravagant gift. I don't know what to say."

"Try 'thank you'," he suggested, taking her hands.

"Thank you."

"You're very welcome." He smiled one of his rare smiles, lifting her hand to his mouth. "The color matches your eyes. You look so beautiful you take my breath away." He bent to pick up her suitcase. "If you're ready, we can go."

The snick of the door closing echoed sharply in Isabelle's heart. She had a sense of a door closing on the whole first half of her life. She would be a changed woman the next time she walked through that door and back into her apartment on the first day of the year.

She was a changed woman already.

Somehow, Nicholas had unlocked something in her she hadn't even been aware of. It wasn't just the sex, though God knows that was shattering enough, even the foreplay he'd restricted himself to.

No, it was more than that. It was the closeness, the connection. She'd grown up with two parents who were too embroiled in their own emotional messes to pay any attention to her. And then after her father had abandoned them, she'd been so involved in coping with her mother's depression and illness that she hadn't really had time to form close friendships or date. After her mother's death, it had taken her years of hard work to pay off the worst of the debts.

Her few affairs had been unsatisfactory and she was almost resigned to living alone and without passion.

The response Nicholas had been able to effortlessly coax from her body astonished her. With him, she'd discovered a new side to her nature. An entirely new dimension to life.

It was as if she'd only gone through the motions before, but now … now she was living life to the fullest. Her time with him was almost frighteningly intense. And knowing that she would barely have a chance to open the door on this new dimension of life, glimpsing the warmth and excitement and hot pleasure on the other side, when that door would be slammed shut again in her face forever, broke her heart.

Nicholas had been very, very clear what the condition for their affair would be—they would live together for a short while, they would be lovers in the most complete sense of the term, and they would part on the first day of the new year, never to see each other again.

How would she give him up?

Isabelle had grown used to Nicholas, to sleeping in his strong arms, to having his mouth and hands on her, to having his tall, powerful frame as a bulwark between her and the world. How would she could survive the new year?

By living minute by minute. For now, Nicholas was with her, and she intended to store up memories for a lifetime.

They walked out of her apartment building and she glanced up at the sky.

It had been raining steadily for the past two days and the forecast called for heavy snowfalls over the Christmas season. The rain had stopped by the time Nicholas handed her into his car, but the clouds overhead looked bruised and sullen, heavy with foreboding, like a part of Isabelle's heart.

Excited as she was at the thought of living with Nicholas for a few precious days, of finally feeling him inside her, of being completely and fully his, she knew she was committing herself to heartbreak.

"What are you thinking about?" Nicholas asked as he started the engine.

Isabelle turned her head to study his profile. Like everything else about him, it was sharp, clean, strong. "About afterwards," she said simply.

He froze, his hand still at the key. Slowly his head lowered until his forehead touched the top rim of the steering wheel. He closed his eyes. "Isabelle..." he murmured. "Don't."

She reached out to put her hand over his and lay her head on his shoulder. "Oh, Nicholas," she whispered. "I can't help it."

Nicholas turned to catch her in his arms and kissed her fiercely, wildly. His lips crushed hers, his teeth clashed with hers as he ate at her mouth, bruising her, in a kiss of possession, not arousal.

His arms were so tight she could hardly breathe, but she didn't care because she was holding him just as tightly, her hands running madly over the strong muscles of his shoulders, over his hard neck, into his thick hair which always surprised her with its warmth. It was so black she instinctively expected it to be cold to the touch.

She was arched against him in his arms and she frantically wished she could get rid of the layers of clothes separating them. It was desperation more than passion. She needed to feel his skin against hers and be reassured by his strong steady heartbeat.

She'd never been held so much by another human being. The touch of his skin calmed her on a deep level. She could hardly sleep now unless her hand was resting on his massive pectoral, right over his heart, the beat strong and reassuring.

The feel of his hand on her breast, even through her bra, sweater and coat, made her jump. Though she responded instantly, she pulled back a moment and rested her forehead against his. They were both breathing heavily and several moments passed before she heard herself say words wrenched from the very core of her being.

"I'm going to miss you, Nicholas," she whispered. "So much."

Isabelle looked up and saw his jaw muscles bunch. He didn't answer her, just turned his head to look out the window at the sky. There was silence for a long moment.

"We'd better get home before the storm breaks," he said finally, gently pulling her arms away.

They drove through the streets in silence.

Isabelle had no idea where Nicholas lived. He was a very rich man. She imagined he would have an upscale residence in an elegant part of town—a mansion on White Oak Drive or a luxury condo in Brixton Heights.

To her surprise, Nicholas drove along the river, straight out to the industrial district. She tried to think of why they might be here, but she drew a blank. There was nothing but dark concrete and brick buildings, huge parking lots with trucks lined up like soldiers, two-story steel fences.

Ten minutes down a deserted road flanked by warehouses, Nicholas pulled a remote control from his jacket and pressed a button. He slowed and she could see massive iron gates in a tall concrete wall slowly opening out. Nicholas drove through the gates and into an industrial lot.

Isabelle turned around. Behind them, the gates slowly closed. It was as if she were entering a different realm, leaving her old world behind.

It *was* a different realm. She could see what looked like an abandoned factory and warehouse. Nicholas pulled into what would have been the loading bay, back when the place was a going concern.

Before her was an immense structure. Only a few stories high, it was so wide she had to turn her head to take it all in. Broken windows, cracked pavement, weeds growing up through the cracked asphalt. There was a desolate air of abandonment about the place.

Isabelle couldn't begin to imagine what they were doing here.

Nicholas brought the car to a stop next to a steel panel set in the wall. A halogen lamp just over the panel was the only illumination in the entire area encompassed by the walls.

He got out, took her suitcase from the trunk and came around to open her door. Taking her elbow he guided her to the panel in the wall. It could have been a door, except there was no doorknob and no hinges. It was in a better state of repair than the rest of the building—a slab of polished blue-gray steel.

Nicholas set her suitcase on the ground and pressed his palm against a small square glass pane inserted about five feet off the ground.

To Isabelle's astonishment, the pane flashed a violent green and, a second later, the steel panel opened with a pneumatic hiss. She swung her gaze up to Nicholas and a corner of his mouth lifted.

"Security scanner," he said, and ushered her into a large steel cubicle.

The door hissed shut and the entire cubicle fell quickly. She hadn't been expecting the cubicle to be an elevator and staggered slightly. Nicholas steadied her with his hand for the duration of the ride and with another hiss, the door opened again.

Isabelle had no way of knowing how far beneath the earth's surface they had gone but she suspected several stories, maybe six or seven, given the speed of the drop.

Nicholas had his arm around her waist and moved her forward by the simple expedient of stepping out himself and half-carrying her with him.

"Welcome," he said simply.

She'd never seen any place like it.

The house had obviously been excavated out of the cliffs rising high over the south side of the river. Limestone cliffs, she remembered reading in school.

She was in an atrium at least three stories high, with a vaulted ceiling, black and white marble flooring and a striking Chinese rug. Massive enameled terracotta pots housed lemon and orange trees, ripe with fruit. She could smell their clean tang from across the enormous room.

As soon as the elevator doors opened, a massive crystal chandelier lit up, banishing the gloom of the day. There would still have been enough light to see by since the entire back wall of the house was floor to ceiling window, affording a breathtaking view of the cityscape and roiling river three hundred feet below. Isabelle could see the McClellan Tower and the Solara Building lit up across the river.

"This is magnificent," she said with a breathy sigh

Nicholas took her coat. "If you go to the right, you'll find tea waiting for you."

She didn't need to be asked twice. She turned right, crossing the great hall, into what was obviously a living room.

As she walked in, lamps lit up, picking up highlights. Everything she saw was luxurious and in superb taste—the artwork, the immense area rugs, Chinese vases.

The room was huge, divided up into separate areas by the furniture. Again, one entire wall was floor to ceiling window. On the left wall was an enormous fireplace, easily twenty feet long, flanked by a comfortable-looking black leather sofa and matching armchairs. A fire was burning brightly and a silver tea service gleamed on a trolley.

With a sigh, Isabelle sat down. She loved fireplaces. She hadn't had a fireplace since she had been a little girl living in her father's home.

Nicholas sat next to her, placing a cut crystal decanter with a brown liquid on the coffee table. "Don't bother pouring for me," he said lazily. He poured from the decanter instead, the smell of good whiskey filling the air. "I have my own tea."

"I see you do," she smiled. Isabelle sipped as she watched Nicholas out of the corner of her eye.

He unbuttoned his jacket and sat back with a sigh. He looked... relaxed. Like a king who had finally come back to the palace after a war campaign abroad.

Oddly, for a room that was both enormous and sumptuous, it was also soothing. Maybe it was the dramatic view out an entire wall, where you could watch the city at work and play, like a living painting, or maybe it was the crackling fire in a fireplace big enough to roast an ox in, or maybe just the leather sofa which was unusually comfortable, but Isabelle found herself slowly relaxing.

This house—this kingdom—was where she would spend the most intense ten days of her life. It was where she was going to leave her heart.

Nicholas lifted her hand to his lips. "The entire house is yours while... while you're here," he said quietly. "Go anywhere you want, do anything you want." With the hand that held the whiskey he pointed to a console on the coffee table. "If you need anything, press the button at the top. That's for Kevin. He'll interface with the staff."

The staff. Isabelle looked around. Of course. A house this size would need a big staff to keep it running smoothly. "Where is everybody?"

"The next level down. Four people besides Kevin live downstairs in mini apartments. But don't worry. For the next ten days, everyone has strict orders not to come up here unless I call. I want us to have privacy. I want to be able to make love to you anywhere, at any time. You ready to continue the tour?"

She nodded, her mouth suddenly dry at the images his words conjured up. She put her tea cup down with hands that shook and stood up on wobbly legs.

They went through room after room. A magnificent study, a truly astonishing library, with built-in bookshelves two stories high reached by wooden catwalks. A dining room like a cathedral. And always, always, the back wall floor to ceiling windows showcasing the city on the other side of the river. The windows had no drapes.

"Don't you wonder about privacy?" she asked.

"No. The glass isn't transparent on the other side. It's like a one-way mirror. It's also polarized so I can blank it whenever I want to block out sunlight. And it's bulletproof." He ushered her into another room. As always, the lights dimmed as they left a room and came on as they entered the next.

Isabelle gasped.

Nicholas looked down at her and smiled, his eyes heavy-lidded. Her thighs clenched. She knew that look. It was the look he got just before playing her body like a musical instrument. "This is the bedroom," he said softly.

It was the only room she'd seen which was carpeted. A thick, dark green mantle, like a lush lawn. Another huge fireplace, burning with some fragrant wood, was set in the left hand wall. In the sudden hush, she could hear the crackle and pop as the resin in the wood exploded. In the far corner, so far away she thought she would need binoculars, a door opened onto rich bronze-colored tiles. A bathroom.

Louvered doors covered most of the right hand wall. She supposed they would be the closets.

Here, too, were bookshelves everywhere, filled with what she imagined were his favorite books.

Deep burgundy leather armchairs were angled in front of the fire. There was a Louis XVI secretaire cabinet she had sighed over while reading an auction brochure, knowing she could never afford it. It had been sold for $60,000 to an anonymous bidder, she remembered reading.

At last, she turned to the bed, heart pounding. Obviously custom-made, it was easily double the size of a king, massive and .. and *there*.

His voice was deep in her ear.

"That's where we're going to spend most of our time. And most of the time we spend there, we'll be making love. I want to be inside you."

Isabelle's heart stuttered.

"But first," he murmured, "we have to get you settled in, calmed down. Fed. Relaxed."

She would never be relaxed again. How could she be when just the thought of what they were going to do on that oversized bed was enough to make her mouth dry and her knees tremble?

"Why don't you put on something more comfortable?" Nicholas asked.

Isabelle swallowed and tried to get her nerves under control. "All right." She looked around. "You'll need to carry my suitcase in here, please."

He walked her toward the wall with lacquered louvered doors, a large hand at her back. "That won't be necessary." He reached around her and opened two doors wide. "I've got more or less everything you might need."

Isabelle blinked. The built-in closet, like everything else in the house, was huge, tall and deep. Rack after rack shimmered with the most exquisite collection of clothes she'd ever seen. She reached out a hand to touch a silver lamé evening jacket. Armani. In her size.

"The clothes are new," Nicholas said quietly. "Not another woman's. I ordered them while I was at your place."

The barest glance showed that all the clothes were in styles she would have bought herself if she'd had the money. The color palette was hers, too. Silver, all shades of blue, moss greens, pale peaches. There was easily over a hundred thousand dollars' worth of clothing in that closet. Probably more.

"Is that what you were doing with your laptop?" she asked. He'd sometimes sat hunched over the keyboard while she puttered around the house. "I thought you were making megabucks on the stock market."

"I *was* making megabucks, but I was also asking the boutiques in town to scan and email me some models I thought you might like."

She looked up at him, her heart turning over in her chest at the sight of that strong, impassive face. No, not so impassive. Oddly, he looked slightly anxious, as if wondering whether she'd like what he'd done.

"They're yours," he said, placing his hands on her shoulders. "Afterwards..." he looked away and his jaw muscles bunched. "Afterwards, I want you to keep the clothes."

She didn't make the mistake of protesting. She sensed this was too important to him to refuse.

Isabelle stepped forward, putting her arms around his strong, lean waist and leaning her head against his shoulder. Automatically, his arms went around her. "I'd rather keep you," she whispered.

She could feel his big body jerk and his arms tightened fiercely. He was bending down to kiss her when the black console on an English marquetry side cabinet buzzed. With a sigh and a light kiss, Nicholas released her and pressed a button.

"Yes, Kevin. I'll be right there."

Nicholas turned to her, dark eyes penetrating. "I'm sorry, love. Kevin has strict instructions to contact me only if something important comes up. I have to go see what's happened. Take your time settling in. I ordered dinner to be served in the living room in front of the fire if that's okay with you. We'll meet in about an hour." His mouth tilted up in a half smile. "There's a pale pink silk knit outfit in there. I imagined you wearing it your first night here. Would you wear it for me?"

"Of course," Isabelle said softly. He bent to give her a swift kiss and she watched his broad back as he crossed the large room, the king on his way to check that all was well in the kingdom.

Nicholas stopped at the door and turned around. "Oh, and Isabelle," he said, black eyes boring into hers, "don't wear any underwear."

Chapter Seven

"It doesn't look good, boss."

Nicholas looked down at the papers Kevin had handed him. The pile was thick, but he was quick and in five minutes he understood what Kevin meant.

Separate incidents, but taken together, they were ominous and presaged an assault on RexLine, his largest holding, a sprawling warehouse and shipping complex along the docklands forty miles downriver.

Several hefty payments made into the bank account of the managing director of RexLine. Twenty people suddenly quitting and twenty new hires with ties to Mendoza. Four companies with complaints that goods which had left RexLine's loading bay on container ships had never arrived.

"What do we do?" Kevin asked.

Nicholas appreciated the 'we'. He had no doubt that Kevin took this assault on RexLine personally.

He was fiercely loyal and Nicholas trusted him with his life. More— with Isabelle's life .

"Fire Fred Hamlin," Nicholas said. "And make sure the IRS gets a copy of his bank statements. Keep an eye on the twenty new hires and fire them in batches of two or three. Say we're restructuring. Hire extra guards and have them work undercover in admin and as workers. And, Kevin..."

The young man looked up. "Yeah?"

"Thanks."

Nicholas had been taken off guard for the first time in his life. These were facts he should have caught himself.

It showed him what a fine line he walked. He couldn't afford distractions, ever. Much as he would like to be just an ordinary businessman, he wasn't. Not by a long shot.

The three days he'd spent wrapped up with Isabelle had been three days he hadn't been paying attention and he'd almost paid a hefty price.

God, how he wished his life were different. He'd been forced to do things Isabelle would be appalled at. But he'd done what he'd had to do. He was what he was. Nothing could erase the past.

Mendoza would try to come after him and anyone he loved for the rest of his life. And if something ever happened to Mendoza, there would be another enemy to replace him.

Had he held a faint glimmering of hope that he could somehow keep Isabelle with him, this turn of events had brutally plunged him back into his world. There was no place for Isabelle in it.

Which meant, Nicholas thought, as he strode out of his study, that he'd better enjoy every second of Isabelle while he had her.

Isabelle walked into the living room an hour later.

She'd taken a long, luxurious bath in Nicholas's amazing bathroom, so opulent it was decadent—as large as her living room and kitchen taken together. And the luxuries: a whirlpool, tub as large as a child's swimming pool, multi-headed water massage shower in an enormous glass-brick enclosure, heated towel racks, tanning bed, sauna, connecting exercise room and what seemed like acres of cultured marble countertop.

She'd lain in the whirlpool for almost half an hour, her head against the rim, feeling the water massaging her muscles until the tips of her fingers started wrinkling.

She felt both excited and uncertain as she made her way to the living room. Tonight they would make love fully and she didn't know if she could take it. She breathed deeply at thought of the coming night, of finally having sex with Nicholas.

Foreplay with Nicholas was so exciting she sometimes thought her heart would stop. Last night she had lay naked and spread-eagled on the bed while Nicholas suckled hard at her breasts, his hand moving between her thighs, for what felt like hours. She had climaxed so intensely she had actually lost consciousness for a second or two. Afterwards, she lay completely exhausted in his arms. They listened to the wild drumming of the rain outside her window. Nicholas's slow stroking started turning sensual again and she had protested she had nothing left.

"Oh, yes you do," he'd whispered and brought her to another shattering climax with his hands.

He wouldn't let her touch his penis, but she'd felt it, long and thick and hard. That penis would penetrate her tonight. Finally, she'd feel him inside her.

Isabelle's knees weakened at the thought and she had to grab on to the back of a chair for a second. She knew his size, his stamina and his skill and her heart thudded heavily at the thought of the two of them in the heat and darkness of the night, rolling around on that massive bed.

She was wearing what he'd asked her to. The long pale pink silk skirt with the thigh-high slit whispered sensuously around her legs as she walked.

Nicholas certainly had an eye for what suited her. The outfit was simple—a long buttoned tunic over an ankle length skirt. The luxury was in the delicate color and sumptuous silk knit which flowed like water over her skin.

As Nicholas had asked, she wasn't wearing underwear and she felt completely naked. The smooth silky material highlighted rather than covered her body. She felt wicked and decadent, unused to feeling her breasts swaying lightly without a bra, to being able to see her own nipples, to being aware of her bare genitals as she walked.

She was aroused by the friction of the silk over her bare skin and by the thought that she was so completely accessible to his hands and his mouth.

She stopped at the living room door. Through the open doorway, she could see a long table set for dinner in front of the roaring fire. Those invisible servants, she thought. A white damask tablecloth swept to the black marble floor and a large silver candelabra gave off the only light other than the fire.

She saw him across the large room and her heart rate picked up.

She would never forget the sight as long as she lived. He was in shadow, standing to the side of the massive fireplace, a large hand on the carved granite mantelpiece, the other curved around a glass of amber liquid. He was lost in thought, head bowed.

Just like that, she thought, as she committed the scene to memory. *That's how I'll remember him.*

Outlined against the fire, tall, immensely strong, graceful.

In his underground palace, he looked like a king of ancient times. A monarch of the underworld, strong and powerful but cut off from the world above.

As if he sensed her, Nicholas's head rose suddenly and she heard his sudden intake of breath. Across the distance, his eyes met hers, shadowed and piercing, taking in every detail of her appearance.

His gaze was enough to arouse her completely. As his eyes moved down her body, she could feel her breasts swell, her nipples harden, her sheath grow moist and aching.

He started towards her, walking slowly. His boots might have made a slight noise on the marble flooring but she couldn't hear anything over the pounding of her heart. Her breathing grew shallow as he came up and stopped, so close she had to tilt her head back. He took her hand and lifted it to his mouth.

"You look beautiful, Isabelle," he murmured. "Just as I thought you would." Holding her eyes, his big hand reached out and touched her breast, molding his hand around it, thumbing her nipple. "I imagined you wearing this, and me touching you, just like this."

Isabelle's breath caught. His hand seemed to shoot fire from her breast to her womb. The feeling grew so intense it frightened her, as if he and he alone possessed the secret button to switch her on.

She had been dead, lifeless before she had met Nicholas and now he seemed to have the power to catapult her into a new, frighteningly sensuous world. Her head fell back and she licked her lips as his hand caressed her other breast.

She needed to get herself back again. She straightened and pulled away, walking blindly to the huge window.

It had started to snow, fat lazy flakes for now, drifting slowly and melting before they hit the window pane, but the weather forecast was for a heavy snowfall during the night. The night she would spend in Nicholas Lee's bed.

Even more than before, she felt as if she had been sequestered by the Lord of the Underworld and taken to his subterranean fortress, spirited away from the bustling world she could see across the river.

Nicholas appeared at her back, looming over her. Their eyes met in the reflection of the dark window. She looked pale, insubstantial against his dark strength. He was a head taller than she was, his shoulders almost double the width of hers. Dressed entirely in black, he was like a dark frame for her—a pale column in pink silk.

In the window, she watched him as he pulled a box from his pocket.

"Don't turn around," he whispered. Still holding her gaze in the window, he fixed an earring to her left ear, then the other to her right ear. The earrings were long pendants, a brilliant white which shone brightly in the dark pane, brighter than the floodlights of the city towers.

Isabelle was very much afraid they were diamonds.

"Nicholas, I can't possibly—"

"Shhh."

"Really, I—"

"Not a word," he murmured as he placed his hands on her shoulders, still looking at her reflection, endlessly. She felt like Persephone in Hade's kingdom, helpless in the Dark Lord's grasp.

"You're so lovely," he whispered.

Still holding her gaze, he started unbuttoning the tunic, his hand moving slowly but steadily down. With a gentle flick of his wrists, it slipped from her shoulders. He covered her breasts with his hands.

Watching him touch her and feeling his large, powerful hands caressing her breasts filled her with erotic sensations. He opened his hands and she could see her erect nipples between his fingers. Slowly, slowly, his hands ran down her rib cage, then around to her back.

She couldn't see what he was doing but she could feel and hear. The soft silk skirt loosening, then falling with a whisper to the floor. The sharp hiss of a zipper and his steely erection pressed against her back.

She was completely naked. She watched, and felt, as his hand covered her mound. He was wearing a black sweater; his powerful arm and hand bisected her white belly. Isabelle's breathing grew erratic as he moved through the folds of her sex, stroking her, coaxing moisture from her.

Nicholas bent his dark head to her neck, kissing and sucking and bestowing light nips. Isabelle's legs started shaking as he inserted one long finger inside her, then two.

"I wanted to wait until after dinner," Nicholas whispered, his hand moving slowly inside her. She trembled but she wasn't alone.

His hand was shaking and his breath came in low pants.

"We were going to eat, and then I was going to carry you into the bedroom, undress you slowly and love you half the night before putting my cock in you. But I can't wait," he said harshly.

Holding her apart with two fingers, he bent his knees and she could feel him sliding forward, hot, heavy, enormous, barely inside her. "Brace yourself against the window," he said hoarsely.

She bent forward, her palms against the cool pane of glass, and cried out as he thrust into her, slowly, endlessly, until she could feel the rough hairs of his groin against her bottom. He stretched her—she could feel the tip of him pressing against her womb.

Slowly, slowly, he withdrew then thrust again, then again and again, setting up a heavy driving rhythm, one hand holding her under her breasts, while the fingers of his other hand stroked her clitoris in time with his thrusts.

He curved around her, like a massive falcon mantling its prey. She felt encased in his dark, powerful grip. The sensation was indescribable, impossibly intense. For an instant, she looked up and saw them in the reflection.

She hardly recognized herself—lips puffy with arousal, eyes lost.

Her earrings and breasts swayed as he took her, moving faster and faster as he continued a driving rhythm, pounding into her.

His fingers moved sharply and Isabelle cried out, her orgasm so piercingly strong she thought she would die. He kept rocking inside her throughout the spasms, harder and harder until he, too, stiffened and cried out and poured himself endlessly into her.

Her heart beat in time with his and she knew she would never be the same again. Nicholas was wrapped around her, still shuddering. Isabelle didn't know how long her legs would hold out, how long she could hold his heavy weight.

Their labored breathing sounded loud in the large, silent room.

Nicholas slowly straightened, eyes closed. He pulled out of her so slowly it brought tears to her eyes at the loss. His eyes opened and met hers in the dark glass. Stooping to pick up her clothes, he bent to kiss her neck and then dressed her gently, as if she were a child.

Isabelle's muscles felt like water. She would never have been able to dress herself. She was still quivering inside.

Le petit mort, the French called the moment of orgasm. The little death.

Truly, she felt as if her soul had fled her body and then had come back, transformed. Every sense was amplified—she could feel the air moving in and out of her lungs; Nicholas, strong at her back; she thought she could see every snowflake now drifting in waves from the sky; she could hear the fire, the soft crackle sounding like a loud roar to her too-alive senses.

Gently, Nicholas turned her around and walked her one step backwards, until she bumped her back against the window. His hands bracketed her face and his eyes bored into hers.

"I couldn't wait. I wanted our first time to be in bed, but I simply couldn't wait."

He bent and touched his lips to hers in the gentlest of kisses, softly softly. Isabelle held on to his forearms as he kissed her endlessly, tenderly, as if it were their first kiss. As if they hadn't just had the most raw, carnal sex of her life.

Gently, slowly, the kiss went on forever. She was floating in his arms, her heart lifting. Tears pricked behind her eyelids, the sensation was so sweet. Her heart swelled as he kept the kiss light, oh so light and gentle, as if he were courting her with his mouth alone. As if he hadn't been in her a few minutes before.

He lifted his mouth a moment and she remembered to breathe. "All night, Isabelle," he whispered against her temple. "I'm going to make love to you all night long."

Isabelle's hand crept up to cup his cheek. She felt so buffeted by emotions—the excitement of his lovemaking, the fierceness of his sensuality, shock at his astonishing tenderness.

"But first," he smiled, "I'd better feed you." Nicholas took her hand and led her to the table. He seated her and lifted the silver domes covering the oversized platters. Wonderful smells drifted up and Isabelle smiled dreamily. All her senses were going to be pleased tonight. He deftly uncorked the champagne and poured.

He tapped her glass with his, the clear crystal ring of the glasses quivering in the air, and she sipped. It was icy, dry, delicious. "To us," he said softly.

"To us," she echoed.

The only light came from the huge fireplace, casting a warm intimate glow over the table. The rest of the room was in shadow. The only noise came from the crackling, popping fire and the ting of silver against china. Outside, the snow silently swirled wildly. Isabelle wished suddenly, fiercely that it would just keep on snowing, for days, weeks, months. She wished they could be snowed in forever, just the two of them.

"Open up," Nicholas ordered and her smiling mouth opened. They were at dessert, a luscious tiramisù.

Another spoonful. "Again."

Isabelle shook her head at the spoon heaped with chocolate and cream. "No," she said on a sigh. Delicious as it was, she was full.

"Had enough?" His voice was a deep rumble. He put the spoon down.

"Yes, I—" Isabelle jumped as he pulled aside her skirt and placed a large, hard hand on the inside of her thigh. Her breath came in on a long, shaky stream as his hand moved up then down to caress her knee. He slowly trailed his fingers back up again and stroked the folds of her sex.

Oh God. She couldn't think when he did that. He stroked her vulva slowly, delicately, and she could feel a rush of moisture there, making her slick. His hands had worked magic on her before, when that was all she knew of making love with him. But now that she had felt his penis in her, knew how hard and thick it was, knew how it could fill her... *oh God.* She whimpered as his thumb slowly circled her clitoris.

Nicholas leaned over and kissed her, his mouth slow and hot. His tongue mimicked what his hand was doing. Slowly penetrating, then retreating, leaving heat and longing in its wake.

Needing an anchor, Isabelle curved her hand around the strong column of his neck.

"Open for me," he whispered. She didn't know whether he meant her mouth or her legs. She opened both and was instantly rewarded. His mouth slanted over hers, biting her lips, then plunging his tongue deep into her mouth. His fingers penetrated her harder, deeper. He pulled her tightly against him as he lifted his mouth from hers. His fingers kept stroking strongly, the rhythm increasing as he watched her. Isabelle's mouth was open as she tried to drag more air into her lungs. She was burning up, on the knife's edge of exploding.

"Don't wear underwear while you're here. Ever." Nicholas's voice was low and deep. "Wear things I can unbutton easily, pants I can open quickly, skirts I can pull up. I want you open to me, day and night. I want to be able to fuck you anywhere, any time."

He circled her opening again, now completely wet with her juices. His eyes never left hers. When his thumb brushed her clitoris, Isabelle cried out, shaking. "Nicholas!"

"No! Not yet. I want you to come with my cock in you." Nicholas surged to his feet, sweeping her up in his arms. He strode quickly to the bedroom as she clung to him, almost too dazed to realize what was going on. The bedroom, too, was in shadows except for the fire burning in the grate. Nicholas quickly stripped her and put her down on the bed. She was grateful for the cool sheets against her back. They anchored her, brought her back from the fevered place of pleasure she'd been drowning in.

Good.

She wanted to remember clearly every moment with Nicholas. She'd waited 26 years to feel this way and deep in her heart she knew she would never experience anything like this, ever again. These were memories she would take out and examine during the long lonely years stretching endlessly ahead of her. She wanted to live these moments to the fullest.

Nicholas looked down at her in his bed for a long moment. Isabelle knew that he was fixing this moment in his memory, too.

Without taking his eyes off her, he shucked off his shirt. His hands went to the buckle of his pants. Isabelle watched in fascination the bulge and play of muscles as he stripped, letting his clothes fall soundlessly to the thick carpet.

He was magnificent. A male animal in its prime. The power and grace evident in every line of his big body took her breath away. He was the only man alive who could turn her liquid with desire.

The fire burning at his back rimmed his body in an orange glow, like an eclipsed sun. He leaned down to grasp her ankle, as if even that short separation from her body were too much to bear. His engorged penis lay flat against the hard muscles of his abdomen, reaching almost to his navel. He was as beautiful here as he was everywhere else. He opened his hand to run his fingers along her leg, tracing her calf, trailing up her thigh, then cupping her mound.

Isabelle opened her arms and legs and heart. "No foreplay, Nicholas," she whispered. "I don't need it. All I need is you."

With a groan, he lowered himself over her. He braced himself on his elbows and entered her with one hard thrust. She cried out in surprise and shock. He held himself still. "You okay?" he whispered.

She couldn't answer, couldn't form the words. Her body did the speaking for her as she began the sharp contractions of orgasm. He smiled down at her and started moving—slow, deep thrusts, as steady as the sea tide. His heavy movements inside her prolonged the contractions. Her thighs opened wider and she locked her ankles behind his back, her heels riding his buttocks as he moved inside her.

She was drowning in mind-numbing pleasure. Isabelle held him as he rode her, her arms barely reaching around the immense shoulders. The muscles along his back felt as hard as concrete slabs. A drop of sweat from his face fell on her shoulder and she opened her eyes.

Nicholas's face was taut with concentration, jaw muscles bunched, eyes tightly closed. He was controlling himself, holding himself back.

Isabelle turned her head and licked his ear, smiling as he shuddered. She arched herself even more tightly against him, rubbing her nipples against his chest, rotating her hips, curling her fingernails into his back. Nicholas trembled and another drop of sweat fell on the pillow.

"Let yourself go, Nicholas," she whispered.

"I'm… afraid I'll hurt you," he gasped.

"The only way you can hurt me is by not loving me. Love me, Nicholas, love me hard."

Her words were like a starter gun to a race horse. He bucked, then started hammering into her. She shuddered with the force of his thrusts, opening herself to him as completely as a woman can.

As she held him, as she listened to his groans, as she felt his heart pounding next to hers, she knew, with exultation and despair, that she had never been as happy as this before. And never would be again.

Chapter Eight

New Year's Eve

Our last night together, Nicholas thought as he searched the depths of the glass of whiskey in his hand. There were no answers in the amber liquid as to how he was going to live without Isabelle. However much he tried to drown his rage and grief in alcohol, it wasn't working.

He stared at the door to the bathroom, waiting for Isabelle to emerge. They were going out tonight for the first time. They hadn't left his house and they hadn't seen another human being in the past ten days. Tonight was a commitment Isabelle had taken months before. She had offered to cancel and he'd been tempted, but she needed to move on with her life after he pushed her out of his. It wasn't fair to ask her to forego something that would further her in her career.

Nicholas would have ripped the heart out of any man who tried to stand between him and Isabelle. The irony was that *he* was that man. He would find the strength to put Isabelle out of his life, even though his heart felt as though it were being ripped out of his chest. Taking another huge gulp of whiskey, he savored the burn down to his stomach.

He contemplated another useless swallow when the door to the bathroom opened. Nicholas looked up and his breath tangled in his throat.

She floated towards him, graceful as a princess, lovely as moonlight. She had on a long silver beaded jacket over a floor-length multi-layered chiffon skirt, her long, slender legs barely visible through the layers of sheer material.

There wasn't a man alive who wouldn't try to make her his and, after tonight, Nicholas thought bleakly, after tonight any man was free to try. Free to fuck her.

He heard a crack and glanced down blankly at his hand. The smell of spilled whiskey drifted up to him. He'd crushed the shot glass.

"Oh, Nicholas," Isabelle said in dismay. "You've hurt yourself. You're bleeding." She rushed back into the bathroom and came out with a cotton towel.

Nicholas stared down at her shiny platinum hair as she bent over his hand to bandage the small cut. She had her hair up in a complicated style and had put on makeup. Already she looked different from the woman he'd shared his heart and his bed with for the past ten days. The makeup emphasized that she was going back out into the world now, after having been secluded with him.

She was going back out into the world where men would look at her and desire her.

Isabelle's eyes widened as Nicholas rose on a rush.

"Nicholas?"

He couldn't touch her hair, kiss her mouth, as he wanted to. He could only touch her where it wouldn't show. He stroked the soft skin of her neck and felt the life pulsing through a vein. How many times had he touched her, caressed her, stroking, feeling her skin warm under his touch.

"Yes," she murmured, knowing from his touch what he wanted. She exhaled softly, her head falling slightly to one side, a rose too heavy for its stem.

He reached out to unbutton her jacket and her eyes closed. "Isabelle." His voice was the merest whisper as he slid the jacket off her shoulders. It fell soundlessly to the carpet and her lace bra followed.

He cupped her breasts. He loved the heavy feel of them and had spent hours fondling them, suckling them. Her eyes closed as his thumbs rubbed over her nipples.

"Christ, you're lovely." His voice came out low and rough.

When they came back tonight, he intended to get in her and stay in her all night but now, right now, his hunger was sharp-edged, as if he'd never had her and would die if he couldn't enter her *now*.

He couldn't get the image of another man's hands touching her, another man's cock inside her, out of his head. It drove him crazy and his hands turned rough as he opened her skirt and pushed it down.

She had on sheer silk stockings held up with lace garters and panties. With a low, maddened growl, he ripped her panties off and pulled her to him. He turned with her held in one arm. With the other he swept his desk clear. A vase and books thudded to the carpet but he was beyond caring as he lay her down on the smooth cherrywood surface.

He stopped a moment, checked by the sight of her long pale figure laid out like a sacrifice, naked except for the garter, the stockings and strappy sandals. He was hard as a rock, his penis straining to be inside her. "I need you, Isabelle," he muttered, opening her legs by stepping between them. "I need you so much."

Her eyes opened and their gazes locked. "I'm yours, Nicholas," she whispered. "I always will be."

His own eyes closed in pain. His hands shook as they traveled up her long legs. His thumbs opened her and he dropped to his knees.

She was as beautiful here as she was everywhere else, smooth folds of skin surrounded by fine gold hairs. The pale pink lips he'd entered countless times slowly deepened in color as he stroked her gently. He watched as his fingers coaxed the cream of arousal from her. Her back arched and she moaned as he slid first one finger then a second finger into her, touching her as he knew she loved to be touched.

He brought his mouth to her and heard her sharp intake of breath. He kissed her deeply, exactly as if he were kissing her mouth. His tongue circled her clitoris then slid lower to plunge back into her vagina. His thumbs opened her wider as his tongue imitated his cock. Isabelle's thighs shook and she suddenly cried out and pulsed against his mouth. He could feel, taste her climax. Rising swiftly, he opened his pants and thrust into her hard, gritting his teeth to keep still as she continued climaxing.

She'd thrown her arms up over her head and lay stretched out before him, pale and slender, impaled on his cock. Her breasts shook with the force of her wildly beating heart. The pulsing of her vagina matched her pulse beats and he could feel himself become impossibly harder inside her.

As the contractions faded away, Isabelle opened her eyes. "God, Nicholas," she whispered, sounding dazed.

"Rise up," he said harshly and waited until she levered herself up on her elbows. "Look at us." He used his thumbs to open her more fully to his gaze and hers. "Look."

Flexing his buttocks, he pushed with the force of his hips until he felt the tip of her womb. He clenched his jaw and pushed further. The hairs at the root of his sex meshed with hers, jet black and pale gold. He ground against her, opening her up even more to his possession. "Mine," he gritted, his voice guttural. "All mine."

"Yours," Isabelle breathed.

They stared at each other, joined in every way a man and a woman could be joined, sex to sex, heart to heart, gaze to gaze.

Nicholas was the first to look away. He closed his eyes and leaned back. His hands gripped her hips hard enough to bruise and he began thrusting with all the strength of his body, hard and fast, in a hammering rhythm which he knew would have hurt her if she hadn't already climaxed. For all the force of his thrusts, he could feel her sheath soft and wet and welcoming.

His passion was too violent to last. A hot wire flashed down his spine, his back prickled. It was as if a freight train barreled into him and he erupted in her, jetting in wild spurts so intense he shuddered under the impact. His orgasm seemed to last for hours as he shook and groaned and spilled into her.

His knees were trembling as he pulled slowly out of her. Amazingly, he was still semi-erect even after that shattering orgasm. He could never get enough of Isabelle.

Capable of gentleness at last, his fingers closed over hers and he pulled her slowly up. Her fingers clutched his, silver eyes wide in a pale face. She'd been as affected as he had by the intense sex. A pulse beat wildly in her throat. He lowered his lips to lick along the vein, teeth closing on the nerve in her neck. Isabelle arched, moaning.

Nicholas slid his other hand around her back and down to her buttocks, helping her off the table.

"This is our last night together."

"I know." She shuddered.

His voice was strained to make its way past the constriction in his throat. "Men will look at you tonight, but you're not going to be aware of them. You're only going to be aware of *me*." He bent to pick up the beaded jacket, ignoring her bra which had fallen nearby. He slipped the jacket up her arms and paused. Arching her over his arm, he suckled slowly at one breast, then the other. When he finally lifted his head, her nipples were wet and distended, flushed a deep pink. He pulled the jacket up over her shoulders and buttoned it, his knuckles brushing against the soft skin of her breasts.

"They'll be talking to you and you won't hear a word because you'll be feeling your nipples against the material all night. All you'll be able to think about is my mouth on you, sucking hard."

She drew in a sharp breath.

He kicked away her torn panties and held her skirt open. Shakily, she stepped into it, one hand on his shoulder to balance herself.

Nicholas slid his hand under the skirt and felt his semen on her thighs. "And all evening," he whispered, his voice harsh and ragged. "All evening you'll feel my come in you and you'll remember my cock moving in you, filling you." He moved his hand further up and caressed her, slick and warm.

"When no one's looking, I'm going to take you around a corner and touch you like this and make you come." He bent his head to her neck as his finger explored her sheath. His voice was a mere breath against her skin. He could smell her sweet fragrance and the smell of sex. Other men would smell it, too, and he intended to make sure that there be no doubt about the man she'd had sex with. He pressed more deeply into her until he felt her sharp intake of breath and then a moan. "You won't think of anyone but me." His thumb circled her clitoris and he shuddered. "No one but me, Isabelle. No one."

She tugged sharply at his hair and he lifted his head. Her pupils were dilated and her hand trembled as she caressed his cheek.

"There *is* no one but you," she whispered.

Our last night together, Isabelle thought five hours later as she and Nicholas stood outside his house for the last time.

She looked up at that hard, beloved face, drinking in his features. After tonight, she'd never see him again. She bitterly resented having had to share him these past hours.

They'd been to an elegant reception at the Marriott, hosted by a major publishing house. She'd been the keynote speaker. Isabelle would have given anything to spend her last evening alone with Nicholas but the contract had been signed six months earlier. This night was significant if only because this was the first and last time she'd been in society with him.

For the past ten days, they hadn't set foot outside his palatial fortress. Each day, he'd offered to take her anywhere she wanted to go. To the finest restaurants. To first run movies. To all the most popular plays, including those for which tickets were impossible to find. He'd even offered to hire a jet to take her to Aruba for a few days.

When he'd asked, her answer was always the same—*I want to stay home with you*. His face always relaxed at her words.

They hadn't needed the outside world at all. Both of them had been perfectly content to spend their time together watching videos, playing chess and going for a swim in his heated indoor pool as the snowflakes drifted past the window.

And making love, endlessly.

She remembered his hard words, and how shocked she'd been at them.

I want to make you scream with pleasure, over and over again. I want to fuck you so much your body will be molded to mine, your cunt shaped to my cock, your skin smelling of me. I want you to forget where you end and I begin.

It had been nothing less than the truth. Her body was so attuned to his, she couldn't begin to understand how she could live without him. But somehow she would have to because this time tomorrow night she'd be back in her own home, alone.

Isabelle shivered as Nicholas put his palm to the scanner and the entrance door hissed open.

She stepped slowly forward. The next time she crossed that threshold, she would be leaving. Forever.

Snow had fallen all evening, but now the clouds had cleared and a million bright stars shone, remote and cold and beautiful. The deep mantle of snow reflected the light of the full moon, almost as bright as day.

They descended, Nicholas's hand at her waist. He'd never been more than a hand span's distance from her all evening. She shifted and felt her nipples brush against the heavy silk of her evening jacket.

He'd been right. His lovemaking had sensitized her body so much that she could hardly think of anything but being possessed by him. She felt him everywhere—her breasts, her belly, between her thighs.

She'd given her speech and, judging from the applause and the delighted look of the author and his publisher, she'd been successful. She had made literary small talk with two editors, a journalist-turned-book reviewer for the *New York Times Book Review*, a world famous publisher, and the editor-in-chief of the local newspaper. They, too, had shown signs of interest in what she was saying, though she couldn't remember what had come out of her mouth. She didn't care about Mailer's retro machismo or the structure of Joyce Carol Oates' latest novel.

Not with Nicholas brushing his hand down her arm, standing so close behind her she could feel his body heat, his arm around her waist.

The slightest sway brought her up against that powerfully muscled body. All it took was one glance out of heavy-lidded eyes and she could feel her body preparing itself for him. Her nipples beaded and she had to clench her thighs against the sharp desire, so sensitized by his lovemaking just moments before leaving the house that it was almost as if she could still feel him, hot and hard and deep inside her.

She'd found it impossible to concentrate on anything but him.

Before midnight, he'd quietly suggested they leave and she'd agreed, relieved that the charade was finally over. She wasn't interested in talking to or being with anyone but Nicholas.

There would be time enough tomorrow to have pleasant cocktail party conversations with her wide circle of acquaintances.

The rest of her life, in fact.

She wasn't going to cry.

She'd promised herself that. It would only make her anguish deeper and make Nicholas suffer. She didn't want to do that. She loved him.

Of everyone there tonight—the best and the brightest the city and the state could offer—the only one she'd really wanted to talk to was Nicholas.

She wanted to know what he thought about the book she'd presented and its overly anxious author, she wanted to know whether he'd found the Senator's prissy wife as ridiculous as she did and whether he agreed that the champagne was too sweet.

Isabelle could spend the rest of her life with only Nicholas and be happy.

Pity she wouldn't be given the chance to find out.

Her eyes stung with unshed tears and she lifted her face to his, wanting—no, *needing*—his touch. He must have been watching her because he immediately bent to take her mouth. She opened to him, reveling in his taste, familiar and yet wildly exciting, like nothing she'd ever tasted in her life.

The elevator came to a smooth stop and he lifted his head, dark eyes glittering. "Isabelle," he said, his voice low and rough. "I—"

The elevator doors slid open. The chandelier came to life and Isabelle looked out into the atrium and cried out in shock.

Nicholas went past her in a rush, a dark lethal shadow, moving so quickly he was a blur.

Isabelle could hardly take in what she was seeing. Kevin—Nicholas's right hand man—lying in the center of the marble floor in a pool of blood, half his head blown away.

Nicholas pulling aside a painting and slapping his hand against a panel. A flash of green and then he was pulling guns out of a safe in the wall. Isabelle didn't even have time to see how many weapons he had pulled out when, with another slap at the panel, the room was plunged into darkness.

She felt a strong hand clamp down on her arm and then they were running. Despite the darkness he ran straight, pulling her after him. She didn't even have time to protest. Loud reports echoed in the huge room as bright flashes seared the darkness.

Someone was shooting at them.

Nicholas plunged to the ground, rolling with her, ending up against a wall, his body protecting hers. Bullets hit the wall above them, where they'd been a second before. She closed her eyes as plaster dust rained down.

"They're all dead, Lee," a harsh voice with a faint Hispanic accent called out. "Everyone's dead in this house and you and your lady friend will be, too."

Nicholas's hand tightened on her arm at the sound of the voice. His entire body was hard and tense.

"When I start shooting, run with me to the living room. The door is five feet to your right." Nicholas's voice was low in her ear, so soft the sound couldn't possibly carry. She put her cheek against his and nodded to show she understood. His mouth touched her ear. "On the count of three."

He tapped her arm once. She tried to draw in her breath without making any noise. He tapped again and she pulled up into a crouch.

Three.

They were up and running, Nicholas a strong presence at her back. Slamming the door open, he pushed her through, turning for a second, weapon drawn and streaked a continuous blur of fire into the room. Isabelle heard him grunt, then heard a scream as he hit one of the men in the atrium.

He pulled the door shut behind them, Nicholas twisting until she heard the loud, solid click of the lock. A fusillade of bullets whined harmlessly against the steel door and Isabelle blessed Nicholas's obsession with security. They were safe for the moment.

Nicholas pulled something from his jacket pocket and reloaded his gun's magazine, the movements practised and smooth. The magazine slid home with a soft click.

"Lee!" The deep voice outside sounded maddened. "You're a walking dead man. You and that woman you've got there—you'll never walk away. I've got Semtex and I'm going to blow that door right off its hinges. And then I'm coming in after you, you fucker. And then I'll take over your business—me. Luis Mendoza."

Nicholas took her arm and rushed her towards the fireplace.

There were scrabbling sounds on the other side of the door and Isabelle drew in a terrified breath as she leaned her hands against the wall for a moment. Shock must be running through her system because she saw red.

No, her hands really were red. She looked down with a frown. How...

Nicholas staggered and she almost slipped as she took his full weight for a second. And then she saw the bloody mass that was his side.

"Oh my God," she breathed. "You're hit."

Her hands and her whole right side were drenched with his blood. Frantically, she bent to rip a large strip out of her skirt. She bunched the material against his side to create a pressure bandage, cursing the fact that her terror made her clumsy. She ripped another piece of skirt and tried to wrap it around his waist.

Nicholas's hands stopped her. She looked up, numbly, terrified to see the pallor beneath his dark skin.

"Don't do that, love," he said gently. "It's not necessary."

"What do you mean?" He must have lost even more blood than she thought. "We've got to pack your wound."

"Isabelle..." Abruptly, Nicholas's legs gave way. He slid down the wall next to the fireplace, leaving a trail of blood, and Isabelle knelt next to him. There were loud scratching noises on the other side of the door and Isabelle could hear the voices of at least three men, maybe more. The whine of a drill started up.

"They're setting the charge," Nicholas said. He leaned his head against the wall and closed his eyes. Isabelle reached around him to tighten the bandage. Blood had already seeped through. She worked frantically, hoping the bullet hadn't taken an artery or a vital organ.

"You have to go," Nicholas said. His voice was weaker now, his breathing labored. He grunted in pain when she pressed down on the bandage, hoping to stop the steady flow of blood. Beads of sweat appeared on his face.

"Are you crazy?" She took his hands and her heart gave a lurch. They were stone cold. Nicholas, whose body was a furnace. "Come on, stand up," she said. "You can do it." She tried to fit her shoulder under his arm. Tears ran down her face and she wiped them on his sleeve. "Come on, darling. Get up."

Nicholas didn't budge. Slowly, he reached into his pocket, grimacing with pain. He pulled out a gun and pressed it into her hand. It was small, gray, light. He curled her hand around the stock.

"That's a Colt 22, Isabelle. It's a semi automatic. All you need to do is aim and keep pulling the trigger. Put your thumb here—" he guided her hand and she heard a small ominous snick. "The safety's off now. It's ready to shoot."

Isabelle opened her mouth and he put a finger across her lips, leaving bloody stains. His eyes bored into hers, willing her to pay attention.

"Mendoza won't stop until I'm dead and he'll have to kill you, too. I won't—" Nicholas broke off and his jaw muscles jumped as he struggled against the wave of pain. "I won't let him. Listen, Isabelle," he said with urgency, his voice a harsh whisper. "Next to the fireplace is a secret passage out of here. Press the third wood panel and it opens up. At the end of the passageway is a keypad. The code is 7928. Press the numbers and then run as fast as you can. Four minutes later, this house will blow up. You have to do it quickly before Mendoza gets here. Mendoza has to die now, otherwise you'll never be free."

Isabelle stared at him numbly . He was asking her to... "No!" she cried. "I'd kill you, too. I can't do that, Nicholas. Don't ask me to."

"I'm a dead man already." He gripped her arm, his fingers digging into her flesh. "Do what I say, Isabelle," he gritted. "I can't risk having Mendoza leave here alive. He'll come after you. You'd never—" He gasped and gritted his teeth. "*Do what I say, dammit!*"

He was sweating profusely now, lines of pain bracketing that beautiful mouth. Isabelle studied his face, the face of the man she loved. She'd never thought to have love in her life, but now she'd found it. Nicholas was the greatest miracle of her life.

No way was she going to lose him.

She was going to have to move quickly. The drilling on the other side of the door had stopped. She had no idea how long it took to set charges, but she suspected not long. Soon, Mendoza and his men would come blazing through the door.

Standing, she picked up the gun Nicholas had been using. It was huge, heavy and lethal-looking. She knew it was fully loaded.

Whipping off a tablecloth, she barely heard the sound of broken crockery and a pewter bowl rolling around on the marble floor. She bunched the tablecloth at Nicholas's side, taking away the bloody bandage. Holding the bloody material carefully, she wrung the bandage as she walked to the window, leaving a trail of blood spatters a blind man couldn't miss.

There is no such thing as bullet-proof glass, she remembered reading. Only bullet resistant.

Let's see if you resist *this*, she thought, bringing the muzzle of the gun up until it rested against the pane and pulled the trigger. The massive gun bucked in her hands, but she kept it pressed against the pane, moving it in as large a circle as she could. The blasts rang in her ears and her hands became numb as she kept pressure on the trigger.

Finally, she ran out of ammunition. A circle of holes starred the dark pane. She had no idea if her idea would work, but she was willing to die trying. Isabelle looked around desperately for something solid and heavy. In the corner next to the door was a wrought iron floor lamp. She pulled out the plug and dragged the heavy lamp to the window.

There was a sudden silence from the other side of the door. It could only mean one thing. The charge had been set and Mendoza and his men had backed away so they wouldn't be hurt by the blast.

She had mere seconds left.

Holding the lamp in front of her like a battering ram, Isabelle charged at the window, striking the pane in the middle of the circle. The stars widened but the pane held. Panting, she backed away and charged again. Diagonal cracks appeared. She charged again and... *yes!* Chunks of pane fell away. Wielding the floor lamp like a bat, she swung again and again until an opening three feet across had been created.

Outside the door, she heard a male voice cry out. "Twenty."

She had twenty seconds.

Running back to Nicholas, she crouched down to look into his eyes. Though his face was pinched and white, his gaze was sharp and aware.

He reached out with his big hand and caressed her face, leaving a bloody trail. "God, I... love you."

"I know, darling." Isabelle managed to get the words out past the huge lump in her throat.

"Go now, Isabelle." His voice was a mere whisper.

"Nicholas," she said. "You're going to die."

He nodded and closed his eyes.

"And I'm going to die, too."

His eyes snapped open again. "No!" he croaked. "Get out of here!"

"Ten!" a man called from the other side of the door.

"Both of us are going to die and then we're going to live again. Somewhere far away. We're going to start a new life together somewhere else, where no one knows who we are. We're going to leave our past behind us. But first you've got to get up, Nicholas." Isabelle bent down to him and tried to lift, grunting with the strain. "Help me here."

He shook his head.

"Nicholas," she whispered. "*Please.* I'm not leaving here without you."

His eyes looked intently into hers and she knew he could read the truth of what she said. She wasn't leaving without him. Either they lived together or they died together.

He gritted his teeth and Isabelle gave up a silent prayer of thanks as his legs bunched under him and he stood. He shook, but he managed to stand on his own two feet. She walked them to the side of the fireplace.

"Five!"

With her shoulder under Nicholas's arm, she reached out and touched the third panel. Nothing.

"Four!"

She started to panic when suddenly it swung smoothly open. She stared into the dark corridor.

"Three!"

Nicholas staggered and Isabelle braced herself against the wall. "Nicholas, *please*..." she whispered. "We have to make it out together."

"Two!"

"If you love me, Nicholas ... *move!*"

"One!"

Nicholas lurched forward and Isabelle half-carried, half-dragged him through the door. It hissed shut behind them as a muffled explosion sounded in the next room.

Isabelle shuffled forward as fast as she could. Nicholas's arm was heavy around her shoulders and she bore most of his weight. She didn't know how long she could last but was grimly determined to take him with her or die in this corridor.

"They're going to think we escaped through the window. It's a straight drop down but it's dark and they won't know if we had equipment with us or not. Put your left foot forward, Nicholas, then your right. That's wonderful, you can do this, darling. You're the strongest man I've ever met. Did I ever get a chance to tell you how much I love you?" She sneaked a glance up and saw his lips curve faintly in his pale face. He shook his head.

"I didn't think so. There wasn't any point before, was there? We were never going to see each other again, so what was the use of telling you that leaving you was going to break my heart? Keep moving, Nicholas, you can do it."

She kept talking, hoping to distract him. He shuffled along like an old man, barely lifting his feet. The corridor stretched before them on a sharp incline, dimly lit with a few neon lights. She had no idea how long this passage would go on. However long, though, they would walk it.

"My best friend in college went on to get a degree in medicine, did you know that? She lives about twenty miles from here." Nicholas's eyes were closed. "Open your eyes, Nicholas, and listen to me."

He looked down at her, eyes slightly glazed. She shook him and he swayed. It was terrifying to see a man as powerful and vital as Nicholas look so weak. "Listen to me, damn it. Listen. We're going to live. We're going to go to my friend and she'll take care of that bullet wound and I'll take care of you until you recover. And then you're going to get us some false documents and we'll get out of the country. But right now, my darling, I need for you to walk out of this place. I need you to help me. Can you do that? I love you so much and I don't want to live if you die and I need you to help me *now*. Can you do that?"

"Yes."

Isabelle closed her eyes in relief. His voice was weak, barely a croak, but she heard his determination. She had no idea where he found the energy, what depths of reserves he had to dip into, but miraculously, he straightened.

She nearly gasped in relief as some of the pressure lifted from her shoulders. She hurried them as fast as she dared. Nicholas staggered but was upright.

The nightmare trip up the steep incline seemed to take hours. She dripped with sweat and Nicholas swayed on his feet when she finally saw the steel door at the end of the corridor.

Wheezing, she leaned against the corridor wall for a moment, allowing her screaming muscles a chance to rest, then pushed away again.

A thump came from far behind them and Isabelle's heart clenched. Her red herring hadn't fooled Mendoza and his men for long. He'd found the secret passageway and they would be coming through any moment. They were strong, healthy men. She had no idea how long the corridor was but they would come up running.

"Nicholas." She glanced at him. He was slumped against the door, breathing hard. "Darling, do you have the keys to the car on you?"

Opening his eyes, he stared blankly at her. She didn't think he understood what she'd said. Hands shaking, Isabelle reached into his pants pocket, sending up a prayer of gratitude as she felt a key chain and the remote control to open the gates.

From behind them came the sound of an explosion. Isabelle felt the heat and the rush of air. She punched the numbers into the key pad and pushed Nicholas out the door. They were at the entrance. Some god was looking down at them and protecting them. Nicholas's Lexus was only three feet away.

By her side, Nicholas lurched and fell to the ground. Isabelle fell on her knees beside him. Frantic, she put her fingers to his neck and cried out as she felt a thready pulse. He was unconscious, not dead, and she sagged in relief.

She still held a section of tablecloth and ripped the last piece into a long thin strip. Grunting, she turned Nicholas over on his back, terrified at his waxen pallor. *Please God, let him live*, she repeated to herself over and over.

Twisting the strip to make it more resistant, Isabelle tied his wrists together, looped his tied hands around her neck and shuffled forward, pulling his body after her. The snow lay heavy on the ground and it must have been at least ten below but she was sweating profusely by the time she dragged him to the car.

Grunting, terrified, she managed to get him up and into the back seat. Running around to the driver's side, she got behind the wheel just as the door to the corridor opened and men spilled out.

Isabelle took off with a squeal of tires and the driver's door still open, punching frantically at the remote control to open the gates.

Shots sparked off the reinforced steel gates as the men started shooting. She slid on the ice and a bullet went straight through the back window and out the front window of the passenger seat scattering shards of glass all over the car. She brushed the glass from her lap, barely noticing the cuts in her hands. The blood made the steering wheel slippery and she tightened her grip.

She accelerated hard, aiming at the gates. She didn't dare stop and prayed that a bullet wouldn't blow out a tire. Sobbing, she drove straight towards the still-closed gate, stabbing at the remote.

Slowly, the gates started opening. Another bullet hit the back of the car and she almost lost control. She floored the accelerator and shot through the gates with barely an inch to spare.

Skidding wildly on the icy road, Isabelle fought the wheel as the car made a complete circle. She had no idea which direction she should go in. All she knew was she had to get away *now*.

The wheels spun, then bit into a rough patch and she shot down the street. In the rear view mirror she could see the first of Mendoza's men run out the gate. He stood in the middle of the road and assumed the gunman's stance, feet braced apart, weapon held in both hands. She watched in the mirror, knowing he was close enough to take them down. The man brought the weapon up and steadied.

The explosion ripped the calm night air. The gunman was blown sideways as a bright flash nearly blinded her. A fiery cloud rose up into the night sky, followed by smoke billowing up. The roar came a second later.

Isabelle concentrated on the road ahead and was astonished to see an explosion on the horizon, ahead of her instead of behind her. She wondered if she was hallucinating, then recognized the stars and pinwheels and brightly colored bursts of joyful light.

Fireworks.

It was midnight. The new year had begun.

Isabelle drove into the sparkling night.

Epilogue

A thousand people had seen Isabelle Summerby and Nicholas Lee together at the Arkana Publishing Corporation reception at the Marriott and had seen them leave together. When no trace could be found of Isabelle Summerby, it was assumed that she had gone home with Lee and perished in the blast.

Isabelle Summerby's tragic and untimely death shocked the community. Her TV station, WKRC, dedicated a ten minute special to her memory.

The police investigated the explosion, but no tears were shed at the deaths of Nicholas Lee and Luis Mendoza. The case was considered closed.

Six months after the explosion, a couple travelling on Maltese passports settled on Kondalu, a tropical island an hour away by plane from Fiji. The mysterious couple kept very much to themselves. The locals knew only that the husband seemed to have more money than God and was crazily in love with his beautiful and bookish wife.

About the Author:

Lisa Marie Rice is eternally 30 years old and will never age. She is tall and willowy and beautiful. Men drop at her feet like ripe pears. She has won every major book prize in the world. She is a black belt with advanced degrees in archeology, nuclear physics and Tibetan literature. She is a concert pianist. Did I mention the Nobel? Of course, Lisa Marie Rice is a virtual woman and exists only at the keyboard when writing erotic romance. She disappears when the monitor winks off.

Flights of Fantasy

by Bonnie Hamre

To My Reader:

I am *thrilled* to be back in a Red Sage collection! Since my first two Regency novellas in *Secrets* 1 and 2, the collections have generated fantastic reader appeal and I have to tell you, I'm impressed.

I hope you'll enjoy this story about a stressed-out, seen-it-all contemporary woman with a very specific fantasy, and a determined, no-holds-barred man...

Chapter One

Chloe Atkinson dropped her duffel bag on the dock and stared. She'd been wondering what to expect, but never in her wildest fantasies did she dream of a sea-going Taj Mahal. It was too late to catch it on film now, but maybe she'd have another chance to capture the sunset tones of russet, peach and rose washing over the sleek silhouette of the yacht anchored in Monterey Harbor.

"Ma'am?"

She glanced behind her. A young man dressed neatly in dark pants, dark tie and a white shirt with nautical insignia on shoulder epaulets, looked expectantly at her. "Ms. Atkinson? Mr. Yancy is expecting you. You're the last guest to arrive."

Guest wouldn't exactly be the right word. Hostage? Blackmailee? What word would explain her being here or else, as her boss at the news service put it. "Chloe, you're falling apart at the seams. Your photos aren't worth a shit, your writing sucks."

"Sheesh," she'd protested. "Don't they teach you anything in those touchy feelie seminars you go to?"

"Touchy feelie is what you need. Go swim with the dolphins, commune with a seagull. Come back at the end of the week like your old self, or get a job somewhere else."

"You want me to interview this guy?"

"Nope. He doesn't do interviews."

"Then why me? Why ask a journalist if he's not going to talk to me?" Her boss had just shrugged.

"Ma'am?" the young man prompted.

"Yes," Chloe sighed. "Lead the way."

He helped her into a glossy launch, then stowed her camera cases and duffel bag aboard, treating her well-traveled luggage as though it were Vuitton's finest. She'd brought her cameras, her laptop and some books she hadn't gotten around to reading. She planned to hole up in her cabin, sleep, read, and shoot a few pictures. That should satisfy her boss and get him off her back.

Pleased with her plan, Chloe sank back against a banquette bench as the young man smoothly edged the launch away from the dock and headed across the bay. A few drops of salty spray flicked across her face. She looked behind her, watching the sailboats in the marina, Cannery Row, Fisherman's Wharf, and the green forested hills of the Monterey Peninsula recede, severing the connection to her everyday world.

The launch slowed as it approached the boat. Chloe swept her gaze from one end to the other, noting the three decks, shadowy now in the dusk, water frothing from an idling propeller, windows showing lots of light. The word *Fantasy* was written in fanciful lettering across the stern. For sure a rich man's plaything, but maybe it wouldn't be too much of a hardship. Excitement bubbled within her. "That's some boat!"

The young man grinned. "We call it a yacht."

"Oops. Yacht it is."

A few minutes later, after welcoming her aboard, a crewman led her across the main deck into an elegantly furnished salon, down a short, narrow hallway, and opened a door. "Your stateroom, ma'am."

She stared at the creamy woodwork and opulent ivory furnishings, at the huge bed dominating the lavish room. "Oh, there must be some mistake!"

"No, ma'am. This is the stateroom you were assigned."

Her eyes widened. "Are they all like this?"

"The staterooms on the lower deck are each different, ma'am." He gestured to a phone. "The buttons will call your stewardess, the galley or any of the staterooms."

The young man left, closing the door softly behind him. Chloe stood in the middle of the room and slowly turned to take it all in. Unbelievable. Fantuckingfastic. She'd slept in tents, on the bare ground, in the back of trucks and sometimes, three to a bed. Having this all to herself was indulgence beyond belief. This was a room made for sex. Pity she had no lover to share the cozy conversation area formed by a plush loveseat, two armchairs and a coffee table. Or frolic in that decadent bed.

She ran her fingers over the silky white duvet, tempted to snuggle into the plump pillows clustered against the padded headboard. Behind the bed, twin swags draped a large window overlooking the dark water.

Lamps on either side of the bed shed a mellow glow. Several doors led from the room. She tried the one nearest her and found it locked.

Another stateroom, no doubt. Underneath her feet she felt a fine tremor, the rumble of engines. Touching the band on her wrist, she hoped it worked. She'd never been on a cruise before, didn't know if she'd get seasick. For that matter, why this one?

She'd been assured that everything was on the level, that her host, Mr. Yancy, was well known with a spotless reputation. Though he preferred to keep a low profile due to the nature of his business, she had nothing to fear. All she had to do was rest. She was due a break, after pushing herself, going after the telling story, the perfect picture, for too long. She was supposed to put work out of her mind and be pampered.

She grinned. Pampering she could handle. Comforts like these, after time in the field where amenities like hot water and flushing toilets were scarce, felt almost surreal. But good, very good. Since she had to be here, she was going to enjoy every bit of this treat. Who knew if she'd ever have another chance?

Chloe kicked off her sandals and sank down on the bed. The fabric under her bare feet was soft, silky and sensuous, a tactile reminder of the difference between her lifestyle and this plush boat, er, yacht. Above her head, the lowered ceiling had hidden light sparkling on reflective tiles… sheesh, mirrors! Now that she looked, she saw her body in a dozen different angles. Just as she'd thought. This was a room for lovers. What a waste.

The knock at her door had her up and crossing the deep pile carpet to open the door. A young woman wearing a white shirt with nautical insignia with trim black pants smiled at her. "I'm Lisa, your stewardess. We've brought your luggage, ma'am."

Chloe stood back and watched a crewman stow her camera cases in the closet. He left her duffel bag on a luggage rack.

Lisa closed the door behind him. "I'll unpack and then press anything that needs a touch up."

"That's not necessary," Chloe protested. "All my clothes are wrinkle free."

"We'll see, shall we? Have you seen the activities schedule?" When Chloe shook her head, she gave her one.

Chloe scanned the itinerary. First night, cocktails and buffet. Okay, she could handle that. She'd need to meet her host and make polite noises. Each morning had a buffet breakfast served on the boat deck, whatever that was, followed by discretionary recreation, then a buffet lunch, more activities, dinner, evening entertainment and a midnight supper. She pulled the waistband of her slacks away from her body. If she weren't careful she wouldn't fit into these by the time she got home again.

There were several "fantasy" activities with no descriptions. Her eyebrows lifted. Thanks, but no thanks. No doubt someone being cute, playing on the yacht's name. She stifled a chuckle. She could imagine playing with several very wild fantasies but none of them were likely to come true. It was a good thing she had an alternate strategy in mind.

In short time, the stewardess had unpacked and put away everything but her long black skirt, the red silk tank top, and the black jersey dress that went everywhere with Chloe. "I'll just take these with me while you get ready for the Welcome Reception," Lisa said. "What will you wear tonight?"

Chloe hesitated. "What do you suggest?"

Lisa held up the black skirt and tank top. "These will do very nicely. Tomorrow is more formal." She looked distressed. "Is this all you brought for evening?"

"It's all I own," Chloe admitted. There wasn't much call for fancy dress when she was working.

Later, after a shower, and an uncharacteristically long time spent brushing and doing up her long black hair in a simple knot, she applied her makeup and dressed in the outfit Lisa had returned. She stood back to see herself in the long mirror over the dresser. She never wore makeup on assignment in war-torn areas, but now she'd applied her own war paint. Blusher enhanced her pale complexion, drawing attention to her black eyes and lips that she'd painted a bright red. Dangling silver and onyx earrings completed the look. Grinning at her reflection, she flicked her thumb up in approval. "Looking good."

Chloe left her cabin, following the sounds of voices, a deep male laugh and the tinkle of glass and ice to the salon. She paused in the doorway to get her bearings. Like her stateroom, this room looked inviting and lush, yet definitely masculine. The furniture was oversized in bold, earthy colors, the sculpture and works of art a mixture of modern and American Indian motifs. The young man who'd escorted her aboard stood at the bar, mixing drinks and pouring champagne. Beyond a laden buffet table, groupings of furniture offered comfort and conversation.

In the middle of the room, a tall redhead in a skin-tight red dress flirted with three men clustered around her. One man, taller than the others, stopped a glass halfway to his mouth at Chloe's entrance. He put the glass drink down, then moved toward her.

"Chloe, it's a pleasure to have you aboard."

She looked up into his lean, dark face, cheekbones starkly carved, a wide slash of mouth, obsidian eyes beneath black brows. Light from the wall sconces gleamed on his skin, highlighting the bronzed tones of his shaven head. She suspected it was vanity that prompted him to keep his beautifully curved head on display. His face was ruggedly compelling and intriguing, one the camera would love. She didn't do commercial portraits, but he'd be an excellent subject. As she studied him, thinking about camera angles and lighting, she realized he examined her as intently.

"I'm Yancy," he said.

"Of course." She extended her hand, recalling what her boss had said about her host's professional accomplishments, his vast wealth, and his rapid rise to a position of power and influence. "Thank you for inviting me, Mr. Yancy—"

"Just Yancy," he interrupted as he took her hand. He smiled broadly, making a little dimple appear in one cheek.

"While I'm here, maybe we could do an interview?"

The dimple disappeared. "No interviews. Ever."

"Then why am I here?"

"You don't remember me?"

She narrowed her eyes and looked up past his broad shoulders covered with custom-made suiting, to his face. He smiled at her, softening the no-nonsense lines of his mouth. One slightly crooked tooth marred the perfection of otherwise even white dental work.

Her breath felt trapped in her chest at the way he stared at her, expectantly and oddly demanding. It was her business to remember faces, but she couldn't place his cryptic, intense face. Quelling the strangest urge to run her fingers over the curve of his head to learn if it was as smooth as it looked, she retrieved her hand from his warm grasp. "We've met?"

"A long time ago." His smile warmed his black eyes. The dimple deepened, giving him the look of a mischievous boy. "You sat at the front of the room, I was at the back. I think I paid more attention to you than to Mr. Braganti's theories—"

She wrinkled her brow in concentration, then made the connection. "You were in my poli-sci class? But that was in college, years ago!"

"It took me a while to find you."

"Why would you want to do that?" She took a step back, putting space between them. Just because he knew her college class schedule didn't mean he'd actually been there. She'd encountered stalkers before, met men who expected her to trade her body for an inside scoop.

"Relax. You're among friends."

Friends? Hardly. Did he think his money gave him the advantage? She put more space between them.

He smiled, as if he'd guessed her thoughts. "I've wanted to get to know you, but the time wasn't right. Now it is."

"Right for what?"

"For you."

"That's ridiculous. We've never even spoken."

"We'll remedy that on this trip. There'll be plenty of opportunity to get to know each other." He touched her elbow. Did she imagine that slight caress? If not, it just made her more uncomfortable. "Come, join my guests."

Friends? Hardly. She glanced at the others, saw strangers and returned their curious looks, then glanced behind her. Oh, no! Two men she'd never thought she'd see again entered the salon. She stiffened. First Yancy keeping tabs on her, then ex-lovers? "What's going on?"

"As soon as everyone else is here, I'll explain." Yancy nudged her forward, urging her across the thick carpet.

She stood her ground. "I want to know now. Why am I here?"

Yancy studied her. She didn't temper her expression. If she looked stubborn and demanding, tough.

"Fair enough," he said quietly. "If you still have questions later, then we'll talk."

As he moved forward, she heard a quick laugh and turned to see two women come up the stairs from a lower deck. The smaller one was dressed all in black, her black hair cropped close to her skull. The taller one wore her hair in multi-colored spikes. Her grunge outfit and heavy boots were a stark contrast to the hedonistic furnishings.

Behind them, as if choreographed, came two blondes. One had hair so pale it looked white, falling in a straight cut that emphasized the delicacy of her face. Next to her, the one with a no-nonsense short haircut looked sturdy and sensible.

If Yancy wanted to get to know her better, why all these people? Chloe stood rigid with her back against the wall, as far away from her ex-lovers and Yancy as she could get. Yancy looked around, as if counting noses. A man rose from a corner seat and caught his eye. Yancy nodded and went to stand in the middle of the salon.

"First, let me thank each of you for accepting my invitation aboard the *Fantasy*. It's short notice, I know, but I'm pleased you were able to clear your schedules." He noted each face, smiling an individual welcome.

Looking directly at Chloe, he continued, "Please sit, make yourself comfortable. The steward will offer you a drink, then leave. When we are alone, I'll have a few things to say."

Chloe accepted a flute of champagne, then perched on the arm of a chair upholstered in bronze suede. She looked at the other guests as inquisitively as they regarded each other, all the while avoiding the eyes of the two men standing by the door leading to the deck. Even though she didn't look at them, she sensed they were staring at her. Why now? And why together?

With her career taking her all over the world, she'd never been able to give a relationship the care and attention it needed. Yet, the two times she'd been swept into thinking that this time, with this man, it might work, she'd been wrong. Absolutely wrong.

Why were they here?

After the steward left the salon, Yancy resumed his welcoming speech. "There are a few safety regulations which the Captain will explain later. Until then, I have some suggestions to ensure your enjoyment during the five days you'll be aboard." He paused, as if waiting for complete attention. "I've already said this to a few of you, but I'll repeat: the first rule is confidentiality."

Chloe's head snapped up. Several of the other guests looked puzzled.

"That's right. Discretion, for your ease of mind. If you are not already known to each other, you may use only your first names," Yancy continued in a firm voice. "What you do after we return is up to you. In a minute, we'll introduce ourselves, and mention our chosen occupations, but beyond that, no shop talk. You are here because you are at the top of your professions, over-stressed, near burnout, and need rest and recreation. You need a complete change of scene." Chloe noted he looked directly at her. "Understood?"

She inclined her head and looked at the other guests. Some looked puzzled, others smiled and nodded.

"As you came aboard, you received the itinerary for this cruise. No doubt you're wondering what the surprise and fantasy items are?"

More nods.

"You'll have to wait to find out." Yancy's grin was unexpectedly contagious, and most of the guests laughed. Chloe rubbed her fingers over the soft suede. Oh, what she was going to email the boss when she got back to her stateroom... .

"There are some items aboard for your pleasure. TVs, DVDs, stereos in each of the staterooms as well as here in the salon. Don't bother to try the phones except for onboard calls. If there is an emergency, the ship's crew will handle it, but as my guests, you will not be allowed contact with your offices. That includes web connections and mobile phones."

Chloe's head snapped up. Yancy dismissed her protest. "You'll find protected sunning areas on deck. Clothing is optional." He ignored a few raised eyebrows. "There's a library in the small den, with cards, board games and such. We'll anchor at selected spots twice. We have scuba and diving gear aboard, WaveRunners, Zodiacs, snorkeling, fishing and exercise gear. If you need lessons in using the equipment, certified crew members will instruct you."

Several men looked eager with the promise of adventure. The redhead tossed her hair back in a curly swathe.

"Okay, to start the introductions, I'm Yancy. I've been fortunate enough to do well in aviation, but the sea is my passion. I spend as much time sailing as I can."

"My name is Saul, I'm in banking. This is your boat?" a tall, dark man asked.

"The *Fantasy* belongs to me, yes." Yancy nodded to the man on his right, the one who had risen from the corner.

"I'm Mark." A blush climbed his throat and stained his cheeks, matching the strawberry blond buzzcut. "I'm in electronics."

Yancy nodded to the woman next to Mark.

"My name is Ali," the black-haired woman all in black said. "I'm in… communications, I guess you'd call it."

"I'm Shelly," the brunette with the multi-colored hair spoke next. "I'm in theater."

The blond man next to her looked like a farm boy straight off the wheat fields, but his voice as he introduced himself was cool and sophisticated. "I handle imports and exports. You may call me Perry."

"Is that your real name?" the redhead cooed.

"Possibly." He looked her up and down. Even from several feet away, Chloe noted the way his glance lingered on the tight red dress. "What's yours?"

"Lane. I'm in advertising."

"Obviously," Perry murmured with a glance at her breasts.

The sturdy blonde woman laughed. "I'm Wynne, a pediatrician. I don't expect any of you to need my services."

Relaxing a bit, Chloe chuckled along with the others. The delicate platinum blonde waved her fingers. "Nor mine, I hope. I'm what you'd call a legislative reformer."

"Your name?" Saul asked.

"Tracy."

Yancy looked around. "Only three left. Who'll go first?"

The compact man in the doorway stepped forward, flashing an engaging grin. "I'm Adam. I fly Yancy's test planes."

Chloe looked away, afraid that his grin would melt her insides as quickly as it had at the experimental airshow she'd covered three years ago. A recently retired Air Force jet jockey then, Adam had swept her into a heady, short-term affair that had left her gasping for air. She'd thought at first that he might be the one, but their relationship fizzled when their schedules kept them apart. She hadn't seen him since they'd agreed to go their separate ways.

"Ladies first," came the deep voice of the man at Adam's side. Chloe flicked a glance his way and automatically adjusted the slit of her long black skirt to cover her thigh. He'd always admired her legs, claiming them to be the secret weapons she kept hidden under her serviceable twill pants. "I'm Chloe, a photojournalist."

Several pairs of eyes turned to her in recognition. Yancy intervened. "No questions."

Did he really expect his guests not to talk about themselves? Chloe looked at him curiously as the others turned expectantly to the last guest.

"Brad," he said in authoritarian tones. "I sometimes consult for Yancy." About what, Chloe wondered. Why did Yancy need military expertise for his aviation business? She could understand Adam, but Brad was not a flyer.

Yancy stepped to the middle of the room again. "Good, now we all know each other. Have another drink, eat, indulge yourselves." He looked from one guest to another. "That's the prime rule for the *Fantasy*. No limit, anything goes. Anything legal, that is."

Laughter followed him as a number of the guests mingled, refreshed their drinks and congregated around the buffet table. Chloe edged closer to Yancy. "What gives?" she murmured. "Am I the only one here who isn't a stranger to the other guests?"

Yancy's dark eyes lingered on her face, moving from her eyes, to her mouth and back again. "Confidentiality, remember?"

Chloe hissed. "Why are Brad and Adam here?"

"They're valued associates. They need a break, too."

"Just keep them away from me!"

"Tell them yourself. Here they come."

Chloe stiffened. At her back, she could feel the heat of Brad's body much as she'd felt it in dark, dangerous places when he'd protected her with both his person and his weapons. He spoke her name.

Reluctantly, she turned and looked into his deep, blue eyes. Combat had etched lines around his eyes and mouth, but couldn't lessen his appeal. If anything, he looked tougher, more in charge in his civvies than he had in battle-stained camouflage.

It wasn't fair that her body should respond so quickly. Not after the struggle she'd had to forget him. She swallowed hard. "Brad."

"It's good to see you, Chloe."

Adam shot him a glance. "You two know each other?"

Brad didn't take his eyes from her. "We met in the Middle East," he said in his clipped voice.

Adam made a sound in his throat as he studied her quizzically. "When was that, Chloe?"

"Several months ago," Brad answered for her. His lips thinned as he turned to Adam. "Something to you?"

Yancy's eyes narrowed as he watched the two men, his body tensed for action. Chloe was aware of his changed breathing as they waited for Adam's answer. Though he said nothing, Yancy was in command, virile and, she was appalled to realize, exciting. Under her thin silk top, her nipples felt full.

Adam put up his hands and gave them his trademark grin. "Nope. Chloe and I were over long before that."

Brad gave Adam a long, considering look. Chloe knew she should leave them to their macho posturing, but she was rooted by her sudden arousal. She hated the thought that it was caused by the thrill of Adam and Brad fighting over her. Whatever she'd shared with each of them was over. Adam by mutual consent, Brad abrupt and brutal. Her scars from that encounter still hadn't healed. She couldn't imagine either one wanting to start something up again, so why the attitude?

Yancy took her arm and led her away. "Let's get something to eat. The chef is particularly talented with seafood."

Chloe noted the smooth transition from a man ready for action to urbane host. Moving away from his grasp, she said, "Thank you, but it's not necessary. I'm leaving."

Yancy gave her a quizzical look. "Haven't you noticed?"

"What?"

"We're underway. We sailed almost an hour ago."

"Oh, no!" She'd forgotten she felt the engines start up. "Turn around and take me back."

"Can't do that, Chloe. If you don't want to have anything to do with Adam or Brad, don't. Ignore them, do as you please. Make new friends. Lots of interesting people aboard." A slow smile lit his face, coaxing her out of her anger. "Or spend time with me. Forget about them."

She glanced over her shoulder at the two men staring at her with tight faces. "Oh, sure."

Chapter Two

Chloe rested her wineglass on the deck railing. A thin band of fog obscured the horizon, and far above her head, the stars winked at her. The breeze coming off the water was cold, but she welcomed the fresh air.

There was something going on here, undercurrents and emotions she sensed, but couldn't quite identify. It made her uneasy to know that Yancy had more on his mind than providing a stress-free break from work. She believed the other guests were strangers to each other, but why had Yancy invited her here with Adam and Brad? Yancy had to be aware they knew each other, since he hadn't been at all surprised at her reaction to seeing them.

It had to be a set-up. Had he brought her on board to play match-maker, to patch things up between her and an ex-lover? If so, he was way off base. She'd learned her lesson. When—and if—she was ready for a new relationship, she wasn't going to settle for anything less than everything. She craved excitement, yes, but she also wanted something deeper. She wanted more than the passionate affairs she'd had with Adam and Brad.

As for that, how did they come to work for Yancy? She wouldn't have expected either to give up his military career. What had Yancy offered them to resign? Or had he? He was a puzzle. More than once she'd looked across the room and found his intent gaze focused on her. What was he thinking?

"Here you are."

She didn't need to turn to recognize Brad's voice. "I'd rather be alone."

"Tough. What are you doing aboard?"

"I was invited." She glanced at him from the corner of her eye. "What's this all about? Why me, why those people?"

"I have no idea. I'm as surprised as you are. Waste of time when I've got other things to do."

"Same here. But I got told no cruise, no job."

"The agency would let you go? No sweat. The others would snap you up in an instant."

"Thanks." Brad made her feel confident, secure, but then he'd always been able to do that. Except when he'd left her without a word. "So why did you come if you're so busy?"

"Yancy calls the shots."

"I would have thought Yancy would only hire flyboys. What's a Marine like you doing for him?"

"Ex. No shop talk, remember?"

"Same old Brad. No comment, no excuses, no good-byes."

He stiffened, standing almost at attention. "That couldn't be helped. I had orders."

"Oh, well, that's all that matters, right?"

"You know I would have told you if I could. I didn't like leaving you."

"And that's why you called me the very first chance you had, to let me know you were alive and I could stop worrying."

He flinched at her bitter tone. "I can only say I'm sorry." He edged closer and touched her shoulder. "We're here now, we can forget about that and get on with things."

"Wouldn't that be convenient?" Chloe moved away and crossed her arms. "Just throw off our clothes and hop in the sack. Oops, I forgot. We didn't get to do that too often, did we? Just get off enough to get it off. No, thanks."

The glow from the salon lighted the narrowing of his eyes. "We had something good going. Why the cold shoulder now?"

It had been good while it lasted. They'd come together, so quickly and completely; she'd thought that maybe she and Brad were destined to be together. How wrong she'd been.

"It's over, Brad. If you'd wanted a warm reception you should have called me when you dropped your uniform." She emptied the last of her wine over the side rather than dashing it in his face. "See you." She placed her glass on a table and moved away. "On second thought, keep away from me."

He took her arm, halting her. "Can't do that, honey. I didn't have anything to do with getting you aboard, but now that we're together again, I'm not letting you go."

"Too late." She moved out of his grasp.

"Is there someone else? Another lover? What do you do, change men as often as you do your film?"

She recoiled. "I cried for you once. I'm not going to do it again."

"There won't be another time. I swear."

"No need for that. Leave me alone."

"Not a chance."

Chloe felt his gaze on her as she strode across the deck to the lighted salon. She didn't look back. She entered the room at the same time the captain introduced himself.

He made a few general remarks, then cleared his throat. "In case you are wondering, the *Fantasy* is a power yacht. Our cruising speed is fifteen knots, and we normally have a crew of ten aboard. This cruise we're down to nine, but we'll do our best to make sure you have a pleasant, safe cruise. We're air-conditioned for your comfort when the fog isn't around. We carry more than enough fuel and water, can make more fresh water, so you needn't worry about bathing.

"Our zodiacs do double duty as lifeboats, and we have lifejackets for everyone. Your steward will show you where they are located in your staterooms, and show you how to put them on. We have more in all of the public rooms." He gestured at a cabinet and a crew member opened it to reveal a storage locker with bright orange lifevests. "If you hear the warning siren, put on a life jacket and meet on the boat deck. At once!

"We don't carry a medical team aboard, but if you need something, your steward will know what to do. In cases of emergency, we can land a Med Evac helicopter on the aft sun deck. In any case, we won't be far offshore." He looked stern for a moment, then smiled. "If there are no questions, I'll say goodnight."

As the captain left, Yancy stood and tapped at the side of his crystal glass for attention. "Welcome again to the *Fantasy* and all she has to offer. Don't forget you're here to relax and recharge your batteries. I'm going to say goodnight now. Sleep as late as you wish. Have breakfast in bed or join us here for buffet until nine. You don't want to miss the entertainment planned for breakfast."

Ignoring raised eyebrows and the buzz of conversation, he followed the captain below. Saying nothing, Chloe made her way across the room and entered the narrow hallway leading to her room. A woman's brittle voice followed her. "Why does she get that stateroom?"

Good question, Chloe thought. Why was she the only one here, and all the other guests on a lower deck? She went on to her cabin, opened the door and found her bed turned down, a designer chocolate on the pillow, and a bottle of mineral water with a crystal tumbler on her bedside table. The lamps were turned low, spreading an inviting glow over the cream colored sheets.

As she turned to close the door, the stewardess, Lisa, appeared. With a few words of instruction, she helped Chloe try on the life vest and re-hung it in the closet. She gestured at the bed. "I'd have put out your night-gown, but I didn't find one."

"That's because I don't wear one." On assignment she'd often had to sleep in her clothes.

Lisa grinned. "You'll find a terry cloth robe in the bath."

Chloe thanked her, and after Lisa left, she undressed, cleaned her face and slipped under the covers. She wriggled and stretched, enjoying the luxury of silk sheets on her bare skin. The fabric was cool, sensitizing her nipples and falling gently between her opened thighs. For a moment, she allowed herself to remember making love with Brad. The few times they'd been able to find a bed and be totally naked had allowed her to play with his fit body. His physique and training gave him stamina, and he'd been a powerful lover, bringing her to orgasm again and again.

Much of the heat and fierceness of their passion was owing to the dangerous times, the risk and the heat of battle going on around them. Sometimes she'd longed for lingering foreplay, the escalating need, the sweet torment of holding off just one more moment. No matter how many times she came, sometimes she'd hungered for more, to have every one of her needs fulfilled.

It wasn't likely that total immersion in physical gratification would fill the empty space in her heart, yet sometimes she'd wondered what it would be like to make love with more than one man at a time. How would it feel to indulge all her senses at once? To have every bit of her body caressed, stroked, kissed?

Her nipples peaked, firming in anticipated pleasure even as her center warmed and went liquid. Contrary to Brad's accusation, she hadn't made love since he'd left her without a word.

Tough, Brad had said. Tough, she told her body.

Adjusting the pillows behind her head, she settled in with a book. When the phone rang, once, twice and again, softly but insistently, she stared at it, willing it to stop, then reluctantly lifted the receiver. "Hello?"

"Chloe, sorry if I've woken you. Can you talk?"

"What is it, Adam?"

"I didn't get a chance to tell you how good it is to see you again. Surprised me, but it feels fine. How have you been, sweet lady?"

Chloe relaxed into the pillows. Nobody but Adam had ever called her that, ever even thought of her in that way. Sweetness wasn't a trait that would get her ahead as a photojournalist. Persistence, determination and a knack for getting to the truth of the matter: those were the traits she cultivated. Yet, every now and then it felt good to be complimented for her softer, feminine nature. "I'm surprised to see you, too. When did you go to work for Yancy?"

"About a year ago. He made me an offer I couldn't refuse. And that's all I'm going to tell you."

She heard the laughter in his voice. If there were planes to fly, he'd be first in line. "So, what's this cruise all about?"

"Dunno. Yancy came in one day, big smile on that poker face of his, gave his secretary a list of people and told her to get the invitations going."

"Why? Why these people? Why me?"

"Beats me. He keeps his plans to himself. All I know is he handpicked everyone here."

"Are we the only ones who know each other? From before, I mean?"

"I think so. In fact, I met Brad only a week ago. Didn't know he'd be here until I found we're sharing a stateroom."

Oh, no. Two gung-ho, macho men bunking in the same room. Both of them having a history with her. Both of them pawing at the ground when they found out about the other. "Sounds like bad news. Can you get another room?"

"Nope. Only six of them, and they're all full. Yancy's already in the crew quarters—"

"He is? Why?"

"Well, I'll be... you're in the owner's stateroom, Chloe. Yancy gave that up for you."

She sat up straight. The covers fell, leaving her breasts bare. "Why did he do that?"

"You don't know? This gets curiouser and curiouser."

"I had no idea." She pleated the sheet with her fingers. "Something's fishy."

"Why don't we put our heads together and see if we can figure it out?"

"Now?"

He laughed. She could just imagine his big grin, the crinkles around his hazel eyes. "I guess that's out by the sound of your voice. See you at breakfast? We can talk then."

They hung up a few moments later. Chloe sank back under the covers, confused and suspicious all over again. Adam's pleasant manner and quick grin often fooled people into thinking he was mellow and easy going. He wasn't. He liked to be in charge, to dominate the situation, to have all the answers. It wasn't like him not to know what was going on.

Why had Yancy brought them all together like this?

Chapter Three

Chloe considered the eggs, potatoes, bacon, sausages, fresh fruits and pastries displayed on the dining table. She placed a slice of melon on her plate.

Adam joined her. "Is that all you're going to eat?"

"No." She added two strawberries and some sections of orange. "This is."

He added bacon and eggs to his plate. "You'll be hungry by lunchtime."

"Better than not fitting into my clothes by dinner time."

He scanned her from tip to toe, his gaze lingering where her red fleece sweatshirt covered her breasts, then moving indolently down her torso, past her khaki shorts to her bare legs and sandaled feet. "You can always take them off." He grinned. "Remember, Yancy said clothing is optional."

"Oh, sure!" Chloe rolled her eyes but she laughed.

Adam replaced the silver tongs on the toast platter and turned to look at her again. She felt his gaze crawl over her body. All at once, she felt naked, poised under him while he took his time touching, kissing and licking her, stroking her into mindless passion. "Stop that!"

He gave her another quick, engaging grin. "Let's take our plates out on deck," he suggested. He led the way past groups of breakfasting guests to the side door, slid it open and gestured her through.

She hesitated between the warm salon and the cool, misty deck where fog and the plaintive cry of gulls were their only company. It was June, officially summer, but her clothes weren't warm enough for the annual summer fog. "Your eggs will get cold out here."

She stepped back inside and found a pair of empty armchairs and waited for Adam to join her. Some of the other passengers nodded and said good morning. Perry, the farm boy with the sophisticated voice, winked at her. She smiled back.

"One man at a time, if you don't mind, sweet lady."

Chloe smiled. His words reminded her of her thoughts last night, how she'd fallen asleep dreaming of fantasy lovers.

Adam ate his eggs. "Okay, so you don't know why you're here, and in Yancy's stateroom, and I have all sorts of ideas."

She leaned forward. "Like what?"

"Like why would he make sure you have the biggest bed aboard unless he plans to share it?"

Her fork clattered across the china and dropped to the floor. "I don't even know him!"

He handed her the utensil. She placed it and her plate on the coffee table in front of her. "There has to be another explanation."

"Like what? Why would he make sure we all understand this is a confidential, fantasy cruise? No last names, discretion all the way around? Sounds like he's set the scenario for a no-holds barred, sex-til-you-drop week. And baby, that's okay with me."

She glanced at the other guests. "They're all strangers."

"We're not. And," he gestured at the couple sitting on the couch, "they won't be much longer."

She followed his gaze. Perry and the redhead, Lane, huddled close together. Lane wore tight red leggings that didn't leave much to the imagination. Her nipples were clearly defined under a striped red and white tee shirt as she leaned into his body.

Chloe whispered, "She looks like the barracuda type. Maybe someone should warn Perry."

Adam grinned. "He's a big boy. He can take care of himself." Chloe bit back a smile. By the looks of Perry's tan Dockers, he was a very big boy.

"And check out those two." Chloe looked over her shoulder. Saul stared intently into Tracy's pale face, listening closely as she spoke. It was hard to believe that they'd met just yesterday. Or had they?

"Bet you a buck those couples will be in the sack by lunchtime."

Chloe snickered. "I don't take sucker bets."

"We could steal away ourselves. Make use of that big bed, run a tub—"

"How do you know so much about my room?"

"Been aboard before." He saw her look and continued quickly. "Business meetings, nothing like this. All guys."

Chloe just looked at him, but he was saved an answer when Yancy and Lisa entered the room. She carried a silver bowl and stood just inside the door while Yancy made his way into the center of the room.

"Good morning. I hope you slept well. Our captain tells us the fog will burn off shortly, and we'll have sun and warm weather for the afternoon. We're cruising to our first anchorage and expect to reach it some-time during the night. To make it interesting, we're going to have a little contest. Anyone who guesses the time of our arrival, as clocked by the captain, wins a prize."

"And what's that?" called Ali. This morning, she wore black again; a short miniskirt and belly baring top displaying a black bead in her navel.

"All the prizes on this cruise are selected first for the occasion, sec-ond, for the sex of the winner."

"His and her prizes?" Wynne asked. Her jeans and navy blue cotton sweater only hinted at curves.

"His or her prizes," Yancy corrected. "If they choose to share, that's up to them." Laughter rose up as Lisa moved around the room, handing out paper and pens. "Write your guess and sign it," Yancy instructed. "I'll give you this much of a hint. We'll arrive while you're sleeping." He gave them all a wolfish grin. "While some of you may be sleeping."

Chloe frowned at Adam. "This is sounding more like a frat party ev-ery moment."

Adam nodded. "Probably going to get raunchy."

She took pen and paper. Firmly, she wrote, 1:35AM while I am sleep-ing. Alone. Chloe

Adam glanced at her slip of paper. "That definite, sweet lady? I may have something to say about that." He jotted down his estimate and folded the slip of paper before she could see what he wrote.

The stewardess collected their guesses and left, taking the silver bowl with her.

Yancy rubbed his hands. "Good. Now, your time is your own. Play, nap, enjoy yourselves. I'll see you back here for lunch."

Chloe watched him leave the salon, enter the passageway leading to her, no, his stateroom, then rose and followed him. She caught up with him as he was turning the key in a closed door. "May I have a word with you?"

"Sure. Come on in." He opened the door and gestured her in. She stepped into an office. Bookshelves held leather-bound volumes and a selection of antique nautical equipment. Yancy went to sit behind a curved expanse of cream-colored wood that served as a desk. Behind him, an open laptop and some file folders waited for his attention.

"You're working but we can't?" she asked.

"I make the rules. My guests need a break. I don't." Yancy gestured to the plush couch facing the desk. She sat, sinking deeply into supple cop-per suede, as he eased back in his large, rust colored leather desk chair.

He seemed relaxed in black trousers and a tan knit shirt that set off the shadowed planes of his face.

"What's up, Chloe?"

"I want some answers."

He spread his hands. "Ask."

"First, I understand you gave up your cabin for me. It's beautiful, and I thank you, but you should take it back. I can sleep somewhere else."

"With whom?"

"By myself, of course!"

"There are no other sleeping accommodations available. You'll have to stay where you are."

She leaned forward and placed her hand on his desk. "Why invite so many people that you have to give up your cabin?"

"I didn't have to." He looked at her hand, then at her mouth. "It pleased me to do it."

"Why me? Why am I on board?" She put her hand in her lap, covered it with the other. "I've been wracking my brain, but I just don't remember you. Are you sure you knew me?"

"We didn't speak, but I knew you." His gaze roved over her face, dropped lower, then returned to meet her eyes. He smiled. "You weren't quite so thin then, and you wore your hair longer than now. Sometimes in a pony tail," he gestured at the back of his head. "But most often hanging down your back. Like black satin. You wore jeans, but I really liked one of your skirts. It was long and had flowers on it and with it you wore a yellow sweater. It looked soft."

She remembered that skirt. Black, ankle length, with little daisies scattered here and there. She'd loved that angora sweater. She shrugged. "You could have seen pictures."

"True, and someone could have told me that you argued with Braganti about third world countries and their right to make their own decisions. But they didn't."

"Okay. So you were in class with me. So were a lot of other people. I can't place you."

"It might come to you." He settled back in his chair, and linked his fingers behind his head. She noted once again the breadth of his chest, the swell of muscle under his clothing. She licked her lips. His breath hitched. His gaze lingered on her face, particularly her mouth. They stared at each other until Chloe broke the connection.

"Why wait all these years? You could have arranged to meet ages ago.

Why this cruise?"

"I told you." He dropped his arms. "I wasn't ready. Now that I am, I thought I might as well give you the chance to relax and unwind while I was at it."

It sounded reasonable on the surface, but she was sure there had to be more to it. "What do you mean, you weren't ready?"

"Let's say that I didn't have much to offer then. Now I do." He made a vague gesture that took in the whole yacht.

"Impressing me with your money?"

"Something like that," he agreed on a dry note.

"That doesn't say much for me. Makes me sound like a gold-digger."

He chuckled. "You're not. Otherwise that playboy prince might have had more success with you."

Her mouth dropped open. She found her voice. "You have been keeping tabs, haven't you?"

"Only because I wanted the time to be right."

"For what?"

"Perhaps I'll tell you later, after I see how things go."

"You're confusing me."

"Good. Now, if you'll excuse me, I have work to do."

She stood up, dismissed and frustrated. She pointed at the closed door. "Where does that lead?"

"To the owner's stateroom." He studied her face. "It's locked."

She nodded and left his office. Instead of rejoining the others, she went to her room. Knowing that it was Yancy's usual quarters made her uneasy. She could see him here, his large body at ease, slipping naked between the sheets. She swallowed hard, imagining his burnished skin against the ivory sheets, his body dark against her pale flesh.

Hers? Where had that thought come from?

Now that it had, it slipped insidiously through her, warming her, making her skin quiver. Or was she only responding to his blatant interest? Either way, she felt overheated, stifled by his presence even though she was alone. She needed air!

She glanced out her window. The sea looked flat and gray, with an occasional white cap creating a contrasting color, white froth flicked into peaks by wave and wind. There was nothing unusual about it, but maybe she'd get some atmospheric shots to steady her nerves and clear her head.

Eagerly, Chloe took out her cameras, and checked her equipment. Photography wasn't only her occupation, it was her passion. She inspected lenses and light meters, filters and battery packs, then made sure she had all her repair equipment with her. She had become adept at fixing her own equipment since camera shops came few and far between in the field. She took what she wanted and securely repacked the rest.

Alone on the sundeck with nothing but the cool breeze ruffling her ponytail and chilling her bare legs, she took a few deep breaths, expelling her fantasies of Yancy and drawing in moist, salt-laden air. She turned in a circle, scanning the horizon. A still-weak sun was burning off some of the fog. A thin, dark line looked like coastline, but wasn't worth the film. Behind her, the wake streamed steadily and white against the grayish-green water. The churned up colors caught her eye for a moment, then receded.

Far out to sea, a small dot might have been another boat.

She sat on a padded bench seat, out of some of the wind, checked the light meter and looked over the side. Water rushed by, rising and falling with the boat. She moved to the front, and peered over the railing, to the front of the boat. The prow, as the captain had called it.

She aimed her camera as a crewman walked across her field of vision. In his uniform, wearing a black windbreaker, he offered contrasting color against the white ship and the gray sea and sky. He looked up, saw her and called a greeting. She lowered the camera and waved.

She snapped a few more shots, then repacked her camera gear and headed for the lower deck. She met Yancy as he was coming out the door to the salon. His shoulders all but filled the doorway. Instantly, the fantasized sight of him naked swept through her, tantalizing her with the imagined feel of his bare skin against hers.

He held out his hand. "I'll take that."

"What?"

"Your camera. I thought I made it clear that this cruise is confidential. That means no photos. No working. Give me your camera."

Sensual thoughts disappeared in a flash. "I wasn't working, just amusing myself. You did tell me to enjoy myself, remember?"

"Not by taking pictures. You can have your gear back when we dock. Hand it over, please."

She'd never been stripped of her cameras while she was on assignment, never been confronted by angry officials who denied her the right to capture on film what the world needed to know. Acting purely on instinct, she swung her camera case behind her back.

He reached for it. His long arms went around her. She felt his torso, his muscled arms enclosing her, his hands on hers. She tried to wrench free. His grip tightened. She became aware of her breasts pushing against him at the same time he did. She felt her nipples harden, felt his cock thicken and rise against her belly. Her eyes widened as he went still. Heat spread up from her nipples, climbed her throat and clogged her breathing. He looked down, she looked up.

Camera bag forgotten, they stared at each other. His black eyes were intent on hers, his face a mixture of determination and awareness. She tried to step back. His arms tightened, then dropped. His gaze never left hers.

He blew out a breath, fanning her temple with warmth. "The camera."

Without another word, she handed it to him and fled, not slowing down until she reached her room. She closed the door behind her and breathed hard. Her breasts were still flushed and sensitive. What was happening here? She'd sworn off men, and here were Brad and Adam wanting to renew the passion they'd shared with her. Here was Yancy, striking new sparks. She ran her tongue over her lips and licked away salt. What would his mouth taste like?

She headed for the shower, adjusted the temperature to cool and stepped in. She scrubbed her skin, then turned her face up to the water, letting it pelt on her temples and closed eyes. Gradually, her body chilled and she turned off the water.

She dried herself, drew the warm terry cloth robe around her and wrapped her head in a towel as she entered the bedroom.

"Are you all right?" Brad rose off the bed.

"What are you doing here?" she demanded. "How did you get in?"

"Your door was unlocked. You seemed upset, so I came to see if I could help."

"He has some nerve!" she exploded. "Taking my camera away from me!"

"Is that all?"

"Isn't that enough?" She whirled, looking for the rest of the equipment she'd left in the closet. All her camera cases and gear were gone. So was her laptop. "That rat!"

"Who?"

"He came in here and got all my camera equipment when I wasn't looking! Even my laptop!"

"You'll get it back."

Chloe ignored his soothing tone. "What gives him the right to take my things!"

Brad reached out and pulled her down on the bed next to him. "Don't you remember the meaning of the word discretion? Yancy's protecting all his guests."

"I didn't take pictures of them. Only the water, the sky and a crewman. What's the harm in that?"

"Nothing in that, I agree. Next time, who knows? Yancy's just making sure there isn't a next time."

She narrowed her eyes to a slit. "Whose side are you on?"

Chapter Four

"You don't sign my paychecks." Brad laughed. "C'mon, relax." He toppled her over on the bed and came down to rest on her. "Forget it. Your cameras will be safe."

He was heavy on her chest, his mouth inches away from hers, his breath mingling with hers. Chloe breathed in his aroma, a discreet mix of subtle aftershave and his unique scent that had never failed to turn her on. Still didn't, she realized in alarm. She pushed at him but he didn't budge.

"What gives, sweetheart?" His index finger traced the *Fantasy* insignia embroidered on the breast pocket of her robe. She felt his touch as though she were naked. "We've got a little unfinished business to take care of."

Maybe that accounted for her crazy hormones. Maybe an unacknowledged yearning for Brad made her extra susceptible to Yancy's powerful masculinity. "I didn't want to come on this boat with a bunch of strangers, then I find you here, and…"

"Adam," he supplied dryly. "Old home week."

"And Adam, and I thought I was over you—"

"How about Adam?" He slipped a hand between the folds of her robe and caressed the underside of her breast.

"That was over long ago. Don't do that." She pushed his hand away. "I can't think."

He came back and nuzzled her throat, then her ear. "Don't think, just feel. I've missed you, missed this. Let me love you." He cupped her breast, then kissed his way down from her ear, past the hollow in her throat, to the moist valley between her breasts. "You smell good. I've dreamed of the taste of you in my mouth."

"Oh," she sighed. She should insist he stop, shouldn't start up with him again, but not now, not when what he was doing to her felt so good. With his hands and mouth on her body, it was hard to recall why she was angry with him, or how rejected and alone she'd felt after he'd left. His cock rode up. In a moment, he'd pulled the edges of her robe apart.

He licked her belly, sampled her and slipped a finger between her folds. She knew he'd find dampness, from the shower, from the arousal she couldn't hide. With his thumb on her clit, and a finger inside her, he teased her, prompted her, encouraged her. "That's it, baby. Show me what you want."

She moaned, she sighed, she wriggled. She opened. He drew back long enough to shuck his clothes, pull a condom from his pocket and slide it on.

"Now, baby?"

For the moment, the heartache she'd suffered for him disappeared. All she knew was the wrenching desire to be filled, to be consumed. "Now."

He lifted her legs, anchored them around his waist and drove into her with the sureness of lovers. He set the rhythm, thrusting and withdrawing as her ankles locked about him and her heels dug into his firm ass. With his elbows locked, arms braced against the mattress, he gave himself up to the moment.

Her hips rose, sucking him deeper, deeper still, until she felt she'd burst. She clutched at his shoulders, pulling him closer, trying to kiss him, licking whatever she could touch. Sweat popped out on his brow, dripped down his chest and made their bodies slick. She panted, he breathed laboriously. She cried out, he groaned. Her inner muscles clamped down, held him tight, refused to let him go as she convulsed around him.

He came an instant later, his entire body in spasms. He held himself still in her for a moment, then pulled out and dropped beside her. With his eyes closed, he fought for breath. "Damn, baby, even better than before."

She drew her legs free. Her thighs still trembled. Breasts heaving, she rested, her face close to his chest. He'd made her come, so good, so hard, and they hadn't even kissed. He'd always been a physically demanding lover, using her body hard, sometimes roughly, but always leaving her sated. This time was no different, but as her reason returned, she realized there was something missing.

She thought back to the times they'd made love knowing that at any moment fighting would erupt and they'd be separated. As her breath evened out, it came to her.

The feeling of connection she'd shared with him then, when danger surrounded them, was gone. Then they'd made love. Now, they'd had sex. As satisfying to her body as it was, it wasn't enough. She sighed, feeling the emptiness expand within her.

A short nap later, Brad rolled to a sitting position, He placed his hand on her hip, running slow circles over it, down her belly, back up and down her bottom, tracing a line between her cheeks. "Mind if I use your shower, baby?"

She opened her eyes, edged away, and closed them again. "Go ahead."

He patted her butt and rose. Chloe didn't hear him leave, but when she woke several hours later, bright sun flooded through the window and bathed her in a warm, golden glow. She stretched, feeling lazy and lax, even as she thought of the best way to tell Brad that their affair was over. For sure this time, over and done with. Her choice.

She showered again, glad the captain had said fresh water was no problem, and drew on her favorite black and yellow tankini. She covered it with a yellow tee shirt, and left her stateroom for the deck. Maybe she'd find a quiet corner, stretch out, grab some rays and think about her career. Commune with the seagulls, as her boss had ordered. Now that she thought about it, there was something that didn't make sense about his insistence she accept Yancy's invitation. She could have found a quiet beach nearer home, snuggled into the sand and watched just as many seagulls there as here. Why aboard the *Fantasy*?

She crossed the dining area of the salon as one of the stewards cleared lunch. She paused, suddenly ravenous. He caught her hesitation and asked if he could bring her something. Shortly after, she was lazing in a comfortable deck lounge, a crab salad on a tray on her lap and a large glass of iced tea at her side. The sun was warm and a windbreak kept the breeze off her body as she finished her salad and placed the tray on the deck. She pulled her tee shirt off, and after applying sunscreen, she stretched out and closed her eyes.

She recalled her orders to rest, recover her edge and go back to work as sharp as she had been, or else. Or else what? What else was there but her work and her passion for recording the human situation? What else demanded so much of her and satisfied her so completely? At least it had until lately. She hesitated, afraid to admit the truth even to herself. She'd returned from her last assignment tired, dispirited and weary. The never-ending supply of misery was getting too much for her. She was burned out. She needed to find some good will, some joy, to balance out the ugliness…

"You missed lunch."

Chloe opened her eyes to see Ali wearing a black tank suit and a towel draped over one shoulder. "I took a nap."

"You missed the vote."

"What was it this time? How long it takes the anchor to get pulled up?"

Ali giggled. "We voted whether we wanted to cruise around or continue with Yancy's program."

"And?"

"The vote was 10 to 1 in favor of the program."

"Oh?" Chloe sat up. "Who was the dissenting vote?"

"Mark. He discovered sailing. Can't talk of anything else now."

Chloe laughed. "It's peaceful out here. I'd have voted with Mark."

Ali shrugged thin shoulders. "You might be sorry. Yancy mentioned something big." She walked off and stretched out on a mat.

"She's right." Adam hunkered down on the polished deck by her chair. Chloe turned to him and made a face. "Don't tell me you're taking part in those juvenile games?"

"I'd be stupid not to, when the prize for one of them is an all-expenses paid week in Fiji." He named a very expensive, very exclusive resort.

Her lower lip dropped. Adam tipped it up with a finger. "Looks a little different now, doesn't it?"

She batted his finger away. Yancy had to be extremely generous to ask everybody aboard and then give away a week in Fiji. He didn't appear to be flaunting his money, but she couldn't deny his largess. "I wish I knew what was behind all this. What does Yancy expect from us? Why is he doing this?"

"Who knows? Stop thinking like a reporter." Adam rose and pushed her legs aside to make room for him on the lounge. In baggy swim trunks, his body tanned and fit, he was attractive as ever. The warmth of his bare thigh pressed against hers made her remember how he looked nude. He was compact everywhere but his groin. She raised her glass of tea to her lips and drank deeply.

Adam ran a finger down her leg. "You're looking good, sweet lady. Very fit."

"Must be from carrying heavy equipment and running from bullets."

He glanced at her, hazel eyes sparkling. "Or bouncing about with our ex-marine? Someone works fast."

She drew her leg to the side. "No comment."

His grin flickered with a touch of resentment. He touched her leg again, lightly. His finger followed the curve of her thigh into the shadow between her legs. She stiffened and closed her legs. "Open," he coaxed. "Remember how it used to be? We could make it happen again."

"No," she murmured, even as her insides shifted and melted. He'd always been able to arouse her with just a touch, keep her humming and melting until he allowed her release. How could he do that now, when she was still sated from sex with Brad?

His finger burrowed deeper, then his entire hand slid between her clenched thighs. Remembered sensations from past lovemaking swept through her, leaving her wet and shaken. She put her fingers on his wrist. "Stop."

He took his hand away, then sprawled the length of the lounge, resting on his elbow. "Yancy says no shop talk, so I can't ask what you've been doing. Can't tell you about me, either, so what's there to talk about?" His slow grin went from engaging to suggestive. "Since we're on board to relax, let's play together."

Playing with Adam had been a favorite recreation of hers. She remembered stripping him out of his flight suit, yanking down his shorts and sitting on his lap. Other times, he'd liked to take her from behind, her head and shoulders on the bed, bottom elevated, while he played with her body, plucking her nipples and teasing her clit while he pumped into her. At times, they'd used bedroom toys until he'd exhausted her into begging him to stop.

Chloe flicked a glance at him. He looked relaxed, lying back on an elbow, head cocked as he watched her. The sun glinted on his fair hair, bringing out a hint of red, lighting his trim body with a touch of gold. His wiry physique was right for the cockpit, and just the right size and stamina to pleasure her for hours. Deliberately, she swung her gaze from him and looked out to the horizon, where cobalt water met the hazy blue of the sky. Overhead, traces of clouds scattered and reformed.

It was a peaceful sight, calming and eternal, but it did nothing to soothe the clamor within her. How could she be thinking of sex with Adam again, when they'd agreed to have nothing more to do with each other?

"Go away, Adam." She opened her book. "If I have to de-stress, I'm going to do it alone."

"That's why I saw Brad leaving your room with a big smile on his face?" She frowned at him. "Is this what this is all about? A pissing contest?"

"No." He shook his head. "No contest, sweet lady. You know I don't operate that way. I don't share." He rose to his feet, stretched, and ambled down the deck. Chloe watched him join a group playing dominoes. He perched on the arm of Ali's chair, said something that had her lifting her face to give him a flirtatious smile.

Chloe shook her head and turned her attention back to her novel. She read a few pages, then let the warmth of the afternoon coax her into sunbathing.

Voices and laughter flowed around her, barely breaking her sun-induced drowsiness. She heard an appreciative whistle and opened one eye to see the bare-breasted redhead, Lane, easing the bottom of her bikini down her legs, revealing a closely shaven mound with a center strip of red curls.

Chloe closed her eyes. For all Yancy's words about professionals at the top of their fields, some of his guests were beginning to act like adolescent show-offs. How quickly the professional veneer wore off, revealing basic sexual natures. The laughter got louder, the jokes bawdy. All this extravagant leisure was eating away common sense. Sighing, Chloe sat up, gathered her things and left the sun deck.

On the main deck, Yancy, Mark, Wynne, Brad and Tracy sat comfortably around a table littered with glasses and coffee cups. Brad gave her a slow smile. Yancy beckoned her over. "Black and yellow. My favorite colors." His eyes invited her to share in the shared memory. "Join us."

She drew up a chair and sat between Yancy and Wynne. A steward appeared to clear the table and offer refills. Yancy said something to him. The steward grinned. Chloe decided she liked the easy-going way Yancy treated his crew. Evidently he didn't need to rely on his wealth and position to command respect. She watched him talking with his guests. They were sought after for their expertise, according to Yancy, but he surpassed them all. She wasn't sure how she knew this, but she knew it was true.

A burst of laughter had Wynne cocking her head at the upper deck. "What's going on up there?"

"Not much, unless you like exhibitionism."

Mark flushed. Wynne smiled. Brad winked at Chloe and stood. "Maybe I should check this out."

"Down, tiger," Tracy murmured. "I'm sure there's nothing you haven't seen before."

Brad wiggled his eyebrows. "But not those particular nothings."

They laughed. Yancy turned to Chloe. "Are you settling in? Comfortable?"

"Yes," she responded, noting that somewhere during the day she'd lost her anger at his high-handed confiscation of her cameras. "Some of the company may be a little immature, but the *Fantasy* is fabulous."

"You don't like the other guests?" Yancy asked.

"Not much. Present company excepted, of course," she added hastily as Yancy grinned.

"I'd guess regressing is a reasonable reaction to huge amounts of stress," Wynne said, echoing Chloe's earlier thoughts.

"Careful," Yancy warned. "No shop talk."

Wynne nodded. "Just an observation. If we all didn't do the work we do, coiled up tighter than a spring, then we wouldn't fly loose quite so easily."

"I can understand that," Tracy agreed. She wore a floppy hat to protect her face, but from the shadows, her light blue eyes sparkled. "If we weren't who we are, we wouldn't be here. Thanks, Yancy."

"Right," Mark mumbled. "I need the break. Sometimes I get so tied up, I forget to eat."

Tracy nodded. "It's the way we are." She paused, then spoke slowly. "If we had a choice, would we be anything different?" She looked at Yancy. "If you could be anyone or do anything besides who you are and what you do, what would that be?"

Yancy crossed one long leg over the other, then lifted an ankle to rest on the opposite knee. In baggy, well-worn Bermudas, shirtless and barefoot, he looked like a man who did nothing but sun and surf all day. Chloe leaned a little closer to hear his answer.

He strummed an imaginary guitar. "A musician. Rock group, even a roadie. Anything to do with music."

Wynne laughed. "I can see you in a band, dressed... hmmm, with your features and coloring, I'd say dressed like an Indian... sorry, make that Native American."

Yancy grinned. The dimple popped out, making him look younger, more approachable. "You wouldn't be far wrong. Crow."

"You're Crow?" Mark asked. "Man, that's something else."

Chloe sat back and studied Yancy. She had the strongest urge to poke his dimple, to see what he would do. What he would feel like. She kept her hands to herself, yet looked her fill. He was deeply tanned, his belly flat and well muscled. There was only a hint of hair across his pectorals and none arrowing down his stomach, but she had no trouble imagining what lay beneath his shabby shorts. Despite her sensual awareness of his body, an image formed at the back of her mind.

Of course, she should have noticed it before. If she'd continued to study him through her mental camera's eye, she'd have realized why his high cheekbones, slanting brows and deep-set black eyes teased her memory. Now she had a faint recollection of a longhaired guy in black braids, a band around his forehead, sitting in the back of the political science classroom, silent and intent. "I remember!"

Yancy smiled.

"Remember what?" Brad asked, looking from Chloe to Yancy and back again.

Yancy waved his question away. He held Chloe with a look as a tangible, private connection grew between them.

Now that she remembered him, she also recalled that he'd been active, in… what was it? Something to do with his heritage, a protest group, probably.

He'd come a long way. She couldn't look away from his dark-eyed gaze, or draw back from her awareness of him as more than host, more than a sexually attractive man. What had he been doing all these years, to become such a powerful, wealthy man? What would it have been like to have known him then, to follow his rise to prominence?

"What would you be, Chloe?" he asked softly.

"I don't know," she murmured, still dealing with her curiosity about Yancy. She knew it was more than her journalistic training that had her wanting to know everything about him. He appealed to her on so many different levels. What was happening here?

"Chloe?"

She noted the others waiting for her answer. "I've never thought— oh, I know. I'd be a painter, live somewhere beautiful and paint huge, colorful canvasses. Like Georgia O'Keefe."

Yancy smiled, teeth flashing white against his bronzed skin. "You do know people see erotic images in her paintings?"

"People see what they want to see," she retorted. Now that he'd mentioned it, Chloe visualized some of O'Keefe's most famous paintings, calla lilies and iris and poppies all with overflowing color, fluid lines and suggestive female shapes. To be able to paint like that, to imbue contours and forms with symbolic interpretations, to meld her love of photography with vibrant art, that would be heaven. To express her own sexuality in paint and imagination, that would be sheer bliss.

Aware of Yancy's gaze still on her, she lifted her ponytail to cool her nape. His eyes dropped to her breasts, lifted high by the motion. She was glad she'd worn the tank to her bikini, glad that the high neckline covered most of her chest. And then she wished she'd worn the tiny little top, the one that cupped her breasts and held them up for all the world to see. For Yancy to see.

"I like you in yellow," Yancy murmured.

Brad made a noise, low in his throat. Chloe saw the expression on his face, and rose smoothly. "I think I've had enough sun. I'll see you all later."

Brad rose, too, "I'll walk you to your quarters."

"Just a moment, Brad," Yancy intervened. "There's something I'd like to discuss with you."

Brad's lips firmed. "Sure." His voice sounded relaxed but as Chloe entered the salon, she knew he'd have questions for her later.

Questions she didn't know how to answer. Didn't want to answer.

Chapter Five

Chloe scanned her reflection in the mirror. The long-sleeved matte jersey dress was her basic black, the skirt draping softly to her knees. The bodice had three hidden snaps that either closed the vee neckline at a modest level, or unsnapped to bare her skin almost to the waist. A hidden bra supported her breasts no matter how much skin she chose to reveal.

She released the top two snaps. The jersey parted to reveal the cleft between her breasts. She undid the last, and the bodice fell completely open. She straightened her shoulders, pleased with herself. With her hair up and a few tendrils curled around her temples, her appearance was chic and sophisticated—a far cry from the usual multi-pocketed vest and khaki twill slacks she wore on assignment.

Brad thought so, too, she noted when she entered the salon as drinks were being served. He moved quickly to her side. "You look fantastic, baby."

"Thanks."

He put his hand on the small of her back to guide her to the bar. "Drink?"

"A small one," she agreed as she looked around the salon. "Looks like some of the others have been drinking all day."

"No doubt." His thumb stroked her spine. "Nothing else to do except go around in circles."

She eased away from his hand. "Aren't we on our way to some mysterious location?"

"We've passed the same headland three times today."

"I hadn't noticed."

"Maybe you're not as attuned to mapping coordinates as I am, baby."

"Listen, Brad, I need to talk to you."

"We're talking."

"Privately."

He studied her expression, then nodded. "Your stateroom?"

They started across the salon, pausing as the steward tapped a gong, calling them to dinner. The table was lavishly set with an ivory damask cloth, heavy silver and white china with a gold and cobalt trim. Crystal stemware sparkled. Chloe stopped. "Later, I guess."

Brad nodded, his eyes lingering on hers. She read his curiosity easily.

"Place cards." Shelly held hers up to show the sleek outline of the *Fantasy* with her name written in ornate calligraphy. "Here I am, Brad, you're next to me."

Brad held Shelly's chair, then looked at the card next to his. "Chloe?"

She sat as Mark took his place on her right. He whispered, "All those forks and things." He touched one. "How are we supposed to know which one to use?"

"Follow my lead," she whispered back.

"What are you two plotting?" Yancy asked as he placed himself at the head of the table.

Mark flushed. Chloe smiled. "We're admiring the silverware. It looks very elegant."

Yancy lifted an eyebrow, holding her gaze, but she said no more.

Across the table, Wynne sat at Yancy's left, then Saul, Tracy across from her, Perry and Ali with Adam sitting at the other end, opposite Yancy. Drawn into conversation, Chloe realized she was enjoying herself. The other guests were intelligent, in touch with world events and not afraid to voice their opinions. Table talk was lively as the steward served the meal, course after course of exquisitely prepared dishes. The chef had used fresh seafood, local produce and Monterey wines, and by the time he prepared zabaglione at the table, she could only savor a bite or two.

She lifted her wineglass. "Compliments to the chef for a wonderful meal."

"Hear, hear."

The chef inclined his head. "My pleasure." He was still smiling as he left the salon.

The steward topped wineglasses, poured coffee or tea and set out liqueurs with thimble sized glasses on a silver tray in the middle of the table. Next to Yancy, he placed the same silver bowl Chloe remembered from the evening before. She stifled a sound of derision. Not another silly game.

The steward placed a slip of paper and a pen by each guest, then left quietly. Yancy cleared his throat. "I see some of you are curious. No doubt you're wondering what pleasures await you."

Chloe groaned. Yancy laughed. "It's not that bad, I assure you. If you remember your bedtime stories, some of them involved magic lanterns and genies who could grant three wishes."

Chloe noted the increased interest on Lane and Ali's faces as they leaned forward to hear Yancy's explanations.

"Now, I'm no genie, and this," he held up the silver bowl, "this is no magic lantern, but we'll see what we can do about making a fantasy come true. Take a moment, think of something you've always wanted, no matter how wild, then write it down."

"Like what?" Mark asked.

Shelly giggled. "Like your deepest sexual fantasy."

"Or your childhood dreams," Wynne added.

"Seriously?" Saul inquired.

Yancy nodded. "Whatever you desire, short of a trip to the stars. Even I can't arrange that."

"No need," Tracy said. "I think I can come up with something more earthly."

"Or earthy," Perry added as the others laughed.

Chloe held the pen in her hands, gazing at the slip of heavy white paper. What should she write? She'd already mentioned her alternate dream of painting. The other guests seemed to have no trouble. One by one, they wrote, folded their papers and dropped them in the silver bowl.

Adam caught her eye and winked, then wrote quickly. He dropped his paper in the bowl and sat back in his chair to watch the others. Next to her, Brad shifted in his chair, then printed in neat caps. She glimpsed his words, felt her eyes widen and averted her gaze. Lane and Perry exchanged passionate glances, then wrote. They added their slips of papers to the growing pile. Lane reached in and swished the papers around. "There, no one will know whose paper is on top."

"Except there are still two to go," Perry reminded her.

Two left. Yancy and herself. He held her gaze for a moment, his eyes dropped to her mouth, then to the deep slit of her neckline. She felt her nipples peak, her breasts warm as warmth coiled low in her abdomen. He smiled, a tiny, thin smile that told her he knew what he was doing to her. That he intended to do more than seduce her with his eyes.

She wanted that. Wanted him. The more she learned about him, the more fascinating he became. He triggered intimate thoughts, visions of lovemaking. A mental picture of Yancy, naked and aroused, grew in her mind. Would he be as superb a lover as he was a seducer? Given the way he made her feel right now, she had no doubt he'd be a virile and demanding lover.

Abruptly, she knew what she would write. It could be the frank and sensual surroundings, her increasing awareness of Yancy as a desirable man that prompted her sexual fantasies, but why not be honest? No one would know it was her wish. She shielded the paper from curious eyes and wrote, *I want to be made love to by three men, all at the same time.* Without looking at any one, she folded the notepaper and dropped it in the bowl.

Mark handed the bowl to Lane who gave it to Yancy. He shuffled the papers around. "Now, no one knows. I'm not joining in. Wouldn't be right to draw my own fantasy, now would it?" He poured himself a snifter of brandy and then pushed the tray forward. As it came down the table, some poured themselves a drink, others passed.

Chloe sipped her coffee, keeping up a pretense of casual unconcern, talking and laughing with the others, but her gaze went repeatedly to the bowl. What had the others written? What if they were as simple as tickets to a ball game? A hidden crush? What if the fantasies were read out loud? She bit her lip. How could she have written something so private, so secret? How could she retrieve her note?

At last, Yancy tapped his crystal glass. The tiny tinkle caught everyone's attention. "Now, according to the rules I've made for this evening's entertainment, all the fantasy wishes here are anonymous. If you want to reveal yours, that's up to you. As I stated before, in the way of genies everywhere, I'll read three wishes, but I'll grant only the third one."

Ali leaned forward. "When?"

"On board, if possible. Else as soon as practical. Does that suit everyone?"

Saul took another sip of port and nodded. Tracy made small patterns on the damask cloth with her demitasse spoon. Adam cleared his throat and sat straighter. Ali shrugged.

Brad sat motionless. Chloe could hardly breathe.

"Ready?" Yancy asked. He drew the first slip of paper, read it and laughed. "Wish number one: I'd like this cruise to go on for another week." He looked around the table. "Wouldn't that be fun, but sorry, no."

Chloe dropped her hands in her lap. They were shaking so hard she was sure everyone would see. Yancy opened the second note. "Wish number two is in two parts: a) can the captain marry us and b) can we use that week in Fiji as a honeymoon?"

Yancy looked around the table. "Congratulations, whoever you are, and sorry, no to both questions." He waited for the laughter to die down, then reached in and ruffled the remaining wishes. He pulled one out and held it up, unopened.

Chloe's fingers clutched at her thighs. What were the odds Yancy would draw her note? She shouldn't have written that - should have written something casual, something she wouldn't have to worry about, hoping it wouldn't be granted.

Hoping it would...

"Now, the last wish. Remember, if this is in my power to grant, I'll do it." He unfolded the slip of paper, read it and smiled, long and slow. "Wish number three: I want to be made love to by three men, all at the same time."

A hush fell over the table, then Lane demanded, "Who wrote that?"

"I'll volunteer!" Perry said.

Chloe said nothing. She couldn't say anything. Her throat closed. Her heart beat so fast she was sure people could see it pulsing beneath her skin. She didn't dare look at Yancy. If she left the table now, people might guess who had made that wish. She made herself sit, smile at the ribald remarks, the assessing glances from woman to woman.

"One of you six ladies is in for the treat of your life," Saul said, as he looked from one woman to another. "Want to tell us who you are?"

"Confidentiality, Saul, remember?" Yancy intervened. "If the person in question wants to identify herself, or himself, that's their prerogative."

"Aha," Wynne murmured. "A new twist to the proceedings."

"How are you going to grant that wish, if you don't know who wrote it?" asked Mark.

Yancy looked at his guests, one by one around the table, as if trying to guess the fantasy wish winner. He picked up his glass and drank. "I have my ways."

Chloe felt her heart pounding faster. The merriment, the laughter, the lusty remarks all seemed directed at her. She pushed back her chair. "I think I've had too much wine. I need some air. Excuse me, please."

She had taken only two steps before Adam reached her. He took her elbow, opened the door for her and ushered her out into the cold night air. Chloe immediately shivered.

"You're cold. Let's go back in."

She ran her hands up her arms. She couldn't go back in, not until she'd gotten control of herself.

"Put this on, then." Adam stripped off his jacket and draped it over her shoulders. The warmth from it felt so good, so welcome, that Chloe burrowed into it, wrapping it around her like a life vest.

"That was some wish. Wonder who wrote it? Or how Yancy's going to make it come true?" He chortled and edged closer, putting an arm around her waist. "You're still cold. How about if I get you to bed, warm you up all the way?"

Chloe looked up at him. "What's this all about, Adam? Why this obsession with sex? We agreed it was over years ago. Why bring it up again?"

Adam dropped a kiss on her temple. "I guess I'd forgotten how good it was between us until I saw Brad pawing at the ground."

"You didn't want me before that, but because you think he does, now you do?"

He shrugged. "That about sums it up. I'd make it good for you."

"Sheesh." Chloe gazed out at the ocean, at the moonlight dancing on cresting waves, at the deep shadows in the troughs. "No way, Adam."

Chloe gave him back his jacket and left him standing at the rail. On her way to her cabin, she was passing the door to Yancy's office when it opened suddenly.

"Just the lady I wanted to see," Yancy said. He'd taken off his jacket, and loosened his black tie. His white shirt was rolled up at the sleeves and gleamed in contrast to the bronzed skin of his muscled forearms. "Have you got a minute?"

She averted her gaze from his broad chest, trying to ignore the heat coming from him. She made her voice cool and calm. "Nothing but time on my hands until we dock, but if you don't mind, I'd rather be alone."

"In a minute or two. Come in." He seated her on the plush couch, then closed the door behind them. "Can I offer you a drink?"

"No, thanks. I've had more than enough."

He sat on the couch, far enough away that she didn't feel crowded. "I was worried when you left the table so suddenly. Are you sick?"

"No." She realized belatedly that she hadn't needed the anti-sea sickness wristband she'd forgotten to put on this morning. "I guess I'm a better sailor than I thought. I just needed some air."

"Were you upset by the fantasy thing?"

She felt her eyes widen. Could he be referring to her wish? "It's a silly game. No one is expecting anything of it."

Yancy smiled. "On the contrary. I've had a steady stream of men offering their services."

"Oh." She swallowed. "Well, I'm sure whoever wrote that isn't expecting it to come true. It seemed to be way out of line."

He reached over and plucked the silver bowl from his desk. "Some of the wishes were even more explicit. Take a look."

Chloe hesitated, then reached for a slip of paper. In feminine, upslanted writing, someone had written her desire to be bound and whipped. "Oh, my." She took another, then another. Variations on sexual bondage, a man wanting a golden shower, a woman asking to be covered in warm wax. She tried to suppress it, but her imagination responded to the suggestive wishes. Her nipples grew hard. Deep in her belly, warmth curled and melted. Her inner muscles contracted, as if already enclosing a heated, hard cock. Her breathing altered, becoming faster, lighter.

Yancy watched her closely. "Want to tell me which one is yours?"

"I prefer to remain anonymous," she replied as she leafed through the written fantasies. She paused at the one where Brad had wished to pleasure six women at once.

"How is that possible?" she whispered.

Yancy moved closer to read over her shoulder. She glanced at him and caught his slow, tantalizing smile that made her think of cats and cream. "A man stretches out, and with his mouth, he eats one woman. Another rides his cock. He uses his hands and his big toes to fondle the clits of four other women until they come."

Chloe dropped the paper. Without any trouble, she imagined a man stretched out on the plush carpet, then realized it wasn't Brad she was seeing, but Yancy, his big body nude, hands, feet, mouth and cock busy. She imagined five women crouched around him. She was the sixth, riding his rampant cock. Her flesh warmed as she imagined him deep within her. Was his shaved head his own phallic reference to another, smooth as silk head? Her pussy muscles clenched.

"I can guess what you're thinking, Chloe," he said in a low voice that sent shivers down her back. "I wouldn't want any other women. Just you."

His eyes locked onto hers. With a fingertip, he traced the neckline of her dress from the pulse beating madly at her throat, down the edge of fabric to her waist, and partially up the other side without touching her skin. She waited, barely breathing, as his light touch focused all her attention on his hand.

At the valley between her breasts, he nudged the jersey aside and slipped his hand inside her dress. His warmth seared her. She glanced down, fascinated by the sight of his big, tanned hand against her pale flesh. He cupped her breast, squeezing lightly as she forgot how to breathe.

"Do you like that? I do," he murmured without waiting for her reply. "All evening I've been watching you, watching your breasts move under this dress, wondering what you feel like and now I know. Soft, warm, trembling, your nipple already hard in my hand. I wonder how you taste."

He reached behind her neck and undid the long zipper. He slipped the dress off her shoulders. The soft folds drifted down, revealing her bare breasts. Chloe didn't have to look to know they were already swollen, tender at the tips.

He murmured appreciatively and nuzzled her. "I am going to make love to you all night."

"Do I have any say in the matter?" she managed as he flicked one nipple with his tongue.

"No." He raised his head. "You want this as much as I do."

She couldn't deny it. All the shared glances, the curiosity about his body, the intensity between them - all led to this moment. He bent to her breast again, his closely shaven head hot and smooth against her skin. The feel of flesh against flesh teased her, made her yearn, made her wet. She caressed his head, running her fingers from temple to nape, enchanted by his smooth heat.

She could feel his smile of satisfaction. She ran her hand down his cheek, felt his dimple and pressed her fingertip into it. He looked up, still smiling. She took her hand away and traced his lips with her tongue, then touched his dimple, poking the tip of her tongue into it. He moved quickly, catching her tongue in his mouth, nipping it gently, then settling into a deep kiss. She sighed into his mouth, then sighed again when he left it and ran his mouth down her skin.

His lips closed over her nipple, pulling it into his mouth. He pulled at it gently, alternating suckling with tongue strokes, round and round her nipple. He experimented with little nibbles until her nipple hardened in his mouth. He sucked harder then, pulling on her, stretching her. He raised his head, licked the tip and pushed her back into the soft cushions before he moved to her other breast. He suckled her as before, harder and longer, as his fingers plucked at her other nipple, keeping it hard. Aching. Needy.

Chloe closed her eyes and concentrated on the feel of his mouth on her, his warm wet tongue swirling around her areolas, a hand kneading her other breast. Warmth and wetness flooded her panties.

She tried to hide a moan, then opened her eyes when he pulled back. His face close to hers, his eyes fixed on hers, he commanded, "Don't hold back. I want everything from you. Give it all to me."

Cool air on her bare breasts chilled some of her fever. She retreated from the imperious tone. "This isn't right. I can't do this."

"You will." His eyes, seen this close, were very dark, almost obsidian. The whites were clear, a startling contrast to the rest of his face. "I've been waiting for you."

She tried to break the connection between them. "You could have gotten in touch."

"Not while you were sleeping with another man."

"I hadn't been…" She swallowed. "That is, until this morning—"

"I know about Brad," he interrupted harshly. "I allowed it since we hadn't gotten to this point ourselves, but not again. Stay away from him."

"Allowed it?" She pushed him away and sat up. "What makes you think you can tell me what to do?"

He lay back apparently relaxed until she noted the fierce look in his eyes. "When the cruise ends, you'll be staying with me."

She stood. "Dream on, fella. I have commitments to keep."

His gaze lifted from her breasts to her eyes. "Your only commitment will be to me."

Chloe refastened her dress. "That might be your fantasy, but it's not mine."

He stopped her at the door to the passageway. "You need time to get used to the idea, that's all."

"Listen. I don't know what your game is, but count me out. Oh, you're a good kisser, and you turned me on back there, but—"

"That's only the beginning, Chloe." He leaned closer, letting some of his weight rest against her. "There's more. I want you, and your body tells me you're ready for me."

His prick rose hot and hard against her. The thin jersey material did nothing to conceal her reaction. Her breasts peaked again as her nipples rubbed against the soft cloth. He pressed against her as he bent his head to trace the rim of her ear with his tongue. She quivered, held immobile not by his body, but by her own response. How could she want him, want another man, after being with Brad earlier in the day? "I can't do this," she repeated. "I don't have sex with one man in the morning, and another one at night."

He frowned. "You're not going to have sex with me. We are going to make love."

She edged away. "You know what I mean."

Yancy brought her back to him. "Are you afraid I'll think less of you? Or do you think less of yourself?"

Before she could speak, he kissed her. "I think very highly of you, Chloe. From now on, it's going to be my job, my pleasure," he corrected himself. "My pleasure to keep you satisfied. Whatever you want sexually, I'll provide. Everything. Anything else you want, I'll get it for you."

"Just like that?" She tried to snap her fingers and found them shaking too hard to connect.

He caught her hand in his, brought it to his lips and stilled her trembling. "Anything. Everything you want."

"Is this how you treat all your women?"

His grip tightened on her hand. His mouth firmed then softened into a slow smile. "You're the only one I've ever brought aboard the *Fantasy*. The only one I've ever wanted to do everything for, give everything to."

"How can you say that when we've never even talked?"

"I can say it because it's true. You weren't ready for me before now."

She tried to shrug off that statement, dismiss his words as the smooth, sweet syllables men used so easily. She failed.

She stared at his face, trying to read his expression, and saw only truth, as naked as his desire. Such a simple explanation from a complex man. His words had hidden meanings, ones that set off alarms within her even as they challenged her to be as honest with him as he was with her. He'd arranged this cruise, a fantasy world in itself, for her. How could she find fault with that? Chloe dredged deep, but found no guilt, nothing to prevent her from admitting the truth. She felt only warmth, a rightness that spread through her and burned out everything but her deepest needs.

She wanted Yancy. She wanted him in her, over her, anywhere and everywhere. This was her choice, her decision. Without a word, she lifted her hands and loosened her dress. As the jersey fell, she took her breasts and offered them to him.

He grinned. He drew her away from the door, locked it and turning, unlocked the way to her stateroom. She went through and waited, eyes on him, wanting only him.

He closed the door and came to her. With his eyes holding hers, he took off his tie and dropped it on the dresser. His hands went to the buttons on his shirt.

"Let me," she whispered. She undid the top buttons quickly, then slowed as she came to the middle ones. She put her lips to his chest as she parted his shirt and licked.

He groaned. Encouraged, she took her time with the rest of the buttons, kissing and licking his smooth chest, the ridges of his ribcage and the flat torso. He yanked the tails out of his pants and threw the shirt on the floor.

She laughed, blowing warm air on his belly, and unzipped his trousers. He sucked in a breath when she slid her hand in, found the opening in his shorts, and caressed him. He was slick and hot, pulsing in her hand.

She clasped him for a moment, enjoying the feel of his cock, anticipating what would come, then took her hand away and brushed pants and shorts down together. Only when he stepped out of them, did she realize he was barefoot. "How convenient," she murmured as she slid to her knees in front of him.

She took a moment to admire him. He was erect already, large, taut and when she placed a fingertip on the head, throbbing. She traced him from scrotum to tip, pleased with the way his cock expanded at her touch. She placed her palm under him, weighing the length and weight of his rod and smiled. When she placed her lips on the tip, licking away the drop of fluid and kissing him before taking him into her mouth, he shuddered.

Pleased, she took her time, learning him with intimate strokes of her tongue while she very gently took his balls in her hand. He was hot and heavy and hard. Murmuring her delight, she sucked him, drawing him deeper into her mouth, releasing him with reluctance, only to suck him back in. With the tip of a finger, she stroked the soft, sensitive skin behind his balls and slid up between his cheeks.

He groaned, breath coming fast, and lifted her to her feet. "No more now."

She made a face. He laughed softly and kissed the pout away. She opened her mouth to him, and he accepted, tracing her lips with his tongue, then entering, tasting her. He explored, leisurely at first with slow thrusts of his tongue, then more quickly, claiming her, a preview of what was to come. Chloe leaned into him, giving him what he wanted.

He brushed her dress from her hips, following its descent with his palms, murmuring when his hands found bare skin at the tops of her thighs. The dress fell as he brought his thumbs down the curve of her belly to rest on her mound.

She inhaled his scent and put her hands on his shoulder as he backed her down into the bed until she lay on her back, her legs open, extending over the side.

He stood between her legs, looking down at her with possessive intent. He moved back to slip her barely-there black silk panties off, crushing them in his fist and bringing them to his face. "My woman's fragrance." He held her eyes as he breathed deeply. "Now it is only for me."

She trembled under his gaze, uneasy with his claim to her, thrilled by the enjoyment he took in her body. He dropped her panties to the floor, and took her ankles, lifting and spreading them wide to expose her intimately. Placing her legs on his shoulders, he studied her intimate secrets as he ran his hands down her calves, then her thighs, stopping short of her exposed clit. She murmured her disappointment and arched her hips in invitation. He ignored her enticement, retracing his way up her legs. He turned his head to her ankle, outlining the small bones with his tongue while she quivered.

"My shoes." She wiggled the foot still wearing a high-heeled black sandal.

"I'll take care of them." He undid the strap and nudged it off her foot. He ran his thumb across her sole, chuckling as she flinched and tried to pull away. "Ticklish?"

"A little."

He closed his hand around her foot and pressed his palm firmly on her instep. She jumped as sensation sizzled up her leg. Yancy grinned. "I'll find all your sensitive spots."

She could hardly wait. Impatiently, she waited for what he would do next. He removed her other sandal, then let her legs slide down his body until they rested on the floor.

She gave him an expectant look.

"Would you like my tongue in you?" When she nodded, he sank between her outspread knees, keeping them apart with the width of his body. "Are you giving yourself to me, Chloe?"

She licked her lips.

"I take that as a yes?"

She clenched her knees around his shoulders. "Yes. Right now!"

His laugh gusted across her mound, and blew warm air on her plush folds. She quivered, waiting for his tongue, and when it came, lightly at first, no more than a delicate tasting, she quivered.

Yancy slid his large hands under her bottom to lift her to his mouth. His fingers kneaded her cheeks; his thumbs held her in place. He buried his face in her muff, inhaling deeply, rubbing his mouth across her mound. She closed her eyes, all her senses concentrated on her clitoris. When his mouth closed over it and pulled it gently into his mouth, much the way she had sucked on his cock, she whimpered.

He pleasured her with long strokes, lazy licks, even tiny nibbles on her flesh, pushing her ever closer to the edge. One thumb ran along the valley between her cheeks, going deeper with each pass until it rested on her rosebud. She clenched her buttocks.

"Open to me."

She made herself relax, unclamped her muscles and spread her legs wider for him. He dipped one finger into her warm juices, then eased the tip into her bottom even as he penetrated her pussy with his tongue. Wicked pleasure swamped her, feeding her craving for more. His tongue and his finger worked together, alternately driving in and withdrawing, propelling her even higher. Speared with pleasure, she panted and arched her hips into his face.

"That's good." He kept up the dual thrusts for a few moments more, then drew back to push her across the bed. He followed her, resting his weight on her. He was heavy, but it felt good and right. Instead of being smothered or crushed, she felt enclosed in his warmth, protected by his muscular body. He worked his arms under her, lifting himself up on his elbows. He looked down into her face. "Is there something you like particularly? Anything you don't want me to do?"

Her mind was a jumble of sensations, of arousal. "Yes. No. Whatever you want."

He kissed her slow and deep as he positioned his rod at her entrance. He teased her by rubbing against her slit, then withdrawing, pushing into her an inch, and pulling back.

She trembled. She wanted him, wanted him deep in her. Wanted him right now. "Stop teasing me!" She grabbed his hips and tugged him into her, demanding more than the inch he'd given her.

He plunged, satisfying her demand, thrusting deep. His breath escaped him in a long, sibilant hiss as he sank into her. She cried out at his penetration. She'd never felt this way before, never felt so filled, never so involved, her muscles working with his, tightening and releasing as he plunged and pulled back.

It lasted forever. It was over in a moment. It was sheer heat and wild frenzy. It was madness. It was glorious. She came an instant before he did. Her orgasm went on and on, convulsing her inner muscles around him even as her hands gripped his shoulders.

He came long and hard, his body in spasms as he shot deep and high into her. His breath came in furious, hot gusts, scorching her face and temples as his face contorted with passion.

At last, he stopped coming. He dropped his head onto the mattress next to hers. His breath now was labored, deep pants that matched hers as passion ebbed. She clung when he would have rolled off her. "Not yet."

He stilled. As her breath evened out, she became aware of the length of his legs wrapped around hers, his smooth torso resting on hers, his breath slowing, and his cock still buried in her. She lifted her arms and drew him closer, nuzzling at his neck. The pulse in his throat beat hard and fast. He had his eyes closed and his mouth partly open as he recovered.

"I meant to make it last longer," he muttered.

She panted still. "Any longer and I'd have passed out."

He smiled. She watched an expression of supreme satisfaction cross his face. "Next time."

Chapter Six

Chloe woke slowly, dazed and drenched with lovemaking. She rolled over, aware of a slight ache between her legs, and smiling, reached out for Yancy. His side of the bed was cold. So he had left as early as he'd promised. After he'd kept his other promise to make love to her again. In fact, he'd made good on that one several times.

He'd also done something else, something that she didn't expect, and wasn't sure how to handle. He'd made her feel wonderful, of course, since he was an expert lover. He'd touched her, stroked her, lifted her high, held her tenderly as she collapsed, then caressed her, each time whispering impassioned love words, showing her with his body how much he craved her. More than that, he'd made her feel truly special, unique, and appreciated.

Laughter and a raised voice roused her enough to sit up and peer out her window. She blinked as two WaveRunners dashed past, cresting the waves and zipping through the troughs. They were here then, wherever this mysterious here was. She pulled a pillow up against the headboard and watched the antics as Mark and Saul played like little boys with a new toy.

When the phone rang, it took her a moment to tear herself away. "Hello?"

"Good, you're awake. I'm sending Lisa up with some coffee. Meet me on the deck in twenty minutes."

He didn't give her time to agree or to protest. She shrugged, then dragged herself out of bed and into the shower. She winced at the bruises on her hips, put there by Yancy's large hands while he'd pounded into her from behind, but the lingering pleasure obliterated the aches. Fantuckingfastic!

When she came out of the bathroom, still drying her hair, a pot of coffee, juice and a warm croissant waited for her on the coffee table. She poured juice and coffee, drank them and nibbled at the roll while she dressed in shorts, a tee shirt and athletic shoes.

Yancy was alone in the salon. He rose at her entrance and tilted her face up to his. "How are you? Not too sore?"

Remembering how he had used her body brought a flush to Chloe's breasts. "I'm fine."

"I wasn't too rough?" The thought of his hands on her body made her skin sensitive all over again. Her knees wobbled. She felt moisture gathering in her pussy even as her breasts felt heavier, more tender. She leaned closer to him, absorbing his heat and scent. "I loved it."

He smile was slow, possessive and hot. "Spend the day with me."

She looked beyond him to the guests gathered on the deck. "Won't the others need you?"

"They can take care of themselves." He ran a finger down her arm, barely touching the fine hairs that quivered at his caress. "I want us to be together."

She looked into his eyes, saw the scorching heat behind the obsidian gaze, and felt it burn deep. "Yes."

"Good. I'll take care of you."

And he did just that for the rest of the morning, as he helped her into a wetsuit, checking her gear, and went over the side with her. Their time underwater was magical, sharing the cold waters with him at her side, fins idly kicking them along, bubbles surfacing, enclosed in an alien world of their own.

At lunch, served on deck with plenty of finger foods and laughter, they found a private spot on the sun deck. He sat close to her, urging her to eat. "I can't," she complained. "I won't be able to fit into my clothes."

"I'll buy you more."

She looked at him appraisingly. He was serious, she could tell, but instead of pleasing her, his offer made her uneasy. "No, thanks. I take care of myself."

"I know that. You wouldn't be where you are, who you are," he corrected himself, "if you weren't fully capable."

"Meaning?"

He studied her face. "You have a delicate look to you. As if you'd break or shatter if touched. Many men would be deceived. I'm not. You're tough. Independent. I like that."

She was pleased. "I wouldn't get far in my business if I was easy to crack."

Instead of chiding her for talking about work, he looked at her thoughtfully. "You've had to deal with situations that would make others weak. Your pictures show that."

"You've seen them?"

"Who hasn't, Chloe? You're in all the newsmagazines, on TV, on the wire services. You see and you show the world."

She stared at him. He understood what she was trying to do. To make her photographs speak for people devastated by war and disease, for orphaned children who knew nothing about play and too much about death. The realization that he shared her vision warmed her to the core. Then she thought of the subject matter of her work.

He seemed to read her mind. "Don't think about it, Chloe. You do a great job, but put it aside now. Don't let it consume you."

"I can't forget what I've seen. What I've experienced." She closed her eyes to shut out the images of her last terrible assignment. "And I'm on the fringes. Those people live it everyday."

"That's what makes you so good at your job, but you can only do so much. Give it a rest."

"I can't. I see… things in my dreams. I think I'm losing my edge," she admitted.

"Maybe it's time to do something else?"

"I can't."

"Think about slowing down, at least." He cupped her cheek with the palm of his hand. "You don't have to make that decision yet."

She leaned into his warmth. "Thanks for inviting me aboard. Even if I wasn't very gracious, I appreciate it."

"I'm glad." He moved closer, faces almost touching. "I want you to forget all that ugliness. Relax. Let the water and fresh air do their job."

"They already are." She looked into his eyes. So dark, so compelling. "What's happening here?"

"What I've wanted for years." He eased away, straightened his shoulders. "You need to know that I've kept track of your career from the beginning. I've sweated out some of your riskier encounters, celebrated your achievements. When you won that award, I was in the audience."

"Why wasn't I aware of this?"

"Do you know everyone who admires your work?"

Put that away, it sounded reasonable. "No, but—" If she'd known this earlier, she'd have been convinced he was stalking her after all. An earlier question interrupted that unpleasant thought. "Did you get my boss to threaten me if I didn't accept your invitation?"

He frowned, the crease between his eyes deepening, making his features more severe. "He did that? Coerced you?"

"He said get myself on this boat or else."

"I didn't expect him to go that far."

She rose and went to lean against the railing, arms crossed over her chest. Having her suspicions confirmed made her stomach churn. She trembled with the force of her fury. "What did you think he'd do?"

"Encourage you, urge you to take a break, that's all."

"In return for what?"

He hesitated. "There was some mention of a new helicopter."

This was worse than she'd expected. "You bribed him with a new chopper? Paid him for his services?" Her voice rose. "For my services?"

"You demean yourself thinking like that," he said firmly. "I did it for us."

"There is no us. Thinking that is as much a fantasy as the name of…" she glanced at the deck below where Perry and Lane indulged in a deep, passionate kiss, "this love boat!"

He laughed. "Sex is a great relaxer."

"That's all it is to you? A way to burn off stress?" The thought cut deep. She'd been so happy this morning. Now, she felt cold, nauseated, as if the boat lurched in heavy seas.

"What is it to you, Chloe? You had affairs with Adam and Brad. What did they mean to you?"

Pride kept her standing upright. "That's none of your business."

He was on his feet in an instant. "You gave yourself to me last night. Everything you do is now my business."

She went rigid. "I didn't give you anything!"

Yancy placed a finger over her lips to silence her. "I asked you if you were giving yourself to me. You indicated yes."

"I did not!" Then she remembered. "That was just last night—just for sex!"

"No, Chloe." His voice was adamant, resolved. "It was more than sex, great though it was. You belong to me now."

"You're out of your mind! Just because you bribed my boss to get me here, because you set up this elaborate, sneaky sham, that doesn't mean a thing to me. I owe you nothing!"

"That's true." She looked up at him, absorbing the heat of his body, the faint tang of sweat mixed with his own unique scent, as he gazed down at her intently. His dark eyes were hooded, making his expression unreadable as he studied her face. Chloe felt her body react to his even as her mind revolted against his underhanded methods.

She shivered as a thought occurred to her. "If you didn't manage to get me into bed, would you have tried one of the other women? Are they here as backups?"

His eyes narrowed. "You ask me that when I've made it clear that this whole cruise is for you?"

"If it's about me, why did you invite Brad and Adam? Did you know about them? And me?" When he nodded, she jerked back. "So you had them come to see how I'd react?"

"In a way. If you were glad to see them, or willing to resume an affair with either one of them, I wouldn't have stood in your way."

"And if I'd preferred one of the other guys?"

"The same. It was a risk I had to take."

"And now?"

"Now I'm not willing to share you." He scowled, his face darkening and looking very fierce. "I wanted to strangle Brad."

She blinked at his admission. "Jealous?"

"I don't like the idea of any other man with you."

Chloe raised her face to the cool breeze tempering the midday heat. She didn't know how to handle all the emotions churning through her. "I hate that you bribed my boss, manipulated me—"

"But? Do I hear a but there?" he asked hopefully.

"But, it is flattering that you went to such lengths to meet me. You could have arranged that without all this fuss."

"I could have. I wanted to give you a good time, a real rest, even if you chose not to have anything to do with me. I was pleased when you weren't happy to see Adam or Brad."

She remembered his smile when she'd demanded he turn around and set her ashore. Now she knew why he'd looked so self-satisfied. She thought of the time she'd spent aboard, of the passion she'd experienced in his arms. More than that, she recalled the way he accepted her work and understood her vision. That understanding was rare. She didn't want to lose it.

Yet, how could she balance the way he'd loved her with the way he'd manipulated her? She'd been beginning to think that there might be something special growing between them, but how could that be? Heady sex, lack of sleep and indignation had made a mess of her mind. Yancy's words, his methods and her feelings about him left her baffled. Hopeful, but confused. "I need to think."

"Why don't you take a nap? Sleep as long as you want. Oh, by the way," he said as she started for the steps leading to the main deck, "dinner tonight is casual."

She nodded. Once in her cabin, she kicked off her shoes and curled up on the bed. The sheets were immaculate and sweet smelling, but she could almost catch the heavy musky aromas of sex and aroused male. She remembered how Yancy had made her come again and again, giving her no respite. He'd taken her repeatedly, in a variety of positions, and each time she'd thought she could take no more, he'd proved she could.

Much later, as the sun set, Chloe dressed in slacks, a cotton shirt and her warm red sweater, then joined the group on deck. Darkness settled over the water with only an occasional whitecap breaking the surface. Candles in glass lamps glimmered over a buffet set up on tables, and many of the others were already enjoying their meal. She selected some seafood and a couscous salad before joining a group in a sheltered corner. Yancy, seated in another group, glanced at the empty chair beside him, then raised an eyebrow. He held her glance until she turned away, ostensibly to hear what Mark was saying about his scuba experiences.

The captain joined them for coffee. After a few sips, he pulled a slip of paper from his pocket. "We anchored here last night at 2:30. The closest estimate was," he glanced at the paper, then at the group. "I think Sam said 2:15?"

Saul stood. "Saul."

"Right." The captain waited while Saul and Yancy joined him. The three shook hands, then Yancy pulled an envelope out of the back pocket of his Dockers and gave it to Saul.

"What is it?" Ali called.

Saul opened the envelope, read the enclosed document and nodded his appreciation. He shook hands with Yancy again. "Thanks. I'll enjoy this."

"What, what?" Shelly jumped to her feet and rushed over to Saul. He showed her the paper, then held it up for all to see. Chloe scanned the writing, saw it was a certificate for a weekend cruise aboard the *Fantasy*. Saul and Tracy shared a look that left no one wondering who would be sharing the weekend with him.

At least two people were making plans for the future, Chloe thought as she returned to her meal. Someone handed her a glass of white wine. She looked up and saw Brad standing by her chair. "Thanks." He looked handsome in a dark sweater and jeans.

He folded into a cross-legged seated position at her side. "I missed you today. Thought we could do something together."

She didn't want to handle the complication of Brad now, but she had to. She should have talked to him last night as they'd arranged. She looked into his clear, open face. He looked so boyish and young, but she knew the steely determination and courage that had fueled his career in the military. He gazed at her now with the same concentration she'd seen so often before in the field. It made her feel like he was assessing the best way to reach an objective. It wasn't fair to let him think she wanted him back in her life. "Yesterday shouldn't have happened. It was a mistake."

"I figured that out. I thought you'd have the guts to tell me yourself instead of hiding behind the boss."

She winced. "I'm sorry, Brad. I…" Her voice faded as she interpreted his expression. "It wasn't anything planned."

"Getting even for getting left in the Middle East?"

His question cut her to the quick. Even though she'd known yesterday that there was nothing more for them, it hurt to know he thought so little of her. "You know me better than that."

He looked at her for a long time before answering. "What's done is done." He stood and began to move away, then turned back. "If you're going to spend any time with Yancy, you'd better be prepared to let him call the shots."

It was an effort to lift her shoulder in a semi-shrug. "I'll keep it in mind."

"Just be warned. He doesn't take no for an answer." He gazed at her for another moment, then moved away.

Chloe looked after him. Sighing, she gave her plate and glass to a passing steward, then rose quietly and went back to her cabin. She needed to think.

She opened the curtains to the window and curled up so she could watch the stars and the dark sea flowing past the sleek hull. They were underway again, to another surprise destination. It still amazed her that a group of very busy people, professionals at the top of their careers and much in demand, could drop everything to accept Yancy's invitation. And what's more, to drop inhibitions and behave so indiscreetly.

She jumped off the bed. After taking a moment to check her hair and makeup, she headed for the door and pulled it open.

Yancy stood in the doorway, his hand lifted to knock. "May I come in?"

His wide shoulders blocked her view of the hallway behind him. "I was on my way out to join you."

His smile lit up his face. "Yeah?"

"Yeah. I realized I've been hiding out here whenever I didn't like the conversation."

"Can we talk?"

She stood back to let him enter. He came in, shut the door behind him and waited. She gestured at the conversation area.

He flicked a glance at the bed but accepted her invitation and sat on the couch. She took a chair across from him, keeping her hands folded in her lap.

He smiled. "You're looking more rested."

"I napped."

"Good." He leaned forward, elbows on his knees. "I did some thinking this afternoon. Want to hear what I decided?"

She shrugged.

"Going to make this difficult, are you? Okay. I can handle that."

She waited.

"You're probably thinking I acted high-handed. Getting you aboard under false pretenses."

She nodded.

He grinned. "You'd be right. I'm not sorry, though."

"Oh?"

"Not when things are working out the way I'd planned. Hoped," he substituted as her eyes narrowed. "Are they?"

The warmth of his smile and the light in his eyes went straight to her heart. She prided herself for looking for truth in her work. She couldn't ask less of herself. "Yes."

In an instant, he was on his feet and pulling her up from her chair. He took her arms and wound them around his neck, bringing her close for a long, tongue-twisting kiss. Any lingering qualms vanished in the fervor of his greeting.

At last, they separated. He lifted her to nuzzle his face into her chest. Holding her close, he nibbled on her long hair as he took the few steps to the bed.

"I was afraid you wouldn't let me in."

"How could I keep you out?" She laughed and kissed his temples, the curve of his brow, the top of his freshly shaven head. She nibbled on his ear. "Why do you shave your head?"

He pulled back, his face almost comical. "You want to talk about my head now?"

She laughed at his expression. "Why not? I like your head." She brought it back to her and ran her tongue over the crown.

He shivered. "Maybe that's why."

"An erogenous zone?"

"Why don't you find out for yourself?" He slid her down his body, letting her feel how ready he was. She smiled and pressed closer. He kissed her again, then moved his lips across her face, relearning her contours with his mouth and tongue. She turned her head to catch his mouth, but he evaded her, and pressed kisses on her ear, tracing the contours, then down her neck.

When he reached the collar of her shirt, he nudged it aside to reach the pulse at the base of her throat. He pressed his lips there, pulling slightly, making her aware of her speeding heart rate. He ran his hands down her back, under her sweater and pulled her shirttails out of her slacks. His fingers were warm against her skin as he slid them up and undid the catch of her bra.

Just in time. Her breasts felt heavy, swollen with need. He pushed her sweater and blouse out of his way, and lowered his head. She expected him at her breast, but he surprised her by putting his lips on her torso and tonguing his way across her ribcage. She shivered. His hands were busy at her waist, undoing the clasp, lowering the zipper, and easing his palms inside.

He dropped to his knees and pushed her slacks off her hips. They fell to the floor, leaving her panties in place. He surprised her again by pulling the waistband just low enough to reveal her navel. Yancy pressed his face into her belly, licking in smaller and smaller circles until he zeroed in on her navel. His tongue delved into it, making her stomach muscles contract. He chuckled and blew into the tiny depression.

"You're driving me crazy!"

He looked up at her, a sparkle in his dark eyes. His grin promised her much more to come. "Good."

He pulled her down on the floor next to him, and eased the sweater over her head. He eased the buttons free, then slipped her shirt off one shoulder, then the other. He tugged her bra free, then put his hands into her hair and loosened the clasp holding it away from her face. Her hair came loose, tumbling over her shoulders. He clutched a fistful and brought it to his face.

"I used to sit in the back of that classroom and watch the sun on your hair. I wanted to touch it so bad I couldn't sit still."

"So why didn't you?" she breathed.

"I wasn't good enough for you."

She stared at him. "Not good enough?"

"I was just another kid off the reservation, in school on a scholarship, working every moment I wasn't studying. What did I have to offer you?"

"You could have let me make that decision," she whispered.

"I needed to do it my way."

She sighed. "Stubborn." Her breasts moved. With one hand still in her hair, he nuzzled his face into the valley between her breasts and licked her. She quivered. He took one taut nipple into his mouth and suckled. She shook.

With his mouth busy on her breasts, she ran her fingers over his shaven head, delighting in the smooth, warm skin. She touched his nape, felt his response and stroked him gently. He sucked harder, then lowered her to the floor. Swiftly, he stripped off the rest of her clothing leaving her naked while he was fully clothed.

The deep pile of the carpet was soft on her back. His mouth was busy at her breasts, leaving a trace of moisture, cool on her heated skin, as he suckled and nibbled.

She arched her back, giving him more. He played with her free breast, kneading it, flicking his thumb against the stiff nipple. He sat up and moved between her outstretched legs, draping her thighs over his. She was open to him, her mons pressed tightly against his groin. The fabric of his jeans rubbed against her pussy, stimulating and frustrating her at the same time.

Yancy ran his hands up her torso, lifting her until she reclined on her elbows. With his palms under her, his thumbs were free to play with her nipples, and he did just that. He lowered his head and licked.

She moaned. "Take off your clothes. I want to touch you."

"Soon." He kissed her open mouth, taking her complaints and whimpers. Flexing his groin against her, he teased her with his aroused cock. She dropped her head back, clay in his hands.

He shaped her, letting her down gently, moving back to rest his face on her stomach. He lifted her legs until her heels rested on the floor by his shoulders and lowered his head to her. She writhed in his grasp, eager to have his mouth ease her torment.

When it came, it was the barest of touches. She wanted his tongue in her, wanted his fingers in her, wanted his hard cock in her. Instead, he gave her butterfly kisses, his eyelashes fluttering against her engorged clit. She whimpered, then cried out as he brought her to the edge of orgasm, and retreated.

"I need you now!" she panted.

"Soon." He withdrew from her and stood. She took his outstretched hand and allowed him to pull her to her feet.

Yancy held her close for a moment, absorbing her shudders, then scooped her up and deposited her on the bed. She lay back, breathing heavily while he undressed. He took his time, giving her time to calm down and imagine what would come next.

She moved off the bed to draw the covers back, then reclined on one elbow to wait for him. He put one knee on the bed, his aroused cock jutting out inches from her face. She licked him. His cock grew before her eyes, then in her mouth as she drew him in and using her tongue, stroked him slowly. He exhaled and flexed his hips.

She took him deeper, swirling her tongue around the ridge, flicking the little nubbin there, and taking pleasure in pleasing him. She felt the tremors in the long muscles in his thighs and with her mouth clasped around his rod, pulled him forward to lie on the bed next to her.

He let her play with his balls and cock until they were wet and hard, then gently pushed her head away. "Enough. I won't last."

"Come in me now."

"Soon." He rolled her over on her stomach, spreading his palms against her back and caressing her in long strokes from nape to thigh. She murmured, sinking deeper into sensuality as his large hands kneaded her cheeks. She pushed back against him, expecting him to position her for entry. He lifted her hips, pulling them up until she knelt with her weight on her elbows. She moaned in frustration, then in embarrassment as he spread her knees as wide as they would go, leaving her open and exposed. She started to close her legs.

"Be still." He moved her back as he wanted her, then lowered himself until his face was on a level with her bottom. He took her cheeks, one in each hand, and gently widened the crack between them. "You are beautiful, every inch of you." He stroked a finger down the crack. "Your ass, your pretty little bud here," he tapped her anus, then moved lower and traced her slit with his fingertip. "Here, your pussy." He dipped a finger into her, felt her wetness. "You are so responsive. So ready."

"Please," she whimpered. "I can't take much more."

"We've only just begun, Chloe. Before we're done, I'm going to see how much you can take. Give you more."

He blew on her inner folds, creating a cascade of ripples along every one of her over-sensitized nerve endings. She was so close! Her hands pulled the sheets as her inner muscles clenched. Her breath came hot and fast against the bed. She begged, she pleaded for Yancy to finish it, to give her release.

He lifted his head and drew back. Only then she became aware of knocking at the door. "No, no," she cried. "Ignore that. Don't stop!"

Yancy patted her on the ass. "I'll get it." He rolled out of bed and stepped into his jeans as Chloe collapsed into the mattress and drew the sheet over her body.

She heard low voices and turned to see Adam and Brad in the open doorway. Brad still wore his jeans and dark sweater, but Adam had stripped down to a pair of well-worn Bermuda shorts. He had a black briefcase with him. Brad carried a bottle of champagne and four glasses.

Yancy didn't seem surprised to see them. She rolled over and sat up, holding the sheet over her breasts. The silky material caught on her pebbled nipples, sending another quiver through her. She eyed the three men.

"What's going on? What are you doing here?"

Chapter Seven

Yancy turned to her. "I asked Brad and Adam to join us. We're going to fulfill your fantasy."

She felt her eyes widen. Her stomach lurched even as her breath caught in her throat. "How did you know?"

"I'll tell you later. May they come in?"

Chloe hesitated. "But… you said…"

"Later, Chloe," he said firmly. He gestured at the men in the doorway. "Should I send them away?"

Her heart beat so hard she could hear it. Her throat went dry. Her nipples ached and deep within her, something wild and fierce clamored for satisfaction. "No."

Yancy stepped aside to allow Adam and Brad entrance. He locked the door as Adam placed his case on the floor beside the bed. Her pulse fluttered as she glanced from that to Yancy and then to Brad and Adam.

Yancy took the bottle from Brad and opened the champagne. He poured and handed a crystal flute to Chloe, then to the other men. He lifted his glass in a toast. "To Chloe. May the reality be as good as her fantasy."

Her breasts felt heavy and hot, hot as the liquid between her thighs. She took a sip, then another.

Adam and Brad drank theirs down. Yancy swallowed, then set his almost full flute on the bedside table. Chloe set hers down too and looked at Brad. "I thought you were angry with me."

His face turned grim. "I was."

"Then why are you doing this?"

He studied her, as if memorizing the sight of her, rumpled and needy. "Why not?"

She swallowed. "You don't have to."

"I want to. End of discussion."

Yancy looked from Brad to Chloe. Satisfied, he opened the bag and beckoned Chloe nearer.

She scooted across the bed, careful to keep her breasts covered, and looked at the contents. Bedroom toys, the kind Adam enjoyed playing with, masks, vibrators, dildoes and a small flogger like the one he'd liked to use on her. He hadn't hurt her, but brought her sensitivity to a fever peak. She glanced up and saw him smiling at her. He was remembering how he'd used the furry side on her, how he'd wanted to use the leather side and she'd refused.

Yancy was watching her reaction, saw her flinch when she recognized the nipple and pussy clamps. "You have a choice, Chloe. Would you prefer the toys? Or the men? Or both?"

Her throat felt dry, swollen. "Men," she whispered.

"Louder, Chloe."

"Men!"

Adam closed the briefcase and placed it by the door.

When he turned back, Yancy asked, "You're willing to let Adam make love to you?"

Chloe's gaze flickered from Yancy to Adam and back again. Strangely, she felt no fear, nothing but excitement bubbling up in her. This was why Yancy had aroused her so thoroughly, made all her senses clamor for completion. He had denied himself, had teased and tormented her, bringing her body close to coming, then withdrawing, cooling her down to bring her up again. He was readying her for this, for three men making love to her at once. Her throat burned. "Yes."

"You're willing to let Brad make love to you?"

"Yes."

"You're willing to let me make love to you?"

"Yes."

"All of us together?"

Waiting for her response, Brad watched her with narrow eyes. Adam wore his jaunty grin. She looked into Yancy's dark eyes, drawn by the hidden heat. "Yes."

"Do you want a mask? So you won't know who is doing what?"

She looked at the three men. Each so different, yet so alike. Masculine, virile, demanding, at ease in their bodies, and so attentive to hers. She licked her lips. "No mask. This is my fantasy and I want to see every minute of it."

Yancy laughed. "Bravo." His smile faded, and his expression grew implacable. "Those are the only choices you'll have tonight, Chloe. Until we leave this room, you are only to experience, to take. From now on, you give your body to us."

She was unbearably excited, could only nod in agreement as she looked from one man to the other. Yancy unzipped, let his trousers fall. He stood at ease, his erection still impressive. He reclined on the bed next to her, propping himself against the pillows.

Brad moved, catching her attention. She watched him pull the sweater over his head, fold it and place it neatly on the coffee table. His jeans followed suit. He wore no underwear. Semi-erect, he came to stand next to the bed, the heat from his body warming the few inches between them.

She rose to her knees, letting the sheet drop from her body. After a questioning look at Yancy, she ran her palms up Brad's legs and cupped his balls in one hand. She licked the tip of his cock, then drew him into her mouth and made him hard. He put his hands in her hair and held her head close to his body. She inhaled his scent and sucked greedily.

"Enough." Brad pushed her away from him. She looked up, saw his expression and knew he was already in the moment.

Chloe glanced at Yancy, saw him relaxed against the headboard, watching her impassively. Adam sat on the far side, undressed, watching her with his mouth partly open.

Yancy held out his hand to her. She went to him, taking it and allowing him to draw her down next to him.

He settled pillows at her back. "Comfortable?"

She nodded. She'd cooled down in the last few minutes, lost the frenzy that had her begging Yancy to take her. As if he sensed the difference, Yancy stood and Adam took his place. Adam turned her to face him, cupped her face with his hands, and then began kissing her. "I thought this moment would never come," he whispered into her mouth. Softly, he kissed her, tenderly at first, then with greater intensity as she opened her mouth to him. His rod swelled and grew hard against her belly.

She felt the bed dip as either Brad or Yancy settled behind her. One hand stroked her back, another her leg and foot. Whoever it was lifted her foot and kissed her toes, then sucked them one by one. She murmured her pleasure into Adam's mouth, then gasped at the slight pain in her toe as someone nipped it.

Adam ran a hand down her throat to her breast. He shaped it, testing its plumpness and gently squeezed. Her nipple hardened under his hand and she lifted her chest to give him more of her.

Chloe gazed over Adam's head to see Yancy at the foot of the bed, his tongue licking the arch of her foot. He looked up and winked. She remembered how aroused he'd made her earlier with his palm on her foot and when he did it again, her body hummed in response. Any trepidation she might have felt vanished in the warmth of his gaze, his dark eyes intent on her, and on her pleasure.

She felt moisture on her spine, and realized it was Brad, tonguing from her nape down to the base of her hips, following the curve of bone and flesh until he had her squirming. Adam latched on to her breast, holding her still for his mouth. Brad's licking gave way to tiny nibbles, barely felt amidst all the sensations in other parts of her body. She felt his finger trace the crack between her cheeks, then part her gently. He blew on the tender skin, creating frissons all over her body. She closed her eyes and gave herself up to pleasure.

Chloe felt Adam move and another body take his place, but she didn't open her eyes to see which man. It didn't matter any longer. Her inhibitions had vanished. All three had loved her well and often. She trusted them to know what enhanced her sensitivity, unleashed her sexuality, what drove her over the top.

The man at her breast pushed her shoulder, rolling her onto her back. He buried his face between her breasts, pushing them up to cradle his face. Hair brushed against her chin, so she knew it wasn't Yancy. Brad then, who liked to place his cock between her breasts and tease them both with his thrusts. She smiled as she felt him straddle her, his hot hard flesh sliding between her breasts and stuck out her tongue to lick him on the forward thrust. His cock pulsed and grew as she lapped at him. With a muttered curse, he pulled back.

Behind him, she felt someone part her legs. She waited expectantly for a tongue, for fingers, but instead, lips brushed up from her ankle, to her knee, turning it slightly to reach the sensitive skin behind it, then continuing up her thigh. She trembled in anticipation.

She inhaled as the lips reached the juncture of her thighs, waited eagerly for the first touch. It didn't happen. Instead, he repeated his ankle to groin touch, barely touching the surface of her skin. It drove her crazy. "Touch me!"

"Just feel, Chloe." Yancy's voice reminded her of her promise. She gritted her teeth as sensation after sensation bombarded her body. Every bit of skin felt caressed by knowing hands. Someone bent to her mouth, pulling her tongue into his mouth, then thrusting his tongue into hers, fast and hard, a taste of what was to come. She opened to him, to the man at her pussy and moaned with desire when at last a tongue flicked at her bud. It licked her folds, running along and between, licking her, then penetrating her.

At last! She quivered and arched her hips. With his mouth still busy, he put a finger into her. She inhaled, caught up in passion, then forgot to exhale as he slid in another finger, then another. In and out, bringing her to her peak again, bringing her so close. Abruptly, they stopped. She opened her eyes.

Brad lifted himself off her body. Behind him, Adam put his fingers in his mouth and sucked them clean. Heat rushed through her.

Brad put his hands on her hips and pulled her down the bed, making room for Yancy who positioned himself on his knees at the head of the bed. He put his hands in her hair as he looked down into her upturned face. "Okay?"

Flushed with desire, Chloe could only nod. He ran his hand along her temple, her cheek and down to her shoulder. "Get on your hands and knees."

Chloe did as instructed, lifting her knee to let Brad slide in under her. In a daze, she straddled him and looked into Yancy's face. He smiled at her and filled his hands with her breasts. He pulled her to him until her mouth opened and took his cock inside. He made a noise low in his throat as her tongue circled the head of his penis and her lips clamped around him.

Chloe felt Brad's hands on her hips, moving her so he could reach her. He placed his palm on her mons and pressed. Chloe gasped as she realized that behind her, Adam was stroking her bottom and worming a finger into her. She tensed.

Yancy stroked her head. "Relax, Chloe."

She didn't know what she felt the most. Yancy's cock thrusting lazily in and out of her mouth, Brad's hand busy on her clit, fingers penetrating her one by one, or Adam applying oil to her bottom. She pulled her mouth off Yancy and peered over her shoulder. Adam spread lubricant on his cock, too. He grinned at her. "Easy, sweet lady. We've done this before."

They had, and she'd enjoyed it, but now, faced with the realization that she was really going to have cock in all her orifices, warmth flashed through her body. Her pulse thrummed in anticipation. She sought Yancy's eyes, saw them half-closed with pleasure. She felt Brad's cock probing as he lifted her, then settled her down on him. She sighed as she took him deeply inside her. Imbedded in her, Brad stroked several times, his hands busy at her breasts. A moan escaped her lips.

Adam held her hips, bending her forward over Brad's torso. Yancy crouched to keep his cock in her mouth. Within her, Brad pulsed, holding back while Adam slowly and deftly entered her from the rear. He gave her time to adjust, stroking her bottom and stretching her before he continued until he was fully seated. "Aaah," he moaned. "That feels so damned good. Hot."

She felt full, stretched, quivering as her inner muscles clamped themselves around the two cocks. Her lips tightened around Yancy. Adam moaned again and gripped her hips hard, as if willing himself to wait until she was ready. Brad gave a tentative thrust as he dropped his hands to grip her thighs.

Adam pulled back as Brad pushed himself in, then between them, they set up an alternating thrust and lunge that had her gasping for breath. She couldn't think, couldn't see. She could only feel, thrust and counter thrust, heat and sensation consuming her. Pleasure seared her to the tips of her toes digging into the luxurious bedding. It was too much. Not enough. She was so close!

Steamy heat rose from the four bodies so tightly meshed. Every forward movement brought Adam's balls against her ass, the rhythmic strokes caressing her intimately, and pushing her against Yancy, who filled her mouth with his cock. His hands were busy at her breasts, shaping them, pulling on her nipples, and pinching them. She felt every touch, every caress, every upward movement bringing Brad deeper into her, completely fulfilling her desire to be made love to by three men at once. Wracked by passion, Chloe felt stretched beyond belief, every pore absorbing sensation, every nerve ending battered by gratification.

She could no longer move on her own. Impaled at every opening, she could only accept and respond. Her body moved at the will of the others. Her breath came fast, as fire scorched through her. She closed her eyes, giving herself up to passion, to each stimulation of her already wracked body. Brad's thrusts went ever deeper. Adam lunged into her, overwhelming her with heat, then came in a long, shuddering burst. He shook with the force of it, inadvertently shoving her deeper onto Brad's cock who eased his hand between their bodies and fingered her taut little bud. Instantly, fiercely unbearable pleasure shot through her.

She convulsed around Brad, her pussy muscles spasming so tightly around him that he yelled and shot high into her. She felt his pulsing orgasm prolonging her own. She'd been kept at such a fever pitch for so long that her orgasm went on and on, draining her completely. Behind her, Adam eased himself from her and dropped to the bed. Yancy held her head away from him, protecting himself from her gritting teeth. She slumped forward onto Brad's chest. He rolled her over, wedging her between his body and Adam's prostrate form. Their chests heaved as they fought for breath.

Chloe licked her lips. Something tugged at her attention, something lacking, but she couldn't imagine what. She'd think about it later, but now she was too exhausted to think clearly. She lay sandwiched between two lovers, eyes closed, dazed and sated.

A hand smoothed hair away from her face. She felt the tenderness and smiled before dozing. She woke as Brad eased himself from her, and drifted off as she heard the shower running. She stretched, moving away from Adam who still slept.

"Rest, Chloe." Yancy's voice sounded close by, but it was too much of an effort to open her eyes to find him. A few minutes later, Brad returned to the side of the bed. She sensed him, fresh and damp from his bath, as he sat beside her. She forced her eyes open as he picked up her hand and brought it to his lips.

"Bye, baby. Hope I made it good for you."

She murmured deep in her throat, smiling as he kissed her fingers. Sometime later, she heard the water running again, then felt herself lifted and carried into the bathroom. She opened her eyes when her bottom touched the warm water, and purred as it came up over her body. The scent of sandalwood drifted up as the water covered her mound, then her hips and waist and slowly rose above her breasts. "Thanks, Yancy."

"My pleasure." He cupped her face in his big, sure hand and smoothed her hair back from her temples. "Don't go to sleep in there."

Yancy left, leaving the door partly open. She heard the murmur of voices, the rustle of sheets and gave herself up to comfort.

The bathroom door closed. Expecting Yancy, she smiled and opened her eyes.

"Almost like old times, sweet lady." Adam hunkered down beside the tub. "Was it what you wanted?"

Chloe felt heat rise from her breasts. Unbelievable that she should feel modest after what she had done, and what had been done to her, but she felt exposed now. She nodded. Adam touched her face, ran his finger over her lips.

"Good. Be seeing you."

Chapter Eight

Chloe heard the voices buzzing even before she entered the salon. What were they doing in San Francisco? She glanced out the window at the distinctive skyscape of the city with the Golden Bridge in the background. And to think she'd been sleeping while they sailed under it. In spite of Yancy's warning, she'd dozed off in the bath last night, and when she'd wakened, Brad and Adam had gone and Yancy was putting her to bed. He'd kissed her and left. She'd been disappointed that he hadn't stayed with her, but was too exhausted to complain.

"How this?"

She turned toward the voice. Wynne placed a black baseball cap on her head. Ali considered it. "No, more at an angle."

Wynne adjusted the fit as Chloe noticed that everyone was wearing a black polo shirt with the *Fantasy* logo on the upper left. Several already wore the same cap. "What's going on here?"

Mark hoisted himself off the couch and brought her a shirt and cap. "Here's yours. Hope it fits since everybody else got first chance at them."

Chloe took the shirt. "What's this all about?"

"Dunno. Have to wait for Yancy."

Even as he spoke, Yancy appeared in the doorway. He looked rested, at ease, tapping a sheaf of envelopes in his hand. He wore Dockers with his black polo shirt and a black belt around his trim waist. The shirt set off his broad shoulders and the depth of his chest. It did more than hint at the power of the muscles it covered. Chloe knew exactly how robust he was, how he looked naked, how his muscles flexed when he made love to her. She couldn't tear her gaze away.

"Good. You're all here." He flicked her a private glance, then turned to the others. "Today's activities combine some fun and games, some competition, some dress up and - who knows what else?"

Shelly waved her cap. "Are we going ashore?"

"All in good time. Listen up, everyone," he instructed as Lane and Perry started whispering. "In these envelopes I have a hundred dollars for each of you." He held his hand up as the sniggers started. "Yes, I know, but you have to spend your money wisely. We are going ashore and you have until five o'clock to spend your bucks."

Lane snickered. "I can spend that in a minute."

"But then you'd lose the prize."

Ali leaned forward. "Explain."

"When we meet at five, whoever has bought the most souvenirs with their money wins first prize."

"Fiji?" Saul asked.

"That's the one," Yancy confirmed.

"Souvenirs? Like from those tourist places on Fisherman's Wharf?"

"The more the better," Yancy agreed over the buzz of conversation. Chloe looked around and saw how serious the guests had become now that the stakes were known.

Yancy's voice cut through the hubbub. "Now, please go back to your staterooms, pack something for this evening. Black tie. One of the crew will take your bags to the penthouse suite at the Hotel Union Square. We'll meet there at five. Until then, you're free to do as you please. Any questions?"

Tracy nodded. "Why the dress clothes?"

"My surprise," Yancy said. He looked around the salon, as if judging the expressions. "Have you been disappointed yet?"

Mark laughed. "You can surprise me any time you want."

"Okay, let's go!" Yancy watched his guests mill towards the steps leading to their cabins. He motioned Chloe to stay.

"Are you all right?" His voice was low and intimate.

She was sore and tender in her anus, but her body felt sated, well used and relaxed. She'd awakened this morning remembering what had jiggled at her mind last night. "I'm fine." She moistened her lips. "About last night—"

"We'll talk about it after everyone else goes ashore."

"That doesn't give me as much time as the others," she grumbled. "They'll have a head start."

"Did I forget to mention that you are excluded from this race?"

"But what if I want a week in Fiji?"

"All the time you want, Chloe. With me."

Put like that, how could she complain? She nodded. He left her and went to supervise the proceedings. Chloe sank into the deeply cushioned sofa and let her head again fall back against the pillows. If anyone had suggested that she'd have her most secret fantasy so completely and delightfully fulfilled, she'd have laughed herself silly.

She didn't feel like laughing now. Instead, she waited impatiently for Yancy to return, to be alone with him. Once, she would have thought making love with three men, indulging her fantasy, would have been mechanical and devoid of emotion. Maybe even demeaning. Now she knew it hadn't been that way at all, and she had Yancy to thank for that. He'd made it very special, tender and loving. He'd fulfilled her fantasy in ways she'd never have dreamed of. She wanted to share her happiness with him, wanted to savor the closeness between them.

She wanted to ask him why he alone hadn't climaxed last night.

She heard laughter coming up from below, then Perry saying, "I think I'll call my office while we're here."

"I will, too," Saul said.

"Not me," Ali rejoined. "I'm having too much fun."

Laughing, they passed Chloe and headed for the boat deck. Shelly lingered. "Aren't you coming?"

"In a bit. I'll catch the next launch." Chloe rested her head against the back of the couch and lightly dozed while the others were taken ashore.

A short time later, Yancy came back into the salon. Chloe opened her eyes as he sat beside her.

"You look very comfortable." He took her hand in his, playing with her fingers while he looked her over carefully. "Are you sure you're all right? We weren't too rough with you?"

"Sssh!"

"It's all right," Yancy soothed. "Everyone else is gone."

She looked him right in the eye. "I'm fine. Thank you for arranging… that. For making my fantasy come true, even after we had that fight." She waited for the lump in her throat to go away. "You made it very special."

"My pleasure," he said once again, and Chloe could see that he meant it.

"Where are Brad and Adam? I didn't see them with the others."

"They left the *Fantasy* soon after we anchored last night."

She questioned him with a look.

"They won't be back." He forestalled her question. "It's better this way. You won't be embarrassed or skittish around them."

"I'm not either of those things. I wanted to thank them."

"You trusted them with your body. That's thanks enough."

She accepted his harsh tone. It couldn't have been easy for any of them last night. She'd been so aroused and eager to come that she hadn't considered their feelings. Maybe they were embarrassed to face her. She'd have to think about that, and contact them privately once she was ashore again. Thank them, and make sure they understood this was a once-in-a-lifetime thing. There was no possibility of a repeat.

"What's got you frowning?"

She put her thoughts of Brad and Adam aside and focused on today. "I have to do some shopping for your fancy dress thing tonight. I don't have anything dressy enough with me."

"Don't bother. That's part of the surprise."

"You're planning to have me pop naked out of a cake?"

He laughed. "I hadn't thought of that. Tempting, but maybe another time."

"Then what?"

"Why don't you use put yourself in my hands and see what happens?"

"I'd rather you answered some questions."

"I can guess what they are. Can they wait?"

"No."

"Very well. I'll tell you anything you want to know. Come." He stood and gave her his hand. She took it and allowed him to pull her up and lead her back to her stateroom.

It had been thoroughly cleaned in her absence. There were clean sheets and towels in the bath. The room was scented with sea air and the fresh flowers on her dresser and the coffee table. There was no trace of anything that had happened last night. Yancy shut the door behind them. "Have you had breakfast?"

"No, but—"

He lifted a hand to silence her and picked up the phone. He ordered breakfast for two. Chloe glared at him. "Nothing like broadcasting this situation."

"There are no secrets from the crew. And it doesn't matter." He settled comfortably into an armchair. "Okay, what do you want to know?"

"Did you kick Adam and Brad off this boat?"

"They chose to leave on their own. Why are you surprised?" he asked when she made a dubious face. "They are discreet."

"Are you sure? I don't want what happened in here… last night, I mean, to get around."

"They will keep it to themselves," he assured her.

"I hope you're right." She paused. "Why did you go ahead and arrange that scene last night?"

Yancy crossed his legs, balancing one ankle on the other knee. One large hand smoothed his trouser leg down. "Yours was the third wish. I was obligated to honor my promise."

"Nobody would have known or cared if you didn't."

"Not true. I would have known. So would you. I don't intend to deprive you of anything you want."

"That's crazy, Yancy, you can't—"

She stopped speaking when she heard the knock on the door. Lisa entered with a tray in her hands. She placed it on the coffee table in front of Chloe and looked at Yancy. "Will there be anything else, sir?"

"Nothing, thanks."

Without the slightest indication that Lisa knew anything existed between them, she left. Chloe watched the door close behind her. Yancy poured coffee.

"You can't arrange my life. Make things happen the way you want."

"Eat your breakfast before it gets cold."

A tense silence grew between them while they ate. Chloe was hungrier than she knew and ate a soft-boiled egg and two pieces of wheat toast with blackberry preserves. She reached for an orange.

Yancy took it from her. "Let me."

She watched him peel the orange. His long fingers stripped the peel, delicately separating the sections. The aroma rose from the fruit, scenting the air with citrus fragrance. Instead of handing pieces of orange to her, he held one up to her mouth.

"You don't have to feed me."

"I want to. I want to do many things for you. To you."

She paused, her mouth partly open to accept the segment. "We have to talk about this obsession of yours, Yancy."

"Sure." He touched her lip with the orange and, automatically, she took a bite. A drop of juice dribbled down her chin. Before she could wipe it away, Yancy licked it clean.

Immediately, she wanted him. He knew it. He placed the orange back on the plate and led her to the bed where he tenderly undressed her.

"Your body fascinates me. You are stronger than you look. Your stamina amazes me. You took the three of us last night and never complained."

"Why would I complain when you were doing exactly what I wanted?"

He touched the bruises on her hips, and turned her to see the redness around her anus. "We were rough."

"Not you. You didn't even come last night. Why not?"

He pulled the sheets back and stretched her out with her hands above her head. He smoothed his palms over her wrists and down her arms to the curves of her armpits. He cupped her breasts, running his thumbs over her nipples, which peaked immediately.

"Why, Yancy?"

"I didn't want to share you."

"But you did. You brought Brad and Adam in here. You made my fantasy come true."

He smiled. "Was it good for you?"

"You know it was. I've never come so hard or so long. It was so much more, so much better than anything I'd dreamed about." She smiled at the memory. "You made it wonderful for me. So special. Only one thing was missing. I want to know why you didn't come."

"I thought I would, but at the last moment, I didn't want to be just another cock pumping into you." He moved her legs apart, spreading them so he could explore her intimately. He touched her clit, gentling his touch when she jumped. "Are you sore here?"

"Just tender."

He put his mouth on her. His tongue flicked out, soothing any rawness away. He probed her gently, his tongue and lips learning her all over again. He inhaled. "I love the way you taste. Your sweet smell."

She squirmed under his touch. He kissed her again, tongue stroking her into fevered arousal once more. When she whimpered, he stood and shucked himself of his clothes. He stood before her, naked and aroused. "This time I am going to come. This time you'll feel only me. Can you take it?"

"I want you. Only you." Her gaze intent on his erection, she opened her arms to him. He came into them easily, fitting himself against her. She was so wet he slipped into her easily and he began to make love to her, so slowly and tenderly that she felt nothing but his big, unfaltering body giving her everything she craved. He kept up his rhythm, building excitement while he kissed her face, her eyelids, her throat, everywhere he could reach. He pleasured every inch of her body, and filled her heart with tenderness, with love.

She blinked, clearing her eyes of tears and looked above them. The mirrored recesses reflected their bodies, his large bronzed one covering hers, his torso bending and his buttocks clenching with each thrust. She couldn't see much of herself under him, only her pale legs clasped around his and her hands clutching his shoulders, but it didn't matter. She knew how she felt.

She felt cosseted, surrounded by his heat and finesse. Her arousal peaked so slowly she wasn't aware she was coming until she did. He took it all from her, encouraging her with words and caresses, before he let his own orgasm overtake him. He stiffened in her arms, going rigid for an instant before his back arched and he came in great heaves. She sucked in every drop of him, taking as much from him as she had given him.

At last, he took the weight off his elbows and rested beside her. He pulled her close to him, and rested his head on her breasts. She stroked his temples, then smoothed her palm over his head. "Why did you wait so long?"

His breath gusted over her belly. "I didn't want you thinking of anyone but me. Be open to anyone but me."

She flicked a glance at her nude body, lying a-sprawl as he'd left her. "I couldn't be more open than now."

He chuckled as he ran a hand down her torso, caressing her skin from armpit to groin. She quivered under his touch. "Not just like this. Open to me in every way. No secrets between us." He stood and walked naked to the bathroom. She heard water running, then he returned with a wet washcloth.

He began to bathe her, gently reaching between her legs, wiping softly between the folds still sensitive from lovemaking. "I was reluctant at first to set up that threesome."

"Why did you do it?"

"I want to give you everything you want. You wrote your fantasy and I wanted you to live it. Last night, I wanted you to experience everything, feel every passion, feel every bit of your body put to use. I wanted to satisfy you in every way, push you farther than you'd gone before." He finished cleansing her and dropped the cloth on the floor. Turning back to her, he took her face between his hands and looked steadily into her eyes.

"I wanted to make sure you experience your fantasy. With me. I wanted you to have three men at once so that you'll never have to wonder again about it. So you won't have to turn to anyone else to satisfy your sexual needs. So you'll choose to stay with me."

"But why Adam and Brad? Why not any of the others?"

He grinned. "I was pretty sure you'd called it off with them. Even so, I thought you'd be more comfortable with men you already knew intimately."

"But if I hadn't agreed?" she pressed. "What if I'd wanted somebody else?"

His hesitation lasted only an instant. "I'd have arranged it."

"Maybe I'd have preferred someone new?"

"Not a chance I was willing to take. Not then. Not now." He paused.

"Is there someone I don't know about?"

"No-o," she admitted, a little bit ashamed of herself for pushing the issue. These emotions were too new, too raw to handle them properly.

"How did you know that was my fantasy?"

Yancy looked very pleased with himself. "I made sure you got a heavier paper. I knew which note was yours by the feel of it."

"Sheesh! That's cheating."

"No. That's being prepared."

"What if I'd wished for something different?"

"Like what?"

"Oh, let me think. A new Jaguar? No, a new Mercedes—"

"What model? Color? I'll have it delivered."

She narrowed her eyes at him. "You're joking, right?"

"No."

"Are you trying to buy me, Yancy?"

He leaned back and relaxed on one elbow. "If I told you no, would you believe me?"

"After all this?" She waved her hand, meaning the sumptuous surroundings, the *Fantasy* and everything. "You've gone to a great deal of trouble and expense to set this all up."

"Worth every penny."

"I wish you'd called me."

"And say what?" He put his hand to his ear, mimicking a phone call. "Hello, this is Yancy. You probably don't remember me, but I've lusted after you since college and I want to entice you into spending the rest of your life with me?"

Chloe laughed. "I guess not. There are other ways though."

"I considered them all. Getting you here, relaxed, where we could get to know each other, that's worked out okay, hasn't it?"

"Very okay."

Hours later, after they'd made love again, napped and lay in each other's arms talking about everything and nothing, Yancy glanced at his watch. "Time to get going. We have to meet everybody at five."

"Do we have to?"

He gave her rump a swat. "I'm the host, remember."

"But I don't have a thing to wear!"

"Yes, you do." He pressed a button on the phone, and spoke into it. "We're ready."

He got up, dressed quickly and opened the door as Lisa arrived carrying a long dress encased in a plastic bag and several other bags imprinted with the logo of an exclusive boutique.

Yancy thanked her and took them from her. He turned to Chloe. "I'll leave you to dress or we'll never get out of here. Is an hour enough time?" She stared at the bags in his hand. "What's in those?"

"You'll see." He winked and left. Chloe jumped out of bed and tore open the bags. Underwear, sheer thigh-high stockings, shoes and even a beaded evening bag. What was Yancy thinking? She picked up the phone and asked to speak to him. A moment later, she heard his voice. "Listen, Yancy, I can't wear these things!"

"Are they the wrong size?"

"I haven't even looked, but I can't—"

"Lisa checked the sizes for me, and I had an assistant pick them up. I don't know if there's enough time to exchange them."

She cut into his worried words. "That's not the problem! They're much too expensive! And if I wear them, you won't be able to return them."

"Why would I want to do that? You're mine now. It's my pleasure to give you beautiful things."

"I'm not yours…" but she was talking to a dead line. He'd hung up on her.

She replaced the receiver, thinking how she could accessorize her black jersey dress. She threw open the door and found her closet empty. She swore. He'd left her no choice. Or so he thought.

Chloe sank down on the edge of the bed. What was Yancy thinking? Arranging this cruise, buying her clothes and setting up that fantasy game just so he could fulfill her wish? Why was he doing this? Going to all this effort and expense? After the passion and the closeness they'd shared, did he think he had to pay her?

The thought soured her stomach. She considered staying in her cabin, demanding the return of her clothes, and putting an end to this fantasy cruise. She could go ashore in San Francisco, rent a car and go home. She could write Yancy a polite thank you note and chalk these last few days up to an unforgettable experience.

She could. But did she want to? Did she want to leave Yancy? Everything between them had happened so fast. The sex was out of this world, but more than cosmic orgasms were at stake here. Her feelings bewildered her. She wasn't used to dealing with so much emotion. Did she dare trust him? Or herself? Her track record with men wasn't good. Did she dare risk trying again with Yancy? But then, could she bear to leave him? The quickening of her pulse gave her the answer.

She bathed quickly, and applied her makeup with a shaky hand, so nervous that she jabbed herself with her mascara wand and had to start all over. She ran a brush through her air and pinned it up, not caring that tendrils fell in wisps around her neck and ears.

She picked up the fragile silky underwear. A whisp of a white bustier, a garter belt, and—where were the panties? She shook the bag upside down but nothing fell out.

Chloe slipped into the white underthings. She took the shoes from the box, glanced at the label and puckered her lips into a silent whistle.

Her whistle became a gasp when she opened the garment bag. Something white, something chiffon. Delicate, soft, feminine, tempting. She held the dress up against herself and sighed. Carefully, she lifted it over her head, and felt it float into place over her body. She stared at herself in the mirror.

She recognized the design, the Greek goddess look of wrapped bodice, one shoulder bare and soft folds wafting out as she moved, settling as she stilled. She was so focused on her reflection that she didn't hear Yancy come in.

His pleased murmur brought her eyes to him.

"You're beautiful, Chloe. That dress suits you." He stood behind her, placed his hands on her shoulders and smoothed his palms down her arms to her hands. He folded them under his across her waist and kissed her neck. "Stunning." He turned her to kiss her fully, his mouth taking hers thoroughly, sweetly and softly.

Her knees had softened by the time he withdrew. Such tenderness from a fierce looking man dressed elegantly in black from neck to toe, his freshly shaven head gleaming in the soft lamplight, made her tremble.

"There's just one thing missing." He reached into a pocket and withdrew a jeweler's box. He opened it, and tilted it so she could see the sparkle of diamonds, the luster of pearls. Her breath hitched. "They're fabulous."

He took an earring and held it to her ear. "Just what I thought. White, virginal."

"Hardly that."

"You are to me." His mouth tightened. "We start from this day. Fresh. A new beginning for both of us."

Chloe shivered. His gaze on her was intent, possessive. Without looking away, she took the earring he offered and put it on. She did the same with the other one.

He studied her. "Mine."

Chapter Nine

Chloe stretched, then curled herself more closely into Yancy's body. He slept soundly even as his arm tightened around her waist and his hand cupped her breast.

The evening before had seemed enchanted with tickets to the Black and White ball, a San Francisco tradition to support the San Francisco Symphony, next a late supper, dancing, and then sailing away from the lights of the city, still bright long after midnight.

Yancy had made it an extra special evening, surprising her again with his careful preparations and attention to detail. All the women had worn either black or white. Yancy had made a ceremony of awarding the grand prize, the week in Fiji, to Wynne for her accumulation of tourist souvenirs.

Amid clapping and laughter, Wynne explained, "Those years in med school taught me how to stretch a dollar!"

Chloe and Yancy had come aboard, talked for hours about themselves, their lives and their dreams. They'd made love and fallen asleep together. Now, she could tell it was morning by the soft light filtering through her window. The absence of engine noise told her they were anchored again for their last day of recreation before leaving the ship in Monterey that evening.

She tried to ease out of bed, but Yancy's grip tightened, then eased as he woke. "Going somewhere?"

"Shower. You didn't give me a chance to take my makeup off last night. I must look like a raccoon."

He opened an eye. "Yeah." He rolled over.

She whacked him with her pillow, and smiling, went to shower and dress. She took her time, working out the kinks as she let her thoughts float by. Today was their last day together, and she wanted it to be special. How to make it memorable, though, after all Yancy had already done, was a puzzle.

She shampooed and soaped, rinsed and dried while she considered.

Scuba again, perhaps, as they'd enjoyed that. Maybe he'd let her try her hand at underwater photography. She'd brought a new camera just for that. Maybe he'd appreciate some photos of him as a thank you gift. It seemed so paltry after his largesse, but maybe once she returned to work, she'd be able to take some shots just for him.

Pleased with her decision, she left the bathroom, all steamy and scented, and found herself alone. She went in search of Yancy. He was not in the salon, or on any of the decks, so she took some fruit and a cup of coffee and climbed the steps to the sun deck where she settled into a deck chair. The yacht seemed quieter this morning with few of the guests up and around. She watched the water, almost calm now under the usual morning fog. Painting the sea this morning would be a challenge. Indigo, azure, cyan, slate, ultramarine… she ran the colors through her mind, matching them to the water, seeking just the right shades of blue. If she had her camera, she might be able to capture some of the hues for later, when she had her palette at hand.

"Why so thoughtful?" Yancy sat beside her, a steaming cup of coffee in hand.

She looked up, then back out to sea. "I was trying to decide what colors are in that water."

"Blue."

She laughed. "So it is. Which shade?"

He lifted his cup and drank. "Any color you want it to be."

"Wish I had my camera." When he made no response, she added, "If we go scuba diving today, I'd like to take some underwater shots, try out some things."

He lifted an eyebrow.

"Not people. Fish maybe. You, for sure."

"Me in goggles?" He laughed. "Maybe another time." He reached out for her hand and clasped it in his. Warmth spread up through her arm, to her heart. She wished the moment could go on and on.

"Quiet today," she commented. "Where is everybody?"

"Wynne had an emergency. Saul decided to stay in San Francisco for another day or so. Tracy decided she'd stay, too."

"I thought I saw something developing there. I wonder if they'll stay together?"

Yancy studied her. "I'm more interested in what's going to happen with us."

She looked back to study the water. "It's been a fabulous vacation.

Thanks for inviting me."

"You're welcome. Now stop avoiding the issue."

She waved her hand in an airy gesture. "You know what they say about shipboard romances."

He looked pained. "Is that what you think this is? Fun and games at sea and see you sometime when we dock?"

She shrugged and made her voice cool, as though her insides weren't trembling, already missing him. "It's been an experience, that's for sure."

His eyes narrowed even as they glinted with anger. "Why are you making so little of it? I thought I'd made it pretty damn clear that I'm not letting you go."

"It's not your choice to make!" she snapped.

"What's making you so uptight, Chloe?"

"What's making you so persistent?"

He looked startled, then frowned. "Maybe I haven't made myself clear. I want you to stay with me. I want us to be together."

Her throat tightened painfully. She couldn't speak.

"Is it because I'm Crow? Absaroka, if you want to be precise. One of the bird people."

Maybe that's why he loved flying. She shook her head, denying his thought. How could he think she'd be prejudiced?

She looked out over the dark water lapping at the yacht's hull, feeling pulled two ways at once. She loved making love with Yancy, loved the way he aroused her and then satisfied her so completely. She loved talking with him, sharing experiences and viewpoints. She enjoyed his company. She'd never felt this intimacy, this connection, with any other man. When she let herself dream, she could see spending her life with him. It pained her to think she couldn't, but she couldn't live with his commanding manner.

It grated that he'd made decisions for her, even if she'd enjoyed the results of those decisions. That might work for the short time they'd been together, however, she couldn't see continuing in this unbalanced manner for any length of time. She was used to making her own decisions, to working hard, taking chances, and evaluating risks against the good she could do with her photographs. She couldn't change into a well-dressed mannequin, to be there when Yancy wanted her or to wait quietly in the background when he was busy.

She couldn't throw away everything she worked for, all the work she had ahead of her, just because Yancy wanted her, because he claimed she belonged to him and wanted them to be together.

She turned to face him. "I can't do it, Yancy."

"Can't or won't?"

"Same difference. I'm used to living my own life. Being independent and in control of my career. I can't toss that all over to be your... plaything."

"Plaything?" he said harshly. "Hardly that."

"What then? What do you think I feel like when you give me all these expensive things? When you insist I wear the clothes you choose—"

"I like to do those things for you. I want to do them. I will continue to do them," he added firmly.

"In return for what? Sex?"

He looked pained. "Hell, yes. And a damn sight more. Your company, your attention. You."

"Meanwhile I'm giving up my independence, my free choice, my work—"

"Who asked you to do that?"

"—my life..." She stopped in mid sentence. "You did."

"Where did you get that idea?"

"You said... you said you wanted me to stay with you, stay on board. Oh. Did you mean for another few days?" She considered her schedule. "I think I could manage that."

"Don't do me any favors, Chloe," he snapped. "I never asked you to stop being who you are. Why would I want to change you? Have you stop doing what you're so good at?"

"But—"

"I asked you to stay with me, yes. You belong to me and I expect a commitment from you."

"That's it!" she cried. "That's it exactly! You want me to commit to you, belong to you, and what is there in it for me?"

His face darkened. "What more do you want, Chloe?" he asked in a soft, even voice. "I'm already offering you everything."

"Anything money can buy, you mean! What about your feelings, your commitment, your heart?"

His eyes widened. "What do you mean 'my heart'? You've had that all along."

"What?" Her knees wobbled. She sank down onto a deck chair. This changed everything. Sweetness flooded her, pushing out her scruples and doubts. "You didn't say anything."

"What else would this be about, Chloe? Why would I arrange this fantasy cruise if I didn't want to do and experience everything with you? Why would I set up that threesome for you if not to please you?"

"Why, Yancy?"

"Because I wanted to see if my fantasy of marrying, you, making babies with you and living with you for the next fifty years had any chance of happening!"

Her eyes misted. "The words, Yancy," she managed through the lump in her throat. "I need the words."

He didn't hesitate. "I love you, Chloe. I guess I fell for you more each time I read your reports. I'm continually awed by the power of your photographs. You make a difference in the world. I want you to go on doing what you are so good at, but not to the exclusion of everything else. I want you to make a difference in my world. Our world."

It took her a moment to breathe properly. Her reservations vanished, making her wonder why she'd worried about losing her independence. Her heart full, she reached for his head, holding the smoothly shaven curve in her hand. She pulled his face closer, and kissed one cheek. "I." She kissed the other cheek, pressing another kiss into his dimple. "Love." She kissed his mouth, taking her time, savoring his taste, the way he parted his lips for her, letting her take charge. Eventually, she released his mouth long enough to whisper against it, "You."

"I love you, Chloe. Never doubt it."

She swallowed hard. "We've wasted so much time."

"No. Now is the time for us. Now and tomorrow. All the tomorrows." He kissed her slowly, promising her all the days ahead. "Will you stay with me, Chloe? Be with me, marry me, belong to me?"

She wanted to dance and sing. She wanted to take his picture, capture forever the tender, loving look on his face. She wanted it all, her work, her photos, him. More than anything, she wanted Yancy.

"Sheesh, fella. All you had to do was ask." Her voice cracked. She threw her arms around him, hugged him tight. "Yes, yes!"

He returned the hug in full measure, and then some. He released her only long enough to kiss her the way she had kissed him. Long, sweet and loving, giving her everything, committing himself to her.

Chloe sighed. "Some fantasies are worth the wait."

About the Author:

A degreed historian, Bonnie Hamre puts her travels in the US, South America and Europe to good use in her novels. Multi-published in contemporary and historical romantic fiction, Bonnie lived in a coastal resort town of California, and has recently moved to the Northwest, where new adventures await her. She is busy writing her next book.

To learn more about Bonnie's books, visit her website http://www. bonniehamre.com or write her at bonnie@bonniehamre.com.

Dear Reader,

We appreciate you taking the time out of your full and busy schedule to answer this questionnaire.

1. Rate the stories in **Secrets Volume 9** (1-10 Scale: 1=Worst, 10=Best)

Rating	Wild For You	Wanted	Secluded	Flights of Fantasy
Story Overall	_____	_____	_____	_____
Sexual Intensity	_____	_____	_____	_____
Sensuality	_____	_____	_____	_____
Characters	_____	_____	_____	_____
Setting	_____	_____	_____	_____
Writing Skill	_____	_____	_____	_____

2. What did you like **best** about **Secrets**? What did you like **least** about **Secrets**?

3. Would you buy other volumes?

4. In future **Secrets,** tell us how you would like your *heroine* and your *hero* to be. One or two words each are okay.

5. What is your idea of the **perfect sensual romantic story**? Use more paper if you wish to add more than this space allows.

Thank you for taking the time to answer this questionnaire. We want to bring you the sensual stories you desire.

Sincerely,
Alexandria Kendall
Publisher

Mail to: Red Sage Publishing, Inc.
P.O. Box 4844
Seminole, FL 33775

If you enjoyed *Secrets Volume 9* but haven't read other volumes, you should see what you're miss-

Secrets Volume 1:

In *A Lady's Quest*, author Bonnie Hamre brings you a London historical where Lady Antonia Blair-Sutworth searches for a lover in a most shocking and pleasing way.

Alice Gaines' *The Spinner's Dream* weaves a seductive fantasy that will leave every woman wishing for her own private love slave, desperate and running for his life.

Ivy Landon takes you for a wild ride. *The Proposal* will taunt you, tease you, even shock you. A contemporary erotica for the adventurous woman's ultimate fantasy.

With *The Gift* by Jeanie LeGendre, you're immersed in the historic tale of exotic seduction and bondage. Read about a concubine's delicious surrender to her Sultan.

Secrets Volume 2:

Surrogate Lover, by Doreen DeSalvo, is a contemporary tale of lust and love in the 90's. A surrogate sex therapist thought he had all the answers until he met Sarah.

Bonnie Hamre's regency tale *Snowbound* delights as the Earl of Howden is teased and tortured by his own desires—finally a woman who equals his overpowering sensuality.

In *Roarke's Prisoner*, by Angela Knight, starship captain Elise remembers the eager animal submission she'd known before at her captor's hands and refuses to be his toy again.

Susan Paul's *Savage Garden* tells the story of Raine's capture by a mysterious revolutionary in Mexico. She quickly finds lush erotic nights in her captor's arms.

Secrets Volume 3:

In Jeanie Cesarini's *The Spy Who Loved Me*, FBI agents Paige Ellison and Christopher Sharp discover excitement and passion in some unusual undercover work.

Warning: This story is only for the most adventurous of readers. Ann Jacobs tells the story of *The Barbarian*. Giles has a sexual arsenal designed to break down proud Lady Brianna's defenses — erotic pleasures learned in a harem.

Wild, sexual hunger is unleashed in this futuristic vampire tale with a twist. In Angela Knight's *Blood and Kisses*, find out just who is seducing whom?

B.J. McCall takes you into the erotic world of strip joints in *Love Undercover*. On assignment, Lt. Amanda Forbes and Det. "Cowboy" Cooper find temptation hard to resist.

Secrets Volume 4:

An Act of Love is Jeanie Cesarini's sequel. Shelby's terrified of sex. Film star Jason Gage must coach her in the ways of love. He wants her to feel true passion in his arms.

The Love Slave, by Emma Holly, is a woman's ultimate fantasy. For one year, Princess Lily will be attended to by three delicious men. She delights in playing with the first two, but it's the reluctant Grae that stirs her desires.

Lady Crystal is in turmoil in *Enslaved*, by Desirée Lindsey. Lord Nicholas' dark passions and irresistible charm have brought her long-hidden desires to the surface.

Betsy Morgan and Susan Paul bring you Kaki York's story in *The Bodyguard*. Watching the wild, erotic romps of her client's sexual conquests on the security cameras is getting to her — and her partner, the ruggedly handsome James Kulick.

Secrets Volume 5:

B.J. McCall is back with *Alias Smith and Jones*. Meredith Collins is stranded overnight at the airport. A handsome stranger named Smith offers her sanctuary for the evening — how can she resist those mesmerizing green-flecked eyes?

Strictly Business, by Shannon Hollis, tells of Elizabeth Forrester's desire to climb the corporate ladder on her merits, not her looks. But the gorgeous Garrett Hill has come along and stirred her wildest fantasies.

Chevon Gael's *Insatiable* is the tale of a man's obsession. After corporate exec Ashlyn Fraser's glamour shot session, photographer Marcus

Remington can't get her off his mind. Forget the beautiful models, he must have her — but where did she go?

Sandy Fraser's **Beneath Two Moons** is a futuristic wild ride. Conor is rough and tough like frontiermen of old, and he's on the prowl for a new conquest. Dr. Eva Kelsey got away once before, but this time he'll make sure she begs for more.

Secrets Volume 6:

Sandy Fraser is back with **Flint's Fuse**. Dana Madison's father has her "kidnapped" for her own safety. Flint, the tall, dark and dangerousmercenary, is hired for the job. But just which one is the prisoner — Dana will try *anything* to get away.

In **Love's Prisoner**, by MaryJanice Davidson, Jeannie Lawrence experienced unwilling rapture at Michael Windham's hands. She never expected the devilishly handsome man to show back up in her life — or turn out to be a werewolf!

Alice Gaines' **The Education of Miss Felicity Wells** finds a pupil needing to learn how to satisfy her soon-to-be husband. Dr. Marcus Slade, an experienced lover, agrees to take her on as a student, but can he stop short of taking her completely?

Angela Knight tells another spicy tale. On the trail of a story, reporter Dana Ivory stumbles onto a secret—a sexy, secret agent who happens to be a vampire.She wants her story but Gabriel Archer believes she's **A Candidate for the Kiss**.

Secrets Volume 7:

In **Amelia's Innocence** by Julia Welles, Amelia didn't know her father bet her in a card game with Captain Quentin Hawkc, so honor demands a compromise — three days of erotic foreplay, leaving her virginity and future intact.

Jade Lawless brings **The Woman of His Dreams** to life. Artist Gray Avonaco moved in next door to Joanna Morgan and now is plagued by provocative dreams. Is it unrequited lust or Gray's chance to be with the woman he loves?

Surrender by Kathryn Anne Dubois tells of Lady Johanna. She wants no part of the binding strictures of marriage to the powerful Duke. But she doesn't realize he wants sensual adventure, and sexual satisfaction.

Angela Knight's **Kissing the Hunter** finds Navy Seal Logan McLean hunting the vampires who murdered his wife. Virginia Hart is a sexy vampire searching for her lost soul-mate only to find him in a man determined to kill her.

Secrets Volume 8:

In Jeanie Cesarini's latest tale, we meet Kathryn Roman as she inherits a legal brothel. She refuses to trade her Manhattan high-powered career for a life in the wild west. But the town of Love, Nevada has recruited Trey Holliday, one very dominant cowboy, with *Taming Kate*.

In *Jared's Wolf* by MaryJanice Davidson, Jared Rocke will do anything to avenge his sister's death, but he wasn't expecting to fall for Moira Wolfbauer, the she-wolf sworn to protect her werewolf pack. The two enemies must stop a killer while learning that love defies all boundaries.

My Champion, My Love, by Alice Gaines, tells the tale of Celeste Broder, a woman committed for a sexy appetite that is tolerated in men, but not women. Mayor Robert Albright may be her salvation—*if* she can convince him her freedom will mean a chance to indulge their appetites together.

Liz Maverick takes you to a post-apocalyptic world in *Kiss or Kill*. Camille Kazinsky's military career rides on her decision—whether the robo called Meat should live or die. Meat's future depends on proving he's human enough to live, *man* enough, to make her feel like a woman.

Men you've been dreaming about!

Secrets

Satisfy your desire for more.

*F*eel the wild adventure, fierce passion and the power of love in every *Secrets* Collection story. Red Sage Publishing's romance authors create richly crafted, sexy, sensual, novella-length stories. Each one is just the right length for reading after a long and hectic day.

Each volume in the *Secrets* Collection has four diverse, ultra-sexy, romantic novellas brimming with adventure, passion and love. More adventurous tales for the adventurous reader. The *Secrets* Collection are a glorious mix of romance genre; numerous historical settings, contemporary, paranormal, science fiction and suspense. We are always looking for new adventures.

Reader response to the *Secrets* volumes has been great! Herc's just a small sample:

> *"I loved the variety of settings. Four completely wonderful time periods, give you four completely wonderful reads."*

> *"Each story was a page-turning tale I hated to put down."*

> *"I love Secrets! When is the next volume coming out? This one was Hot! Loved the heroes!"*

Secrets have won raves and awards. We could go on, but why don't you find out for yourself — order your set of *Secrets* today! See the back for details.

Secrets, Volume 1

Listen to what reviewers say:

"These stories take you beyond romance into the realm of erotica. I found *Secrets* absolutely delicious."

—Virginia Henley,
New York Times Best Selling Author

"*Secrets* is a collection of novellas for the daring, adventurous woman who's not afraid to give her fantasies free reign."

—Kathe Robin, *Romantic Times* Magazine

"…In fact, the men featured in all the stories are terrific, they all want to please and pleasure their women. If you like erotic romance you will love *Secrets*."

—*Romantic Readers* Review

In *Secrets, Volume 1* you'll find:

A Lady's Quest by Bonnie Hamre

Widowed Lady Antonia Blair-Sutworth searches for a lover to save her from the handsome Duke of Sutherland. The "auditions" may be shocking but utterly tantalizing.

The Spinner's Dream by Alice Gaines

A seductive fantasy that leaves every woman wishing for her own private love slave, desperate and running for his life.

The Proposal by Ivy Landon

This tale is a walk on the wild side of love. *The Proposal* will taunt you, tease you, and shock you. A contemporary erotica for the adventurous woman.

The Gift by Jeanie LeGendre

Immerse yourself in this historic tale of exotic seduction, bondage and a concubine's surrender to the Sultan's desire. Can Alessandra live the life and give the gift the Sultan demands of her?

Secrets, Volume 2

Listen to what reviewers say:

"*Secrets* offers four novellas of sensual delight; each beautifully written with intense feeling and dedication to character development. For those seeking stories with heightened intimacy, look no further."

—Kathee Card, *Romancing the Web*

"Such a welcome diversity in styles and genres. Rich characterization in sensual tales. An exciting read that's sure to titillate the senses."

—Cheryl Ann Porter

"*Secrets 2* left me breathless. Sensual satisfaction guaranteed…times four!"
—Virginia Henley, *New York Times* Best Selling Author

In *Secrets, Volume 2* you'll find:

Surrogate Lover by Doreen DeSalvo
Adrian Ross is a surrogate sex therapist who has all the answers and control. He thought he'd seen and done it all, but he'd never met Sarah.

Snowbound by Bonnie Hamre
A delicious, sensuous regency tale. The marriage-shy Earl of Howden is teased and tortured by his own desires and finds there is a woman who can equal his overpowering sensuality.

Roarke's Prisoner by Angela Knight
Elise, a starship captain, remembers the eager animal submission she'd known before at her captor's hands and refuses to become his toy again. However, she has no idea of the delights he's planned for her this time.

Savage Garden by Susan Paul
Raine's been captured by a mysterious and dangerous revolutionary leader in Mexico. At first her only concern is survival, but she quickly finds lush erotic nights in her captor's arms.

Winner of the Fallot Literary Award for Fiction!

Secrets, Volume 3

Listen to what reviewers say:

"*Secrets, Volume 3*, leaves the reader breathless. A delicious confection of sensuous treats awaits the reader on each turn of the page!"
— Kathee Card, *Romancing the Web*

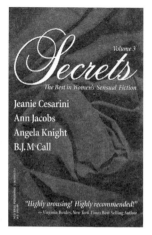

"From the FBI to Police Dectective to Vampires to a Medieval Warlord home from the Crusade — *Secrets 3* is simply the best!"
— Susan Paul, award winning author

"An unabashed celebration of sex. Highly arousing! Highly recommended!"
—Virginia Henley, *New York Times* Best Selling Author

In *Secrets, Volume 3* you'll find:

The Spy Who Loved Me by Jeanie Cesarini

Undercover FBI agent Paige Ellison's sexual appetites rise to new levels when she works with leading man Christopher Sharp, the cunning agent who uses all his training to capture her body and heart.

The Barbarian by Ann Jacobs

Lady Brianna vows not to surrender to the barbaric Giles, Earl of Harrow. He must use sexual arts learned in the infidels' harem to conquer his bride. A word of caution — this is not for the faint of heart.

Blood and Kisses by Angela Knight

A vampire assassin is after Beryl St. Cloud. Her only hope lies with Decker, another vampire and ex-mercenary. Broke, she offers herself as payment for his services. Will his seductive powers take her very soul?

Love Undercover by B.J. McCall

Amanda Forbes is the bait in a strip joint sting operation. While she performs, fellow detective "Cowboy" Cooper gets to watch. Though he excites her, she must fight the temptation to surrender to the passion.

Winner of the 1997 Under the Covers Readers Favorite Award

Secrets, Volume 4

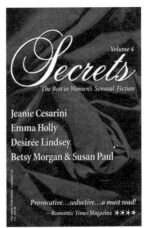

Listen to what reviewers say:

"Provocative…seductive…a must read!"
— *Romantic Times* Magazine

"These are the kind of stories that romance readers that 'want a little more' have been looking for all their lives…."
— *Affaire de Coeur* Magazine

"*Secrets, Volume 4*, has something to satisfy every erotic fantasy… simply sexational!"
—Virginia Henley, *New York Times* Best Selling Author

In *Secrets, Volume 4* you'll find:

An Act of Love by Jeanie Cesarini

Shelby Moran's past left her terrified of sex. International film star Jason Gage must gently coach the young starlet in the ways of love. He wants more than an act — he wants Shelby to feel true passion in his arms.

Enslaved by Desirée Lindsey

Lord Nicholas Summer's air of danger, dark passions, and irresistible charm have brought Lady Crystal's long-hidden desires to the surface. Will he be able to give her the one thing she desires before it's too late?

The Bodyguard by Betsy Morgan and Susan Paul

Kaki York is a bodyguard, but watching the wild, erotic romps of her client's sexual conquests on the security cameras is getting to her — and her partner, the ruggedly handsome James Kulick. Can she resist his insistent desire to have her?

The Love Slave by Emma Holly

A woman's ultimate fantasy. For one year, Princess Lily will be attended to by three delicious men of her choice. While she delights in playing with the first two, it's the reluctant Grae, with his powerful chest, black eyes and hair, that stirs her desires.

Secrets, Volume 5

Listen to what reviewers say:

"Hot, hot, hot! Not for the faint-hearted!"
— *Romantic Times* Magazine

"As you make your way through the stories, you will find yourself becoming hotter and hotter. *Secrets* just keeps getting better and better."
— *Affaire de Coeur* Magazine

"*Secrets* 5 is a collage of lucious sensuality. Any woman who reads *Secrets* is in for an awakening!"
—Virginia Henley, *New York Times* Best Selling Author

In *Secrets, Volume 5* you'll find:

Beneath Two Moons by Sandy Fraser

Ready for a very wild romp? Step into the future and find Conor, rough and masculine like frontiermen of old, on the prowl for a new conquest. In his sights, Dr. Eva Kelsey. She got away once before, but this time Conor makes sure she begs for more.

Insatiable by Chevon Gael

Marcus Remington photographs beautiful models for a living, but it's Ashlyn Fraser, a young corporate exec having some glamour shots done, who has stolen his heart. It's up to Marcus to help her discover her inner sexual self.

Strictly Business by Shannon Hollis

Elizabeth Forrester knows it's tough enough for a woman to make it to the top in the corporate world. Garrett Hill, the most beautiful man in Silicon Valley, has to come along to stir up her wildest fantasies. Dare she give in to both their desires?

Alias Smith and Jones by B.J. McCall

Meredith Collins finds herself stranded overnight at the airport. A handsome stranger by the name of Smith offers her sanctuaty for the evening and she finds those mesmerizing, green-flecked eyes hard to resist. Are they to be just two ships passing in the night?

Secrets, Volume 6

Listen to what reviewers say:

"Red Sage was the first and remains the leader of Women's Erotic Romance Fiction Collections!"

— *Romantic Times* Magazine

"*Secrets, Volume 6*, is the best of *Secrets* yet. …four of the most erotic stories in one volume than this reader has yet to see anywhere else. …These stories are full of erotica at its best and you'll definitely want to keep it handy for lots of re-reading!"

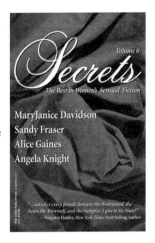

— *Affaire de Coeur* Magazine

"*Secrets 6* satisfies every female fantasy: the Bodyguard, the Tutor, the Werewolf, and the Vampire. I give it Six Stars!"

—Virginia Henley, *New York Times* Best Selling Author

In *Secrets, Volume 6* you'll find:

Flint's Fuse by Sandy Fraser

Dana Madison's father has her "kidnapped" for her own safety. Flint, the tall, dark and dangerous mercenary, is hired for the job. But just which one is the prisoner — Dana will try *anything* to get away.

Love's Prisoner by MaryJanice Davidson

Trapped in an elevator, Jeannie Lawrence experienced unwilling rapture at Michael Windham's hands. She never expected the devilishly handsome man to show back up in her life — or turn out to be a werewolf!

The Education of Miss Felicity Wells by Alice Gaines

Felicity Wells wants to be sure she'll satisfy her soon-to-be husband but she needs a teacher. Dr. Marcus Slade, an experienced lover, agrees to take her on as a student, but can he stop short of taking her completely?

A Candidate for the Kiss by Angela Knight

Working on a story, reporter Dana Ivory stumbles onto a more amazing one — a sexy, secret agent who happens to be a vampire.She wants her story but Gabriel Archer wants more from her than just sex and blood.

Secrets, Volume 7

Listen to what reviewers say:

"Get out your asbestos gloves — *Secrets Volume 7* is...extremely hot, true erotic romance...passionate and titillating. There's nothing quite like baring your secrets!"
— *Romantic Times* Magazine

"...sensual, sexy, steamy fun. A perfect read!"
—Virginia Henley,
New York Times Best Selling Author

"Intensely provocative and disarmingly romantic, *Secrets, Volume 7*, is a romance reader's paradise that will take you beyond your wildest dreams!"
— Ballston Book House Review

In *Secrets, Volume 7* you'll find:

Amelia's Innocence by Julia Welles

Amelia didn't know her father bet her in a card game with Captain Quentin Hawke, so honor demands a compromise — three days of erotic foreplay, leaving her virginity and future intact.

The Woman of His Dreams by Jade Lawless

From the day artist Gray Avonaco moves in next door, Joanna Morgan is plagued by provocative dreams. But what she believes is unrequited lust, Gray sees as another chance to be with the woman he loves. He must persuade her that even death can't stop true love.

Surrender by Kathryn Anne Dubois

Free-spirited Lady Johanna wants no part of the binding strictures society imposes with her marriage to the powerful Duke. She doesn't know the dark Duke wants sensual adventure, and sexual satisfaction.

Kissing the Hunter by Angela Knight

Navy Seal Logan McLean hunts the vampires who murdered his wife. Virginia Hart is a sexy vampire searching for her lost soul-mate only to find him in a man determined to kill her. She must convince him all vampires aren't created equally.

Winner of the Venus Book Club
Best Book of the Year

Secrets, Volume 8

Listen to what reviewers say:

"*Secrets, Volume 8*, is an amazing compilation of sexy stories covering a wide range of subjects, all designed to titillate the senses. ...you'll find something for everybody in this latest version of *Secrets*."
— *Affaire de Coeur* Magazine

"*Secrets Volume 8*, is simply sensational!"
—Virginia Henley, *New York Times* Best Selling Author

"These delectable stories will have you turning the pages long into the night. Passionate, provocative and perfect for setting the mood...."
Escape to Romance Reviews

In *Secrets, Volume 8* you'll find:

Taming Kate by Jeanie Cesarini
Kathryn Roman inherits a legal brothel. Little does this city girl know the town of Love, Nevada wants her to be their new madam so they've charged Trey Holliday, one very dominant cowboy, with taming her.

Jared's Wolf by MaryJanice Davidson
Jared Rocke will do anything to avenge his sister's death, but ends up attracted to Moira Wolfbauer, the she-wolf sworn to protect her pack. Joining forces to stop a killer, they learn love defies all boundaries.

My Champion, My Lover by Alice Gaines
Celeste Broder is a woman committed for having a sexy appetite. Mayor Robert Albright may be her champion—if she can convince him her freedom will mean a chance to indulge their appetites together.

Kiss or Kill by Liz Maverick
In this post-apocalyptic world, Camille Kazinsky's military career rides on her ability to make a choice—whether the robo called Meat should live or die. Meat's future depends on proving he's human enough to live, man enough...to makes her feel like a woman.

Winner of the Venus Book Club
Best Book of the Year

Secrets, Volume 9

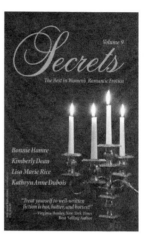

Listen to what reviewers say:

"Everyone should expect only the most erotic stories in a *Secrets* book. ...if you like your stories full of hot sexual scenes, then this is for you!"
> — Donna Doyle Romance Reviews

"**SECRETS 9**...is sinfully delicious, highly arousing, and hotter than hot as the pages practically burn up as you turn them."
> — Suzanne Coleburn, Reader To Reader Reviews/Belles & Beaux of Romance

"Treat yourself to well-written fictionthat's hot, hotter, and hottest!"
> —Virginia Henley, *New York Times* Best Selling Author

In *Secrets, Volume 9* you'll find:

Wild For You by Kathryn Anne Dubois

When college intern, Georgie, gets captured by a Congo wildman, she discovers this specimen of male virility has never seen a woman. The research possibilities are endless!

Wanted by Kimberly Dean

FBI Special Agent Jeff Reno wants Danielle Carver. There's her body, brains—and that charge of treason on her head. Dani goes on the run, but the sexy Fed is hot on her trail.

Secluded by Lisa Marie Rice

Nicholas Lee's wealth and power came with a price—his enemies will kill anyone he loves. When Isabelle steals his heart, Nicholas secludes her in his palace for a lifetime of desire in only a few days.

Flights of Fantasy by Bonnie Hamre

Chloe taught others to see the realities of life but she's never shared the intimate world of her sensual yearnings. Given the chance, will she be woman enough to fulfill her most secret erotic fantasy?

It's not just reviewers raving about *Secrets*. See what readers have to say:

"When are you coming out with a new Volume? I want a new one next month!" via email from a reader.

"I loved the hot, wet sex without vulgar words being used to make it exciting." after *Volume 1*

"I loved the blend of sensuality and sexual intensity — HOT!" after *Volume 2*

"The best thing about *Secrets* is they're hot and brief! The least thing is you do not have enough of them!" after *Volume 3*

"I have been extreamly satisfied with *Secrets*, keep up the good writing." after *Volume 4*

"I love the sensuality and sex that is not normally written about or explored in a really romantic context" after *Volume 4*

"Loved it all!!!" after *Volume 5*

"I love the tastful, hot way that *Secrets* pushes the edge. The genre mix is cool, too." after *Volume 5*

"Stories have plot and characters to support the erotica. They would be good strong stories without the heat." after *Volume 5*

"*Secrets* really knows how to push the envelop better than anyone else." after *Volume 6*

"*Secrets*, there is nothing not to like. This is the top banana, so to speak." after *Volume 6*

"'Would you buy *Volume 7*?' YES!!! Inform me ASAP and I am so there!!" after *Volume 6*

"Can I please, please, please pre-order *Volume 7*? I want to be the first to get it of my friends. They don't have email so they can't write you! I can!" after *Volume 6*

Finally, the men you've been dreaming about!

Give the Gift of Spicy Romantic Fiction

Don't want to wait? You can place a retail price ($12.99) order for any of the *Secrets* volumes from the following:

① Waldenbooks Stores

② Amazon.com or BarnesandNoble.com

③ Book Clearinghouse (800-431-1579)

④ Romantic Times Magazine
Books by Mail (718-237-1097)

⑤ Special order at other bookstores.
Bookstores: Please contact Baker & Taylor Distributors or Red Sage Publishing for bookstore sales.

Order by title or ISBN #:

Vol. 1: 0-9648942-0-3 **Vol. 6:** 0-9648942-6-2

Vol. 2: 0-9648942-1-1 **Vol. 7:** 0-9648942-7-0

Vol. 3: 0-9648942-2-X **Vol. 8:** 0-9648942-8-9

Vol. 4: 0-9648942-4-6 **Vol. 9:** 0-9648942-9-7

Vol. 5: 0-9648942-5-4

Secrets Mail Order Form:

(Orders shipped in two to three days of receipt.)

	Quantity	Mail Order Price	Total
Secrets Volume 1 *(Retail $12.99)*	_____	$ 8.99	_____
Secrets Volume 2 *(Retail $12.99)*	_____	$ 8.99	_____
Secrets Volume 3 *(Retail $12.99)*	_____	$ 8.99	_____
Secrets Volume 4 *(Retail $12.99)*	_____	$ 8.99	_____
Secrets Volume 5 *(Retail $12.99)*	_____	$ 8.99	_____
Secrets Volume 6 *(Retail $12.99)*	_____	$ 8.99	_____
Secrets Volume 7 *(Retail $12.99)*	_____	$ 8.99	_____
Secrets Volume 8 *(Retail $12.99)*	_____	$ 8.99	_____
Secrets Volume 9 *(Retail $12.99)*	_____	$ 8.99	_____

Shipping & handling (in the U.S.)

US Priority Mail
1–2 books .... $ 5.50
3–5 books $11.50
6–9 books $14.50

UPS insured
1–4 books $16.00
5–9 books $25.00

_____

SUBTOTAL _____

Florida 6% sales tax (if delivered in FL) _____

TOTAL AMOUNT ENCLOSED _____

Your personal information is kept private and not shared with anyone.

Name: (please print) _____

Address: (no P.O. Boxes) _____

City/State/Zip: _____

Phone or email: (only regarding order if necessary) _____

Please make check payable to **Red Sage Publishing**. Check must be drawn on a U.S. bank in U.S. dollars. Mail your check and order form to:

Red Sage Publishing, Inc.   Department S9   P.O. Box 4844   Seminole, FL 33775

Or use the order form on our website: **www.redsagepub.com**

Secrets Mail Order Form:
(Orders shipped in two to three days of receipt.)

	Quantity	Mail Order Price	Total
Secrets Volume 1 *(Retail $12.99)*	_____	$ 8.99	_____
Secrets Volume 2 *(Retail $12.99)*	_____	$ 8.99	_____
Secrets Volume 3 *(Retail $12.99)*	_____	$ 8.99	_____
Secrets Volume 4 *(Retail $12.99)*	_____	$ 8.99	_____
Secrets Volume 5 *(Retail $12.99)*	_____	$ 8.99	_____
Secrets Volume 6 *(Retail $12.99)*	_____	$ 8.99	_____
Secrets Volume 7 *(Retail $12.99)*	_____	$ 8.99	_____
Secrets Volume 8 *(Retail $12.99)*	_____	$ 8.99	_____
Secrets Volume 9 *(Retail $12.99)*	_____	$ 8.99	_____

Shipping & handling (in the U.S.)

US Priority Mail
1–2 books .... $ 5.50
3–5 books $11.50
6–9 books .... $14.50   _____

UPS insured
1–4 books $16.00
5–9 books .... $25.00   _____

SUBTOTAL   _____

Florida 6% sales tax (if delivered in FL)   _____

TOTAL AMOUNT ENCLOSED   _____

Your personal information is kept private and not shared with anyone.

Name: (please print) _____

Address: (no P.O. Boxes) _____

City/State/Zip: _____

Phone or email: (only regarding order if necessary) _____

Please make check payable to **Red Sage Publishing**. Check must be drawn on a U.S. bank in U.S. dollars. Mail your check and order form to:

Red Sage Publishing, Inc.   Department S9   P.O. Box 4844   Seminole, FL 33775

Or use the order form on our website: **www.redsagepub.com**